In the ORCHARDS of SHADOW and LIGHT

In the ORCHARDS of SHADOW and LIGHT

ARTHUR McMASTER

IngramElliott

In the Orchards of Shadow and Light

Published by IngramElliott, Inc.
www.ingramelliott.com
9815-J Sam Furr Road, Suite 271, Huntersville NC 28078

Book design by Maureen Cutajar, gopublished.com
Cover design by H.O. Charles
Map illustration by Mary L Eggart

ISBN Hardcover: 978-1-952961-40-3
ISBN Paperback: 978-1-952961-41-0
ISBN E-Book: 978-1-952961-42-7

Library of Congress Control Number: 2025949782
Subjects: Fiction--Historical Fiction--General. Fiction--Thriller--Espionage.

Published in the United States of America.
First Edition: 2026, First International Edition: 2026

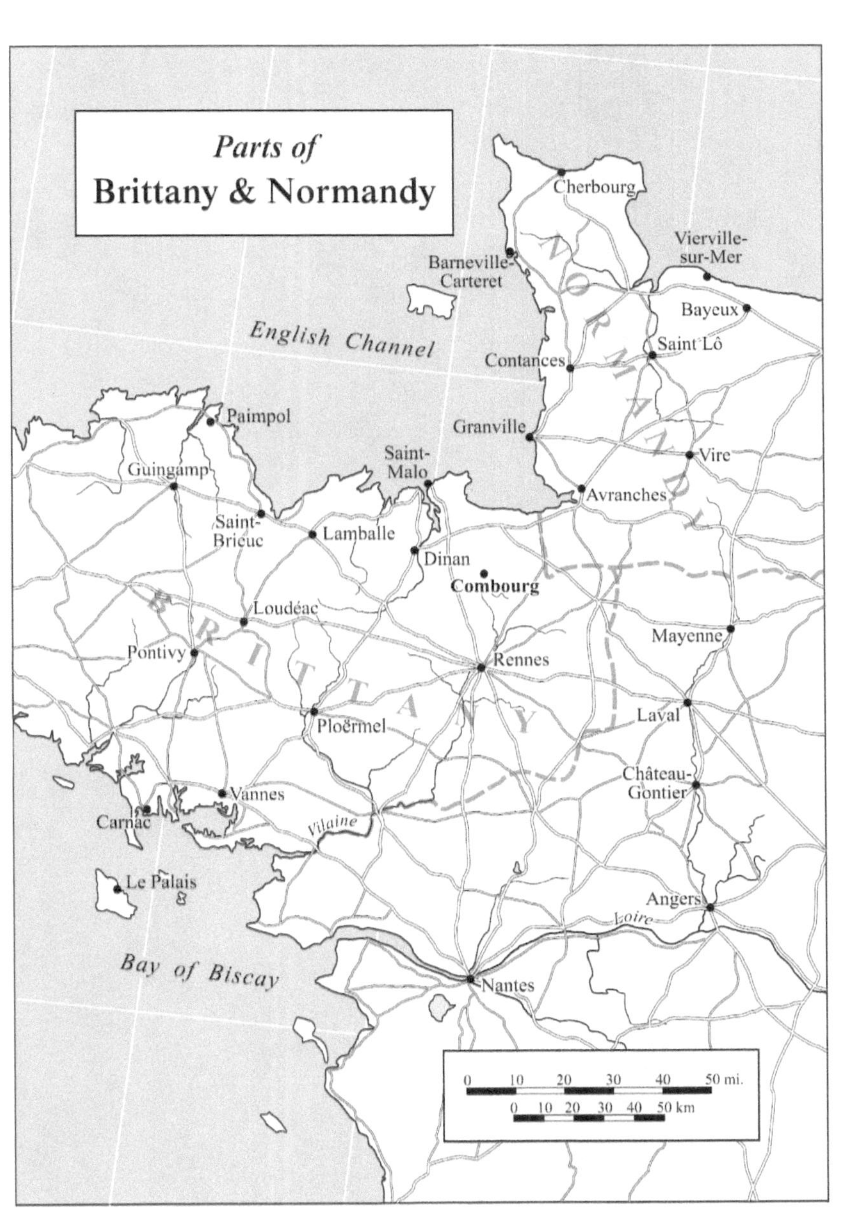

Parts of
Brittany & Normandy
English Channel
Bay of Biscay
NORMANDY
BRITTANY
Cherbourg
Vierville-sur-Mer
Barneville-Carteret
Bayeux
Saint Lô
Contances
Granville
Vire
Avranches
Saint-Malo
Paimpol
Guingamp
Saint-Brieuc
Lamballe
Dinan
Combourg
Loudéac
Mayenne
Pontivy
Rennes
Laval
Ploërmel
Château-Gontier
Vannes
Carnac
Vilaine
Le Palais
Angers
Loire
Nantes
0 10 20 30 40 50 mi.
0 10 20 30 40 50 km

In an orchard there should be enough to eat,
enough to lay up, enough to be stolen…"
JAMES BOSWELL

In memory of the Skiffington sisters:
Madolyn, Clare, and Rita

PROLOGUE

Mourners came to the cemetery behind Église Saint-Martin that grim November morning, a day cold as iron. Two of Corporal Mathis Berlangier's buddies stood together—one with damaged lungs, the other missing an eye. Also present were three of his farm workers and their ever-steady foreman, Émile Chalfant, too old for service. A few elderly women in black had gathered as well, souls strong in purpose. The women always seemed to be about the Catholic church's business, perhaps more so its sacred duties.

The Breton town of Combourg was small, a commune popularized nearly a century before by one French romantic author for its stunning stone castle overlooking enchanting Lac Tranquille. Apple orchards and farmland had long given it purpose. But many of its good men were gone, killed in the third year of the war. *Der Weltkrieg*, as the proud Germans called it. The World War was what Canada's news magazine had dubbed it in 1914. The Great War.

Little Nina Berlangier looked to her mother, adjusting her black shawl against the stiffening breeze. When encouraged, Nina stepped to the head of the grave and placed her small clutch of flowers upon it. Primroses. One stem had fallen away from the rest, and the young girl knelt to correct it, conscious of her brother watching. Adèle drew Nina to her side, her daughter distracted by a sudden flock of excited rooks overhead. She'd seen that behavior before. A dreamer, Nina was given to drift. Adèle pulled her closer, the troubled young person. Adèle and her husband had struggled to discipline and, when they could, to please both children. Not that she would have said they'd done that well on either count. Mathis Berlangier was dead and buried, killed along with three others by a German sniper guarding a useless, nearly destroyed bridge. 1916 had been a harrowing year for French forces, more so for the families of the war's dead. Thiepval, the Battle of the Somme, had changed everything. Or almost everything.

Adèle turned to her sixteen-year-old son, Jacques, stronger and more practical and four years older than Nina. The young man had been speaking with Chalfant, their trusted foreman. Jacques, she knew, was made of sterner stuff. His perception of what had just occurred among them, however, was quite different, and what he saw irritated him, feeling something close to envy as he watched his sister garner their mother's solace and affection. He had loved his father too, had worked by his side; he was a good man who'd taught him much about work and commitment. Honor too. Perhaps no two members of any family ever see things the same way.

Walking from the grave, Adèle reached into her pocket and fingered the sharp edge of the envelope her husband had handed her the year before. A just-in-case letter to be given to Jacques should Mathis be killed. She motioned for the boy to come to her, and she showed him what she held, but he didn't take it. Nina, trembling, looked to them both, then back to the grave.

"We should get back," Jacques said, blowing on his hands.

Nothing more to do.

"Jacques," Adèle said, beckoning him to her side. "Take this. It is from your father."

He put the envelope into his pocket. He'd want to be alone when he read it. With Papa gone, family business would be his responsibility. He looked again to his sister; she was staring at the cold ground. She took her mother's hand.

That night, alone, hurt, bitter, and not a little ambivalent as to what lay ahead, Jacques sat down on his bed and opened the letter.

My son, if you are reading this, you will know that I have done my duty to France and to my fellow soldiers, and I shall not be coming back. I know you will be a strong young man and will look after your mother and your sister. I have loved you all, and I pray you will care for one another.

Keep the farm strong, Jacques. You will make it prosperous. War has taken much, but it cannot take your heart, my boy. It cannot touch your will. This land belonged to my father and mother as it will now belong to you. You, Maman, and Nina. The future is yours. And your childrens', someday, if you are blessed with your own family. Our past and our future. Where you are raised is a forever thing. This I know well. The Berlangier farm will always be your home. Honor me by making it so.

PART 1

CHAPTER 1

Claire Skiffington left Bodney just before 2300 hours for her first operational assignment, ostensibly an uncomplicated courier job. Betty McIntyre, a dear friend and her OSS supervisor at RAF Bodney, accompanied her to the otherwise empty flight line. Waiting for the aircraft, Claire looked to the darkening sky, searching not so much for what was up there but perhaps what awaited her on the other side. She reflected on what the previous day's visit to agency headquarters in London had meant, what it had brought about.

"How good is your French, Claire?" Colonel Peter Hibbert had asked her. She'd told him it was perfect, or as perfect as any non-native speaker can get. Fragments of the conversation came back to her as she reflected.

"Well, it is going to have to be. I've asked for the best, and I am told that is you. Can you handle a weapon?"

The question had startled her. She'd said she could, or at least she had qualified. Not that she had ever shot anyone, nor hoped she would ever have to. That decision, she knew, would be instinctive. In short order, the general mission had been made clear. Details would follow from Betty. She could do this—assume a false identity behind enemy lines. All that was on the line was her life.

Claire's visit to London's Office of Strategic Services had also provided common-sense security procedures. Briefings. Debriefings. Hibbert could give her what he called the broad strokes. All the required preparation. One network in Brittany had been rolled up, forty-eight hours before, a man shot in Brest, the agent trying to link up with a blown resistance contact at some ill-lit boulangerie, four resistance people subsequently found and taken. OSS assignments in support of French resistance were nothing but dangerous.

"Lessons for us all," Hibbert had said, sharing the awkward intelligence from behind his polished desk, secure in Mother London, Blitz-scared though the city still was.

"Do we know how or why?" she recalled asking him, sensing this news was given as much as a test of her resolve as well as out of common decency.

"Sadly, no." He turned back to the great window, adjusting his tailored shirt cuffs. "Someone stumbled onto it somehow. And now the game is afoot," he'd added, riffing on a catchphrase from Sherlock Holmes. Someone? *No one's fault,* was what he meant. Well, there was nothing to be done about it. Claire understood the risks.

"You go out tomorrow night, my dear, if I am not mistaken."

"Yes. All right."

Fidgety and eager to get going, Claire peered at one small book in her bag. Something was concealed within, the details of which she did not need to know. This first-timer, this rookie, was eager to get the mission over with. Her own identity was Celine Mercier. A name she rather liked.

Betty took her arm, bringing Claire back to the moment. "Your contact is Corbeau."

"Corbeau, yes. I give this to him or her?" She set her jaw so as not to show her nervousness. Simple enough. The word, she knew, meant raven. A very smart bird, if not particularly social.

Betty nodded. "The book is not for her. Corbeau is your escort. She'll know who it goes to." Both understood the small operation was a test for Claire.

Betty took her hand, and Claire said, "I'm going to make sure she gets it. I will."

Her affable friend, Flight Officer Owen Terfel, was not her pilot that early-spring night. He said little to Claire except that they'd need to fly lower than he liked once they crossed land at Le Val-André. No choice. There was no instrument flight capability in the Lysander. Visual all the way. Having never been a comfortable flyer, she gripped the seat tightly with both hands. The plane was as noisy as a brass band. Complicating matters, a storm threatened over the channel. Her brother-in-law, Ott, had always said she had the balls of a burglar.

"Foggy nights mean we do what is expedient, Miss." "Of course." Nothing to like or dislike. One coped.

Their destination was a farm south of Mégrit, where they would meet one local operative code-named Corbeau. She asked whether he knew the contact. "No," the man replied, not even turning his head, a hint of weariness in his voice. He had no operational intel. "I'm just the ferryman, Miss," he said.

"Yes, of course," she whispered. He was her own private Charon.

The plane touched down at just past two a.m. Claire was forced back sharply in her rear passenger seat as the pilot reversed thrust. She did a quick survey of the site. Four small flares illuminated the beginning and the end of their makeshift runway. There was no movement at the tree line.

"Hold on back there!"

"Yeah, I got that."

Claire felt the craft turn a hard one-eighty and pull to an abrupt stop. As she stepped down, the pilot said something, waved once, and immediately taxied away. She'd be on her own for the next twenty-four hours. It was OSS protocol. She could not help checking her watch, a small Bucherer with an inexpensive leather band. Peter Hibbert's clothier, in the stately old building's basement, had also made sure that her kit was consistent with working-class French tastes. She searched the tree line. Claire Skiffington also carried a small automatic, and she looked at it in her bag.

Two figures approached. No names. One man and one woman—both in black slacks and sweaters. Partisans. These must be her contacts. Claire helped the stocky woman douse two nearby flares. The man ran the few hundred yards to extinguish the far ones.

"*Vite!*" the woman said. "Quickly!"

Together, they raced for a grove of scraggly pines. Some ten minutes later, reaching another clearing, Claire spotted a dark farmhouse. The man entered; he went to a kitchen cabinet and immediately pulled out a bottle of what might have been a locally made brandy, taking a pull. The woman put apples and cheese on the table, sat, and spoke to Claire.

"Call me Corbeau," she said. Straight-faced, staring.

Claire knew these people tended to be more reticent than Americans. Vigilant, Claire thought. She took the woman to be about fifty, sturdy, a good bit shorter than Claire, who was athletic and trim, though, even at five foot seven, she would never be called solid. A burst of brownish freckles covered Corbeau's long nose. One tooth argued with conventional alignment. Corbeau? There was nothing about her look or demeanor to suggest a raven, Claire thought.

"Celine," said Claire. Operational at last.

The man left the room. So, she had made it this far. Were they man and wife? Claire had to admire their efficiency. Whatever their private reality, the woman was in charge, responsible for making certain the linkup took place. She was in charge of Celine's safety, at least for the next twenty-four hours. Half the job was successfully establishing contact, confirming bona fides. Claire surveyed the room once again, studying the place, looking, perhaps, for something to make her feel less anxious, maybe something to focus the mind. Occupied France in 1944 meant proximity to a kind of tension, a measure of danger that she'd never fully appreciated until that moment.

The woman had not asked about anything Celine had carried with her. The man went to tune the radio. Corbeau, she understood, would act as a conduit between rural French resistance and any Allied assets in play for coordinating covert operations against those Germans or Vichy traitors trying to inveigle French cooperation in Brittany. Claire hefted her travel bag; felt the outline of the book she'd have for whomever Corbeau was to connect her with. So far, so good.

From the radio room, she heard the man yell out. Something had him exasperated. Any OSS activity in this narrow part of the region likely came through these two. Claire suspected the woman had been doing such work for years, or from the day when the Germans came knocking in September of 1940. She'd not ask. It mattered little, so long as Claire remained alert to potential weaknesses in her own cover.

Corbeau took the bottle from the table, put it into the closet, and showed Claire what looked like a wardrobe off the small main room. There, she recognized a makeshift transmitter, receiver, and power pack—two liquid-filled plastic batteries. The man sat with the headset cocked at an angle. He would not break radio silence until three when, on Claire's behalf, he could signal to the code clerks at RAF Bodney she was in place. The woman explained that, after first light, they'd travel some distance northeast to Dinan, to the train station. The news startled Claire. *My Lord*, she thought. *I cannot be late for my return.* Not that she would say anything to the woman. Claire had expected—hoped—to take care of business right there.

"We go to meet another man. He is Hibou; the one you are to connect with."

"I see," she said. "Hibou, of course."

"Celine, everyone is anxious. We must only stick to the plan."

She would make contact with this resistance leader—Hibou—at the train station, where Germans would be everywhere. Wehrmacht. SS patrols checking papers making things difficult for all.

She needed only to give the man whatever it was she'd carried in the book, then go back to the station and rest. She could do that. So, there'd be another bird, an owl this time. Two cover names. At the train station, a common connecting point, everything would be in motion.

Claire knew from briefings that any such gathering point offers good cover—to be among many others, coming and going. Still, the enemy would know that too. Pétain's Vichy goons were all over.

Corbeau read the American's worried face. "No safe place, Celine."

"I understand." Had she ever been so vulnerable, this first timer? The Dinan job would be a far cry from the work she was given to do just two years ago when she'd first agreed to help—handling classified message traffic at headquarters, on Washington's busy E Street. Initially on orders for Algiers, Claire's operational assignment was changed to Europe because they needed someone who spoke fluent French for courier duties in England at Station 141, known more commonly as RAF Bodney. And, there she was.

"Pardon?"

She shook her head in reply. "Nothing." Had she been thinking out loud? The older woman was studying her. Trust cannot be forced. There could be no time for worry. Celine ran her fingers through her hair. *Be attentive. Be alert.*

The farmhouse had one room with a bed, a living room with a wooden table and one weary sofa, a kitchen, and an adjoining work room with the radio. If there were others about, if there were children, or had been, there were no signs of them at that point. The fireplace was cold; Claire stared into it. The dark well of the stone pit gave nothing of its story away. It was what she had trained for, that sense of being alone while being with others. The man looked in, whiskey in hand. One double-barreled shotgun rested, stoic, against the cabinet of dishes in the kitchen.

Claire tried to stretch out on the musty sofa, taking off her shoes. Corbeau told her they would leave at 0630, then gave her the pretty comforter, and she pulled it up over her feet and chest. A low humming came from the small radio room, then static. At just past three, exhausted, she dozed off, the woman's words playing back to her: "They are all around, Celine." German patrols. Vichy spies.

The couple came for her at six. She used the toilet and washed her hands and face. The man handed her a chunk of soda bread. He raised his eyebrows as if in solidarity, still not speaking. A quick ersatz coffee, and they'd walk to the train station. Two kilometers. Something unseen browsed among the hedges as they left the house. Maybe a cat, or opossum? Or the dark silhouette of something else not wanting to be found.

A twenty-minute walk, Corbeau told her. The train would leave at seven. Two hours' travel. Then, "We shall see."

CHAPTER 2

Claire settled with the others into a smoky, hazy-windowed third-class compartment. She looked into her bag and loosened the wrapper and read the cover of the book, the purpose of the trip. Guilloux's *Le Sang Noir*. Black Blood. How fitting. Was there a code embedded there? Money concealed beneath the book's cover? She put it back into her bag and forced herself to look out the window.

Corbeau leaned toward her in their booth. "You have your papers, yes?"

"I do."

The man got up, checked the hallway, and returned. He took a breath and looked to Claire, eyes fixed, as a banker looks at a suspicious loan applicant, and she thought maybe he doubted her. No need for her to engage either of them. No talking where others might overhear. Her cover was that of a pastry girl—a *boulangerie* assistant traveling to Dinan for ingredients. Simple. If pressed, she'd say something about being short on yeast. In Vichy France, one may well be short of anything save courage. Their despicable history of collaboration, subterfuge, and hostilities against loyalist French had only darkened since the winter of 1941.

Claire had a good idea what lay ahead. Peter Hibbert's guidance came back to her. "Trust your training," he had encouraged. "Sometimes, Claire, all that will be necessary is to meet a field op and take information. You are a courier. We are not asking you to blow up anything. Take a bawling out if necessary. Listen to your people," he'd said. "They need not know exactly who is helping, as long as it's someone they think they can trust." He had told her something else as well. "Be the psychologist if need be. If that is what the game demands." The game makes many demands. The truth was malleable. "Keep these people in the fight, Claire, at all costs. They count on you, and so do I."

She'd closed her eyes for what seemed only moments when her companion tapped her on the knee. "Dinan, *mon dieu*." Corbeau kept her voice down, but they all knew something was wrong. The station roiled in chaos, German troops pushing people apart. One sinister-looking young soldier in field-gray uniform held back two dogs straining at the leash.

Out on the platform, a whisker-thin officer in a tight, black uniform held a pistol high above his head, a body at his feet. A statement of raw power—holding the gun, pointed straight up. Looking down at what he had done or could yet do. Had the dead man been hurrying away? A *résistant?* A Jew? The fear was palpable. What had Claire gotten herself into?

Other soldiers were selecting people at random, stopping every few, making angry faces. Did they know something? Who was the victim?

Claire looked to the older woman. "Can you see? Is it Hibou?"

"Poor man. I cannot see. But whether it is or is not, there will be no contact today. If alive, if Hibou saw this, he will have disappeared." Corbeau looked to her partner. His palms rested on his knees. They must only blend in. But why had this one been shot? The American looked at the couple, at the taciturn man tamping his pipe. Intuitively, the play was to make eye contact with no one.

"We get off the train and walk away now," said Corbeau. "Slowly."

Claire knew the only objective was to stay alive by staying apart. Wait and watch. Be prepared to take the next train back. Otherwise, what? Avoid the Germans and the pernicious power in their impressive dress and demeanor. Soldiers were taking the man's body to their vehicle, the crowd excited by the fear.

Corbeau would lead. "Keep a good distance," she said. The man clasped his hands behind his back and took up the rear. A show of indifference, perhaps. No threat from them. Simple farmers. Claire had to think this older fellow had been a soldier in the first war. His apparent age would suggest so. The stillness about him said as much. A listener. A watcher. Corbeau's companion.

More Germans rushed to the station house, perhaps thinking to discover someone else hiding.

"We cross the track for the train back. Do not look at anyone," said Corbeau. Two men in black coats walked toward them, haughty, unhurried, passing by.

With her sleeve, Claire wiped the perspiration from her forehead. How should she process such craziness? A shooting? No doubt part of the Nazi plan to keep everyone anxious. But who and why? And what of Hibou?

Back on the return train, she thought about the dead man. Someone's father? She adjusted her scarf, pushed at her skirt. Moments later the train pulled away. She looked out to the fast-rushing fields, where one saw only the ragged surface and nothing of what lay beneath.

Returning to the farmhouse that afternoon, Corbeau pulled off her heavy shoes. After an indifferent hour of cards, a nap, and some light music, the three sat down to a poor, gamey meat pie and one hefty, wrinkled potato to share. The strong red wine helped.

Claire needed some affirmation. "My God, what has it been like here for you? How do you manage?" Corbeau looked at the back of her rough hands. "For many, there was simply not enough to eat," she began. "Especially in the first years of occupation. Everyone was desperate. Coming from the store, seeing German soldiers. . . I avoided looking at them for fear they would be able to see the panic in my eyes."

The woman was recalling a particularly bad incident. Corbeau's voice grew quieter. "There were times, especially if I was alone, running an errand in town, when I would be seized by anxiety. I might see a man in a trench coat through the reflection of a window. I'd come home from the store with little to show for my effort. Food, rationed as it was. People traded for things. Fruit. Meat was scarce." She half closed her eyes and continued: "Eggs—some, for the fortunate. Not the black market. That was in the cities." Was that what she wanted to know?

"We had a few chickens, so we could make do," she continued. "People on farms had it better. But in the bigger towns? No. Terrible. Germans on the street corners. So haughty, smoking and laughing, eyeing me, or any woman, as if they were thinking what they might do. Never could I look at them. My cousin, in Tours, lost her ration card, or it was stolen."

The man got up, gathered the plates, and went to the radio. He said nothing, but rubbed his eyes, mumbled something, and walked away—the radio was his weapon. Claire saw that he transmitted only at set times. Radio security. Broadcasts never lasted more than a minute. But listening was pretty safe, and he had another radio, something commercial. He might tune to BBC war reports or find music. He came out of the room at just past nine. Excited, he let out a whoop. He'd picked up one vital BBC broadcast—a secret code meant for the French underground—alerting them that the long-awaited Allied invasion of France was imminent.

"They are coming," he said, startling her. His voice rising, he exclaimed, "*Mon dieu, ils arrivent enfin.* They are coming at last." He shook his head as if in disbelief, then went to Corbeau, who raised her arms to the ceiling. The couple laughed and embraced, did a little dance step, and she kissed him on the forehead. It seemed so out of character. Claire, too, felt caught up in their joy. The man went back to the closet and pulled out the bottle. He poured three glasses and roared again, raising his glass. He said something to Corbeau, his wife or, maybe, his sister. Claire could not quite catch it, but Corbeau told her the man would make contact soon, affirming that Celine was to be picked up for return. She grinned and felt her shoulders release some tension.

The American would meet the RAF pilot at two for the night return. Celine was going home. History had taken a breath and would find a quicker, no doubt more violent, thrum. The bands and gears of time had restarted. The American military was coming, and nothing the enemy could do would slow their historic pace.

Claire also had to think that if the Allies were planning something, the Germans knew it too. Or soon would. The question was, where? Whatever help Hibou needed, if the man were still alive, whatever he would have gotten from the book, or perhaps would have asked of her, all would have to wait. At least for a little while.

Claire's ride back to Bodney touched down nearly on time, and came in blacked out, four flares and obligatory prayers doing what little they could. One strong hand reached down, that of a grinning Owen Terfel. Claire could not have been more delighted.

"Owen!"

Corbeau and the man—these mysterious partners—were gone as quickly as they could kill the flares and head back to a cove of trees. There may have been a wave, a safe travels kind of thing, or she just thought there would be. She had no idea whether she would see them again, these partisans. She was optimistic because the Americans were coming. Her people. At long last.

Back at Bodney, the pilot taxied to the spot on the tarmac being held by his technical sergeant. The smell of spilt aviation fuel was strong. Could he see her to her quarters? Claire shook her head. She was tired. "No, but thank you for being on time, Owen. I did not want to spend one minute longer there than needed."

Owen touched his cap jokingly and left her at the door to her wooden hut, which she found locked, and on which she had to knock a few times. Momentarily, Paula answered, wearing an oversize, green cotton nightshirt. She seemed pretty much still asleep at nearly four a.m.

"God bless. Get yourself in here, girl."

Claire secured the door. Keyed up from so much that had happened, and oddly enough, she thought, that which had not, the uncertainty of it all tasted almost bitter. She could not help but think about missing the resistance leader, Hibou. She'd say a prayer for this owl, this cautious and observant man. One cot over, Miss High Energy, Jilly Bates, was talking in her sleep.

Claire sat on her bunk, slipped off her shoes in the near-total darkness, and looked into her bag to feel for the book, which she'd return to Betty. Betty would want a debrief. Claire ached to sleep but sensed she was too adrenalized from the horror at the train station, from the long rush of danger. She heard another plane land somewhere in the dark.

When would she travel back? Another mission. Another grasp at something barely within reach. And her pilot friend, Owen Terfel? How would she manage if she actually were to become attached to him? Given how urgent it all seemed and how much at risk she felt, did she need someone?

Soon, the other women would awaken from the warm mist of sleep. *Mother of God, what am I doing here*? An unmarried, unsettled, far-from-home gal from small-town central New York, Claire Skiffington was thirty-five years old, and what did she have to show for it but a facility for language, a false identity, and a desire to prove something? To herself, at least, if to no one else.

CHAPTER 3

Jacques arrived at the Dinan station thirty minutes early, bought a paper, and sat to survey the busy waiting room. He noticed one restless, middle-aged fellow holding a small package, his knee jumping restlessly. When two German soldiers entered, all power and intimidation, Jacques saw the man look up, stand, and scurry to one exit. Then, two shots. Foolishly, the man had tried to bolt from the soldier who'd called out to him. Jacques had no idea who the dead man was, but he saw the shooter—the German—young, irritated, four pips on the collars of his black SS uniform. A major—*sturmbannführer.* Had he been looking for that unfortunate fellow? Someone who fit a description? A deadly tip, perhaps? Was the man an agent, and, if so, whose?

The ill-lit room pulsed with fear. As people scrambled, pushing away from the horrific scene, Jacques made the decision to abort. He climbed into his truck and made it safely onto the road; it was half an hour's drive home if no soldiers stopped him. German surveillance was always relentless. And there, not a half kilometer up the road, sat two German soldiers on powerful motorcycles, just off the southbound side. Jacques's best play would be to ignore them. One watched carefully as Jacques drove by. The other leaned back, adjusting his helmet and pulling at his black gloves. Evidently, they'd both just gotten there and were about to begin making random stops. His timing had held.

Working through a long-trusted associate, Corbeau, a local, Jacques Berlangier was to have met with an American OSS agent at Dinan, one who would have something for his team, likely a message and, maybe, money. Everyone had expenses. The murder of one unlucky soul at the train station put quit to that plan, but he knew it could be reset quickly. There was nothing to do but await further instructions. It was always a waiting game.

What some would learn that evening by BBC coded radio was that the long-expected allies-in-waiting were coming. There was nothing about timing. The hornet's nest that was deadly German overwatch would be buzzing too, matched, and perhaps trebled by, despicable Vichy collaboration. With word of the Americans' imminent arrival known to the partisans, the *Résistance*, the bad guys would know it as well.

Alert to possibilities, Jacques could expect another assignment soon. If so, he'd find it in the town's Roman Catholic church.

The next day, ostensibly in town on business—business associated with his apple farm north of town—he stepped through the heavy, weathered doors of Église Saint-Martin and looked into ambivalent sunshine. The weathered clock on the tower next to the church seemed to be watching what went on below. Jacques fingered the message in his pocket. He had another mission. His undercover work necessarily took him to that church, where all such dead drops were managed.

A woman wearing a light-blue beret peddled by, head down and determined, the past out of reach, the future out of her control. People living in or near town were not keen to show their faces. Several stores had been shuttered thanks to German harassment of local businesses. The centuries-old Romanesque church, with its small cemetery to the back, graced by stoic hardwoods of beech and ash, had been a respite for Jacques in more ways than one. Saint-Martin's was also his sanctuary. In such times, he felt a reconnection to his long-dead family, to a mother and father who had worshipped there during the last war, both buried behind the building. Jacques had read the message twice. Sapper work. Once again, their target would be a train. Jacques—*nom de guerre:*

Hibou, Owl—was experienced at such demolition work. He'd need to put his small team together, beginning with his close friend.

Jacques crossed the cobbled street and stepped into the aging stone building belonging to a farm supplies vendor. Most of his team had survived their dangerous work for going on three years. The one he'd lost the previous winter was arrested and shot. No one had discerned how he'd been exposed, and that concerned them all. Remi had been his best explosives man, and, until he could be replaced locally, Jacques would have to rely on uncertain assets and exercise care in what kind of people were brought into the circle. All good operatives understand their first imperative must be to remain observant. Secondly, trust your instincts.

Jacques walked into the store. Behind the counter stood his affable friend, Fabien Brun, a ruddy-faced character with a big laugh and a most atypical French sense of humor. Jacques liked and trusted him.

Fabien spoke first: *"Ça va?"*

Jacques shrugged his shoulders and chose an apple from a large dish on the man's counter, then tossed it into his other hand. Jars of nails and screws sat beside the cash register. The few yellow-pearl case knives Fabien had been so proud of had been confiscated some months ago by a German patrol. "One of mine?" he asked, looking around.

"Difficult to say."

Jacques turned his head to check the door again. No one was lingering, listening. Then, he said, "Some can be too tart, you know." This phrase alerted Fabien that Jacques was not shopping; he had a message. Their own private code. Jacques was in the store on resistance business.

"Tart. Like so many other things these days," Fabien replied, giving the necessary message to proceed. Their agreed-upon two-step waltz—de rigueur—meant both were clear to speak candidly.

"You know what is coming, yes?" Jacques asked.

"I think perhaps you mean *who* is coming."

"All a matter of timing," Jacques said.

The work to free France from Hitler's war machine and his collaborationist minions raged on in the fourth year of German occupation. No two cells were the same—in manpower, or in purpose. Jacques's people worked well in large part because he kept them focused on foiling the enemy's lines of supply. Sabotage. He left the underground newspaper work, the espionage, the hiding of Jews, and selective assassinations to others. Some elite cells did nothing but assist downed British pilots in getting safely into Spain, or, more rarely, straight back to England. In most cases, those saved would again fly bombing, recon, or courier missions.

The networks to protect the flyers and usher them out of harm's way were intricate. Such teams often involved counterfeit identifications and travel permits, which were tricky to manage. Such teams were the most at-risk, for, when one of their members was caught, they could all be rolled up.

Jacques's people blew up bridges, derailed trains, destroyed other materiel bound for Germany, or did so as well as they could. Such work was not steady—maybe two or three jobs a month. That was risky enough. All assignments originated in London, specifically from the British Special Operations Executive, the SOE. "We have a job. Sorry to ask, Fabien, but will your brothers help?"

"Yes, of course. When?"

"We meet tonight. At one," Jacques told him. "Twelve hours," Fabien said, checking his watch.

"A night train to Köln. There can be no hesitation." Jacques looked to be sure his meaning was clear. One brother, Raoul, had a young family. His reluctance to participate in the last op was understandable. The other, Paul, was a bachelor, a barber, and an able partisan. Fabien's wife, Emma, supported her husband, as long as he promised he would take no foolish chances. Not that he would throw his life away, but Fabien understood what his brothers must be going though.

"I am sorry to have to ask."

"No. I understand," he said, crushing out a cigarette. "Such are the times. Both will be with us."

"Tonight, then."

The men had known each other for more than twenty years, but their tricky, clandestine game made them anxious.

Jacques walked to the window. "Fabien, come look. Who are those men at my truck? Can you see? Look there!"

The storekeeper peered out and shrugged. "Strangers?"

"Well, yes," Jacques insisted. "Not Germans. There are two." Fabien asked, "What's in the truck?

"Just Cleo."

"They may be Romani."

"Who?"

"Gypsies. The Germans are kicking them hard, at least those they have not locked up, not already interred in Drancy with the Jews." The reference stung, and Fabien immediately regretted saying it. He knew Jacques's dear girlfriend Martine and her mother had been caught up in Hitler's manic obsession, the Nazis' pursuit of the Jews.

"I cannot imagine what they want." Jacques opened the door to take a closer look and saw they were gone. Walking out, he told Fabien, "Tonight, then."

"Tonight."

His lady spaniel, Cleo, sat up as Jacques approached and climbed into the truck. He ruffled her fur, gave her a chin scratch, and nursed the vehicle back through the town and onto the narrow road heading for his farm. He thought of Brun's brothers. He could not help but think he, too, would be reluctant to participate in such missions had he anyone in his life, any loved one or close family to count on him. To matter. The woman he had loved for three years, his brilliant, beautiful Martine, had been taken, along with her mother, by gendarmes one night in May of 1942. That was just over two years ago. In his hours of optimism—fewer every month—he thought it possible he might see her again. He tried to keep hope alive. Much of what he did, not as Jacques Berlangier, but as Hibou—for the resistance, the struggle—was to speed that day.

Working in coordination with Britain's SOE had far-reaching implications. Cells operated throughout the country as well as in villages and cities, mostly in a disconnected fashion; it was safer that way. Vichy control of what briefly had been called Free France, south of the Loire, had been brought under ever-tighter German control, in part because some resistance teams had been too successful. The collaborationist Vichy relished shooting their countrymen and not a few teens when they caught them. The menace was relentless.

What Jacques had been made privy to was that senior resistance people knew the Allied attack was imminent. Paul Verlaine's poem *Autumn Song*, broadcast on June 1, was the signal to prepare. Knocking out rail lines was a priority.

If the Americans were coming and the enemy could well know it, those conditions would only get worse. Thus, the resistance needed to hit German supply lines, degrade their capability. With the enemy controlling access to and security at train stations, airfields, and shipping ports, it became harder to interdict vital German supplies, and yet it was never more important to do just that. Any matériel for the Nazi war effort, or even the sustainment of German citizens, became prized targets. If a shipment of ammunition, weapons, or even a truckload of barley oats could be destroyed or delayed, that is what Jacques's people would do when ordered. The team always operated some distance away, most often to the north, in and near Dinan and Saint-Malo, which meant the team could hit quickly and readily disperse after any strike. Fabien had said on more than one occasion that they lived only on borrowed time, a nation in peril, as if infested with a deadly black mold.

Jacques and Fabien had agreed to meet at half past twelve, to be joined, at one a.m., by Fabien's brothers and a man Berlangier knew little about but who had been vouched for by people he did.

M. Bérubé was a short, stocky, heavy-browed man—a trusty railroad engineer from the south who lived in the nearby village of St. Léger. Jacques had worked with him once before.

A Nazi ammunition shipment would pass just north of Rennes late that night, enroute to the Ruhr. Another work-a-day job for his team, but that did not mean it would be easy. German military presence was the real threat. Spies. Scare tactics. Collaborators. Threatening of food supplies. Roughing up the old people and scaring young women. The plan was simple enough. It was better to blow the train when it slowed, near Rennes, than to try to catch it at speed somewhere in Normandy. Bérubé knew the train's braking system. For safety reasons, the train would slow appreciably before the station, given that the tracks there had been damaged before.

Jacques's people would assemble just to the north of the station, and, from there, they would have decent access to the tracks. If required, their key man was sufficiently well known to the platform control cops that he could be seen if need be. Whatever cover story Bérubé had in mind would likely involve something about train safety. In any event, it must be up to him to signal whether to abort or delay, or when to move ahead with the plan. Risky.

Fabien's younger brothers, both armed, took lookout duty, mostly looking out for German soldiers. Not that their handguns would do them much good if they were discovered and apprehended or simply shot on sight. They accepted the danger. Jacques would assist from the unmonitored side—dark, but not impossibly so.

"Coming now," Fabien said sotto voce.

Jacques found he had been holding his breath. He'd been successful in locating supplies of Composition C, called *plastique*. Such material was nearly impossible to acquire. Some had been taken from mines and quarries, but that access was too closely monitored. His best sources were the British—their special operations people—but they were tough to contact safely. He had recently begun using a grizzled Albanian warrior named Gashi, a sixty-something-year-old mercenary living in Rennes who liked money. He liked parties and girls too, but he had other sources for all that. His talents were for sale to the highest bidder. They did business together when Jacques's link to England, mostly through American OSS, was disrupted. One didn't have to like a man to accept his help.

Jacques had bought two kilograms of the putty-like explosive from Gashi a few weeks earlier and, that night, carried the malleable materials, including the requisite timers, in an old haversack, which he was only too happy to turn over to Bérubé when the time came. The plan was to construct two small explosive packs, one for the fourth car back from the engine, typically where the Germans tended to place their vital cargo, and one for the car two back from that, just to be sure—thus employing what was called the center of mass tactic by explosive experts, commonly known as sappers. If the timers worked, even one of them, there was going to be one hell of a bang.

Under a pitch-black night sky, the men took their positions as they had done several times before, accommodating for weather, the gradient, lighting, and the presence of patrol dogs. Their unquiet nerves they managed individually. When one single, strong point of white light appeared well up the track, Jacques nodded to Fabien, who signaled that security looked good. The skies above hung low with ponderous clouds. The Cologne-bound train was on time, rushing to the Ruhr valley steelworks. They would see that it would not get there.

The tracks came together at a switching point a half kilometer from the station, a busy terminal. The men knew that some three hundred meters out, the train would have to slow to accommodate other cars arriving or clearing. It was a matter of timing. There, Bérubé leaned into the undercarriage, securing the adhesive-prepared package where it would be most effective. It was a delicate business.

The trains then came hurrying past, little more than a blur. Rails buzzing with the energy of late-day locusts. Seconds later, their man placed the other pack, their three-minute fuses set to explode well past the station itself. No one wanted to take innocent lives, which they would if the train derailed close to the station.

Their mission complete, they could expect to hear at least muffled explosions even as they made their way back to their assembly point and away from the railyard. If successful, they would know soon enough. The train would blow, its cargo damaged or destroyed, or it would not. Some things, most things, they had no control over. Each man returned to his vehicle, to family, to his conscience. The double explosion minutes later confirmed their skill.

Returning to his ever-demanding work at the farm, Jacques had plenty to think about. His resistance work came from a deep sense of obligation, and that night's work had gone well. Still, that was one train of how many? Thousands? Other sapper teams contributed, but everyone's war was somehow unique. For him it was a counterblow to what they had taken from him: his Martine. Jacques's war was, in a sense, a half-measure war in that he never directly faced the enemy. Still, it was satisfying to hit back at the bastards. It was all anyone could do just then.

Jacques approached his farmhouse and saw his best friend there. Cleo must have heard the truck as he pulled up to the house. The dog was at the window.

"I'm home, girl," he said, hurrying to the door.

The large fruit-tree farm inherited from his father constituted everything he had. He would give the world for someone to pass it along to. There was nothing, he understood, that he needed more. But Martine was gone, and the timing for any other romances had always been wrong.

None of his five farm workers—his regulars—he considered true friends. One man, the oldest of the crew, had assisted Jacques when, in 1918, the farm came to him. His mother dead that year from Spanish flu. His father had died in the grotesque war two years earlier.

The next evening, relishing the quiet, Jacques ruffled Cleo's head and went into the kitchen to refresh her water, then he knelt and gave her a good rubbing behind the ears and along the back of her neck. Eleven years old, she was more about love and homey comfort than hunting. She had eaten all her food and was asking to go out. Taking a glass of port, resting in his oversized armchair, Jacques let his thoughts return to the previous night's train strike, to Fabien and his brothers. They'd done well, though it would be nearly impossible to judge the importance of one derailed German train. And the Americans were coming. His missions would change, would become more frequent. His crew of honest, dedicated men was truly a blessing. Not all the people he had to work with, he would come to discover, were to be trusted. Not everyone is what they first seem.

CHAPTER 4

Cleo ambled into the room the next morning and nudged Jacques's hand. He looked to his nightstand, found his watch, saw it was eight o'clock.

Jacques walked to the sink and splashed water on his face. He'd drive to town and check in with Fabien, find out what degree of success they'd had the night before. But more importantly, what blowback there could be. The Jerries would not let this go. There'd be inquiries. Arrests, maybe. Still, no one looking would put a target on Combourg. Too many small towns separated them from Rennes, including nearby Saint-Grégoire, just five kilometers from Rennes, which had stung the Boche last year. Someone shot at a passing German auto, killing the passenger. Local boys punching back.

Cleo gave Jacques a "hurry-it-up" look, then headed out the front door. Jacques walked back to the kitchen and switched on a burner. He could enjoy eggs in those days of strict rationing, less a problem in small villages than in cities, only because he kept a few hens in a pen behind the house. Still, it was a dark time for all, given German reprisals for anyone showing anything but deference. Their wanton savagery kept most people afraid. No doubt that's why he did the work he did.

Jacques made what passed for coffee in the old glass press— that ancient bronze plunger pot of his mother's—a staple in the house since he was a boy. No sugar, but Jacques didn't care. He liked it strong, strong enough to float a carpet nail—an expression he'd heard his father use. Soon, the dog was back at the door. Jacques put some scraps of chicken mixed with leftover squirrel gravy into her bowl and changed her water. When the coffee and eggs were ready, he sat down at the small table and picked up the notes—more of a prioritized to-do list—work he wanted to catch up on.

Raccoons had been ravaging his trees again, especially in one section by the stream. He hated to set traps and snares, but they had proven effective. He'd tried aluminum sheaves last spring to protect a few of the trees, but such material was no longer available given the military embargo on metals. He'd make do with the snares. No need to protect every tree, but control of the raccoon population was a priority.

Before the war, he might have shipped as many as a hundred barrels of cider in a season, much of it to Paris. He could not do that then, nor would he expect to any time soon. Still, there was nothing wrong with being optimistic, he figured. Problems with the Germans. Problems with the raccoons. Cleo looked up at Jacques tapping his pencil on the pad, calculating. Just the two of them. What would his parents have made of his idea—expanding into the apple brandy business? Might there be a legal issue regarding Calvados branding? He'd check. He turned on the radio and found some Berlioz—*Harold in Italy*, recognizing the viola solo. One of his favorite works. Martine had played violin beautifully, Fritz Kreisler's work. Jacques listened for another moment, transported, then turned it off. His thoughts drifted to his long-dead father.

Mathis Berlangier had owned and worked the property first acquired by his own father over eighty years ago. There were fewer trees, but, even then, they'd had several thousand. Called to war, he met his untimely death on the hard-frozen ridge where his unit engaged the Germans at the infamous battle of the Somme. The river took its name from a Celtic word for tranquility. Such irony.

Jacques looked at a framed photo of his small family on the mantelpiece over the stone fireplace—him and his parents, Mathis and

Adèle, probably taken at some time when he was ten or eleven, and his sister, Nina, four years younger. She was in a bad marriage in Nantes, as he knew the story. He looked at the image of his mother, smiling warily at the camera. Adèle's strength had brought them through the arduous post-war years—Nina and Jacques, just teens when their father was killed. He could still hear her words: "You are the man now. Work this farm."

And with the help of their trusted foreman, he'd kept it all going, and he would keep it going through the devastating war. His father's letter, given him long ago by his mother, had enjoined him to do so. He studied the photo, willing himself to understand.

"Hello, Papa . . ."

Thinking back to the night before, Jacques figured Fabien would have heard something, having been close enough to any rumors or news of how successful their attack had been. He'd also stop at the church to find, or not find, any further instructions. Thinking about who could be servicing that dead drop pew, he figured it could well be the monsignor, a man who had long ago taken a personal interest in him. It was Arnoux, a friend of his father's. Evidently, he had a secret, a deadly one, and kept it well. Any successful clandestine operation, Jacques knew, simply meant this: Every man knows just what he must, and nobody knows too much.

Since his days as an altar boy, he'd disliked the smell of incense, heavy in the church as Jacques slid into the aisle seat two pews up from the back. On that day, all was still—a spiritual sense of grace. No votive candle was burning, which meant no message. When he had knelt at the pew for long enough not to be suspicious, he left and walked the short distance to Fabien's store.

"Heard anything, my friend?"

"Nothing certain, but I think there may have been some transportation difficulties for our foreign guests. Two men came in when I opened."

"Strangers?"

"Oh yes, and from their accents I would say most certainly near neighbors. If I had to guess, I would say Gestapo."

"Not good," said Jacques. "What did they want?"

Fabien told Jacques that one of them asked if he sold explosives. "They asked if I knew anyone in Combourg who did. They told me they were interested in digging a well on a farm they had just purchased over in Dinan."

"Dinan? Not good. What did you tell them?"

"I said that there were safer ways to dig a well and that, no, I did not carry such merchandise and did not know who might." Fabien took a moment, grinned slyly, then added, "I told these bright, stern-faced gentlemen, neither looking like he was ever going to dig a well or farm any land, that to have such materials was against the law."

"I'll bet they liked that."

"They seemed to take it as an impolite correction and left with no cheery goodbye!"

"Well, so much for new friends," added Jacques. "Fabien, I will not be back for several days. We should let this situation play itself out. And, meanwhile, in order to keep the line in the water while the trout considers it, let me have a bag of this dog food. And a small bottle of milk, if you have any."

Walking back to the truck, thinking about the Germans inquiring into explosives, he knew he had to keep his head down. Dinan—only a couple of nights earlier, he was to have met up with an OSS operative there. Another close call. Still, he needed money to pay his people—French francs, not the worthless script the Vichy were printing. There'd soon be more assignments, more linkups. He must be patient.

Meanwhile, back at Claire Skiffington's temporary quarters at RAF Bodney in East Anglia, another set of cautionary flags were being raised.

CHAPTER 5

The airbase saw operational planning and flight activity peak the morning of the 4th of June, in anticipation of the next major phase of this war—the invasion, the expected game changer. For weeks, there had been rumors of an Allied assault into Normandy, but where? Maybe Calais? Dieppe? Running directly against that tide of speculation was the proviso to keep one's mouth shut. Need to know the watchword. Security was job one.

Corporal Paula Evers, WAAF administrative chief, stood in the open doorway of the women's hut. "Something has the brass excited," she said, looking left and right, seeing one vehicle pull up to headquarters. Rays of an insistent sun pushed through the jagged tree line from behind and created a kind of illuminated stage at the entry to the cement, two-story command building. "Look," she said excitedly. "There's Major Holmes, hurrying out of his car. And it looks like he's got something hot in his hand." The man's jeep engine pinged for several seconds and quieted in front of the building; the Union Jack on the left fender of the American vehicle settled. Holmes's message for the base commander and his senior staff, no doubt from Special Operations in London, likely signaled the Allied invasion was imminent and would mean a sea change to the operations of the base.

Claire came to stand next to Paula at the door. "God Lord. Well, we've been expecting something big," she said. Unable to resist, she added, "It's about time, if you ask me. I wonder what it is." The girls knew Major Brian Holmes, chief of the comms section, a bright light in a place not infrequently seen as dark and ever anxious. On several occasions, the good man had led an impromptu host of off-duty club regulars in song with his rich, agile voice and guitar.

Jillie Bates, a vibrant ripple of Bedfordshire energy, squeezed between the women and peered out. "Lemme see." She had just returned from a rendezvous with her husband over at Lakenheath. "Sweet Jesus. Aren't you nervous, ladies? I sure as shit am."

Moments later, a loudspeaker blared from the building. All personnel were to meet with their respective division or department heads: Operations, Security, Support, Communications, Transport and Logistics—everyone. This must be the big one, Claire realized. The allied counterpunch. The reason for Claire's presence at Bodney was casually protected by a cover identity, that of liaison to American War Department Plans. Anyone who did not see through that thin mask wasn't trying. Permanent-party Americans on base were assumed to be OSS. A couple of others might show up. Temporary duty types, on classified assignments, maybe signals or codebreaking. Or propaganda—air-dropped or electronic. False photo IDs. False flag operations. Claire had seen several men and women come and go. The energy was palpable. By that point, all ops and support personnel understood this break in routine meant something massive, and whatever it was would impact everyone. The base commander rarely met with the full complement, being given to let his next-level supervisors handle such matters.

What few of them would have known was that, for the past several days and into the previous evening, the Allies had staged one of history's boldest military deceptions—Operation Bodyguard. This super-secret ruse, complete with dummy landing craft and rubber tanks, sufficiently fooled Hitler and his general staff into looking to Calais and the beaches of Dunkirk. Maybe the misdirection worked as well as it did because Brit radio chatter and practice fighter runs complemented the faux military hardware on the ground in southern England, some of it at Great Yarmouth, not far from Bodney. The 5th of June was to have been the day, but the weather said no.

"That means us," said Paula, nodding to them all. "Each to her own section, ladies." Paula went to Claire, who was looking at a photo and sitting on her bunk. Paula took both her hands. "You will be fine, Claire. You know you are ready for whatever comes next. Betty will be expecting you." Claire hugged her friend, retied her shoes, and headed directly to McIntyre's quarters, gathering both confidence and courage for what she expected would soon bring another mission for her in support of the French.

What Claire could only assume was that French resistance operations would also change immeasurably. Assignments were certain to be more difficult and more dangerous. SOE would signal French resistance to engage in enhanced strikes against vital railways, electrical grids, and Nazi troop transports. The *Résistance*, which for years had had no true center, would bond. For Claire, one vital rendezvous was imminent, a rendezvous that would change her life.

Betty was writing something at her desk. She looked up and signaled for Claire to come in and sit by her. "You understand this is what we've all been expecting," Betty said, looking relieved to be able to state this so directly. As chief of OSS operations at Bodney, she was keen, at last, to get things into gear. Claire nodded and crossed her arms, which was her habit when nervous. "Of course." Betty offered Claire coffee, and she settled the saucer on her lap. "We are going to have to be ready at any time, dear girl. Air and ground attacks will be underway. I don't know any more than that. We just have to give it the time it takes." The coffee was hot, and Betty blew into her own cup, looking to her friend to see how she was taking the news. Betty had to keep her own composure. She set her cup down, took a deep breath, and finished what she had to tell her friend and subordinate. "People are gonna need our help. Your help"

"Yes. Thank God," said Claire. "That's why I'm here."

The early morning of June 6 brought the full-scale allied assault known as Operation Overlord. A new front had opened, an invasion fleet of some 5,000 ships, including 3,000 landing craft, supported by 12,000 aircraft, all en route to Normandy's five designated beachheads, driven by the will and courage of 150,000 men, including elite airborne units from Britain, Canada, and America. There had never been anything like it in the history of warfare.

CHAPTER 6

With Allied landings progressing through that seminal morning, word was beginning to reach French partisan teams, and, by noon, radio broadcasts confirmed the Allied assaults. There were few details, as of that point, but no one doubted what the arrival of the Americans meant. Jacques and his team would have work, and likely soon. Difficult work. Dangerous work. The exact nature of it, of course, was unknown. Only one way to know, and that was for Jacques to check the dead drop locale in the church daily. The first full day following the landings yielded no assignment, but then Brittany was not in the path of that Allied advance. Any work he and his team would be given would necessarily be one of rear-guard support. Still, the probability of left-behind enemy units heightened the anxiety.

And then there was the air battle, bringing even more complications.

Early the next morning, Jacques gave Cleo her breakfast and walked into the living room; he went to the mantle above the fireplace and picked up the photo of his family. What he did and would do for France he was doing at least as much for them—all gone. Well, his sister was another story: Nina was reportedly down in Nantes. His parents were long dead.

If he thought about his own lack of family, a wife and children, as any single man his age might do, someone to carry forward the Berlangier name, it was only for a moment. A gesture to the ineffable. A ruffling breeze of what might yet be, then gone.

On the morning of June 9, Jacques walked into the Romanesque Église Saint-Martin anticipating another assignment. Three days of unexpected quiet had left him feeling on edge. Surely, he'd be called upon soon. The covert operational procedure that would signal an assignment was both simple and reasonably secure. So much depended upon one candle.

He stood at the back of the church. Six worshippers were at prayer. Jacques crossed the nave to get a better look at the altar and at the bank of votive candles set to the right and just next to the sacristy. All assignments and their secret codes and instructions were handled, he was certain, in the shadow of the able Saint Martin—more specifically, Martin of Tours, a fourth-century figure who had served in the Roman cavalry in Gaul and, subsequently, became known for his attention to the needs of the poor and the disadvantaged. *Deo et patriae*. For God and country.

"Here I am," he whispered. "What have you got for me?"

The low mass that day, a Friday, brought only the few regulars to the church. Jacques looked around for anything or anyone that looked out of place. First things first, he understood, and that was to be cautious. He watched for another moment, sensing nothing unusual, then settled into a pew. As expected, the white-haired Monsignor Eduard Arnoux was at the altar, a man accustomed to going about his spiritual business quietly. Perhaps other, more dangerous matters equally so. Was he a hero of France in holy orders? And was he Jacques's resistance controller? The priest held up the chalice, a man apart, perhaps close only to the Holy Ghost, and he whispered his ritual benediction.

Jacques looked to the rack of candles by the beige colored wall, hard beneath the faded statue of Saint Martin, and there, in the center, in the third row, one lone candle burned brightly. The signal was clear. He had a mission. He need only wait until mass was over, then go to the designated pew and retrieve it.

Twenty minutes later, he opened the requisite book and secured the folded paper that awaited him. He pocketed the note and sat for several minutes more, his heart racing, needing to be certain he was alone and no one had seen this small act. He would not read it there, even as he burned to know what lay ahead for him.

And what of the man, this priest, Eduard Arnoux?

Jacques had long felt close to the cleric given how kind and supportive he'd been when Jacques's father was killed nearly twenty-seven years ago. He cherished the memories of how the priest had come to the house, maybe just to look in on the family. Did the young man have anything he needed to talk about? What the good father had shown him was simple decency.

The mass over, Jacques walked to the back of the church and headed out to his truck. When he arrived home, he pulled the coded note from his pocket. Someone needed help. And this one would be an assignment unlike any he'd had been given before. No demolitions. No cash to be delivered. With OSS assistance, he would meet a go-between agent in order to render direct support. But to whom, and where? The war, or his part in it, would take on a whole different dimension, and this operation would be a game changer.

In those long, hard days and nights following the landings, as Allied troops had fought their way inland, orders for any and all guerilla operations grew exponentially. With so many air engagements over north coastal France, resistance action would focus on the problem of downed aircrew. Three days into the attack, one such challenge resulted from German BF 109 fighters in support of the 21st Panzer Division engaging American P-51 Mustang fighters. There was one downed American asset just northeast, bordering directly on Berlangier farmland. So, the operation was imminent. He looked at the message once more.

Friend of family en route this evening.
Praise Brother Erwan for valuables.
Rendezvous delicious.

That meant OSS, friend of family, was coming in tonight. The valuables would be one or more clandestine operators in danger. Somewhere. He knew who Erwan was, and where to meet up. He'd met him once several months ago in Dinan. Delicious meant expect complications. Jacques looked to his Cleo and gave her a chin scratch. "*C'est une nouvelle journée, Cleo,*" he said to the dog, who looked up at him eagerly and barked. "We are going on a journey."

CHAPTER 7

Betty came to Claire's hut with a better understanding of what the mission would entail. "Claire, you will need to prepare to fly out tonight."

"Yes. Of course. I'm ready." She set her shoulders. "What is my mission?"

"We've got one of our people in trouble. Maybe injured. We don't know much more. Your orders are to get him to where he was supposed to go before losing his ride. You'll partner with a French resistance agent."

Claire nodded instinctively. "Do you know where?"

"I don't, but your connection will. A typical partisan cutout kind of thing. Failing that, get him back to us. It will be a fluid situation. Sorry, I don't know any more."

She had to process this. "How many days?"

"It could be several."

Claire knew she would carry a few packs of military or Occupation currency as well as a few French francs for the journey. But, more importantly, she'd also have French citizen identification cards, corroborating papers, and requisite permissions for travel within and exit from the Occupied Zone. All would be given to the American operative.

Betty lit a cigarette and offered one to Claire, who shook her head. "You'll make contact through a local partisan. Our man is a high-value asset. Claire, this will not be easy. It certainly will be dangerous."

"Yes, of course. I know that. . ." She felt her face flush.

Interrupting them, Paula came into the hut silently, so as not disturb. She went to her bed and sat. Bad timing. Betty apologized and asked if she might give them a moment of privacy, just for a few more minutes. "Sorry, I know I'm being difficult, Paula. I don't mean to be. But we just have some private business."

Paula pulled a long face and left without saying a word.

"Your contact is known as Hibou," Betty told Claire. "He's been reliable. He will take you to meet the OSS man you are going there to help. It's not much, but it's all I know."

"Yes, I was to meet him several nights ago." She instantly recalled the shooting at Dinan. The panic. How everything fell apart with that killing. The man Claire and Hibou were to assist had flown too close to an ongoing fighter battle raging several kilometers south of Saint-Malo. Stupid. Their slow, lightweight aircraft went down. The passenger may have jumped. He probably did. No one was sure, and no one knew what kind of shape he was in.

"Do you know who the pilot was? "No."

"Okay," said Claire. Her first thought was of Owen, and she prayed it was not him.

"Sorry. Hibou will give you more detail on site. You fly out tonight. I'll bring you the money and the classified materials ahead of that, which means eleven. Pack a light haversack and be sure to include clothes for rough terrain. And bring your weapon."

Jacques, meanwhile, was on site just after midnight, ready for whoever was coming. He and the ever-able woman he knew as Corbeau had set two small fires some forty meters apart, and another had been set downfield, but they had trouble keeping them going in the heavy rain. They'd worked together several times. Jacques knew she worried about her brother, a man seriously injured in 1916 at Verdun. He helped when he could. Jacques checked his watch. If the plane was to be on time, it should have been there by that point.

"Go home. I've got this taken care of," Jacques told her, squeezing her arm.

"No, you do not. The weather has its say, and it is saying no," she replied.

"Weather be damned. Go. I can manage. You are needed at home."

Corbeau shrugged, shook her head, and turned back to the tree line where she'd left her bicycle. Jacques looked into the dark, rainy sky, knowing he'd not hear any plane until it was nearly on top of him. Two more of his small signal fires, he saw, had once again gone out. After nearly an hour with no sign of the Brit plane, he, too, turned back toward the woods to shelter and watch. Maybe they'd had to abort. He would wait as long as it made any sense to do so. Meanwhile, her visibility poor and unable to locate the designated makeshift strip where she was to meet Hibou, Claire asked her pilot if there might be an alternative place somewhere nearby. "I need to get down there."

"It will be rough," the pilot told her. "Are you sure, Miss? We can turn back."

Claire's pilot, yet another new face to her, then said he could maybe shoot for a spot he could just make out—not far, maybe half a kilometer from the intended landing. The rain was letting up a little, and the open terrain he saw below was something he thought could work. Small trees in tight rows gave way to a decent-sized clearing. The tough part, he told her, might be getting the plane turned around in that tight space and back into the air. Claire said she was willing if he thought that was their best option.

The landing was rough, jarring her lower back. On the ground, with a few more jolts than usual to the Lysander and their weary bodies, she detected no one. Claire needed to trust her instincts. Whether or not it was foolish to insist on this landing, the linkup plan, which had been scotched, was immaterial. There was an OSS colleague out there, and she would find the man who was to take her to him. She also suspected that Hibou was probably looking for her.

"Just don't let the bleedin' Jerries or local gendarmes find you first," her pilot said.

She climbed down and helped the pilot turn the small plane around; he was eager to make his way back to Bodney. Her clothing was soaked;

she wiped rain from her face and pulled her cloth coat up as far as it would stretch to give her any extra protection. The plane's engines strained.

"I've always been a decent hider," she yelled. "Be careful too." He waved a thank you, and the plane pumped its way along the sodden ground, lifted more quickly than she thought it ever could, and made for home. Claire watched the single engine sputter and rise up for the short while it remained visible—one woman left staring into the odds. The rain picked up again.

Checking the compass in her kit, finding a route east and back to the tree line, she tightened her bootlaces and made her way into a nearby grove. *Green apples,* she thought. *Well, at least I won't starve.* Putting the best face on the situation.

One twenty, she noticed. *Full dark.* Claire walked toward what she took to be the intended landing area. Imprecise, but best she could do. Keeping track of time would tell her about how far she'd walked as she made her way onto what looked like a pathway, something a vehicle might manage. What she did not foresee was one well-camouflaged animal snare at the base of a small tree that snapped hard around her ankle when she wasn't looking.

"Oh, God. Shit, that hurts!" she cried out, looking around. She tried to open it, her fingers slipping on the cold, hard ring. *Don't panic.* She slid down to work at it. *Figure it out.* She told herself not to be upset. But what the hell was she thinking, stuck in an animal trap, in the rain, in France, in the middle of a war? The last thing she'd done before flying out that night was to reread an old letter from her sister Rita, a mother and a full twelve years her junior. While there was Claire, the educated one, wet, trapped, and angry.

Just then, from a small road maybe 100 meters off to the south, she saw a black vehicle—German? Yes, "Damn." Was she about to be taken? Her heart was racing.

The car had a rotating spotlight on the hood, what her Brit friends called the bonnet. These men must have been looking for someone, possibly her. Two got out. Angry. One talking fast and loud. No uniforms. Gestapo, maybe. She figured they were German from the make of car, an old black Mercedes. One man peered in her direction and began walking toward her, the vehicle light fixed and pointed. Claire took a sharp breath and held absolutely still. Leaning against the tree for support, she tried again to loosen the wire that bound her. Claire reached into her kit for the .32, racking the slide, and holding the gun under her coat to keep it more or less dry. Was he coming for her? Held in place as she was, her line of fire would be limited. Her foot was beginning to hurt all the more, the wire biting through her woolen socks. The man's pace quickened.

Claire's worry eased when she saw him stop next to a tree some forty meters from her to unzip. His partner had not come into the woods but evidently wanted to give up any driving responsibility as he tugged on the brim of his hat, walked around the car, and climbed into the passenger seat, while the other finished his business and returned to take the wheel. He backed the car into the tree line, then headed in the direction from which they'd come, smoke pouring out of the back of their vehicle.

She'd been holding her breath, determined to make no sound. She needed something to sustain her strength. She found several small apples nearby. Taking a bite from one, she put the gun back into her carryall and checked her watch. Nothing to do but wait to see what, or who, would come along next. Morning and its early light were still hours away; her injured leg felt almost numb. She had made choices, far less conventional choices than others, such as her sisters Madolyn and Rita. Maddie, as everyone called her. She and Ott with two fine daughters. She thought of her parents, John and Julia. Arguments now and again. Never any extra cash in the house. But they had cared. What hurt more than her leg just then, which was feeling miserable already, was a pervasive loneliness that could not be denied. "We make our choices," she said to herself. And not for the first time. Losing her Robert had hurt. They'd planned a future. The man she'd met and loved in Paris, had been gone for seven years. Well, she had work. People were counting on her.

Just then, startled, Claire detected someone else approaching. A man. A good-sized fellow carrying what looked like a rifle. She froze. "Not again," she whispered. Then a single flashlight beam— gone in an instant. Someone was looking for her.

CHAPTER 8

Jacques put a small flashlight into his jacket pocket, picked up the automatic he'd come to trust, checked the magazine, and left to take a look. Whatever else Jacques was feeling about the missed OSS connection, other than irritation with himself for taking a job well out of his expected remit, he knew it would be impossible to give up. Dicey weather or not, just maybe someone had come in. Jacques tried to think where anyone could have made it work, via small courier plane. If his contact was out there, he had to find him. Or her. But how?

Growing up on the land and knowing intimately its layout, he had one idea where such an aircraft could possibly get down. One spot lay fairly nearby. Carefully making his way, some twenty minutes later, he spotted something at the base of one tree. Not an animal. Someone was nestled tight against the trunk. That someone had spotted him. Judging by size, he'd guess it was a woman. Jacques flashed his light.

Cautious, Claire looked up and attempted to stand— determined to control her voice. "My God," she said. Struggling. Wanting more than anything to be vigilant. There'd been Germans there not thirty minutes before. But in a car. This felt different.

"*Qui est là?* Who is there? She held her breath. No answer.

The possibility of some German or Vichy traitor wandering in an orchard in the rain in the middle of the night was slight. This was a local.

Jacques came closer. "Well, what do we have here?" he asked, astonished, peering at her trapped leg. He knew this could only be the OSS American. Vulnerable, soaked, and mad.

"We have a lady in a blessed trap," she said. "And you could help." Her anger was rising again.

"So I see. And what is the lady, a lady eating my fruit, I might add, looking for here on my farm?" He considered the snare she'd found. The realization made him grin, yet he suppressed it. How ridiculous she must feel.

"Well, I'm not bird watching," she said. "And I would appreciate it if you would help me remove this damn thing. It really hurts."

"I suspect it does," Jacques agreed, all the more interested, as he squatted down to release the catch. "If you were to be watching for birds, and you have told me you are not, what kind of bird might you be watching for?" He wanted to help, but he needed to take this by the book.

"Oh, that's better." She stared at him a moment. What should she say? "*Je cherche un hibou.* I am looking for an owl. If you can believe that," Claire said, rubbing her ankle and looking fearfully defeated.

"An owl? Here? Any owl in particular?"

"I do not know what kind. Damn it! Just Hibou." She said the word again. She was mad at herself and feeling foolish.

Jacques pulled away the snare and tossed it. "I am Hibou," he said. "Let me help you up." He asked how long she had been there. Maybe as long as forty minutes, she said, adding there had been Germans, just there, pointing. She told him what she had witnessed, described their car.

"Germans, in a car? You heard them speak?"

"Yes. Just there. One of them was angry."

"I'm sure." He got a kick out of this very idea. Someone finding a dead-end road. "This is most peculiar. That road was abandoned years ago. It ends just where you pointed. I take my truck in there sometimes, for harvesting. But it's a dead end."

Well, she thought, *someone else had been made a fool.*

"Tell me your name."

"Celine."

"Welcome to my apple farm, Celine."

"Thank you." She let out a big sigh. What would Betty say? What a mess. What a poor start for the mission. Jacques studied her for a moment. Having done this kind of clandestine business for years, he knew he had a rookie with him. He'd help in any way he could. Although she was the one who had come to help him. He squared his shoulders, reached, and made to pull her up.

"Thank you." She rubbed her ankle and settled her carry bag. She tried to smile. "Look, I'm sorry, I don't have much experience hiding like this."

"Well, you knew not to confront those lost Germans. So, I would say you are doing pretty well," he said, pushing his own English skills. "Let me get you out of here, and maybe into some food and drink. You do have experience with food and drink, don't you?"

She wanted to laugh but would not, still angry about her absurd predicament. Claire took a second to decide how to take the fellow, knowing things had come right, in spite of her absurd circumstance.

"Yes, of course, that would be wonderful."

He grasped her arm, assisting her first steps. "Let's get you decently dry and maybe warm." Jacques helped her up into his nearby truck. Looking at his watch, he saw the time was two-thirty. "What happened?" he asked. "You missed the landing site?"

She told him her pilot was unable to see the prepared opening. "Too much rain and no clear lighting to get us down. We agreed to make do. I was not about to be turned back."

"Of course." He found her courage and relentlessness admirable, all the more so in that weather.

"We picked a spot that looked reasonable—doable—to him. I pretty much insisted. And then, I stepped into that damn trap. It must be yours."

"Guilty. And it's a snare, actually. Sorry, it's for raccoons."

"Does it kill them?

"No, it just keeps them from climbing and eating my apples." He did not tell her he shot most of them anyway, since they would only return, the creatures not being analytical enough to learn to leave the apples alone, or to move on for their scavenging.

Claire smelled a trace of smoke coming from the chimney. A fireplace. All she wanted just then was to get warm and dry. When they entered the house, the amiable Cleo was waiting at the door. She'd been taught not to bark when strangers appeared, though she did look to Jacques, perhaps to detect any anxiety in her master's manner. Her curiosity evident, the dog's tail suggesting her degree of excitement, she sniffed carefully at Claire until the stranger gave her some rubs and spoke to her, as people tend to do, as if the dog were a small child.

Jacques found a full-sized towel, which he brought to the woman.

"Thanks."

"Cleo is happy for the company. I think she may get bored alone with me." He suggested that he take a look at that ankle. "Let me see, did it break the skin?"

"Only a little, and it will be fine. Never mind. I think my dignity hurts more."

He asked if he might put some salve on it, wrap it in gauze. There was not much swelling. Heavy socks had helped. He gave her a pair of his to change into, and a soft woolen shirt, which she looked at with satisfaction. She asked for the loo. Using the British term. He smiled again and pointed. Having settled the woman, Jacques went to heat up some stew, having also offered her a small glass of brandy. Momentarily, she followed him into the kitchen, still on edge, but interested in how a man tended to domestic chores. Handily enough, she thought, gathering the plates and flatware. He set a bottle of red on the table.

Raising his glass, he said, "So, to Celine and Hibou. Contact made," and he smiled.

She thought this fellow was going to be fine. Maybe she'd been lucky after all. Later, as they ate and enjoyed the warmth of the nearby fire, he said, "I am thinking that you are new to this secret mission business, Celine. How many linkups have you made— more or less?"

"Well, not many," she said, and looked to her near-empty plate. She did not want to tell him she was on her first real assignment, that she had, only months ago, been a code clerk in Washington. She made to bite her lower lip, which she was given to do when agitated.

"Oh, this is for you," she said, reaching into her nearby haversack, and handing him a wrapped packet. "It's something I understand you need. And I am told you have another, bigger job for me as well." The rest of what she carried with her would wait for the downed OSS man, assisting him being their actual mission. She looked to the dog, who was studying her.

Jacques peered into the envelope.

"Perfect. And just in time. Thank you," he said. "Yes. The other matter can wait until morning. Are you warm enough?"

She took a moment to answer. She was. Claire thought him strong. And, actually, quite attractive. Medium build. Curly hair— lots of it. Nice eyes, a surprisingly light grey in color, and a dry sense of humor, which she liked. Cleo came to her, sensing the woman a welcome addition. She could see the dog was well settled. A good sign, she thought.

Claire petted the spaniel for a moment, pensive, then said, "Can you tell me anything about this other business? About the papers I've brought along in my bag? It's on my mind."

"Identity papers for the downed American, I would imagine. That can all wait."

She let out a sigh. "Good. Because I'm tired, and the wine is wonderful." Claire told herself to slow down. She'd be spending the night and was still feeling that all this was surreal. The next day, when more clear-headed, she'd give further consideration to security protocols. The enemy has many faces, but she sensed this fellow was on the right side. He and his Cleo. He had done all this before, she figured. He'd be a good partner. Claire knew she needed confidence in herself. She needed to establish some sense of trust as well. "This place is marvelous, and so homey." She put her hand down, showing Cleo that she'd like to pet her, make a friend, vexed as to what was proper at that point. Their work together would begin the next day.

Jacques went to the fireplace and adjusted the logs; he looked into his own glass. "Thank you. I grew up here. It's all I've ever known." The dog had not gone far from Claire's chair since they'd sat down to eat. Cleo stuck her nose into her hand, giving the woman a few quick licks.

"Cleo must think you are a friend, Celine, even if I think this is all an elaborate plan to finish up the lamb stew I'd been saving for a rainy day."

She laughed nervously and put her hand to her mouth. He was easy to be with. So different from Corbeau and her taciturn partner. "Well, it was rainy enough for me."

"Oh, me too."

From across the small table, an old oaken piece that had belonged to his parents, Jacques looked at the woman, taking in her unaffected self-confidence, the American deep into French partisan activity. He saw how she adjusted one wisp of her auburn hair behind her ear. She had short bangs, and he wondered whether it was an American style. The light from the dying fire flattered her eyes. They talked for another quarter of an hour about the excitement of the invasion, the stepped-up activity on both sides of the battle. When Jacques stifled a yawn, she thanked him for the meal and told him she needed to turn in, lest she fall asleep right there at the table. Jacques showed her to the spare bedroom and gave her a fresh towel.

"We'll get to work in the morning. Get some sleep; we have some traveling to do. People to meet."

He opened the front door for Cleo, but she turned back and lay down on her rug. Jacques thought for a moment about the work he was about—dangerous and unpredictable—and about how, while its ending could not be foretold, the good men and women he worked with were giving up so much, all a part of something larger than themselves. The new one would make a good partner, the American. Smart and quick.

What lay ahead for the newly born, enterprising team would be totally unexpected.

CHAPTER 9

The next day, Claire helped Jacques to load three mixed barrels of apples and one of Guyot pears into his truck. Having checked the map, they headed out for the commune of Saint-Léonard, not a twenty-minute drive, past the north edge of his orchard farm. The fruit run was a cover, of course, but Jacques was well known to the gendarmes controlling road access and conducting spot checks. There were rarely German troops that deep in the countryside, but one never knew and would need to stay alert to the possibility of a roadblock and an identity check. The trip would look like routine business to any curious Vichy official. Still, if stopped, Claire's French was good enough to pass for a native, though not local. He figured they'd be okay. For the moment.

For her part, Claire had agreed to wear a doleful brown headscarf to better feel the part. Poor Celine, she thought. Her slacks had dried, and the shirt fit her well enough. They saw no one on the road until a man on a dark green, powerful Alcyon 305 motorcycle came up behind them and followed Jacques's truck.

"What have we got back there?" he said, as much to himself as to her.

"Where?"

"Motorcycle. Behind us."

Jacques said the man had been driving aggressively, and that observation gave them several minutes of concern, but, soon, he passed, and their luck held.

"Bastard," Jacques said, as the man flew by. "What was that about?" she asked.

"Just a local idiot. But I cannot help thinking that the plainclothes Vichy police are a threat around here. And you never know." Jacques confirmed that the man they were to help was an OSS operative whose plane went down south of Saint-Malo, not far from there. American OSS. Claire had been briefed, she said, but added she knew nothing about his mission. Meanwhile, there'd be a middleman, a local, at Saint-Léonard. He'd be the one to take them to the safe house. Always a cut-out in their business.

Jacques met the man at just past ten—a Breton partisan named Erwan. Jacques had connected with him once, several months back. As was the nature of those kinds of jobs, it was vital to keep identities to oneself. Claire was not introduced, though Erwan acknowledged her with a nod. Jacques instinctively wanted to turn his head from the man's breath.

He told Jacques the farmhouse was a few kilometers away, a ten-minute drive, toward Épiniac. Their American would be waiting. And, because people were not accustomed to seeing strangers, Jacques agreed it would be best for all concerned if he and his partner followed in his truck. Both men checked the road to see whether anything or anyone looked out of place.

Moments before Jacques turned onto the road that would bring them to the farmhouse, Claire tapped him on the arm and pointed to the green motorcycle parked in front of a weathered yellow stucco office-type building. A despicable Vichy flag fluttered from below the central window.

"Trouble?" she asked.

"Tough to avoid it, I suppose."

Jacques checked his rearview mirror to see if anyone had come out of the building, trying to decide whether he was being smart or foolish.

Strange how assignments develop, he thought. Their escort and courier parked in front of the farmhouse, and Jacques pulled up behind him, noticing that the curtains in the front-facing windows were drawn. Ushered into the house, they found their distressed American working on some notes and studying a map. A slight smile belied his nervousness. He stood, wincing, as he favored his left leg.

He said hello to Erwan, who was first through the door, then looked at the others, clearly much relieved. "At last. The name is Thomas, Roland Thomas." He looked to Jacques and Claire. Erwan, who had brought the man there two days before, had done his job and turned to leave. Jacques signaled for him to wait. Not all the pieces were in place. Jacques identified himself to Thomas as Hibou. Extending his hand. Whatever mission this fellow had been given was his business. At least for the moment. The less said the better, given so many uncertainties.

"I knew you would come. Or I had to trust that you would," Roland said, and looked to Claire.

"Celine," she said, and extended her hand, almost formally.

Jacques took the American to be about fifty. He was balding, and it was hard to assess any degree of fitness. Medium height. His clothes looked all right. With a change of shirt and some work pants, he'd blend in as well as anyone. Decent boots. Jacques and Claire sat opposite Thomas, Erwan still near the door. Claire knew Thomas was on orders from OSS, but his assignment would have originated with Britain's SOE. Allied clandestine ops shared a common cause. Still, that kind of job was new to Jacques—assisting a downed asset. He'd be all the more vigilant there. He looked at Claire, knowing she would have to establish her own position.

"What do you make of the mood in Mother England, Mr. Thomas?" Claire asked. "What with the successful Allied landings in Normandy?"

Thomas cocked his head. "Please—call me Roland," he said, then answered that he thought the allied landings meant renewed hope. He felt his ankle, evidently injured in his jump from the plane, then began searching for his pipe, finding the tobacco pouch on a nearby pine table and accidently knocking it to the floor. He did so as a youngster reaches for a cloth animal, needing something familiar. Jacques had been trained to spot obvious nerves, and this fellow showed plenty.

Jacques asked Erwan, eager to head out, if he had any reason to suspect that others were aware of Thomas's presence there. Erwan shook his head no. Claire continued to study Thomas, maybe to determine his purpose. Infiltration? Certainly not. What, then?

Jacques looked at Erwan, who left, and the room fell quiet.

"Well, we had best get down to business," he said.

His operation evidently saved, Thomas let out a sigh of relief. "Certainly. And I may as well tell you that I am from the Communications Branch of the organization," he said, again trying to light his pipe. "My assignment—do you know it?"

Claire shook her head. Jacques remained silent but attentive, then said, "No."

"Well, it is nothing more than to set up a portable radio intercept operation as close to the German main battle area as I can. Copy voice traffic, process the information, and get out."

"Nothing more than that, eh?" said Jacques, looking at Claire.

Thomas either missed or chose to ignore Jacques's prickly challenge.

"We are not equipped to fight this war head-on," he added, to which Thomas nodded, as if he couldn't agree more.

"Near the battle zone?" Claire leaned forward in her chair. "What do you mean?"

"That's where the most critical operational intel is to be found," Thomas said, "and it has seldom been done before—apart from what our Army G-2 people are doing and putting together back in Arlington. I'm thinking there may be others now. Signals intelligence." Claire knew that a good deal of that work was being done at Bletchley Park, as well. She added that she thought his was a test case, looking to Jacques for affirmation. "Mr. Thomas, you know how fluid battle zones can be. Distance could work to your advantage. What is the range of your equipment?"

Jacques pushed for clarity. "You must be able to pick up what communications you need from some standoff distance, is that not so?"

Thomas shook his head. "Inadequate range," he said. "Gotta get near the buggers. We need intel on unit assignments, Wehrmacht order of battle, unit movement and tactical engagement." Thomas added, "They need SITREPS. The key is to get reports and analysis to Allied commanders or their G-2s in a timely way. The closer to their command posts the better." He'd been touching the bald spot in his head, a habit, Jacques noted—a kind of tic.

"We had a whiff of this kind of operation at Bodney," said Claire. Did Betty know about it? "You do not need line of sight, but you do need the right radio and antennas. Right?"

"Yes. For HF broadcast. But, and I'm sorry, I have no radio. Our plane, you know . . .

Jacques looked to Claire. She said, "No intercept radio?"

"No. Lost it in the crash."

"What?" Jacques leaned in, shaking his head. "Well then, that's it. No chance. . ."

The man reacted immediately. "Can you help?" Thomas interjected and looked at them both, his face flushed. "My assignment is to copy the bastards' tactical comms. But I need the right radio."

"How? Where are we expected to find such a thing? No. Impossible. We will escort you back. Get you fixed for a return to Britain."

Claire cleared her throat. "Well, let's wait." She put her hand on Jacques's arm. She wanted to know more about the man's assignment, thinking maybe something could be done. Her own radio training gave her an idea. Could they try to find a replacement? "Tell me, Roland, what your general plan was to be. There are so many different radios, you see."

"Yes. Ideally, I'd set up in a barn, somewhere near Caen," Thomas said, trying to be optimistic and looking at the map.

Jacques knew he needed to assert control.

"Caen? That's a good 150 kilometers. Even if you had the right radio, you cannot just set up shop on the enemy's doorstep. That's a death wish. Germans everywhere. Mr. Thomas, what you are talking about is extremely dangerous. And you have no radio."

"I understand. But what you said about help, Celine. The Brits, maybe?" Thomas was near tears.

Jacques shook his head in disbelief at the man's blinkered insistence. He turned to face Claire. "This is nuts."

She had to pursue the matter to her own satisfaction. "Let's go back to the mission." She asked Thomas about his language skills, his French. How much did he understand?

"I had high school French. Two years. I can get by, I suppose." Claire nodded, "Limited, then," she said, smiling, as if to assure Thomas they were there to help. She'd need Jacques on board for finding Mr. Thomas a replacement unit.

Just then, Jacques heard a noise. "Whose house is this?" he asked.

The American pointed to the stairs. "Madame Laurent."

"Who?"

"The house belongs to an old woman. Madame Laurent. She will not be any further involved. A meeting place. The courier, Erwan, he made the arrangements."

"I can go see about this," said Claire. "She may be less nervous talking with a woman."

"I would be less nervous if we just got back into the damn truck." Jacques looked toward the nearest window. He needed to clear his head. "Yes. All right. Go ahead, Celine. See if she'll come down."

Thomas set down his pipe and put his head in his hands. "I know this is asking a lot."

Claire pulled Jacques aside, indicating this was for his ears only. "Now, just maybe we can still help. I have an idea about what kind of radio he needs. If we can find one here, in country, there could yet be a chance."

"Maybe," said Jacques. "That's a big maybe."

"It is. I know. But I'll need your help, your contacts," she said, and headed for the stairs.

CHAPTER 10

Whose plan was it? The Americans', in concert with Brit Special Operations, of course. The Baker Street Irregulars as they'd been called. Jacques had doubted the wisdom of some schemes before, but such divinations were above him. Tactical signals intelligence was risky business. He had no experience in that. Did Celine? He thought about what she'd just told him. That she knew what kind of intercept radio Roland Thomas would need.

He heard her on the stairs and watched her enter the room with a white-haired woman who appeared to be about sixty-five, though Jacques was not particularly good at assigning ages to anyone, least of all older women. Short and round, she wore a yellowing housecoat and a worn-out pair of woolly blue slippers. She held a thin, tawny cat in her large, mannish hands, and she looked at Jacques. She knew Thomas, of course, but who were the others?

"Madame," said Jacques, ever the gentleman. Claire pulled him aside, leaving the woman to head into the kitchen on her own steam.

"She has a brother, a priest," she said. Maybe thinking this, somehow, would help to clarify something about Jacques's involvement.

"Really? A priest? Well, that confirms something." The good Monsignor

Eduard Arnoux was behind the plan, of course. But then, he would be a focal point for local resistance. The old badger was smart enough and bold enough, an old friend of the family. Jacques looked to the kitchen.

"You know him?" she asked. "This priest?"

"Oh, I do. I certainly do." Jacques saw the whole scenario. He'd been selected to take the lead on this operation for both professional and personal reasons. The monsignor trusted him.

The old woman came back to the room, again holding the cat, maybe for comfort. She shook her head. Much put out. "My son should be here," she insisted.

"Your son?"

Claire said something to her the others could not hear, and the woman put the cat down. Claire told Jacques that she'd explained to Madame Laurent that they'd been sent by friends to help the American, Mr. Thomas, who acknowledged the obligation with a weak grin.

"Ask her about Roger. He speaks English. He helped me," Thomas said, looking to his fellow American, who might have been more likely to be sympathetic. "I thought he would be here when you arrived. Sorry, I suppose I'm not thinking straight."

Roger. The woman's son. "Every unknown, every variable added to the operation, creates more chance for failure, for exposure," said Jacques, as much to himself as to the others. Well, the monsignor knew this. Over the years, Jacques had come to feel not unlike a son to the man. There was no bullshit from him, ever. Trust came first. Always. Eduard Arnoux had been good to Adèle Berlangier, encouraging her as she walked from the church after mass. Jacques had to trust that the cleric knew what he was doing. After all, the old fellow knew more about the workings of the clandestine world than Jacques ever would.

Claire turned back to the woman. *"Où est Roger maintenant?"* Where is your son now?

The woman's spirits picked up. He was in town but would be there soon. "My Roger goes to town," she told her with a note of pride. "He is a very important man."

"I see," said Jacques, knowing he'd have to give that some thought. There was no way to gauge his true alliances, but perhaps a man with connections could help. The monsignor would know his skills. So, it was another matter of trust.

"Does Roger have a green motorcycle?" Claire asked the woman, switching back to French.

"Yes!"

"How did you know?" asked Jacques, clearly impressed. Then, "It only makes sense that you are in this house owing to some larger plan," he said to Thomas. "A son who gets around quite freely would likely have been part of the whole thing."

"Yes, of course. I'm sure he is."

"But who is *he* working for?" asked Claire, reverting to French, sensing that Thomas would not follow her rapidly delivered speech.

Madame Laurent, however, had no trouble. "My son works with important people. I know this because he has told me. Police."

"I'm not surprised," Jacques said, and looked to Celine. *Whose police?* was the tricky bit.

Claire looked toward the door, listening. "We have company, it would appear."

No one could miss the distinctive, straight-pipe, loud rumbling sound of a powerful motorcycle approaching the house. Someone's arrival would further change the calculus. Madame Laurent rushed to the door. Thomas stood and looked at Jacques, who, reflexively, touched the handgun beneath his jacket. Claire stepped into the kitchen. Better to have multiple points of egress, she figured. She would listen and decide what to do in the moment.

CHAPTER 11

He will have seen my truck," said Jacques. "Stay sharp."

Thomas stood in anticipation as Roger Laurent stepped into the house, stomping his black leather boots. Roger took a quick look at Jacques, on point in the middle of the room, nodded, then turned to smile at his mother. She opened her arms.

"There is my son." The woman beamed as he stepped to her for a welcoming hug.

"Well, well," Roger said, setting his cap onto a nearby chair, taking in the presence of Jacques. "Hello, Maman. I see we have company."

Jacques assessed the situation as odd but nonthreatening, while watching what Roger did next; he was a man who looked like he could handle himself. After kissing his mother, he moved past her, extending his hand. Jacques took Laurent to be about thirty-five, maybe a little older. They were nearly the same height. His handshake said a lot about what physical strength he likely had. Thomas seemed to stand taller, unconcerned about any awkwardness. Roger grinned at him.

"I know this must be somewhat of a surprise, Monsieur," said Roger to Jacques. "And you will by now know our American friend here," he said, looking to an excited Roland Thomas.

Claire entered last, more the cautious operative. For a moment, no one spoke. Roger knew Thomas was there and that he was American. Would he know why too? Claire introduced herself as Celine and shook Roger's hand. His mother, meanwhile, looked as though all had at last come right.

Roger pulled a small paperback book out of his jacket and nonchalantly tossed it onto the table, next to Claire, evidently looking for a reaction. If he was expecting her to notice, he was not disappointed. Albert Camus's *L'Étranger*, a book written two years earlier and published by the author in Algeria. Jacques took it in as well. A prop? Signifying what? Camus had volunteered to fight for France but was rejected because of a prior bout of tuberculosis. The writer was a fighter.

"Oh, Camus; I must read that sometime," Claire said.

Roger grinned. "For some, it is a must. You are from Paris, Madame?" he tried, testing.

"I am from Reims, but I lived and worked in Paris for many years." This was true enough, or the Paris part was. Confident her language skills were up to the test, she said she'd lived at the southeast edge of the city, teaching and painting landscapes in oil. She knew enough about Reims to make that sound legit if she had to.

"I must make tea," said Madame Laurent, not a little confused, settling the cat. Then, she turned to say something to her son, possibly, Jacques thought, about some cake. Roger ushered them to the small sofa and two chairs. His house, his initiative. Jacques remained standing, alert to where things were leading.

Roger turned to Claire. "You may have this book, if you would like," he told her. "I am finished with it."

"Thank you. Did you enjoy it?"

"It is absurd, of course, is it not? This business about freedom. What is it, I ask—freedom—when man has many responsibilities, yet must somehow first make a living, eh?"

Jacques considered the man's tone as much as his subjective point. Did Roger mean to suggest freedom was over-valued? That it comes after duty? Jacques picked up the book, read the back cover, and set it back, looking to his partner to see what she might say.

Roger turned to Jacques. "Do you know Camus's writing, Monsieur?"

"I do not. Perhaps after the war."

"Of course." Roger turned back to Claire, replying in English, "I adore the cathedral in Reims." Searching for something. A test? "Do you know the lithographs of Fatin-Latour? In the *musée*?"

"Fatin-Latour? Regrettably, I do not. Someday, perhaps." She frowned and replied in faultless French.

"Well, there is so much to see," Roger replied. Still in English.

Jacques took that in, translating for Claire. Trying to protect her cover. What was the man's game, switching languages? "The cathedral is likely everyone's favorite," Claire replied, trying to keep the tension out of her voice. "That adorable smiling angel in the portal." Still in French. She returned her gaze to the Camus, not wanting to make further eye contact with Roger. There were too many uncertainties.

Roger grinned. "I only ask, you see, because that is the kind of question you are likely to receive from the Germans, or from any suspicious and jumpy French police. From people, in fact, like me."

"I do not understand," she said, on edge. "People like you?"

"Everyone is not what they seem, Celine," said Roger, lighting a cigarette, self-assured. He looked at Jacques again, as if measuring the man for any potential trouble.

"What do you mean by that?" asked Jacques, uncomfortable with the mood of the room. The statement felt like a kind of provocation.

Thomas looked to be more interested in the cat than any tests of authority or authenticity.

"Yes, like me," Roger said, taking advantage of the time his mother was out of the room. It was his show at the moment.

Jacques leaned forward to make his irritation clear. "What are you trying to tell us?"

Her timing exactly right, or perhaps just wrong, Madame Laurent walked back into the room with a platter of sweets. Jacques could smell the orange used to flavor the small cakes. How did she get such treats? Someone had privileges.

"We will have tea in a few minutes," she announced, with not a little pride, walking back to the kitchen, smoothing her apron. Thomas considered the cakes.

"Pardon my speaking so directly. What I mean," replied Roger, "is that there are certain speech and cultural tests the Nazis and their Vichy associates will use to trip you up. Foreigners, I am saying. And *résistantes*."

Thomas looked at Roger as if this revelation troubled him too, thought to speak, and held back. Jacques quieted his nerves by opening and stretching his hands and turning his head to relax the muscles in his neck.

Laurent continued. "You are American, if I am not mistaken, Celine," he said. "OSS, yes? How brave of you."

Claire took a sharp breath. Jacques was irritated that he'd figured out the truth so quickly. Her French was good. Had someone exposed the mission? Did it matter?

"Yes. I am. You seem to have all the answers. And what do you mean?" she asked. Then, with a quick look to Jacques, "Who will trip me up?"

Reading her anger, Jacques knew he had to re-exert his own influence. "I think you had better tell us who you are, Roger. And be convincing." Redirecting the tension, if only for a moment. "This is dangerous talk."

"Yes. And being an American in France is dangerous. More so, two of you." With this he nodded to Thomas and grinned again. "Both with your secret missions, eh? Let us all sit."

Claire found a spot on the couch, and Jacques moved to stand behind her. Thomas, taking it all in, picked up the cat, sat down, and put the cat back on the floor. Roger turned to Claire and resumed. "As I said, everyone is not who they seem." Roger showed the palms of his hands as if in supplication. Then, he gave them a big smile. "I will tell you my story, and I would appreciate yours. The real ones, please."

Madam Laurent walked in again with a tea service and five cups. "Please," she said, not actually looking to each of them, setting down the tray on one freshly painted table and seating herself next to Claire, clearly missing the tension. Claire was trying to figure out to what extent any near-term danger might be hanging over them—the proverbial sword of Damocles.

Thomas looked at Roger and cleared his throat. "Well, I should probably go first," he said, lifting his round shoulders and tamping the tobacco in his pipe. "As you know. . ."

"No. No," interjected Jacques, needing to exercise authority. What could or should be said in front of Roger, a man of unknown affiliation, a fellow whose fidelity had not been vetted? This was his op. He'd not let an unknown player call the shots.

"To be clear," Jacques continued, "we know who we are. I think we are curious as to who you are and what your story will be." He looked at Roger.

Laurent crushed out his cigarette and looked to his mother. What he had to say was not for her ears. He asked her, would she please make some coffee? He hated to ask. Unfazed, the woman agreed and moved to the kitchen, asking how many would like coffee. Thomas raised his hand. Then Claire. Roger nodded to the others, and then to Thomas, eyeing him with some curiosity, pausing to be certain his mother was not likely to hear.

"I also know who and what you are," he continued, relishing the power he felt. "This OSS business with our Resistance. Dangerous." He looked at Roland Thomas, who simply nodded. "I would begin by saying I am grateful to all of you who work for the liberation of France or, I should say, for the destruction of the Nazi menace." He smiled again, self-assured.

Claire put her hand to her mouth. Yes, Roger knew she was an American and OSS. Did he know as well why Roland Thomas was there? His mission? Not possible.

"I also know of Monsieur Thomas's task," began Roger. "Also OSS, yes? And you two are here to help." He stared hard at Jacques. "This is all quite clear to me."

"Clear to you, is it?" asked Jacques, controlling his voice. He looked at the unconcerned Thomas, who was searching for his tobacco pouch. Claire stood, recognizing the importance of what was about to be disclosed, and said she'd help Madame Laurent in the kitchen, keep the older woman busy. Thomas drew on his pipe, complacent and in agreement. He was the man who'd already spilled the bouillabaisse.

"Crazy business, this war, and what we are made to do," said Roger, looking to Thomas, perhaps to see whether he would speak. The blasé American stared off into some future only he could see while sampling another orange pastry.

"These are good," he said, seeking neutrality. Jacques took pride in reading other people. Roland Thomas was something of an enigma. Something was not right about him. The cocky young Frenchman, he knew, was a player.

Roger stood and walked back to the center of the room, center stage. "I can tell you this," he began. "I have a position of some trust with the local authorities. In town, and, of course, here—more importantly, in the countryside—under the supervision of the Combourg police. Our *préfecture*."

No one moved. Claire looked in once from the kitchen to see how long she might need to keep the older woman occupied. Jacques nodded to the kitchen, signaling for her to get back and preserve that necessary space and sound barrier. Jacques knew Roger would have more to say. Thomas drew deeply on his pipe.

"I keep an eye on things, Monsieur, looking out for elements of resistance and for related—shall I say, enemy—activity. But all the while, I am doing quite the opposite, trying to protect those I know are working against the Pétain puppet and Nazi interests in France.

"So, you are telling us. . ." began Jacques.

"I am saying that I am likely to be shot by either side." Roger delivered that notice with less drama than Jacques had expected, sensing that killing would not be new to Roger Laurent. "My mother has difficulties," he continued. "She does not know what I do. She knows only that I work for France, and she is not given to wonder which one. Just police, you see."

"Well, the fewer people who know such business the better," Jacques insisted. "And we must keep it that way."

Roger shrugged. He could come to his final point. "My uncle has spoken well of you, Jacques Berlangier." Then, he added, "Quite often, in fact." He offered this last as a juror foreman delivers a difficult verdict.

"Has he? Your uncle?" That was more confirmation the monsignor was Combourg's area Resistance controller. The polymath Eduard Arnoux. "Kind of him." He was not taking the bait. Jacques looked to see if Thomas had heard him. Evidently not. Or he seemed not to care.

"Is that what you call it? Kindness?" Roger said and shook his head ever so slightly.

Jacques was left to discern the relationship of Roger and his uncle, which was surely complicated. Still, it suggested some measure of trust—a wartime bond. Jacques's prior supposition had been confirmed; the priest had put him and the clever American woman into the middle of a very loose operation because Arnoux knew Roger, his nephew, could have useful connections to push ahead and perhaps seal up torn seams.

The two women came in from the kitchen. Thomas had been silent throughout the last part of the conversation. Somewhere in his own private world.

Moments later, when all had settled with their teas, coffees, and cakes, Madame Laurent rose and asked Claire if she'd like to see her small herb garden and the clay pottery she used for holding the most delicate plants. Claire said she would. "Maybe you can show me how to take proper care of my tarragon and that wonderful chervil!" Claire told the woman encouragingly, as both headed for the back door. Obviously, the women had taken something of a liking to each other. Jacques recognized that his partner had a good sense of how to provide subtle cover for him to consider and candidly work the problem of allegiances. He continually found more to admire in his new teammate, Celine—her confidence, her style, most surely her situational awareness.

With the women out of the house, Roger asked whether there was anything he could do, other than to provide misdirection to the police. Jacques had no doubt that Roger had brought Erwan, the initial contact man, into the game, the first essential clandestine move. Still, there were too many sous-chefs in the kitchen for Jacques's liking. Standing, then, and walking to the door, Roger turned to Jacques and said,

"Monsieur Hibou, please tell Celine this for me: The *Sourire de Reims,* that smiling angel she mentioned, has a purpose. It is to commemorate the healing following the cathedral's destruction in the first war." He said all that in English, a demonstration of the fellow's control. "Details are important when one's life depends on a good cover story."

With that, they all stepped out of the house together, the partial sun noncommittal. Their unexpected meeting had ended with Laurent enjoying the last word. Thomas stepped out behind them, hat in hand, everyone's friend.

"The angel. I'll advise her."

"Do that." Laurent climbed onto his bike, waved, and drove off. He was a man on both sides of a deadly argument. If Laurent had some false leads for the *préfecture,* he would go and sow them then. Or he would not. Whatever else he was up to was not the most immediate concern of Jacques or Claire. They faced a more immediate problem, that of the missing radio. Could they find a suitable replacement? That had been Claire's idea. He had a thought. Maybe Arnoux?

With Roger Laurent gone, the disruption settled, Jacques turned to the beleaguered Roland Thomas, who was seemingly preoccupied by something in his hat. The men walked toward the truck, where Jacques slipped his handgun into the vehicle's storage compartment.

"I cannot promise anything."

CHAPTER 12

Claire came to the driver's side of the truck and watched as Thomas pulled a map from his jacket pocket. This Quixote-like fellow with another impossible mission.

"What is your thinking on the radio?" Jacques asked her.

"I think I know what we need. Our people with SOE in London might help. They could have the radio. Getting ahold of one anytime soon is the trick."

Jacques pointed to Roland's map. "May I see it?"

Thomas handed it over—a good tourist-quality map of the Normandy beaches and inland territory, a red circle around Saint-Lô. Claire leaned in and looked. She put her hand to her mouth.

"Why is Saint-Lô circled?" she asked. "And Caen? As you know, or you should know, it's dangerous to have such a map on your person. Anyone could stop you. . ."

"Celine makes a good point. It's risky."

Thomas gave a slight shrug. Claire added that any city circled so suggests intent, plans.

"Dangerous practice," added Jacques. Vichy police.

"Roger knows my mission. I told him. He said the Germans are likely to be active there. On the ground and in the air. The SS are swarming too, or so he said."

"Why in God's name would you tell him?" Jacques asked, irritated all the more. "He's just the safehouse man. He has no need to know your mission." Jacques swore again and looked to the house. "Caen. Saint-Lô. German tactical operations? This is fucking suicide. Christ, we are not combatants!"

Thomas looked to the sky and said, "I know. But I have my orders." He rubbed his eyes. The sun settling behind the house cast them all in an early-summer-evening shadow. So much was unknown, unseen. Jacques handed the map back to Thomas and looked to Claire.

"Hibou, can you ask about help in getting a proper radio?" she asked. "Your controller?"

"Maybe." The monsignor, he knew, would be their only source.

"I do have some equipment," Thomas said. The small stuff. Capacitors." Thomas wiped at his nose with his sleeve, then slumped his shoulders and looked away. "I'm sorry. I am doing this for my brother." This last was given as with a great breath.

Claire turned to the bewildered Mr. Thomas. Then to a disbelieving Jacques. She knew what they both must be thinking. Thomas was working out some tacit family obligation.

"Your brother?"

"Our James. He was killed at Guadalcanal, poor lad. Last February." Thomas's eyes were glistening.

"I see. I'm sorry," she said. The news changed so much. Her ill-prepared countryman was stuck fast in an impossible hole. With one ineffable debt.

"How is your German?" she asked. "Assuming we get the equipment, and you press ahead. If you're listening to tactical German comms you must need to know what the Germans are saying."

"Fluent," Thomas replied, lifting his chin. "My French may well be rudimentary, but my German is tops." He'd lived in Essen and Dusseldorf as a boy, he said, his father doing turn-of-the-century steel business with the Germans.

"You lived there?"

"My brother James and I, as kids. Until early 1910. From when I was six until the age of eleven. The OSS was interested in me for my language capability as much as anything."

"And you kept with it?"

"Oh, I did. In school, I was made to do my lessons at home in both languages. My mother was delighted I could read the *Grimms'* stories as a child in the original German. I suppose it was a matter of pride for her."

"Well, this is no fairy tale, and I hope you will be more forthcoming with me." Jacques put his hand on the fellow's shoulder. "If we want to survive this operation, be successful in our part of it, I need—we need—complete intelligence. Agreed?"

Thomas ran his hand over his head, finding determination. "Of course."

So that was that. Claire considered all the man must be working through. No ring on his finger. She thought about the man's conundrum, empathy battling with common sense.

"We'll see what we can do," she said, seeing Jacques look away. "Listen to me," Claire said to Jacques, her voice rising. She knew he was angry. "We can help by finding a replacement radio. This is my mission. I just need you to work with me." She stared at Jacques. "I was sent to do a job. Mr. Thomas is my countryman." She lowered her voice, gathered her strength. "I need you!" Claire clenched her jaw and looked at him.

Jacques took a moment, shifting his weight. "I got you this far," he said, trying to convince himself, then looked to Thomas, as if that preposterous fellow might yet come to his senses, obviating the unholy mess. "You are right. We will do what we can, Celine." Jacques understood that it meant starting over. It meant paying a visit to Monsignor Arnoux. The logistics burden would lie mostly on him. Or it would all collapse. Different teams. Different protocols. But the same goal. Same dead end, perhaps, as well. This cleric—Madame Laurent's brother and Roger's uncle—was at the center of it all. So, just maybe it could work.

"Tomorrow," said Jacques, "We take a short trip." He put his arm around her, knowing she'd used common sense and showed real courage.

Come evening, the men walked into the garden while Madame Laurent, with Claire's help, was preparing a light dinner. Jacques looked back out to the road. Could they find a replacement? Get Thomas in position for his mission? That would be the most dangerous aspect. No one had accurate, up-to-date intelligence on where anyone's combat forces were engaged. Troop positions were fluid. Caen and Saint-Lô sat about fifty kilos apart. Someplace closer could work if they could get the radio hardware. Give Thomas an opportunity to fulfill his mission in memory of his brother. "We will come up with something," Jacques said.

"Wonderful. Who's hungry?" asked Roland Thomas, suddenly more confident. Claire said Madam Laurent had told her she had a soup stock as well as chicken, carrots, and a hearty loaf of bread.

"Well, that's the first good news in a while," Jacques said. Arnoux would be their best hope going forward. Jacques understood that that the American, Celine, had her own strong sense of duty. She would contribute in any way she could. She had become a trusted, determined, reliable partner.

Sitting at the table, not ten minutes later, she looked to Roland Thomas. "We will need to locate some things for you. Oh, and I have your travel documents."

Thomas nodded again. "Thank you." He rubbed his head, a habit.

So much was out of his hands.

"This will take some time." said Jacques. "You stay here with Madame Laurent for another couple of days."

He could. Doing just what, he didn't know. He said he thought maybe Roger would have some ideas as well.

Jacques told him, "No. Leave Roger out of this."

After supper, Jacques asked Claire what she was thinking. How lovely a quiet moment alone with that fascinating woman might be in normal times, but the business ahead was anything but normal. They both had to take a deliberate breath and settle down, make a plan. The next day, early, they'd pay a visit to the able cleric in Combourg.

Jacques studied Claire's face in profile, the sun going down behind her. How astonishing, he thought. This woman. "We head out at first light. All right?"

She said yes. "For the radio."

"And we will bring Cleo along when we come back. Can't leave her." That last part was delivered with a grin. "In fact, the dog would likely add to our cover of a working apple farm."

She said she liked that idea, thinking the dog might help settle her nerves. Claire studied the man, constantly amazed by his grasp of small details. He was, certainly, a fitting partner. "Yes, to Cleo," she said, adding, "Thank you." She took a deep breath. "So, first thing tomorrow."

With the dishes done and the kitchen swept, Madame said goodnight and went upstairs to her room. Thomas collapsed on the sofa in the far corner of the room. The two were alone. Claire and Jacques pulled their heavy chairs close to the big stone fireplace where the glow of dying embers lit and warmed their faces. Feet propped on the raised hearth; they welcomed the small respite of companionable silence.

"I have something to ask you," Claire said. Her voice suggested an uncertainty about what she would say. "Of course," she said, "I have nothing against owls." She looked to see how he would react.

"So you say." He took a moment. "Why do you want to know, Celine?"

"Well, because I know that Hibou is your cover name." She paused. "I was told by Corbeau that we would travel to Dinan to meet Hibou. That was just about two weeks ago."

He gave her a look to say he found their conversation interesting. He stood and said, "We all operate with some degree of cover. You know that. Security. Standard practice."

"Right, but is it necessary now, between us?" she asked. "We have one Raven—Corbeau—and one Owl. No doubt, someone is assigning bird names to his or her operatives."

"Are they?" Jacques smiled. He stood, ran his hand through his hair, took a moment, and put his hands into his back pockets. Standing with his back to the fire, he said he had grown rather fond of the name. Being Mr. Owl. "Like on a radio show!" He saw her smile. She was still nervous, but perhaps she was relaxing a little. She needed that. Needed a moment of simple truth.

"All right," he said. "We need cover names only for initial contact. To establish—oh what is the word?—bona fides. The French way? You do too, no? But if we do this, only we can know." She had been holding her breath. Then said, yes, it was the same for OSS. "Agents working together need to feel trust. Retain full cover until you do. That's the way it's done. And to everyone else, we are Celine and Hibou. Rules are rules. I understand that." Jacques considered her idea. Was this a kind of intimacy she needed? What she meant by trust? He looked to the inner room, the closed door behind them. Thomas asleep, safely out of hearing range, then said, "Jacques." There was no reason to give surnames. Less was more.

"Jacques. Okay. As in Cartier? The French explorer in North America?"

"Umm, no relation. Canada would be too cold for me." He smiled more broadly than she'd yet seen him do. He asked about her. "Celine, or not Celine?" he said, lowering his voice.

She stood and took a step toward him. She desperately needed this between them. "Call me Claire. This is important to me, Jacques. I do not know what could be more important. So, thank you."

"Claire." Jacques said he loved the name. "Claire. Like *Clair de Lune*. Quiet and contemplative?" The two of them were facing each other, moving closer, warming at the fireplace.

She chuckled. "Oh, I think you have me exactly right. Like the Debussy song." She offered her own more confident smile.

Jacques looked at her and thought about how she had stood up to him. He thought about the very precise, so-American manner of her, which she carried so ably. Yes, they would work well together.

"As far as Thomas knows, we are Hibou and Celine," she insisted. Her papers were solid on that score. "Celine Mercier. A legend is a legend. And that's mine. Pastries!"

He laughed. "Yes, of course." And they had their apples. What better cover than apples? People needed rations. Apples were good for trade and sales. Jacques stretched his long arms above his neck and shoulders, dissipating the tension. The commitment they'd just made was necessary. More so to her. After all, he'd been successful because he knew how to read people, how to adjust to circumstances.

The next morning, Thomas found the two of them in the kitchen. The coffee smelled good. Madame Laurent was not up, and no one would wake her. There'd been enough tension the previous night.

Job one was to get a radio. They all agreed. Logistics would be uncertain. That would take a couple of days. Maybe a short delay would work in their favor. All action was moving eastward. The mission would be dangerous no matter the timing. There could be stragglers, Wehrmacht infantry platoons left behind. No way to tell. "We should get started," said Jacques. He pulled the keys from his pocket.

Thomas picked up the Camus novel from the table, then set it back down, and, with forced bonhomie, wished them safe travels. "While you two are away, I shall discover the identity of the stranger," he said, pointing to the book with not a little satisfaction with his cleverness.

"Right. Two days, maybe three," Jacques told him, placing his hand on the other man's shoulder. "If we are not back by this time Thursday, you should assume we will not be coming."

"And, in any case," added Claire, "you have the necessary papers."

"I'm sorry, Roland, but, if we should fail to return, you must rely on Roger for help, perhaps to get back to Rennes, where things are now not so dangerous. We have agents there."

He said he understood.

"From there, someone can arrange to pick you up and fly you back to England."

Thomas examined the *carte d'identité* with his photo on it naming him Tomas Roland. He held an in-country travel pass as well. His alias was close enough to his actual name should there be any slip in direct address or his own memory. Claire had not opened the packet. She'd not need to know the false name until the point that she did. Operational security.

"I understand, but you will return, my new friends, and we shall all get on with the job." They shook hands. There was nothing more to say, and the two walked into the early-morning light.

Jacques and Claire made their way out to the road that would take them back to Combourg, to meet with Arnoux and explain what they needed, avoiding any enemy troops or stragglers on the move. Just maybe they could pull it off.

Pulling away, Jacques said, "He's an odd one," looking to see what Claire would say.

"He is working through a huge burden, the loss of a brother; it's his motivation. He's an honorable man, Jacques."

"Honorable and foolhardy, I would say. And we are in the hot soup with him."

Making their way over and around sections of broken road, Claire gave thought to what they needed, what Thomas would use to set up his radio intercept operation. She had a mission. She was not just a courier. With help from Jacques, whom she was growing to admire more and more, she had an important assignment. Surely, Betty McIntyre would agree that Claire Skiffington, given her training, must take up that larger role. One hand was always reaching out to the next and the next for the necessary help. All vital parts coming together.

CHAPTER 13

Jacques and Claire pulled into an open space behind the parish house just before 9 a.m. The monsignor would, or should, be done with any morning clerical duties. Timing was important. He'd not want anyone to see him, and, more so, did not want anyone to see him entering the house with a woman. A stranger. He squeezed her hand once, said, "Here we go," and he walked with her to the door.

"Come in. Come in, you two. I have been half expecting you," said Arnoux, placing his reading glasses into his breast pocket.

Jacques grinned and said, "Only half?" as the two stepped into the kitchen, where the monsignor had been working on a baguette. Claire gave her name and offered her hand, held it straight out, as if the meeting were a job interview. She would control her nerves. Arnoux gave her a big grin and put his arm around Jacques and ushered them into the sitting room. Would they like coffee?

"Nothing would be better just now," said Claire, finding him charming and welcoming. She never really knew a priest. Not personally. He reminded her of someone. Maybe Spencer Tracy, but with a shock of snow-white hair. She smiled uncertainly and sat on the nearby sofa, hands in her lap. Jacques remained standing, maybe to see what Arnoux would say or do next.

"I'm sorry, Father, if my being here, our coming to you like this, now puts you in an awkward place," said Jacques. "I mean with respect to our work together. I had long suspected that you were my controller, but . . ."

"No, no. This is most welcome, Jacques. And I figured you knew that all along. You and I were only being smart about all this unquiet business we do. Together."

Claire looked at the man, whom she'd been told was also an old family friend. As a Catholic, even a pretty much a lapsed Catholic, she was naturally nervous. And nothing to confess, she thought! Her mind racing. What would her mother say? Where was the meeting likely to take them? Together, they'd need to make clear that their asset needed a functioning intercept radio and tell him what functionality it needed. Or would he know that already?

Arnoux came directly to the point. "What has happened to the American? Is he hurt? Tell me what you need."

Both knew Arnoux had overseen their rescue operation from the beginning. When ordered to do so from London, he had put them into play. The nominal puppet master linking OSS—Claire—to Jacques. None of that was supposed to be acknowledged, of course, but, for years, Eduard Arnoux and Jacques had shared a much deeper connection, one that went back to Jacques's parents—hence, theirs was a relationship of trust, respect, and an abiding sense of commitment.

"We connected with him. He'd injured his ankle in the jump.

That's all. He's terribly nervous, of course. He's waiting for us back at the Laurent house," said Jacques. "We met her, your sister I am told, and, of course, the son, Roger. I did not know she was your sister. Well . . ."

"Ah, yes, Roger. Quite the fellow, as he will have told you. And my sister is another story."

That last comment made Claire smile. She could sense the mood in the room shift from anxious to something more settled. Honest. Positive. Roger's exalted sense of self was their touchstone.

Jacques continued, "He made it to the safehouse, but his radio did not. I suppose you must know that." He looked first at Arnoux, and then to Claire, inviting her into the conversation. Arnoux told them that the American at his sister's house was not the first or the only such operative with this collection assignment. "Signals intelligence will be even more important now that the Germans are fighting on two fronts." He said that OSS, in concert with Britain's Special Operations Executive, had attempted to put a few other such teams into play with Resistance help. Intercept teams. How successful they would prove no one could say.

"But this mission is so dangerous," said Claire, looking to Jacques, who took a quick, sharp breath and decided to say nothing more. Her OSS experience was limited, and the men knew it. Both waited to see what the monsignor would tell them.

"It is. I have an idea that my counterpart in Rennes might be able to help. I can find out. Meanwhile, Claire, please tell me about yourself. Americans have come to play an unexpectedly large role in my own family. "But first: more coffee? Do you want something to eat?" Jacques said they had eaten. Claire asked if she could do something. Arnoux got up and set a plate of sliced apples on the small table between them. She saw his left hand tremble. Was he unwell? Claire took a small piece of apple, leaned toward the older man, and asked what he meant about Americans in his family. That was interesting. Would he want to speak about that?

"You've met my sister, Odette, Roger's mother. Her husband ran off sometime shortly after the first war. She has never gotten over that sense of abandonment. And I, a priest, seem to have been no comfort to her. Just another man making a peculiar choice, as she once said to me. Our youngest sibling, our little sister, Margot, lives with her husband in the States.

"Really?"

Jacques said that he'd never mentioned her. Not to him. But why would he?

"Your parents knew about her. I think they thought it was perhaps a hurtful memory to me, so not much was said. She is happy, I think, our Margot. She met the man, a soldier, after he'd been wounded. He was a corporal. She was a nurse. That was the battle near Amiens, at Cantigny. In May, I think, 1918. Well, that is now twenty-six years."

Claire put her hand to her mouth. "She cared for him, a wounded American?"

Jacques was taking all of it in.

"It's so sweet. But what was the draw, the attraction, I mean? She must have helped and maybe cared for many soldiers during that time. That awful kind of war."

Margot had told him that the man, her husband, Terry Allen, spoke excellent French. That he talked in his sleep. In French! He was an artist, and he was also what is called a birder. He cataloged birds. She loved that about him. So creative. And that was that. "He came back the next year. They live near Albany now. In New York. Happy, I suppose."

"Some people make the most out of strange and truly scary situations," added Claire. Wondering whether, perhaps, that generalization included her too. "And some do not."

Arnoux told them that he would handle the radio problem. "Come see me tomorrow. Late, I would think. Maybe go back home and get some rest. Gather strength. Both of you. Take that little dog of yours for a good, long walk. Rest. I have a feeling you will need it."

Some thirty hours later, Claire and Jacques placed a heavy but transportable RCA-built AR-88, into the bottom of one large basket of pears. The monsignor had once again proven to be the vital cog among his broader connections. Claire assured Jacques the radio was powerful for its size and, as she knew it, could search in six bands across all HF frequencies.

"What an amazing man," she said as they finished loading the truck, the unit secure in a barrel, along with covers and boxes that would divert attention from the radio in the back.

"He is, and I noticed that he thinks pretty highly of you too."

"Why do you say that?" The observation delighted her.

Jacques grinned, "He served you extra coffee, along with that last, small bite of baguette. I got only a warm handshake."

Claire laughed and said he was just demonstrating good manners, then added, "That radio is just what Mr. Thomas needs to copy Panzer and infantry command and control voice."

That crucial barrel, set well to the back of their truck, would give them halfway decent cover. Given the chances of being stopped and questioned, would anyone want to dump the fruit of seven barrels searching for contraband? The next day, Claire, Jacques, and one excited spaniel, the latter insisting on fresh air and window access, began their return journey back to the Laurent house. Claire sat in the middle, next to Jacques. Cleo's insistence on the window, along with the resulting exuberant tail-wagging, allowed Claire only a small slice of middle seat, her thigh occasionally brushing Jacques's as the truck rumbled along.

"Are you comfortable, Claire?"

"Perfectly."

The return trip to the safehouse and to pick up Roland Thomas proved uneventful. Aircraft flew high above, likely British Lancasters and American B-17s. The hard, sharp popping of anti-aircraft artillery sounded to the north. The good and the bad. How long could such luck hold?

Meanwhile, Thomas had been keeping himself somewhat occupied with the OSS-generated material Celine had given him. His stay at Laurent's place had bored him silly, his only distraction playing with the cat while he awaited the long-absent Roger Laurent, maybe for a card game. His French was not good enough to speak much with the old woman. Nor could he read the Camus. At long last, he heard them arrive, and he hurried out to meet them. Claire and the dog stepped out of the truck.

"I'm so relieved," he said, getting a look from Cleo, who bounded over to inspect him. "I didn't relish the idea of finding my way back to England alone, of not getting the job done."

"What do you mean, alone?" Jacques asked whether Roger would not have helped, if needed. Given him some protection, cover. Where was Roger?

Thomas shrugged, shook his head, and said, "Madame Laurent has been worried."

"What do you mean? Where is Roger?" Jacques looked to the house.

Thomas took a quick breath, let out an anguished sigh, and said, "Madame is in a state. Roger has not returned since you two left here on Tuesday."

CHAPTER 14

Jacques took a moment to process the fact that Roger had not returned, then slammed the door of his truck. "Cleo could use a stretch," he said, stepping away from the vehicle, as if he could get away from all the nonsense. And where in the hell was Laurent? "We need to get our gear together and head out."

"But what about Roger?" Thomas asked.

"What about him?" Jacques eyed Thomas, looking haggard if not sleep-deprived. "I don't trust that man. Something's not right. And we don't need him."

Thomas looked at his watch. "Did you get the radio?"

"Yes."

Claire decided it best to keep her own counsel. "I should check on Madame Laurent again. See if I can help."

"I wouldn't," Jacques said. "I doubt she'd have anything to say."

"We should go, don't you think?" asked a newly inspired Thomas, fiddling with the brim of his hat.

Jacques reached for Claire's arm, meaning to assure her, and said, "Let's go."

"Wait!" she insisted. "Listen to me. Why not ask her? She might know something." Claire, not wanting her idea dismissed, could tell Jacques was unhappy, but she was not about to concede the point. "Maybe a woman's touch," she said.

Jacques looked back to the house. "I say we forget Laurent. And his mother. You know there's nothing to be done now. And the good Mr. Thomas here needs to get on with it. We all do. We have what he needs."

"Listen to me. Why not try?" Her voice firm, she continued, "If Roger has been taken and is discovered for his real purpose, his mission, he could give up the whole show. How long before Roger would be made to give up the monsignor? Right? And, if so, who else would fall? Just think."

Jacques recognized that she needed more clarity.

She pushed. "I say we ask Madame Laurent."

Jacques took a half step toward her. "She knows nothing. . . "

"Listen to me! You can be SO pig headed! It cannot hurt to *try*," she said, undeterred, her mouth turned down. All five feet-five of her seemed insistent. "It's the right move. Think! It's only smart."

Jacques took a step back. Before him was a woman who knew her mind and was not afraid to speak it. Hers was a strong voice of reason. Claire had stood her ground with him twice in as many days. He nodded, his face red. "Yes. Yes, I see," he said. "You go in and ask. And I'll see to Cleo." He moved to Claire's side and added, "I suppose it's possible he could have said something." He leaned in toward her. "You are right. Thank you."

"Of course." Claire said, taking a sharp breath and appearing visibly relieved. Her point had been made.

Thomas just wanted to get going. He was fidgety; he'd been in the house for three days. "I like Celine's idea," he said. Then, "I'll go in too." He was not sure what to do with himself, so he followed the bold American woman, an uncertain grin on his face.

Jacques would tend to the dog. He put some water into a small bucket for Cleo and watched her drink for a moment, then headed back to the house too, still keyed up from the argument. There, he found Thomas in the kitchen with a short shot of whiskey. From the looks of things, it was not his first. Claire stood with Madame Laurent, polishing a small copper pot. The old lady was whispering something—evidently to herself. Claire shook her head. Nothing.

"Madame, do you know where Roger could be?" Jacques asked.

The older woman stood by the sink, totally still.

Jacques stood apart and watched as Claire stepped closer. "Maybe just an idea? Where he goes sometimes? Maybe . . ."

"No. You! Why did you come to my house?" she said, voice rising. She was looking at Jacques in an accusatory way. "You! My son is gone and does not come home. I blame you." And, at once, she began to weep. Thomas sat at the small wooden table, watching it all, picking at his fingernails.

"I am sorry about all this, Madame," Claire interposed, looking to Jacques, conscious of how much help the woman had been to them. Then, in a softer voice, "I know this is difficult. You must be worried." Claire pulled her to her side like a caring monitor.

"Has he been gone like this before?" Claire urged. The older woman made no reply.

Jacques moved from the doorway and whispered to Claire. "Ask if maybe there is a girl."

Thomas indicated with a slight shrug of the shoulders that he, too, had tried. Madame Laurent looked to Jacques, then to Thomas, perhaps thinking all men thought the same way. "He is not with some girl. I know my son. Roger would come home if he could."

"Never?" asked Claire.

"One time," the woman allowed, looking to Claire for understanding. Kindred spirits. "He has a friend in Paris. A woman."

"Do you think he went to Paris?"

She shrugged as if to ask what difference it would make, then repeated he was doing vital work.

Reading support from Claire, the woman added that, several months ago, in February, he'd stayed away for two or three nights. He had mentioned Rennes. "For his job."

Jacques looked to the yellow clock on the wall. It was 10:20 a.m. "Maybe Rennes. Nothing more to be done. Time to go." Thomas stepped to the near-empty bottle on the counter, set his glass next to it, and agreed he was ready. Jacques gave him a look.

"I was just having a taste of some nice brandy."

"I see. Calvados. Good choice, Mr. Thomas."

Thomas offered a sheepish grin. Claire looked to Jacques; she could see he was also eager to get going.

"I like it," said Thomas, coming to a decision once again. "Something unusual. . ."

"It's the soil," Jacques said, adding, "The clay soil." Then, turning away, he told them, "Enough of that. We must get on the road."

Thomas put the much-depleted bottle into his jacket pocket. Heading to the truck, finding a noncommittal sky overhead, halting traces of blue and a heady wind, Claire assured Thomas the radio they'd secured was a good one. Versatile, she said. Hidden in the back. She told him she could help if he needed her.

Thomas turned to both of them and said, "Wehrmacht," as if the threat had just dawned on him.

"Yes. Lots of them. We'll drive to a midpoint, maybe an hour or so away," Jacques said. "Head toward Caen. Then, if the roads stay clear, we decide which direction looks most promising. I cannot overstate the problem—the danger. The trick is to find the enemy troops before they find us."

Jacques asked Thomas to come back around the truck and help pull a few tarps up and over the barrels. "We need to tie these down and get started."

Claire asked whether she could help.

"We have it." Jacques looked to the road. "Let's not meet up with any Bosch armored scouts. Or their left-behind infantry." He looked to see if he was getting through. "This is a dangerous mission."

"I know," Thomas insisted, finding further determination. "You have your documents, and we have a good radio," Claire added, prepared to put the best face on a grueling day. She looked to Jacques and gave him a half smile. Again, she thought back to her first encounter with him—that awful, rainy night, the unseen snare. She replayed how he'd listened to her when pushed. So capable and smart. He had the strength to listen and do the right thing. How able, this Breton apple farmer.

Jacques squeezed her knee and said, "Time to go."

Jacques was in her head at that point. She'd have to decide why and what to make of that. Was it more than the rush of danger, with the able fellow assisting on her first assignment? Studying his face, she decided, no. They were professionals.

Thomas sensed the mood and repeated, "My French is limited."

She gave him a rueful smile. "Just don't speak. Maybe try to look ill."

"I can do that." Then he added, "The sick man of Europe, like one of the Ottomans!"

"That's the idea. It will be crowded here in the truck, with the dog," Jacques said, "but we won't tell Cleo you're sick." Jacques chuckled at his silliness and glanced at the map.

"See, there—we head toward Avranches," Jacques said, turning in the yard and cutting the wheel hard, angling back to the road.

"Then what?" Claire settled herself. Thomas looked straight ahead, a man in character.

"Who knows? If we can get past the town of Vire without being shot or blown up, something I'm not sure we can manage, it might be another hour," Jacques said. "All small roads. Damaged, I'm sure. And combat changes timetables. By then we may well be on top of the fight."

"Maybe we can test the radio near Vire," Claire said, looking at the map. "Decide what to do. If that's far enough."

"Vire?" asked Thomas. "What is there?"

"Well, besides being the heart of Calvados country, a drink you have evidently taken a liking to, probably just about half the German 7th Army."

"Keep your papers handy," Claire told him, "should we be asked for them. Do you know how to say, 'I am sick'?"

"*Je suis malade,*" he offered; then, "No. *Je suis très malade.*"

"That should do it. *Très malade*. Jesus, you do look like death warmed over," Jacques added.

"Actually, I think I look rather like Dickens's Ghost of Christmas Future."

"Let's hope it's not our future."

Cleo scooted to the window, stepping on Thomas and pushing Claire next to Jacques again. Clearly, neither minded. Roland Thomas slumped next to the dog.

"Our story is simple: We're bringing apples to Vire," said Jacques, looking to his partner. "Doing our bit for the brave Germans defending France from the awful English and their lot. It sounds ridiculous, I know, but it's all we have."

She looked at Jacques, considered saying something, but knew he was concentrating. Then, "Well, nothing makes sense in war, except trying to survive."

Jacques adjusted the rearview mirror. He'd already made his thoughts known.

"Can you think of anything better?" he asked. She shook her head no.

Roland Thomas knew he had put them all in an awful situation. Inspired, he took a moment to gather the words, then prepared to speak a few lines from a timely poem he'd come to cherish. He sat upright, cleared his voice, and began.

> "And how can man die better Than facing fearful odds,
> For the ashes of his fathers,
> And the temples of his Gods."

"Roland, where is that from?" Claire asked. She thought she'd heard it years ago. "It's brilliant and timeless, isn't it?" At that point, she looked to Jacques.

"Oh, I forget the poet's name, Celine," Thomas said, terribly pleased. "A Brit. Macaulay, I think. About protecting the gates of Rome from the enemy."

"That's pretty much the larger task," said Jacques. "And I agree the odds are fearful enough. But no dying—for gods or gates. Let's just not get too close. You set up the radio and do a quick listen. Finish the assignment and then get the hell out."

CHAPTER 15

Not an hour later, their vehicle slowing for a barricade in the road approaching Brécey, they came upon a makeshift post manned by one aging, overweight German *Feldwebel*—a sergeant—and two youths, one thin as a broom, the other pulling at the back of his pants. Both were probably local, certainly trouble. The German would be the one to play, keeping the unpredictable youths off balance.

Even so, Jacques saw the older man hang back while the younger two approached from both sides of the truck's cab. Curious. The sergeant gripped an old Mauser, tapping at the trigger guard. Not his first dance party, but likely his last. Jacques rolled down the window, inching the truck forward.

"What do I do?" asked Thomas, trying to make himself smaller.

"Pretend you're asleep. If he raps on your window, roll it down and look pathetic."

Thomas pulled his hat over his eyes, then thought better of it and pushed it into his lap.

Claire nervously suggested they might offer a few apples. "I think we may have just enough back there," she said, patting Jacque's knee. Thomas looked at the Calvados bottle in his kit, said they could offer that. Jacques told him, no—better keep what's left of the brandy for an emergency.

Jacques slowed the truck to a stop with a half-smile of supplication. When one obviously irritable youth, his allegiance wrong-sided, approached the truck, Jacques handed him his identity papers. He'd long since been issued a card showing his occupation as apple farmer.

And who were the others?

"My associates."

When the lad asked, "Is this your dog?" it was all Jacques could do to keep from admitting the dog had no papers. The thin one, sporting a sad wisp of blond mustache, also came around to Jacques's window and asked where they were going.

"St. Lo," he told him.

"You will not get to Saint-Lô," said the bestirred *Feldwebel*, scratching at his heavy jaw bristling with white stubble. He dismissed the others. Everyone in the truck knew he was probably right. Sounds of small arms fire repeated in the distance. A recon patrol? That could be bad news. The high-pitched whistle of an artillery shell echoed from a distance. Then another.

Jacques asked if there was trouble ahead. He pointed up the road.

The sergeant shrugged.

He suggested they leave the apples and return home. Thomas, stirring to life, took the initiative, leaning across and telling the old soldier, in a pathetic voice and in perfect German, "*Wir bringen die Äpfel zu deinen Männern.*"

That plea—that these simple farmers were bringing them apples—gave the old soldier pause enough to change his mind, crazy as that notion may well have been. He shook his head, said, "Apples," tipped his cap, and waved them on. The willing suspension of disbelief—how readily it spreads across the errant fields of war. Thomas turned to them both and smiled.

"We will not get to Saint-Lô, he said," repeated Claire. "And I am beginning to agree all the more."

Moving on, Claire saw to her right the charred remains of a downed bomber, ghostly and oddly colorless. One wing gone. Smoldering at the distant tree line.

"Look there. Whose is it?"

"I think it's one of ours," Jacques said. "Or yours, I should say." Then he added, "Probably a B-17. Americans. Poor luck." German air-defense controllers would be tracking the flights of Allied bomber aircraft, alerting interceptor squadrons across northern France.

"Were you worried? Back there?"

Jacques said one would have to be a fool not to be.

Thomas continued to stare out at the scene, transfixed. His lips were moving ever so slightly. Maybe a prayer. Or was he speaking to his late brother?

They lost time when Jacques had to find a way around a fallen bridge, then drove on through eerily quiet forests and fields. Their serenity was interrupted now and again by concussive booms in the unknowable distance. A couple of planes flew high, heading east. Twice they pulled off the road when German trucks drove up hard and fast behind them, passing and moving on. Two German soldiers sitting in the rear of the last vehicle looked out through the open black tarp at nothing in particular. Their fates were as unpredictable as those of the apple farmers.

"Everybody's war is somehow different," Claire continued. "And everybody's war is, in one respect, the same: death and destruction."

Jacques looked to her and said that it can also bring people together. "Let's see if we can make Vire, or just short, maybe a kilometer or two. Find a place to disappear. Set up camp."

"An old barn would be ideal," Claire said, stating what she knew to be the obvious.

"Better yet, an old, abandoned barn," added Thomas, breathing more regularly now.

"Well, maybe an owl in residence," Claire said quietly, looking for Jacques's reaction, and he grinned. He asked whether she liked owls, and she said she did. More so every day. Thomas seemed to be paying them no attention.

They found what they were looking for near dark. The roof of the building had nearly collapsed, possibly from an artillery shell, but the stone foundation and wood exteriors looked all right, and, after keeping an eye on the place for another ten minutes, driving past it a few times, they agreed the place offered some concealment if not necessarily security.

"Tell me, how do you plan to contact allied operators with alerts or with any intelligence you obtain?" said Jacques. He'd asked Claire that very question days ago, and she'd said she understood Thomas had a plan. Getting the intel out is just as crucial as the gathering.

"Oh, I have that sorted," he told them. Thomas added he would need to find some scrap wood to make a breadboard—the necessary ad hoc piece he'd use to affix the electronics—to set up— and then it would just be a matter of patience and luck.

"Luck is one thing we cannot have too much of," Claire agreed.

Thomas sat up straighter when Jacques asked how he would do all that. Expecting the question, he told them that a simple transmitter was easy enough to build. As for essentials, he had hidden in his clothing enough ultrathin wire to make a simple capacitor, and he had secured some magnet wire.

"Where?

Thomas showed them the interior of his large, canvas hat.

"Right here."

No wonder he never went far without it, thought Claire. Thomas said the crystal oscillator technology, which came about right after the first war, was easy enough to hide. All small stuff. And resistors were tiny. He went on to explain how he would make the coil.

"Easy enough to bring a few diodes from England," he said, "if you have some way to place them into the false heel of your boot, that is." Both Jacques and Claire looked astonished with this news.

"In the heel? Amazing. What if they break?"

"Well then we are out of business, I suppose," he replied, and frowned.

The trick, of course, was to find the necessary wire for an antenna, which Thomas calculated needed to be about fifteen feet long, not something he could bring along, but material that might be found nearby. Thin steel wire was plentiful enough around farms.

"One more question," said Claire. "You need a mic to transmit. You must have managed to bring one. I just know you did. And not in your boot."

Thomas chuckled and said Britain's SOE people had taken care of that. One miniature Western Electric unit fit nicely in the bottom of his eight-ounce jar of shave cream. "Standard kit," he said. "I'll show it to you later, Celine."

Jacques pulled to the edge of the wood line, next to the barn. "We sit here now and wait," Jacques said. "The barn will be decent shelter."

With the falling dark, the moon giving them just enough light, they began hauling the fruit barrels out of the truck. The best attribute of the barn, other than being remote and looking forlorn, was that it sat on a slight hill and offered a good line of sight to the north and northeast, where any German ground force activity would come from. Vire itself was built on high ground.

"Are we sleeping here?" asked Thomas, content to let Hibou make such decisions.

"Unless you have anything fancier lined up," said Jacques, and Claire laughed.

She said they would all make it work, looking at the several stalls, seeing one ladder leading to a loft with an east facing window. The smell of old hay was unmistakable.

Jacques set the radio on the edge of an old tarp.

"How do you signal critical activity as you monitor the Germans?" she asked, finding a bucket with nails, hinges, and scraps of wood. "I'm thinking it would not be in the clear."

"Oh my. I should walk you through the protocol," Thomas said, eager to involve his new friend in the work she had so selflessly made possible for him. He showed her a shopworn copy of a novel, Arnold Bennett's late Victorian masterpiece *The Old Wives' Tale.*

"Do you know it, this book?"

She said she was unfamiliar with the work, adding that it looked like that was about to change. Thomas told her the agent in the field and the watchers on station use a text that would not appear to be anything but a good read. No math books or anything obvious. "This edition was published in 1940." He told them he'd learned the crypto game on Thomas Hardy, and specifically with *Jude the Obscure.* He handed her the Bennett volume. "Take a look. What do you see?"

Claire intuitively went to the contents page.

He showed her how one thing, or name, is agreed to stand for something specific, and only the users had the one-time codes. It was the most usable form of cryptography in the field. American G-2 operators monitor set frequencies. Higher headquarters, too. Corps level, mostly. All very timely.

"I get it," she said, her days in D.C. handling encoded papers fresh in her mind.

Thomas was warming to the task, telling her he would take her through the key rules the next day, but Book One, Chapter One suggested the square, and it indicated a specific region; the page numbers worked like a series of concentric circles, with, for instance, Caen in the middle.

"Caen. Ah yes, like the boroughs of Paris."

Thomas looked at his watch and noticed he'd neglected to wind it at some point in their troubles over Roger Laurent and their hasty relocation from Épiniac. He told her there was also a strict protocol about when he might transmit, and it worked on short, designated time intervals. All unnoticed.

"Best to be unnoticed. But more than once a day, I would think."

"Yes, three-minute windows, beginning at quarter past the hour, and only odd numbered hours."

She nodded, understanding the system in a general sense, where a specific code for any operation, one which could last no more than a few days, was put into play. All stock-in-trade.

"It's getting darker," said Jacques. "The radio looks okay. I think we are set for the night."

Thomas pulled the cover back again to take a quick look.

"We are." Claire put her hand on his and asked whether he was tired from the hectic drive, from the sheer uncertainty of it all.

He said he was. Then, surprising her, Jacques pulled her to him. A quick hug of affirmation, spontaneous and welcome. Was it because of their partnership, she wondered, or more?

"You must be tired too," he said. Then added, "No room service tonight!"

She laughed at his humor, reluctant to let him go. They found a place to sleep; they were restless yet exhausted. She was back in the cab of the truck because the barn smells made her sneeze. The men and the dog found a decent place inside the old barn. Horse blankets, water buckets, and an abundance of hay.

Next morning, having unloaded the truck, Jacques made ready to drive into a nearby village some fifteen kilometers away to buy some food staples and assess any lingering presence of Wehrmacht. Thomas asked him to find a roll of tape. But first, they'd get the radio into place.

Getting it some dozen feet or so up into the loft, where it would work best, was not easy. With Jacques doing most of the work, they were able to wrest the piece up the old wooden ladder and stabilize it on a long cut of plywood the erstwhile owner might have used for a kind of bench.

Jacques connected the small generator they'd hidden in a pear barrel. There was not much petrol to run it, but it had some, and maybe they could siphon more from the truck later.

"Brilliant. It will take me a while to get my shop set up," said Thomas, working on an apple he'd saved and put into his pocket. "I'll want to test my transmitter."

Claire asked if he could think of anything he might need, as they'd be gone for a few hours. No, he was fine. Did he want Cleo to keep him company?

"No, no. She likes the air from the window. She should stay with you two."

Thomas told Hibou and Celine he'd put to good use the time they'd be away. Alone, Thomas began to assemble the remaining parts he'd set aside the previous night, eager to get to work. Any intercept operation required a tuned transmitter. With a sense of pride and accomplishment, he started the generator and switched on the radio. Thomas decided he'd begin his search for active frequencies.

Timing and luck, however, proved no longer his keeper, and Thomas had no way to know that German radio security, operating from within the wood line not a kilometer away, had been searching for just such partisan activity. Nearby German radio direction finding was a threat the man had failed to anticipate.

Near eleven, Jacques's truck approached the barn. There, he and Claire saw two men in black coats putting a third into their vehicle. The barn behind them roiled in flame. From the look of it, the generator had exploded, or maybe they had simply set off some explosives. Jacques and Claire sat far enough back to observe what had happened but not close enough to be spotted.

"Goddamn it."

"My God, Jacques," she said. "They are taking him." Their own luck had held. Thomas's had not. "And he had been so clever. The boot heel. The shaving cream."

"We have to go. Immediately!" Both watched, though only seconds more, until the Germans drove off with their prize, the barn behind them collapsing in flame. "Did you think he knew about Combourg?" Jacques asked her.

She had never mentioned it. They'd only met Thomas at the Laurent farm, in Épiniac. "As I recall, nothing was ever said to him about Combourg."

"He would not know of the monsignor, Roger's uncle," she added. They had kept that secret. Claire rubbed at the palm of one hand, kneading it with the knuckle of the other.

"No. And he does not know our real names," Jacques said. "But Roger Laurent could know."

Jacques took her hand. "Thomas is lost, but what harm Roger could do yet is considerable. If he gives up Roger."

"Will he? Where will they take him?" she asked as Jacques worked the truck around, knowing he was leaving behind his apples and, more importantly, his cover for travel.

"Saint-Lô, I would think. Some Nazi headquarters."

As Jacques wrenched the truck sharply onto the road toward home, where the deeply distressed Claire would be able to arrange for her return to Bodney, a bottle scooted out from under her seat.

"Look at this," she said, pulling it up from the floor. "It's his Calvados." Attempting to hold back tears.

"Keep it. We will finish it tonight in his honor with a tip of the hat to our friend."

Passing near enough to the Laurent farm en route to Combourg, with relative safety still several kilometers away, Jacques pointed to the farmhouse. It was risky, but he had to take a look, remaining well back from potential observation. There, they were able to make out, standing near the entry door, the one thing they had hardly dared hope to see—a dark green motorcycle.

What Roger's return portended was unclear, but given what had happened to Thomas, that outcome was surely the best they could have hoped for. Jacques slowed the truck and looked to the darkened house, their hearts racing.

"Oh my God. He's come back."

Jacques touched her hand.

She thought to say something, leaning into him. "Let's go home, Jacques. Please!" Then added, "You did well, getting us through it all. So brave."

"You and me," he said. "We did. Together." He touched her face tenderly.

In that moment, Jacques and Claire leaned toward each other for a necessary hug, and then a kiss. A kiss of relief. A kiss of what might yet be.

CHAPTER 16

Against considerable odds—Wehrmacht activity focused elsewhere—the couple made it safely back to the Berlangier farmhouse. The war ground on beyond them and above them, relentless. Same as it had and maybe forever would do. Yet so much had changed.

It was not as if the Germans had gone home. Rather, ten days after the first of several successful Normandy Beach invasions, the main battle area had shifted significantly to the east. Bloody ground battles that followed had the effect of scattering German forces across multiple sections of northeastern France, while their Luftwaffe scrambled to blunt Allied advances by air. German troops outflanked by coordinated Allied airborne and ground operations hastened to recover and reconstitute their operational lines. They hung on to Caen for a few weeks, until the Brits and Canadians swept them out. Soon, much of the fight against Hitler's forces would come from Soviet pressure well to the east.

Though Fate had dealt the telling cards, Claire and Jacques's timing proved impeccable, avoiding troop movements passing just north—infantry, with armored escort. In fact, Jacques and Claire had cleared out of the Vire area only one day before the devastating battle of Villers-

Bocage, not twenty kilometers away from that fated barn where the unfortunate Roland Thomas had been dragged from his radio intercept and comms gear.

Claire and Jacques took no incidental German fire. No mortars or snipers. No left-behind enemy combatants, though they saw numerous dead in the fields. They did find one severely damaged Panzer tank, off its tracks, blocking a hamlet crossroads, about thirty kilometers north of Combourg. There were a few fire-blackened buildings looking resolute behind one dead German soldier, hanging grotesquely just below the gun turret. They drove around the vehicle, not a little prayerful.

"Are you shivering?" Jacques asked.

"I think I could be in shock. I mean, I have to put the image of Mr. Thomas being taken out of my mind." She moved closer. "I still see him. Poor man," she said. "My God. . ."

Jacques pulled her closer. "I know. Nothing we could do. We are almost home now."

As the sun began to set, their long and parlous operation finished, they made their way to Jacques's home. Cleo let out a low-pitched whine as they approached the place, happy to be home. Jacques parked by the front door, and Claire let Cleo jump free. The couple stood together by the truck's side a moment. The war for now out of reach, a moment neither wanted to lose.

"You were wonderful in getting us back," she said.

Jacques, rarely one to let his emotions rise to the surface, looked into her eyes, searching for the right words. He'd had to control any drift toward romance for so long. Maybe too long. His Martine gone. Was Claire a new opening? A clearing away of so many difficult locks and channels? He took a moment to decide what to say, and he took her hand.

"I have been in love, Claire. I have. And I can tell you that love can hobble and can be highly unsettling. It does not always come with the promise of happiness. Love can be vexing. So, it's something I must take precautions with."

"I understand. I do. But I want you to understand what I feel. For you," she assured him.

"We are a pair, aren't we?" Tenderly, he pushed her hair away from her eyes and heard her sigh. Those eyes, a shade of green he found irresistible.

And so, one two-person team—a French partisan and one American woman—were considering what they might yet come to. Together. Acute danger focuses the mind, makes men and women aware of what life means, or could mean. The war constituted a kind of catalyst. They had survived, and they both felt horrible about Thomas's tragic death. That brave man. The clandestine German radio DF team that intercepted Thomas's test signals saved two lives by taking one. Arguably, theirs were two remade lives—war was always a portal to a different world. Getting back safely to Jacques's place meant a new start. Where it would lead was something unforeseen.

"For now, Claire, we are safe. But just because we don't see Germans does not mean they are not there. Enemy agents could be passing as friends of friends. Informers. Enemy sympathizers. Spies. A bone cancer in the limbs of the nation."

Claire put her hands to her face. "I hate it all. But I'm grateful for you." She suggested they go in. She needed a bath, needed to get something to eat. "My Lord, Jack, I need to get cleaned up," Claire insisted, taking his hand as they walked into the house. He smiled at the liberty with his name. "But I'm afraid I have little to change into. Even a fresh shirt would do wonders," she added. "I must smell like a barnyard."

He laughed and told her she smelled wonderful. "Let's go in."

Once in the house, he took one of her hands and kissed it. Neither needed to say more. Fortune had given them another chance. And, if possible, they'd take that chance together. He admired the woman's tenacity. Her intuitive mind. Her gift for reasoning and for listening. How she had stood her ground when she had to. All that, and he found her so very desirable.

Claire realized Jacques Berlangier was a remarkable man. She'd not felt this way about anyone for the longest time. His integrity, gentleness, ingenuity, decency. And such good looks. Still, she thought it best to leave any further romantic initiative up to him. She would play it by ear, as her mother used to say.

Jacques said he had something she could change into and handed her a towel, along with what may well have been the last scrap of soap.

"I'll use whatever soap you have left! And I have another light work shirt too small for me. I'll get it."

Claire decided to seize the moment. "We could save water if we bathed together," she said, blushing. Would he take her up on it? Was it too much?

He laughed and said her survival instincts were kicking in again, two being better than one, then took her hand and led her to the bath. Cleo watched as they closed the door. Home meant togetherness. A moment of peace. A future as yet undefined. Perhaps one full of promise.

Later, Jacques opened a bottle of a decent chardonnay, something he'd been saving. To say they were ready to enjoy themselves only underscored how well they had kept their nerves in check. And, at that moment, they shared such wonderful intimacy.

Early that evening, Jacques cooked—more accurately he broiled—a scrawny chicken. He added, as well, the juice of three pears to the broiling pan, adding herb roasted potatoes and hot, buttery cauliflower, the taste of which Claire told him they would just have to agree to disagree about. The meal was a feast. The surviving local bakery, the Armand Boulangerie in Combourg, was famous for their baguettes. Claire told him she knew something about French cooking from her years in Paris but avowed that Jacques's was better. Where had he learned to cook? That meal, he said, was a long-standing family secret that had more to do with necessity than inspiration.

"That was wonderful, Jack."

He grinned and gave a mock British salute, repeating the name, as if to test its possibilities. Claire said giving nicknames and fun names was something they'd always done in her family, an affirmation of love and caring. For her, whatever was happening between them was more than a matter of trust. She felt about any attempt to have a lover again much as a gambler who'd lost his life's savings might look at a fresh deck of cards. Why take a chance? Because she had to. Could she make herself vulnerable again? Could she let herself love Jacques? She ached for such certainty.

"No, *you* are wonderful," he answered, then kissed her nose, her throat, and her long, slender neck. He ran his hands through her auburn-colored hair and brought her to the sofa.

"And you kiss pretty good, too," she said.

How had she come to him, Jacques thought? That charming, full-of-life woman. That gift. Pure luck? It seemed lucky, given that their first partisan meet-up in Dinan had been aborted with the shooting on the platform, then they'd had to rendezvous in the rain not a week later. Fate. He realized that his Martine, gone nearly three years, and Claire had much in common—both with aspirations for love and companionship, each with a generosity of spirit and empathy. Both women touched his heart as few others ever could. Now, a new start.

Sitting with Cleo by the unlit fireplace, Jacques asked the question he'd not dared ask before. "How close did you come to turning back that night?"

"Oh my. That awful, rainy night?" Claire sipped her wine, smiled, and said she had never once thought of going back. "My God, I could not go back. Never. I had a job to do."

"Do you always have to have a job?" he kidded her.

"Yes, I do, and I have to return to Bodney soon." Their teamwork—the professional side of it—was complete. She set down her glass, and looked at him for a moment, taking full measure of that extraordinary man. She wondered where Jacques was going with that question. Would he say more? Would he suggest she stay?

"I feel terrible about Roland. His mission was impossible from the start," she said.

"We did what we could, Claire. He was on a mission for family as much as for country."

"Yes. His James. The loss of his brother drove him when common sense said no. But we did what we had to do," she said. "And, in truth, we met one brave man given a terrible task. We got him into the tactical zone, as he insisted." The wine might have been making her more voluble than she might have been. She continued, "And we cannot hold ourselves responsible for what happened." She put her hand on his.

"No. And now it's just us," he said.

Claire leaned into his arms, an embrace they both needed. She looked up and kissed him. She could not help but think what they were doing was a necessary balm. A comfort. Therapeutic. Compensation for so much loss.

"Where do we go from here? You and I?" he asked.

"We go back upstairs," she insisted, then added, "And this time, let's take our time." Claire let out a small sigh, a woman deep in the hold of an unquiet battle between heart and head.

"I want you," he said.

"I need you," she answered, and she pulled him closer, kissing him, taking him. They were eager for each other, marveling at how their bodies fit so perfectly together. Later, in the afterglow, they felt so warm in each other's arms.

Before falling asleep, they sorted out what they'd been through together, the long hours of danger, the close call, the safe return, and their intimacy; whatever their new reality could come to mean, she knew she had other, more practical, matters to sort through. "Tomorrow, Jack, I want you to arrange for my return."

"The monsignor can manage that. Meanwhile, we have tonight."

CHAPTER 17

Jacques arranged for Claire's return using the ever-reliable dead drop at the church. He lit the requisite candle and left his message, standard operating procedure. Claire felt like a changed woman as she prepared for her departure following those several tumultuous days in northern France, the maelstrom of war, the rush of clandestine work, and Roland Thomas. Even the roles played by Madame Laurent and her elusive son replayed themselves in her mind. And then there was Jack.

After an early dinner, which she'd prepared that time, following much needed rest and music, reading, and more loving, Claire had packed up and sat with the dog. Never had she felt so conflicted. She and Jacques talked about what they'd come to mean to each other, about their days and nights as partners. Both understood those moments could be their last time together for a while. Cleo followed them to the door, where they hesitated. The dog looked up at Claire, then to her master. Claire wiped at a tear and hugged the little spaniel.

"I'll see you soon, girl," she promised, hoping it was true.

Making their way to the courier plane pickup site, neither knew what to say. They had said it all and done it all. Hadn't they? Jacques kissed her and repeated Claire's words to Cleo. "I'll see you soon."

Claire Skiffington better understood her true feelings about that man and could begin to reimagine a whole other future. And past the war, what then? She'd do anything and everything to get back. Of the many things that mattered, where so little could be certain, nothing could mean more than them—together, supporting each other. She gave some thought to the story of the monsignor's sister Margot and her American husband, her injured soldier.

What could Claire tell her roommates back at the base? That she'd fallen in love? What does one say to the serious-minded, ever- able Paula, or to the always-affable Mary Perry, now in London? She'd report the operational details to Betty, of course. She'd have to think about what she might tell her that was deeply personal. After all, she cherished the woman as a friend. But would she understand?

Claire was relieved that her pilot was not Owen. There was another new fellow, one with no way to know how conflicted his passenger felt just then. Flying low, the wind dried her face. What she was flying from would always be a part of her. It was not just a harrowing mission. In another sense, she was flying from the physical difficulties of her childhood, her horrible bike accident as a young teen in Binghamton that broke and scarred her leg as well as her confidence. Her father had made certain she'd overcome that day. And, years later, via one big insurance settlement, preparation and determination led her to a college degree and a career. After that, she'd been led to the man she knew she loved—her owl. Her Jacques Berlangier.

RAF Bodney had not changed, unlike all that was so different for Claire. There'd be more assignments, though not right away. Betty told her to hold tight, knowing her friend was exhausted. Meanwhile, she could help the code clerks. One thing she would do was to write to her sister, Rita, who would surely be a source of help, a sounding board for her angst over Jacques. She'd not write her mother. There was too much to try to say, and Julia Skiffington was not easy to reach when it came to emotional matters. Same thing with her older sister, Maddie. Both would say something about her age. What was she doing in the middle of a war? And why a Frenchman?

During supper, the evening she'd left for Bodney, Claire had toyed with Jacques, not a little silliness in their intimacy. At one point, he'd asked her, "What are you grinning about?" She told him she was just thinking about the old English nursery rhyme "The Owl and the Pussycat." Did he know it?

No, no. His English was decent, but how would he have had exposure to that one?

She recited the first few lines, which were actually all she could recall. "Listen, now," she continued then in her best performance voice:

> "The Owl and the Pussycat went to sea
> In a beautiful pea-green boat:
> They took some honey, and plenty of money
> Wrapped up in a five-pound note."

Jacques looked puzzled, then stood and grinned. "And are you the pussycat?"

"I suppose I must be."

"I am not at all sure we have plenty of money." He grinned again, fetching the wine as he thought about it. "Much less a pea-green boat, but, after this war—and it will end, maybe this year—this Owl will take you to Paris. No secrets. No danger. Just us," he said.

"That sounds better than going to sea," she replied, giving him another kiss. *Paris?*

They had turned on the radio after clearing the table. Glenn Miller's *Moonlight Serenade* delighted the couple. No words had been necessary. They danced more slowly to the piece than they might have done under better circumstances. Their moment. The sun had gone down. A willful, early summer breeze was just whispering past the window reflecting their image.

For several days, Claire sat on her bunk, reading, listening to airplanes coming and going, alert to the prattle and thrum of a rear-guard army. The Allies were making progress that summer through bloody battles—fits and starts. They were taking back much of France. With the Americans finally persevering in the so-called hedgerow battles, most of the country was free of the Nazi menace by late July. With the liberation of Paris in August, the rationing, imposed by the Germans, had begun to abate.

Come mid-July, Claire made two more quick trips. Courier jobs, a timely code book one time, identification papers another. Jacques was always in her thoughts.

She wrote in her diary and then copied out the silly poem for her Jack, uncertain whether she'd see him again. She'd give it to him as a keepsake, yes, but also as a promise. She showed the piece to Betty, needing someone she trusted with whom to share her thoughts. Betty's husband, Bill, also OSS, was serving in the battle-intense Pacific. A naturally curious person, one who never stopped wanting to understand her world and that of her friends, Betty asked about Jacques.

"When and where did he learn his English?"

Claire was happy to praise his language prowess. "One of his aunts was a nurse, as I recall him saying, and she'd trained in England. Liverpool maybe. In the twenties. Jacques told me how determined his mother was that he learn the language. So, he had the encouragement. And he reads English novels," she said, adding that the aunt, from Bayeux, had died some time ago.

"My. Quite a cultured apple farmer," Betty said, only half teasing.

Claire said she thought family heritage mattered a great deal to him, though there had been problems. He worried about his sister, Nina, whose self-imposed isolation he'd mentioned to her. His instinctive patriotism has brought him to the resistance when others hunkered down and left the battles to their neighbors. "His father's example," Claire recalled. "Or he was just waiting for a chance to help the good guys, beginning with Britain."

"Or the right American," offered Betty.

"Yes, I suppose so." She brightened. "Or the right American. And I am ever so happy about the result."

Claire managed an agonizing six weeks before she encountered Jacques again during her third OSS mission into France since her return from the Thomas assignment. Several of her colleagues were flying—or jumping, in the case of the men—into Normandy and even into the Low Countries. Betty knew Claire wanted northern Brittany, and no one would be able to predict when one such task would connect her to Berlangier—Hibou—whose team's focus on demolitions had been broadened to include assisting downed Allied flyers, something he'd proven capable of handling.

They had only the briefest reunion one night in August. The brevity of their meeting only aggravated their forced separation. They had time that night for only a kiss and a promise.

"No snare tonight?" she teased. She had once again brought money and an ID package.

That brought a nervous smile. "Maybe next time," he told her, giving her a hug, something the Brit pilot took notice of. Moments later, turning the plane so that they could take off into the wind, he said, "I suppose you know that bloke."

"I do," she said. "Yes. I suppose I do."

By mid-September, the pace at Bodney had begun to slow. Claire would have done more if she could have, especially if she thought her partisan contact could be the man she was missing so much. How many more such missions could she stand—seeing him not at all or ever so briefly?

Her final assignment before being sent home some six months short of the war's official end was once again to the historic village of Lamballe, near the northernmost coast, carrying maps and codes printed on lightweight, durable parachute silk material. Escape and evasion materials for stranded British Special Air Service soldiers tasked with bringing a high-value German back for interrogation. Codes and cyphers generated by SOE—data the SAS team would need to reach Saint-Brieuc unobserved, where, with any luck, they would rendezvous with British sailors who could get the German prisoner out of the country and over to England.

All went well until she stepped into a crater while helping the pilot turn the airplane around, severely fracturing her left ankle. It was the same leg she had broken when struck while riding her bike as a teen. In the middle of the mission, the leg was further compromised.

Betty requested and arranged for Claire's service to continue back in Washington, once more on E Street, NW. "You've done enough here, Claire. Help us from home. Bring back a touch of operational reality to those Plans people."

She said she would but hated to leave before the job was done.

Betty assured her that this was best for all. "They need to know what you have seen. Be safe, and I'll see you when this damned business is over."

Claire was going home. OSS courier Celine Mercier was no more. Claire asked only that a courier get a message to Jacques— a note that she'd see him again as soon as circumstances permitted. She asked her friend Owen Terfel to try to deliver it, not saying this was the man she loved. Could he do that for her? He told her yes; he'd take care of it.

She did not mention, didn't say, that Claire Skiffington would worry about him too, that he was a friend to count on. "See he gets this note and tell him I have not forgotten that pea-green boat he promised me."

CHAPTER 18

When the war in Europe at last came to its exhausted, inevitable end; when the despicable little man in the burned-out bunker in the shadow of the Reich Chancellery was at long last dead, when Europe could begin once more to take full measure of itself and its way ahead, Jacques Berlangier returned to his apple farm, to his hopes and his enduring aspirations.

Two problems worked to rattle the man's confidence. The first was the loss of a man he respected above all others. The next was the near loss of his beloved Cleo.

The good man and unrecognized hero of France, Monsignor Eduard Arnoux—Catholic prelate, family friend, and brilliant partisan warrior—passed away one morning after a short walk behind the church. Jacques attended the man's funeral Mass at Église Saint-Martin that sunny September morning. Several sisters from the nearby convent of Kermaria, women who had graced the church on numerous occasions, occupied a row in the back of the church, ever- dedicated to the body and the blood, as the catechism insists.

In attendance as well, not surprisingly, were the late priest's sister and her son Roger, the latter looking quite the man of the hour in a somber gray suit, a British-style rep tie and black wingtips. His uncle had taught him something, evidently, though Jacques had no clear idea what Roger's true function for the resistance had been. Roger looked agitated, shooting his cuffs, stretching his neck, patting at his hair. For her part, Madame Laurent stared into the rack of votive candles, perhaps only vaguely aware of what was happening around her. Those same candles had constituted a kind of serving board for wartime secrets shared by Jacques, by Arnoux, and by others he would never know.

From across the aisle, Roger nodded perfunctorily to Jacques, an acknowledgment of something, perhaps. His body language suggested ambivalence or maybe irritation. Jacques gave most of his attention to the priest giving the final blessing, but he could not take his eyes off one rose-colored glass votive that suddenly seemed to burn all the brighter. Returning home, just past noon, he found no sign of his Brittany spaniel.

Jacques drove for nearly two hours around the property, stopping to inspect a few possible trouble spots, one where lightning had mangled a pear tree a week ago, one where a wild boar had been trapped and shot—Jacques had not been willing to take a chance on letting the furious creature go, certain as he was to turn on him. Where could that dog be? He called several times, compelled out of love to do so, though knowing it could come to nothing. If the dog was near and free, she would come home.

Late that afternoon Jacques drove back into town. He knew only one man who would possibly have heard more about what was going on than any other, especially with the monsignor gone. Walking into the supply store, he could not help but recall the many times he had done so to enlist his friend for an operation. That time, he needed quite a different, more personal kind of help.

"Jacques," said the big man behind the counter. "*Ça va?* What's up?"

"I am at a loss in finding my dog, Fabien. I think someone may have taken Cleo."

"Taken? No! But why? Who would do such a thing?"

"Exactly why I've come to you, my friend. Have you heard of such trouble around here? Property theft, animal abuse, anything that could be related to this?"

Fabien pounded his fist on the countertop. "Yes, by God. I have. There was a small house near the village of Lanhélin. Maybe ten days ago. An elegant cottage, actually, renovated by a Dutchman and his wife. She's French. Wealthy types. Untended Muscadet vineyards all around. People from some place north of Paris. They keep the place here for now-and-again stretches. You did not hear?"

"Tell me."

"They had it fixed up after the damage of the war. New plumbing, expensive lamps, and nice carpets. You know, money. Someone burned it. Good thing the people were away. When the authorities looked at it, they found the place had been all but demolished inside—the copper pulled. Things taken. Good money, you know, for copper. Not much of it around now."

"So, it was a money thing," said Jacques. "Robbery, arson, and who knows what else?"

"Or some kind of revenge. And I would not put it past people who did that to the Dutchman to take a man's dog. Everything is money for some." Fabien came around the counter and put his hand on Jacques's shoulder. "Dog like yours, healthy, good training, will command a good price," he continued. "I am sorry. I hope you find your little Cleo. And I hope that is not what has happened."

"But who?"

Fabien grunted and returned to the other side of the counter where he reached beneath and pulled out a bottle of apple brandy, then poured them each a small glass. "Do you recall last year, here in the store? We looked out to see two men at your truck. Cleo was inside."

"I do."

"Gypsies. My thinking. . ."

"Of course." Jacques finally had a lead of some sort. "Thank you, Fabien." Brun told him to be cautious. Jacques took a quick drink, thanked Brun again, and left the store. The more he thought about it, the angrier he became, pounding the steering wheel with his open palm. Well, that was their trade, their view of life. Take or be taken. Still, he had to make a choice. The wrong decision could spell the end for his dog. He could follow the potential thievery angle, which both intrigued and infuriated him, or take what struck him as the more likely course of action and go back to do a more thorough search around the property. Was there not a greater chance she was hurt somewhere by the house? Whichever path he followed would exclude the other. If those people had taken her, they'd not keep her long. Cleo was in peril, and time was running out.

If she was dead, he'd have found her. If hurt, she'd make her way back, or try, and thus would be close. That he did not find her meant Cleo must have been taken. There was a substantial probability it was those thieves. How to locate them was the trick. Find her and bring her home. One man came to mind. A man who may well have contacts with all manner of people. The next day, early, he would look up Roger Laurent.

Jacques saw no motorcycle when he arrived at the house, but there was a snappy little red-and-black Citroën Avant in the drive, looking to be in quite good condition. Jacques had to think that whoever had it during the war must have hidden it well. So, Roger was there. If Madame Laurent was at home, he recognized too late, he should have brought flowers, a show of respect and sympathy for the loss of her brother. Roger met him at the door.

"May I come in?"

"Certainly." Roger shook his hand. "Thank you for coming to the service," Laurent said, stepping back, showing Jacques to the main room, where he could not help imagining Roland Thomas sitting there, as he had those long-ago months back, fidgeting in his chair. "Your uncle was a fine man, Roger, and a friend. He was so much more than what he did for the church. I am sorry for your loss."

Roger frowned, nodded, and asked whether his visitor wanted anything. A drink? Declining, Jacques decided to make his business known. He knew Roger had contacts—underworld people who knew things. Roger's skill was observation. What Jacques did not say was that he also thought Roger likely used them to his own nefarious ends. That cop was one of the most calculating individuals he had ever known.

"I suspect not much goes on around you that you do not have a window into."

"Really? Well, that window has kept me alive." Laurent said in a boastful tone. He said he had been recently made a captain of police in gratitude for his services. "So, I must be observant."

The promotion was news to Jacques. Still, it could only mean a greater spread of contacts. Did he know, by any chance, of any recent problems in the area with gypsies?

Laurent took a moment. "They usually keep pretty much to themselves," he allowed, lighting up a cigarette, thinking what to say, choosing his words carefully. "They keep to their traditions." He then added the obvious note that their behavior sometimes created problems for the police. "The *gadjo*, to them. But why ask?"

"My dog is missing. I have reason to suspect she was stolen, and maybe by these people. A Brittany spaniel."

"Fine hunter. They took her to sell, I suppose. Is that right?"

"That is my thinking." Jacques would not add that she mostly treed red squirrels.

Roger took all that in, intimating he'd heard it before. He drew laboriously on his cigarette and blew out the smoke in short puffs as if he were creating something—an image, a history—using the slight delay to think about how to respond. "There had been reports. Nothing certain. Nothing acted upon. They travel, of course, these people, and will come back to a place from time to time." He said they had a camp sometimes, north, near l'Oisette, up on the river Ruisseau. He thought they were there at that moment, he said. "A place they like. Not far."

"I know it," said Jacques, who stood and again shook hands with the enigmatic man, eager to get to it. "Congratulations on your new position," he added. Jacques figured Laurent would know how to come out right side up no matter who won what war, large or small.

Laurent thanked him. For all he knew, Berlangier might be picking a fight he'd not come out of well. Was there anything else? Jacques shook his head. He wanted to get going.

Laurent put his hand on Jacques's shoulder. "One more thing. Your apple farm, Jacques. Very impressive. You are doing well? Nice profits?" he said.

Jacques said yes. They were doing all right. Gradual expansion. "Labor intensive," he added. Jacques thought that was an odd tangent.

"My uncle said to me several times that you knew what you were doing, that you were a highly successful man."

"Did he?" Jacques was at a loss for words. What was that about? "Thank you. I had great respect for your uncle. The monsignor was a longtime friend." Jacques turned to leave.

"Those gypsies, Jacques. Be careful. Bring a weapon. Such people do not fuck around."

"No. I am certain of it, Roger, and neither do I."

Late that afternoon, coming upon what was clearly the campsite—caravans, a slew of trucks, men and women, many raggedy children—Jacques thought he saw what looked like a few tethered goats. He also spotted a flatbed truck with several pens or cages lashed to the bed. Dogs. He would have to get a good bit closer to know for certain whether Cleo was there, yet he did not want to be seen. He reached into the glove box and pulled out the small Modèle, a gun he'd had for many years. The grip felt right in his hand, though he'd not fired it in a while.

Jacques made his way along a small wood line, having pulled the truck off the road some hundred meters back. From the wood line, he could see the dogs. Maybe eight or nine. There was a good chance Cleo was one of them. No guards. These bastards would not expect to be found or caught. Gaining a better line of sight, he was maybe two hundred meters away and would soon have to break cover. The green conifers above were still and breathless. He spotted his Cleo.

The Romani people had been a plague on France for years—often on the move, always on the wrong side of decency. Many of them were pickpockets in Paris and other big cities, charlatans and cheats in the countryside. Thieves turning their own children into thieves.

Jacques wiped a kerchief across his forehead, realizing he'd begun to perspire. He checked the automatic in his hand; the safety catch was on. The dogs were making a hell of a noise. Cleo was in the pen at the rear of one truck. How to get her out and run off safely was another matter. He could not be certain about how far he'd get or how to get safely back to his own truck without the bastards becoming aware. Should he wait for night? No. That would be hours.

Someone—maybe a teen—was taunting the dogs with a stick. Jacques watched for another few minutes, biding his time—for what he did not know. He did know he'd like to take that stick to that kid. Just then, something behind him snapped. He turned. There was rustling in the underbrush. But no, it was not a person, just a pair of wild turkeys.

Once he got close, Cleo would sound off in welcome. That could be a problem. But other dogs were barking, so maybe that was not something to worry about. Jacques wiped his gun hand on his pants again, chambered a round, and stepped out from behind a dense hedge, calculating how far he was from Cleo. No more than hundred meters. His best bet would be to create a diversion.

Near the animal pens, he heard one great ruckus, shouts and hoots and the distinctive sound of a pistol shot. Someone fishing in the near part of the lake must have landed a big one. The carp in those inland lakes, he knew, could be monstrous. Even the teenagers closest to the caged animals were caught up in the euphoria of whatever was happening at lakeside. No time to second- guess this small miracle.

As the fishing drama pulled everyone to that side of the camp, caravans between the flatbed truck and the lake provided adequate cover, and Jacques raced to the vehicle. He was nearly there when he stumbled on a root. He got up, more or less unhurt, his hand cut and knee bloodied. His heart pounding in his chest, he ran to the back of the truck, found a simple bolt, and slid it back, opening the old wire door. More commotion at the lake. Cleo yelped, leaped out, and jumped down, too excited to bark. She was yipping, then let out a brief low-pitched howl. *What took you so long?*

The spaniel racing at his side, they made it safely back. Neither was really hurt. Pulling away, Jacques slipped the gun into the place from which he had retrieved it minutes before.

"What were you doing here, girl?" he said as Cleo laced him with licks and made more jubilant yipping noises. "You need to rethink the company you keep," he told her. That night, he kept a close watch on the grounds. If he slept at all it was little.

Over the next weeks, Jacques had plenty of time to think about what he needed and wanted; he was closing in on forty. The war had taken not a few years in which he might well have settled down, invested in his farm, taken a chance on expanding his business—something that, for the last year or so, had intrigued and tempted him. Something his Claire—back in sleepy Vestal, New York, teaching—had encouraged him, making the goal more compelling. So much turns on what are often unremarkable choices—those made and those not.

He owed Claire a letter. She tended to write back almost immediately, and so he was always owing one. Her job. Her sisters. How much she missed him. She'd written that she was making plans, exciting plans, but so much was still undecided.

Safe at home, Cleo's energy showed her joy, though for days following the trauma she barely left Jacques's side. When he walked out to the storage shed for tools, she wanted to go too. A team again.

Late the next week, Jacques received the news he'd hardly dared hope for, learning by letter that Claire would be coming back to France. "I will live in Paris again, my dear one. I have an offer," she'd written. Delighted with the prospect, she'd teach at a *lycée* in Montmartre.

Paris! He reread her words, looking for nuance, for all meaning he could discern. "I cannot wait to see you."

Was she coming to be with him? She'd not said that, but he would help her to make that choice. Paris. She could teach and paint. Was this not what he wanted for her too? Jacques would help her to settle into the city, but he had his eye on something much more definitive. The sharp barbs of war were gradually dulling. Fate had been more than considerate to them both up to that point. He loved her, that brave, amazing woman. Could it happen? Yes. Why not? He knew he must move forward. Claire was his way ahead.

Tout s'arrange dans la vie, he whispered to himself. Everything in life works out. Have a little faith. It just takes time. Alone at night, he heard her voice.

CHAPTER 19

Claire stepped out of her crowded *Métro* station to make her way across the busy rue La Fayette, barely avoiding one horn-tooting cabbie. She peered into a cheese shop, thought better of it, and continued home. Two boys pedaled by on old bicycles, bright woolen scarves wild in the wind, ringing their bells and laughing. The cold December wind worked to slow her pace, but her mind was occupied with matters more important than weather. Had she been smart to return to France, no promises made? Jacques's last letter had made clear he wanted her there. But it was best to take it slowly. After all, it had been just over a year. Could that be true?

She'd thought all that through before. Her work was satisfying. Painting and teaching fulfilled her in many ways. She enjoyed her students. She had made friends. Well, a few. Claire had trouble articulating whatever it was that she wanted and needed. After all, the war had been over for more than a year—her life had been too long on hold. "We live our lives forward, not backward," she'd written to her sister Rita.

Those boys on rickety black bikes began waving to her. She waved back, taking it as a good sign, a telling sign. Cheery youngsters on their way to whatever fun they may have had in mind caused her to think again about her situation: the husband and children she did not have. Nearing her apartment, she came upon one establishment certain to improve anyone's mood, and there, she could not resist.

The wonderful old confectioners' store, a mere three doors down and around the corner from her flat, was too good to pass up. The owners at À La Mère de Famille, on Faubourg Montmartre, Paris's best chocolate shop, had placed their famous ganache squares just so in the corner window, as if to deliberately tempt a woman to come sample—and, of course, to buy!

No fair, she thought as she entered, a small bell over the door announcing her.

Claire selected six—enough to last several days. With Christmas only three days away, they would be exactly right, a few sweets to remind her of childhood days in south central New York, where her parents would bring out the best chocolates they could find and afford, along with her mother's delightfully decorated sugar cookies. At such times, Claire had to guard against loneliness, and, for the most part, she did. Dark chocolate was her comfort food.

The owner, a matronly woman whose name Claire could never quite recall—Lisette maybe—asked whether she'd take anything else. "Maybe some ice cream?"

Should she? "Well, I would like a coffee to take along with these, please," she said, after giving the treat some further thought, and, yes, maybe the *glace à la fraise*, a wonderful strawberry ice cream. The strong coffee was also first-rate.

Arriving back at her narrow second floor walk-up with dark hardwood floors and a light shade of yellow walls—an apartment offering just enough room for her bed, a small kitchen and bath, and a studio she'd fashioned from what might have once been a dining area—she set down her purchases and walked over to her easel. Her palette looked as shopworn as her utilitarian brown leather shoes—shoes her brother-in-law Otto Maier had given her years ago. Ott was always looking after others.

Claire took a bite of a truffle and studied what she'd managed so far, keen on the effect the gauzy gray light had on the work she'd begun the week before. Her immediate interest was in a new landscape she was working on, the Seine at its most serene. The Seine as Monet had seen it, or imagined, at Port-Villez—a technique she'd not attempted—something with bits of egg white mixed into the pigment. That was one technique others were encouraging at the Académie Julian. The objective: gradients of daylight. Claire was determined to get the luminosity right. On the way in, she'd stopped to see whether she had mail without paying much attention to the pieces she'd received. Thinking she might have had a Christmas card or two from her sisters and her mom, she had set the mail down on the small oak console just inside the door.

Only when she went to the kitchen to find some milk for her coffee did she think again about the mail. Finding a card from Jacques made her smile. His handwriting was as distinctive as the man himself. Opening it, she found he'd sent a homemade Christmas card with a photo of him and his darling Cleo wearing a holiday wreath and looking embarrassed for the adoration.

"Bonjour, Clee, Clee!"

Claire had asked him weeks ago whether he might come up for a few days. At first, he'd said it would be difficult, but he was coming. He could be with her the day before Christmas. Would that be suitable? "Please let me know if there is a problem with the timing," he wrote, adding, she thought needlessly, "I know you protect your painting time." That last excuse, if that is what it was, made her laugh. He had signed it, "Love, Your Owl." Just then, there could have been no better news.

Their history was clear, if clouded only a touch by the expectations of both regarding his nascent business in the apple brandy industry and her study and painting at the academy. Claire was busy teaching art at an international high school—one situated only a short walk north of her place—the Lycée Jacques Decour. Its very name delighted her for its allusion to her Jacques. She loved working in that old building constructed around its own grassy, central court. The brilliant Fauvist painter Raoul Dufy had lived in a small, vine-covered building nearby before the war.

What had drawn her back to Paris more than a year after she'd been sent home to Washington was more than art, more than the energy that pulled her to Paris a dozen or more years back. It was hope. More than the opportunity to work, to study, and to paint in the City of Light—*La Ville-Lumière.* She could teach in Vestal. She could teach anywhere. Facing the truth, she'd come back to France for what she needed even more, a test of both will and heart, the implied promise of being with Jacques. Be near but be careful. Be close, but not too close. He was never an easy read. How much would have changed for him, so busy, and how would the stakes have changed for both of them?

With Jacques expected in a few days, it would be up to him to demonstrate intentions. He'd always been truthful with her. The Christmas holiday brought its own heightened expectations, of course, and she wanted to give him something special. What would make a suitable gift? Not necessarily anything expensive. Something expressive and unique.

He liked music: swing, big band, and anything from the highly innovative Claude Debussy—very much an impressionist composer. The next day, Claire paid a visit to a charming little place called Old Dominion, a gift shop near Sacré-Cœur run by an older British couple, William and Janet Morrison, English expats she had taken a liking to. The first time they had met was at her school, at Jacques Decour, where their daughter Michelle was also teaching. Her appointment had started some six months ahead of Claire's. Michelle was a math teacher, and much prized by the dean. The two women got on, but they lived in quite different circumstances. Michelle was married, and any free time she had, which could not have been much, was spent with her husband and teenaged children. Claire enjoyed more the company of the older Morrisons, who lived above their store.

The Old Dominion had more tchotchkes than treasures, several things from Mother England—things they'd picked up in their own extensive travels, throw pillows, knock-off paintings, gaudy ashtrays, and stuffed elephants. Antiquarian books, including some Jules Verne. Claire had not stopped by for months. With Jacques's arrival imminent and her school on holiday break, she poked around in the back room for something that might catch her eye, not knowing just what she wanted. Most of the people in the store were speaking French, but she heard Janet talking with one woman in English, and, from the tone, someone was unhappy. Clearly, the woman wanted to pay less for an object than Janet was willing to sell it for. The customer, very much put out, left the desired item abandoned for the moment, leaving Claire curious.

The subject of the incident was a small, dark-green tin box—a keepsake kind of thing—and delightfully ornate. Very fetching, as her mother was fond of saying.

"Janet, is this piece still for sale?" asked Claire, picking up the item. The box was some six or seven inches square. It was a nice size and had quite a good feel to it. "This is charming."

"Well, hello, Claire. My, I didn't see you come in. Oh, yes, it is. The woman who seemed to want it so badly did not want to pay for it."

"Well, I like it. It's perfect. How much is it, please?" Claire was not much for bargaining. Things were what they were. They cost what they cost. Janet Morrison may have been a casual friend, but she was also working at making a living at a time when people were still skittish about nonessentials. The fact that the long war had ended could not put quit to the long-term pain and damage it had caused.

"Thirty francs, dear," Janet said, weighing it in her hand, as if just realizing that that was surely too low. "The woman who left must have confused francs and dollars. I do not know, but she was rude." She added, "So, will you take it? It is a lovely box, isn't it?"

Claire did a quick calculation and understood that, at the going exchange rate of three and a half to one, she was buying the box for a bit over eight dollars. She would think in French, naturally. But in matters of money, she often used the American dollar as a guide to true value. It was certainly worth every bit of that. "I will. Thank you. Do you know where it was made?"

"Let's take a wee look." The woman turned the box over and pointed to a small, distressed label—largely faded. "Well, I think this one is from a company in Sheffield: The Biscuit Company. Ah, yes. We used to have quite a few of these. In red and in dark green. It was made before the war, as it must be a good ten years old, from looking at it. I couldn't say when we got it. Or even where it's been."

"Oh, it's perfect," said Claire, eyes wide with the joy of the find.

Other people were waiting to ask their own questions, perhaps to buy this or that, and Claire sensed she was holding things up. Janet, however, was not about to be hurried. "That company went out of business, you know. In the war. . ."

"Yes, of course." Claire never mentioned what she did during those years.

Mrs. Morrison continued, "So many people lost everything," she said, looking at the box, "and I would not be surprised but that the owner or someone in the family was—" She paused. "—lost." Claire assumed from the way she added that last word that she, too, had known personal loss.

"I'll take it, please."

Claire gave her three ten-franc notes, keeping the fifty she had folded in the purse. She had a special fondness for those 1940 fifties because they boasted a painting of the fourteenth-century merchant and trader Jacques Cœur. How perfect! She associated the name with her own Jacques, or Jack as she had often lovingly called him. Her owl, her Jack of Hearts! She noticed music playing from somewhere in the back of the store. The song was one of her favorites—Johnny Mercer's "Fools Rush In." She thought about how much Mercer looked and sounded like Mercier. But she was no longer Celine. At last, she was happy. Too seldom, she knew, do we recognize the simple fact.

Janet rang up the sale and asked whether she could wrap the box for Claire, but Claire said no; she would wrap it herself as a Christmas surprise. Claire pulled her beige wool scarf up around her throat and walked out into the bright sun and the bracing late-December air. Heading back to her flat, she gave some thought about what to prepare. Turning the corner, the song came back to her: Her heart no doubt above her head.

Jacques was coming!

CHAPTER 20

Travelling from Combourg, coming into the big, modern Montparnasse station, Jacques had to manage the train to Cadet, the station closest to Claire. Should she meet him or wait for him to make his way to her there in the 18th? Either choice was fraught with potential timing problems. Montparnasse could be a nightmare for anyone not familiar with getting to the *Métro*. When arriving at the street-level rail station, Claire recalled, one must figure out how to deal with the underground across the city, negotiating the change through yet another busy station, Gare de l'Est. Worse, that station, much like Gare du Nord, was riddled with thieves.

Time passed like sand through an obstinate hourglass. A woman of great goodwill and, against all odds, an optimist, Claire was nevertheless more fidgety than she had expected to be. The following day, when she met Jacques at the *Métro*, it was obvious there had been trouble.

"Hello, Claire. My sweet. You look wonderful, as always." He embraced and kissed her. Claire saw he had one bag over his shoulder and one small suitcase, which he'd set down in order to hold her. His right hand looked bruised and red.

"Good Lord, Jack, what happened? Are you all right? Your hand."

"It's nothing," he said, pulling it back, sneaking a quick look as if its short history could be read. "Let's wait, and I'll explain it all when we get to your place. I recall it's not far."

Jacques had been to see her once before, a month or so after she had settled in. That was a weekend to remember. But they both knew, as well, that they needed time to figure things out. She'd gone to see him, once, in Combourg, but both visits felt rushed and, somehow, expectations had worked against them. They would have four days before he had to get back.

"Where is my little Cleo?" she asked.

"With Fabien. She's good with him, and it's only for a few days."

"Of course." Claire knew he had a special affection for that dog, no doubt magnified in intensity because he had no children, an ache she understood all too well. Affection finds its own home in its own way. When they arrived, and he'd set his bags just inside the door to her flat, both experienced a moment of, *What now*?

"I have missed you so much," she said, stepping into his arms. "And I've missed you more than I can say," he told her, and he pulled her closer. Their wartime romance had been fueled by a different kind of energy. Their quick visits to each other had left them more confused than assured of where they stood. What this love was and what it meant. Where they were going and how long it would take them to get there remained awkwardly unclear.

That night, after a quiet supper and a delicious bottle of Rhône wine, they took a walk together in the silvery air along the rue Richer, past the infamous Folies Bergère, which they both agreed they must be either too young or too old to look in on, and stopped just down the street for a coffee at a little spot Claire liked. There, they found a table by the front window. The soft, wistful piano of Erik Satie added to a sense of peace. Snowflakes falling softly added another grace note to the evening. She had delayed asking about his hand during the meal; he'd not indicated that he was eager to discuss it. She told him she wished there were more little parks close to her place where they might walk.

"We need more gardens, darling. More green space."

He nodded, and said only, "We do."

She put her hand on his uninjured one. She meant to soothe. "Do you want to tell me what happened?"

What Jacques told her caused him more discomfort than did the damaged hand. He said that, upon arriving at Montparnasse and making his way to the *Métro* to connect to Gare de l'Est, he encountered a team of pickpockets. A team, he said, because he knew they worked with others: a spotter, a man or woman to distract the victim, and the dip—the person, often a child, who steals. Wallets mostly, or whatever they could make off with, things like watches and jewelry.

"I sensed a hand ever so slightly, and only because I recognized in that instant that someone was distracting me with a tin whistle to my other side." He paused to look into her eyes, nearly out of breath with anger. "Alert as I thought I was to the threat, here was this boy, maybe six, snatching my wallet."

"Oh my God."

"Gypsies!"

"Are you certain?"

"I am certain. I can tell those people when I see them," he said, angry again.

"And he got away?

Jacques nodded. "The kid did. He was gone."

"How?"

Jacques explained that with the lift, the strike, he stepped back and away from the train doors, which, with a beeping sound, closed. Claire asked him what happened next. Jacques said that, with the wallet gone and the little one disappearing in the dense, noisy crowd, he turned quickly to the other, the accomplice. The distractor had not been able to pull away; there were too many people—this filthy-looking teen boy. This hard-eyed youth.

"Oh my. No police?"

"There never are when you want them. There's more . . ." Jacques paused before clarifying the rest. "He could tell I'd spotted him. I saw it in his angry face. Instantly, I knew he was part of this dirty game. My wallet gone, I grabbed hold of his shirt, spun him around, and smashed him in the face as hard as I could."

"Oh, Jacques, was that smart?"

"Maybe not. But it felt good to hit the little son of a bitch. I think I broke his nose, and I cut my knuckles on his mouth, several teeth of which are probably loose." Jacques looked at his hand. "But it was worth it. Still, I hate to lose my driver's registration. To get another, I will have to go to Rennes." He looked around as if to see who might be near, even then. "There was not much money in the wallet. Maybe one hundred francs. I keep my money in this clip." He showed her a fine-looking silver money clip with a blue fleur-de-lis on the clasp. "I had some photos in there, as I recall. A picture of you."

"I'm sorry."

"Well, the hand will heal. My pride was damaged more," he said. He indulged in a small laugh, seeing how absurd the whole business was.

"I should have known better. Stupid of me. And they just throw away the wallets. They must get thirty of them in a day."

"Probably," was all she could think to say. "Those people are a scourge. Well, in Paris, at least. Not all of them, of course," she added.

"No, not all. Most? Some? There is no answer to that, but some is too many." Jacques then asked whether she wanted another coffee, and she did. He signaled for the waitress and ordered another for each. She asked about Cleo. He had told her of the scare, how he'd taken the dog off that truck, out of the pen, near l'Oisette. That if he had not gotten an idea about where to look from Roger Laurent, his dog would be gone.

"Oh, that man is full of surprises," she said, thinking of how unreadable he could be. Roger was a fellow, they both realized, who would always put his own interests first. She pointed to his bruised hand. "Did you hurt him badly?" she asked.

"I don't know. Why?" Jacques was uncomfortable suddenly, talking about it. He would rather put it all away. "Why would I care?"

"Well, depending on how angry his family is, or his clan, they do have your wallet and therefore your identification. They could do something. Look for you?"

"You mean a vendetta? I doubt it, Claire. One broken nose is probably of little consequence to these people." She smiled at him and said, "Let's go back to my place. I'll doctor that hand and think of some other ways to make you feel better."

That Christmas morning, Claire gave Jacques a first-edition copy of Graham Greene's 1940 novel *The Power and the Glory*, thinking he would like the exceptional priest—the whisky priest, as the author called him. Graham Greene, she knew, understood something about silent work having worked for the British Secret Service in Africa during the war. The gesture was a proper salute to the good monsignor, another unheralded cleric hiding in plain sight. She also gave him a handsome blue scarf and that marvelous green tin cookie box. Inside, he found something which delighted him; she had placed the Edward Lear poem, "The Owl and the Pussycat." For his part, he had placed his gifts for her beneath the small, cleverly decorated little tree redolent of pine: a pretty pair of lady's tan leather gloves and a hand-carved wooden owl, some four inches or so tall.

"Oh, this is delightful, Jack. Did you carve this?" She flushed with joy and wiped at her eyes.

He said he had a craftsman in town do it. He'd saved the best for last and asked her to sit with him on the couch. There, Jacques gave Claire a box as well—a box of Belgian chocolates. In that box, in its own delicate, silver wrapping paper, was a one-quarter-carat diamond solitaire ring. Claire reacted with cries and tears of joy, an "Oh, my God," which Jacques knew to be one of her favorite expressions, and with kisses enough to keep them both breathless for a minute or more. Careful Claire, erstwhile OSS operative, teacher and painter, had not so much fallen in love as jumped in, harness abandoned and boots unlaced. When she regained some semblance of composure, she said to him, "Well, are you going to actually ask me, or are you just going to sit there grinning?"

He asked. She laughed again, kissed him once more, and said, "Yes, Jacques, yes!"

They would marry! Claire ached to hold him and to have him hold her, to hold on to that moment as well, which had eluded her for so long. He gave her the kind of radiant smile that could only come from the heart, and all old sorrows were expunged.

"Do we want to talk about dates, guests? When, Jack? When?"

"Soon," he said. "We have time. We have all the time we need, my sweet."

That afternoon, before the tasty quail dinner she'd prepared, they traveled by bus to the Luxembourg Gardens. Its nearly sixty acres were the jewel of the Left Bank. A few youngsters were out with their frail sailboats. Even in winter, the park was theirs to enjoy, an impressionist painting in its own right.

The newly engaged couple found a new kind of joy infused in everything around them. Christmas ornaments and lights brought a kind of magic to the grounds. Children were laughing. Dogs were romping. Claire's cheeks reddened with the wind. It was too chilly even for a stand of old men playing boules. And in the air drifted the lightest scrim of snow, lace-like, rather as if it could not bear to actually fall to the ground. They listened to the many ambient noises with a new kind of interest, taking joy in all that surrounded them. Music, coming from some unseen source, Jacques thought suggested Strauss. But no, it was "The Skaters' Waltz," Claire told him, by Émile Waldteufel. Were they walking in a romantic fantasy or real life? At last, a wedding! Claire looked at Jacques's mouth, his smile, his light-grey eyes. She needed that.

"Well, that would be close enough to Strauss," he agreed.

They stepped into a gift shop situated at one garden entrance on Boulevard Saint-Michel, where, later, they would catch their crowded bus back to Claire's place. In that gift store, Jacques bought her a cute little wooden plaque shaped like a watering can, maybe to hang in the kitchen. The message was clear: *Je suis dans le jardin.* I am in the garden. He promised her she would have a fine garden when they lived in Combourg. She thought that sounded ideal. She could paint there, in their home, as readily as in her Paris flat. And, no doubt, with better light.

She thought, as she fingered a few other quaint mementos, daydreaming of their future, that soon she'd give notice at the school.

Before Jacques left to return home three days after Christmas, they set a wedding date for the first Saturday in February. Where? Paris or Combourg? They agreed to have the ceremony in his village. Paris would feel too remote, and he had many friends in Combourg. Église Saint-Martin, of course. The next thing that came to Claire's mind was how to get her family over, especially her mother. Likely, they would not be able to come, but she would ask.

Betty McIntyre, her long-ago college classmate and, more recently, her Bodney OSS boss, who was surely her best friend and closest confidant, would be her matron of honor. What would Maddie and Ott say, back in Vestal? They would be happy for her. What would Rita and Mac say, in Binghamton? Her younger sister and brother-in-law were busy with their first child. Claire told herself that time was still on her side for having children, though barely. And, perhaps, it was risky. She looked to Jacques; he was clearly deep in thought as the bus bumped and plugged its way across the still, wintry Seine back toward her flat. The stoic, black iron lampposts lining the quai suggested vigilance.

Turning to him, she asked, "Who will you ask to stand up with you, Jack?"

"Oh, I will ask Fabien."

He decided he liked being Jack, an endearment and a good American name. If she was willing to live with him in France, he could give her a touch of America in the home. And he knew she would be a strong partner for him in the years ahead, helping to make his new business a success. "Will we have children, Jack? Please say yes!"

"Oh, I think we should get started on that right away," he said. She laughed and kissed his injured hand.

"I do like your sense of timing!" he said with a grin, pulling her to him while she whispered how much she wanted him. He let go of her hands and pulled her to him again, not at all gently. Not sated, they kissed again. A whole world of sensations thrilled them both.

Five weeks to get things lined up, they agreed, sounded just about right. And Saint-Martin would play yet one more major part in Jacques's life. In her life as well. Theirs were two lives that, at long last, looked so full of promise. How difficult it would prove, however, for those two survivors to know what lay ahead for both.

CHAPTER 21

People coming into town to shop—or maybe to gossip, or just because it was Saturday and one went to town on Saturday—found Combourg's village trees, otherwise winter-stark bare, festooned with gala lights in brilliant whites, bright yellows, and several variations of blue. Curious, winter-loving finches and crossbills flew about excitedly.

On the day of their wedding, at noon on the second of February, not five weeks past Christmas but what must have felt like five months, Claire Skiffington and Jacques Berlangier were married, that wartime team, that near perfect fit. Then they'd become lovers, then husband and wife.

In truth, the entire village—maybe some four thousand souls— was not invited to the church wedding, or not invited in the finite sense of the word. But all Combourg was definitely there. The reception, arranged at Emma Brun's direction, with her beautifully linened tables, was large and grand. Who had put up all those lights? Well, Fabien and his brothers, of course. The wedding of one of their hometown heroes was an event.

By actual count, and not including the new priest Father Bogniard, and two altar boys, there were twenty people in the church with Jacques and Claire, the new Madame Berlangier. Men and women who would always be their friends. Fabien and Emma Brun were there, of course, and Fabien's brothers. The Gaillards too. Victor was Jacques's key employee. These were people who respected what the couple had been through, yes, but loved their generosity of spirit even more. Few could afford any other kind of generosity just then. Haunting shadows of war were still impossible to chase away completely.

"Did you know that today, besides being the day of our wedding," Claire told Jacques as they walked together out of church to Combourg school's cafeteria for their reception, "today is Groundhog Day, back in the States. Did you know that?"

He asked her what that meant, and whether he would have to get something for the groundhog, and, if so, whether there need be a toast to the little beast as well. She smiled brightly at his silliness and told him no, that, as she knew it, owls and groundhogs were never on particularly good terms. Jacques nodded and said that would be his sense of the relationship as well.

Standing in a pretty white charmeuse dress she'd borrowed from Emma Brun, Claire had no relatives present. It was not feasible for the Skiffington family to get to France in the winter of 1947. "Why could Claire not be married in Binghamton?" asked her mother.

She did have Betty McIntyre with her, along with her husband, Bill, a tall, handsome man as gifted in languages as he was in telling humorous stories. Claire had also invited a few friends from Paris, including Bill and Janet Morrison. They came early and spent the night in town prior to the wedding to support the happy couple.

The brilliant Mary Perry, herself still single, flew over from London, where she had taken a post-war job working for the Foreign Office. Mary had more Bodney stories, which everyone found interesting, though some were not exactly happy.

When asked about her friend, Mary told Claire that Lieutenant Owen Terfel had been lost, just weeks before the war's end, when his airplane went into the Channel. No one knew why. Maybe running out of fuel. Claire held back her tears, but everyone knew she was saddened deeply by his loss, adding to an already awkward sense of melancholy that evening.

Her parents had sent a lovely card noting how they would have loved to be there.

Claire's father John had written, telling her of his love for and pride in her, something he had seldom done. "Not possible to come. So sorry. We love you." Their absence bothered her, and yet she knew it shouldn't, for it was the natural order of things. Her mother must have known they'd not marry in the States. After all, she would make a life there, in France. Jacques's friends were welcoming to her.

People have long been given to speak of their experience of war in terms of fears and anxieties. Choices made in the throes of any such tumult and destruction would be uniquely their own, yet recognizable each to the other. Such bonds are strong. Jacques had asked Fabien to be his best man. Betty came to stand with Claire. Cleo, garnering a spot of attention, watched from the aisle nearby, next to Fabien's wife, Emma, and his brother Paul. All of them were taking it all in: the music, the magic. "Will there be a honeymoon?" asked Mary Perry, always one to assume anything possible.

"We may find the time, Mary," said Claire, "but not right away." She added, "And besides, when anyone can get to Paris in a few hours' train time, who needs anyplace else to celebrate?"

The supervisor of Berlangier's apple farm, Victor Gaillard, and his young wife, Gisèle, a bright, capable couple, came into the church, expecting to sit in the back, perhaps uncertain of their proper station. Jacques motioned to Fabien, who ushered them toward the front, where they shook hands, whispered together. and stood with Fabien and his brothers. Victor had long since replaced the aging workhorse, the kindly Émile Chalfant. Victor's help was a godsend.

Somehow, Roger Laurent and his mother made it as well; they arrived in his flashy Citroën. The invitation had been sent in recognition of the help given Jacques in finding Cleo, with no expectation that Laurent would take them up on it. A formality. Jacques had never really trusted Laurent. But having him and his helpful, if peculiar, mother with them for the ceremony was as close as they'd get to having the cherished monsignor. Ambivalently, they welcomed them. Predictably, Laurent acted inappropriately. After the service, he suggested Jacques consider purchasing another small and non-contiguous piece of land which would border his own. Everything, to that man, was about money and prestige. His car was a good example.

That evening, when everyone had left the reception and the Bruns had said their goodbyes and congratulations, Claire asked Jacques what Roger had been so disgruntled about. "He struck me as being irritated about something. There's something not right about him."

"There may well be, and he wants land," Jacques told her. "And I think he'd like, somehow, to get a hand on some of mine. Ours."

Claire said she figured it was a personality trait. "He is highly competitive, and his ego must drive much of what he does as well as how he perceives others." Then she added, "He's insecure."

Claire said she thought Madame Laurent looked more settled that day than she'd ever seen her. Her hair had been done, and she'd worn a fine-looking tan suit that looked almost English in its cut. "Clearly, she relishes being with her son. Or maybe she just likes weddings," she said, with a little laugh.

Jacques saw Roger Laurent speaking with Victor. What could that be about? Maybe he wanted to see who would be there, find a bone for himself. That strange behavior irritated Jacques, and he whispered to Claire that he looked to be feeling out Victor.

"Ignore him," Claire told him.

"I should. No doubt, he wants something. I do not like or trust him."

"Probably best to ignore him," she said.

Over the next several days, Claire and Jacques discussed what they would need to complete their household. His kitchen cutlery looked a bit limited. No blender. They would go to Paris and bring back what she needed from the old apartment, things she could not manage before the wedding. They'd spend a few days enjoying the ambiance of a city eager to thrive once again.

As soon as weather permitted, Jacques made a few necessary repairs to the storage building behind the farmhouse. There had been damage to the roof. Hail had broken two windows. He'd need to construct a larger building. Claire wanted a rose garden and took that job for herself. Both were preoccupied with larger plans and weightier dreams. It was clear by early April, to Jacques and his bride, they were expecting a child. Probably early November.

Jacques's business goals were focused on a sizeable Calvados capability. They'd talked about expansion, had worried over the costs and labor. Apple brandy production would be a gamble, Jacques knew, but he was committed. Having stopped to speak with the owners and managers of one small operation in nearby Brémoy, Jacques figured he had a good sense of the project. One family-owned enterprise looked to be about the size of what he would be attempting. Devising a realistic plan would be the key.

Jacques made notes on estimated capital investments: storage buildings, grater tanks and presses, vats. And plenty of cider- apples, which he had. He'd need more pear trees if he wanted a somewhat more mellow taste. Fermentation cannot be rushed, which meant he would have no substantial product to sell for a couple of years, but that only meant he needed to make sure he had all the parts in place and trained staff to make it viable. If any character trait had kept him alive during his days and nights as a clandestine agent, it was patience. That, and a gift for planning and looking ahead. The last Berlangier—not counting the long-absent Nina—he had a reason to plan for a greater future. He had a loving wife, a child on the way.

Claire kept an eye on the books and tended her gardens—flower and vegetable. Together, they planned for the arrival of the baby in the fall. Not surprisingly, she found less time to paint. On two occasions, she'd seen her doctor about intermittent, deep pain in her calf. Never one to be sidelined long for discomfort, she soldiered on with only aspirin. That she'd not even mentioned the problem to Jacques would prove a devastating mistake.

One June evening, after supper, their happy mood was crushed when Cleo came to the door whimpering, limping heavily, surely in pain. Bloody, Dragging one hind leg.

"Dammit, Claire; look at this. She's been wounded."

Claire rushed to the dog's side, and then ran back to the kitchen for a towel. The wound was bleeding, but not heavily.

"What happened?" Claire held the dog while Jacques looked at the wound.

"She's been shot. Poor girl. Small bore I would say, and it looks like the bullet passed straight through. See. Look. The wound is larger here. She was lucky."

"Shot?" Claire gingerly took the dog's head into her hands and asked if he thought it was deliberate.

"Well, clearly it happened on our property, and probably not far from the house. There is no hunting, although some fool could have been looking for rabbits." He found what he needed to staunch the bleeding and wrap the wound as well as he could. "This was deliberate. What I don't know is whether this was done as a provocation, not trying to kill the dog, but trying to get me out in the woods, looking."

"Oh, you cannot go out there now, Jack. Not if someone is looking to shoot you. You can't go. I'll go. I'll take her into town."

"Absolutely not! You stay. She may be going into shock," he said. "I'll drive her to the village vet." He pulled a handgun from a drawer next to the kitchen, thought a moment, and handed it to her. He then wrapped Cleo in a small blanket. "There's a shotgun in the truck," he added. "I'll take that. You know how to use this. Stay here and keep the doors locked. And stay away from the windows until I get back."

Claire took a deep breath and sat at the kitchen table as Jacques rushed out with the dog. She looked to the gun in her hand, put it back in the drawer, and closed the curtains.

Two hours later, she heard the truck pull up. Jacques walked through the door with Cleo, still in that blanket, the spaniel looking dazed and much depleted. "He gave her something for the pain and cleaned out the wound. Bandaged her up but says it will be four weeks or more before she has much use of the leg." Claire kissed the top of the weary animal's head and told Cleo that they both had bum legs.

"Well, it could be worse, I guess. Who could have done this?"

"I have no idea, but I will be watching for anything or anyone that looks out of place."

Had this been a hunting accident, or did it truly constitute some kind of threat? He checked with his foreman, Victor. The several workers around the farm had seen no one. No one had shown up unexpectedly on the property. There'd been no gunfire or signs of anything out of the ordinary. Even so, for several days, Jacques kept that small Modèle automatic tucked under his shirt, in his belt when he went out. That he had not seen anyone did not mean no one was there.

With most things returning to normal, Jacques and his crew got busy with the construction of necessary buildings for the new enterprise, maintaining the production side of the farm with little additional difficulty. Apples came into season at various times over the summer and fall. Sales of several fruits kept them busy and had them nearly breaking even financially. Jacques had put away some money—not much, but it was there—and he'd leave it alone as long as he could. These orchards meant family and constituted what would be their future. His and Claire's. Not that he didn't feel another kind of absence now and again when he thought of his sister. Would he ever see her again? His Nina? His only sibling. Her dimpled smile. That part of his heart.

Jacques had worried for her safety in Nantes, that city having experienced far more Wehrmacht presence during the war, even in its last months. All this had once been hers too. His mother had done all she could, tending the farm for two years after Mathis was killed until she became too ill and Jacques was able to take it over and run it with help from the old hands like Chalfant, who'd stayed on with the family.

Jacques would only use that reserve money should he absolutely have to. Some of it, necessarily, would have to go for new equipment. Fermentation vats were not cheap. One he brought in from a ruined farm in Brécey, and then he bought another from a woman nearer by, who sold off her deceased husband's property. So, he had two apple brandy operations going—the larger, new steel vat for near-term production and the smaller, older oaken vat for his better quality, longer-aged stuff. He needed only to stay solvent in the interim. They worked long hours to get by and fought against the devastating blight that hit the apple trees that spring, which was widespread in Brittany and worse in Normandy. As many as thirty trees were lost before they found the right combination of water and vinegar spray and figured out the necessary pruning to stop the dreaded blight from spreading. Victor had spotted the problem first. Together they'd learned how to manage the unexpected. And Jacques and Claire? They looked ahead. They made a life.

That August, before she got too big, as Claire would put it, they made another trip to Paris. Claire's apartment in Montmartre had been rented to the new arts instructor, an English woman who had replaced Claire at the *Academie*. The school's director had asked Claire to help the new teacher get settled. The transition went smoothly, the two becoming friends, and, since the new girl was on holiday with her parents back in Hastings, during the week of Jacques and Claire's visit, they had the ideal place for a short stay when they came back to pick what they wanted to keep. Cookbooks, some passed along from her mother, were foremost among them.

She had some shopping to do upon arriving and getting settled, especially for the baby—some cute clothes, a stuffed white bunny. Jacques said they had stores in Combourg, prompting Claire to say, "Yes, we have feed stores in Combourg."

She found a darling mobile at Old Dominion to hang over the crib, bright and clever-looking little birds. Jacques joked that Cleo might like to take a close look at those little birds as well—but they'd be safe in that they did not look much like squirrels. They had a late lunch nearby. Janet Morrison joined them. An unexpected reunion—expats simpatico.

"Jack, I'd like to spend some time at Père Lachaise, if that sounds good to you," Claire said as they walked out into the heat of the city at midday.

"At the cemetery? Of course. Why?"

"I always find it peaceful. And it's cool there now. All those stately trees—maple, ash, and hazelnut." She said the mausoleums were gorgeous, and the utter peace spoke to her. "A place one can feel somehow contemplative."

"I suppose it is. Anyone in particular you want to look in on? Maybe Monsieur Proust?"

"Ha!" She laughed. "No, he's much too longwinded for me. Maybe we could just wander. Sit on a bench and think. Think about how fortunate we are. About, I don't know—mortality."

"Not ours, I hope," Jacques said, gently squeezing her hand.

"Not ours. No. Just the understanding that comes from that kind of time spent with the past, with all those quieted souls, time that informs us about living in the moment. We so seldom do, don't you think?" She moved to a nearby bench and patted the spot next to her, where Jacques joined her.

"I suppose all that shade, even that sense of chill, is a metaphor, isn't it?"

"Oh, good for you, Jack," she said, delighted. "You're letting your inner poet out."

He told her he was not sure about his poet but that he, too, liked to sit in a peaceful place.

Upon arrival, for they'd entered through the north gate at Gambetta, Claire wanted to show him Oscar Wilde's outrageous construction—more a testament to the man's unchained spirit, captured by a cement casting of a flying sphinx set on his small tomb. Jacques knew little about the man, he said. He knew Wilde held a special fascination for Claire, who was always in awe of those who broke the proverbial artistic mold. Later, they made their way to a distant corner of the place to honor the distinctive modernist Modigliani. An hour or so after that, both pretty much worn out, she wanted to look at the simple grave of Camille Pissarro, near the front entrance. His impressionist landscapes and his imaginative use of light, she said, had been of enormous influence on her work.

"Oh, and let's look for a gelato."

He agreed and kissed her lightly; he said he could think of nothing better.

They returned to Combourg two days later, a few shopping bags heavier—mostly things for the baby. Claire was delighted to find a letter waiting for them from the Maiers. Ott would take a week from work at the factory, and he and Maddie would fly over for the birth, suggesting that she could help, or at least spell them some in infant care and feeding. Their own two girls were doing well and could fend for themselves for a few days.

The timing was driven by what her obstetrician in Saint-Malo had to say about the likely birth date, projected to be November 9. Aware that, at thirty-eight years of age, her pregnancy could be complicated—no one was saying risky—Claire was due for another check up at the hospital on August 10, her six-month routine appointment. On that day, everything looked good. There'd be no midwife delivery or small-town clinic. Jacques insisted that she get the best care, and that would be the estimable maternity hospital just a forty-five-minute trip north, situated on the sea. Days of anticipation. Nights to ponder their future together.

CHAPTER 22

The pace at Berlangier Orchards grew intense that autumn. Claire worked as much as she was able, doing the kind of work she was best at, which meant keeping an eye on shipments, their finances, and on the inevitable squabbles that arose in the fields. She and young Gisèle took turns baking for the four of them on alternate Sundays. Victor was doing all he could to keep the physical operation going strong, managing and motivating crews, directing storage and bottling procedures. Jacques spent more time with his nascent brandy team, and in directing upgrades to the farmhouse. His most recent such effort had been to erect several honeycomb frames as centrally located in the newest orchards as he could manage. Behind the house, a few honeybees—by nature, caffeine fiends—circled around his coffee cup.

"It's lovely out here this time of year," Claire said, watching a small cardinal preen in a nearby tree. Jacques had placed a green metal table with two chairs at the edge of his wife's flower-and-herb garden. That crested songbird, as the tale goes, was said to bring joy and health.

"We should talk again about names for the child."

He said he had been thinking the same. "You know I favor Eduard, if a boy. Maybe Julia, after your mother, if a girl."

"Eduard because of the monsignor," she said. "Absolutely. Yes. He was so very important to me. We were getting close those last few years. And my father's first name would make a good middle name for the boy."

Claire said she thought that was fine and a splendid tribute to the heroic priest. They would just have to wait to see what colors to paint the baby's room. Claire picked up a small paperback she'd been reading, a thin book lying open on the table. "Have you ever read any Robert Frost?" she asked.

Jacques said he had not. It was too far from his circle of curiously.

"The American poet?"

"That's the one." Claire added that there was a poem in that book that always made her somehow melancholy, even though it was most suitable for them, just then, on that fruit-tree farm, even as everything felt just about perfect. "There is just something wistful about it."

"Don't read things that make you sad," he told her, curious nonetheless as to what it was. He knew she was looking for his encouragement to read it aloud. "What is it?"

"The title is 'After Apple Picking,'" she said. "It was written about the time of the last war."

"I think I know an apple picker or two. Why does it make you feel that way?"

"Maybe because it speaks to the idea of a final reckoning, Jack. One that cannot be foreseen." She added that, for her, apple picking was a strong metaphor for one's work on this earth, while it lasts and when it is done. "But how well done, that's the concern. And what has been left undone."

He asked her to read him a few lines of it, to share what she found so compelling. She offered the book, but he shook his head.

"No, no. You read."

She adjusted her chair, coming closer. She started strong but found her throat constricting as she read on. Claire began the first lines:

> "My long two-pointed ladder's sticking through a tree
> Toward heaven still,
> And there's a barrel that I didn't fill

Beside it, and there may be two or three
Apples I didn't pick upon some bough.
But I am done with apple-picking now."

"Well, my sweet girl, we are not done with apple picking here, are we? I am not, and most certainly you are not. So, don't let us get too caught up in the allusion."

"And the barrel that we didn't fill?" she asked, not knowing if he would attempt to say anything more about what Frost might have meant. What one does and what one must leave for another time. "Do we have an empty barrel?"

He showed her by way of another light squeeze of her hand that her thinking was clear to him. "I cannot imagine what that could be. And soon we'll have a child, my sweet. Our first. A healthy little Berlangier to continue the name and the work."

"You're right, Jack. Of course. We've done all we might." She set the book down, staring into contours and textures of the garden she'd come so much to cherish. The cardinal, she saw, was gone.

Claire's labor began late on a windy, rainy day—the morning of November 8—pretty much as the physician had forecast. Her labor did not go well, and she suffered with hard contractions for close to twelve hours before the infant was delivered. Jacques stayed with her the whole time, holding her hand, reassuring her that all would be fine.

Maddie traveled up with Jacques to Saint-Malo and looked in on her exhausted sister. The risk to the child was considered minor, but the stress on Claire was enormous. Midday on the ninth, one elderly pediatric nurse carried the fine-looking seven-pound, two- ounce baby boy to her bedside twenty minutes after delivery. Claire's joy was incomparable; she could not stop touching the infant's tiny face, smelling his sweet breath, feeling his light tufts of hair. Too soon, another nurse came to take the baby. The medical team told Claire they wanted her to get some rest. Just sleep. No one could have been aware that a blood clot from her left leg had been working its way to her lungs.

Exhausted and thrilled with the baby, his son, Jacques kissed his wife's damp forehead, squeezed her pale hand, and told her how much he loved her. He said he'd be back in the morning. He then drove home to get some sleep.

Claire awoke in startled agony, even as her husband was turning in. It began with severe chest pains, leading to acute shortness of breath. If frightened, she made no call. She signaled no nurse or doctor. Did she possess some bracing courage uniquely her own? Or harbor an insistence on self-reliance? Did she pray? Ever-courageous Claire, for whom faith in splendid outcomes was a given, a virtue, would not see her darling infant again. She would not kiss his head ever again. She would never hear him cry. Speak. Never see him take his first steps. Nearly eleven hours after giving birth, Claire Berlangier passed away from a pulmonary embolism, her stout heart exhausted.

That brilliant woman, that erstwhile, valiant OSS operative, that teacher and artist, at last happily married and settled, at last a mother, was gone. And no one who knew her would ever be the same again.

CHAPTER 23

The telephone rang in the kitchen downstairs—that resonant, insistent double trill—over and over, that sound he could barely tolerate in the daytime. Something about it struck him as ominous. Jacques sat up and looked at the small clock on his bedside table. Had he overslept? No. The phone insisted itself once more. It was nearly two. He'd crawled into bed at only half past midnight.

He pushed the covers aside, stepped over the sleeping Cleo, and walked out of the room, moving deliberately downstairs. As he reached to answer, the machine rang again. Opposite the light-green plaster wall where the phone hung, Claire had painted a good-sized mural of Monet's water lilies in bisque white, rich greens, and cerulean blue. Their mood was hopeful, eternal.

Something told him no. Not to answer. Let it keep ringing while he got dressed and raced up to Saint-Malo, to his wife. His Claire. To kiss her, and to hold her, and know that she and their baby boy were fine. Just to be there, where there would be no fear. He lifted the handset.

Ott came into the kitchen then, in his pale undershirt and some kind of light blue cotton pants that passed as pajamas. He had heard the phone ring, of course, but knew to let Jacques answer. Maddie had not come out of their room.

"I have to go to the hospital, Ott. Something's gone wrong. I don't know yet what it is. Please go back to bed and tell Maddie I will let you know what has happened when I can. When I get back. Sorry. That's all I know."

"Something bad, Jack?"

"I don't know what it is, Ott. Claire or the child. I must go."

Jacques knew when he arrived—when he walked into the hospital and saw the weary, dark-haired woman at the desk, everything so still—that nothing could ever be right for him in the world again. No one had actually told him one of his beloved was dead, but his senses, his intuition, were keen. Something was very wrong.

He replayed in his mind the brief conversation. "Can you come to the hospital right away, Monsieur? We are sorry to have to tell you there has been an incident."

"Now?"

"Yes. So unexpected. We are sorry," the voice had said. "Can you come now?" This *incident*—that was the word she had used. Like a tiny misstep. This event. Some error?

Hurry.

The woman in blue and white, at the desk, set down her reading glasses and looked at Jacques, standing in the bright waiting room lights. She looked as if she knew who he must be. He was bleary-eyed, confused, distraught.

"Where is she? Where is my wife? Claire Berlangier," he demanded, his voice rising. "*Où est-elle?! Où est ma femme?*" The charge nurse, if that was what she was, shook her head.

Immediately, a doctor came through the double doors, doors with opaque glass inserts, doors next to and behind the nurse's station. He shook Jacques's hand perfunctorily, nodded his head and led the man into the bowels of the place. They walked quickly together, as if there yet might be something to be done. Jacques could detect certain distinctive smells—maybe a solvent. The thrum of machines labored behind them like overworked railway watchmen.

Seated in the doctor's office, the man at last spoke the words, "I'm so terribly sorry. Your wife has passed." He shook his head, this man in a faded white coat, behind his desk. He was sorry. "Claire Berlangier," he said, as if they might be speaking of another woman. "We are so sorry," he said. "She expired. Half past midnight. Very sudden." They had tried to resuscitate her. But no. Madame Berlangier had suffered an embolism that stopped her heart. She was terribly fatigued from the delivery. "Weakened," he said. That was the word he used. This man, well beyond Jacques's age, was worn down and wanting only understanding, forgiveness, something much too large for Jacques to give.

He listened to how the man's voice trembled. This doctor he did not know, this caregiver searching for words. Another nurse looked in, one Jacques had not seen before, then backed out of the room. "An embolism," he said again. Did he know what that was?

"Yes," he said. He knew what an embolism was.

Could he see her? Yes. Certainly.

"Then I want to see our baby. Our son."

"Yes, of course." The doctor told him that there would be a review of procedure. Hospital rules. Jacques looked down to the cold tile floor; his one shoe was untied. He felt himself shaking. He'd never been so hopeless, so bereft.

Lying there on a gurney, a starched white sheet pulled back, Claire looked drained. Jacques touched her hair, as if to correct a few errant strands, something she might have otherwise done for herself. Claire, always wanted things orderly, for things to go where they were supposed to go. For an artist, she was fussy about such matters. Perhaps a sign of her intelligence training. She had many gifts. This loving woman—her mixture of vulnerability and courage, her pure joy for their son, her certainty of their future together, gone. Jacques leaned down and kissed her forehead. He lay his head next to hers and kissed her again. A moment that would have to last a lifetime, their final moment. Willing something more.

Looking at his infant son in the stainless-steel bassinet where the child lay sleeping, he saw standing beside tiny Eduard the same woman who had looked in on him and the obstetrician. She had her own duties to carry out; one was to connect parents with their newborns. With the child's mother dead, the job would be more complicated. The nurse picked up the baby and signaled for Jacques to come into the room, where four other infants slept or cried or just appeared astonished by whatever they sensed around them.

She handed the baby to Jacques, saying something too soft for him to hear, words of encouragement, maybe. The infant was just then waking and opening his eyes—startled—judging by his small, rapid fist movements. Jacques looked into his son's face, maybe to see Claire there, or something of her, although he knew that was not realistic. The baby, only hours old, would show nothing of either parent yet except a predictable pale pink coloration, A tuft of hair no color at all. Jacques held the blessed little fellow tightly, whispered Claire's name. "Oh, my God. My boy, my boy," he said, and began to cry.

Madolyn and Ott somehow knew what must have happened. Knew what to say and what not to say when Jacques returned. Maddie had always been a tough read, but she held Jacques for a moment and asked whether it would be all right for her to make them some breakfast. She had just lost her sister. Ott, a taciturn man, kept his peace. Maddie went to the sink, put her shaking hands to her face.

Ott told Jacques they could extend their stay a few days if he wanted them to do so. How could he say no? Baby Eduard would be coming home in two days. Or he was scheduled to do so. Claire had set up a bassinet in their bedroom. The expectation had been that they would take turns feeding and changing the baby, caring, loving, tending to a newborn's needs. How unprepared he actually was for such responsibilities. Only Claire could be Eduard's mother. And now, with her gone. . .

The Maiers had planned to leave that Friday, but now they would stay until Tuesday, then fly back to Vestal. Claire's funeral could be

Friday morning. The extra few days would give everyone time to think, to discuss the impossible, recognize the inconceivable.

Would Jacques be able to manage? Maddie asked. What choice did he have but to manage? Jacques's foreman, Victor, and his wife, Gisèle, offered support—truly more care and consideration than any nominal second-in-command could be expected to show. They had attended the wedding—Claire had bonded with the younger woman—and Jacques was coming to count more and more on Victor to run things in his absence. Harvesting fell to the field hands. Victor had a knack for the business end of the work. That, and he was smart.

Over the next weeks, Gisèle would prove to be wonderful with the baby. The fact that she was so young with as yet no children of her own no doubt played a part in that degree of attention and affection. "You must just tell us what we can do. Anything," she said, stepping toward him, giving Jacques an unexpected hug.

Claire's funeral—the Mass, reception, and burial—all went as well as anyone could expect. Her plot was next to those of Mathis and Adèle. Jacques stared hard at the impossibility of it. Graveside, he picked up one small, smooth, heart-shaped black stone found at his feet and put it into his pocket. He would keep small, perfect thing, natural and yet remarkable. Like her. Beautiful.

The weather was chilly but not uncomfortably so. The baby had fussed during the service, as he would do, and Maddie had insisted on holding him. Jacques was relieved to see that he quieted in his aunt's arms. Ott held him some during the burial, and that helped everyone as well. Claire's older sister and husband could not have been more caring and attentive.

"What plans do you have for the baptism, Jack?" asked Ott.

"I had not given it much thought," Jacques said. "But now that you say it, I have to do something. I'll take care of that while you and Maddie are still here."

Maddie asked whether she should find the baby a baptismal dress. Jacques told her not to bother; Claire had bought some things. He asked if the couple would be the baby's godparents, and they said yes, of course. They wanted to do that. Father Bogniard, replacing Monsignor Arnoux at

Saint-Martin, would take care of the arrangements at the church. With one phone call, Jacques arranged for the sacrament for Monday morning. Then, Maddie and Ott would leave for New York. It had not been possible for Mac and Rita to come to France. Maddie would bring something of Claire's back to their youngest sister to help in such ineffable loss.

"I know it's probably not something you want to talk about now, Jack," Maddie said, "but you will have to have this recorded in the church."

"What do you mean?"

"Eduard's full name. What is the child's full name to be?" Jacques told her he and Claire had decided some time back to name him Eduard Mathis, the middle name after his father—if the child was a boy. Mathis—French variant on Matthias—the minor Judean-born saint and replacement apostle. But now, with Claire dead, he had decided to give his son another middle name, and it would be Skiffington. His mother's maiden name.

"Yes, and my own," she reminded him.

"Of course."

"I think that's splendid," she said, "and a fine tribute to Claire."

After the baptism, all of them went back to the farmhouse to partake of a light lunch prepared by Gisèle. Jacques, Ott, and Maddie walked up the stairs. Jacques wanted to show the others a painting. There, he would also put the church paperwork into a keepsake box, where he kept valuable papers and documents, along with some special mementos. That tin box, he said, had been a Christmas gift from Claire. The baptism papers and the child's birth certificate were all placed in the box, then the box went back into a wall safe he had built a few years before—a safe in the bedroom covered by a watercolor painting Claire had done of the house that summer, a rendering after a rain: trees, shrubs, and flowers at their most expressive. No one could capture the moody, sensuous light of such a day as could Claire.

Jacques could see how Maddie admired it; she asked whether she could touch the painting, unframed except for the thin wooden pieces of balsa that held the stretched canvas.

"Yes, of course."

"Look at this texture. The complexity of color," she said, as if the reality was too much. She had only one painting done by Claire, and that was something her sister did while at Bodney. A young, smiling, waving airman—a pilot—in a small airplane. Jacques said he had never seen it, but he knew it would be a fine piece. Someone who had meant a lot to her. Somehow, that realization only deepened the grief. He would have to figure out how to manage it.

Coming only a month or so later, Christmas was difficult. As was the cold February day of what would have been their first wedding anniversary. That evening, Jacques put some Erik Satie on the Victrola—his contemplative piano. He listened for Claire's voice in the somber melody. She was never far from his mind, his reverie. And Satie never failed to bring him back to their hours together, and especially that day together in the Luxembourg Garden. *Je suis au Jardin.*

That night, he fed his infant son, then bathed and changed him. The baby was growing fast, he thought. His boy was already two months old, his bright eyes following the mobile above his crib when Jacques would set it in motion. The baby made what Jacques took to be little smiles and burbly noises.

Victor and Gisèle looked in on him that evening, solicitous and caring. Later, he poured a small glass of brandy, toasting the water lilies mural in the kitchen. Several weeks ago, Cleo had stopped following him from room to room, perhaps thinking that Claire was just there—in the next room—yet to discover her. The dog, too, had slowed.

Late that spring, with much work to do on the farm—building maintenance and real property upkeep, repairs to the machinery, and all manner of challenges from pests and even vandals— Jacques and Victor discussed expansion. That would mean a bank loan. Could he? Should he? Just managing the original apple farm and cider production was one thing. The burgeoning apple brandy side of the business needed even more investment. It was not something to do in any marginal manner. Victor encouraged Jacques to think about expanding—

he knew of property for sale just east of Berlangier's current holding. That, Victor said, would represent a growth option that, in three years or so, would allow them to stabilize the cider operation while yielding more for distillation.

"We grow, or we fade," was the way he put it, and Jacques knew Victor was right. Still, he demurred. Jacques said he would consider something in the autumn. He wanted to see how things worked out over the spring and into summer. He would see what fruit they would sell, what had to be set aside, what the markets looked like. More so, he had to see how Eddie was doing. He had little enough time to spend with his boy as it was. He needed time to sort things out. Claire would not want him taking unnecessary risks. All the big Calvados operations, as well as many small holders, were in Normandy anyway. Hence, even more risk.

Victor accepted that, for the time being at least, they had to keep the business manageable, as Jacques put it. They would look for opportunities. Victor, as patient as he was supportive, figured Jacques would go for it sooner or later, and he was right.

Following the gift of an early spring, Jacques revisited the idea. "We can see how we do with this crop," he told Victor. "See whether we have a quality product. Then, maybe."

And so, they left it at that, Jacques dealing with an unsettling sense of absence. Perhaps it was bold aspiration. A calling to succeed engendered by his parents. It had been their farm. No, it was more. Something done for Eddie, in Claire's memory? Yes, the orchards of his wife. The child's mother, his mother—whatever choice he made, he'd do for them.

That November, Eddie was doing well and was about to celebrate his first birthday. With cider sales strong and some demonstrated interest in his Calvados product, Jacques told Victor he was ready to scout for growth opportunities. Victor, a steady voice of support, told Jacques he'd heard of something coming available. Good land. Jacques told his friend to make inquiries.

Over the previous year, Victor had come to supervise not only the property maintenance, but the dozen or so farm hands, and even some of the cider distribution. Victor was content that Jacques kept the brandy business close. Jacques came to embrace the idea that Victor was aiming for some kind of partnership. He was a smart and able man, a friend. That was doable.

A few days following their tacit agreement, Victor asked Jacques to his house. "Come for dinner on Sunday, Jacques. Gisèle will prepare a pork roast, and we can talk. I have something in mind, a piece of land I think you might like."

Eddie was doing well. Crawling, curious, getting into things. Gisèle, so able, had been caring for the child. She had his playpen handy. That night, she kept him occupied with some stuffed animals while the adults ate and talked. After dinner, the men sat by the fire blazing in the central room. Gisèle brought in coffees.

"We should look into one promising property," Victor told Jacques. "I am hearing there are eighteen hectares, and not far from your northeast property line."

"Eighteen! Near Épiniac. That would mean about thirty percent more capacity." He stretched his arms, perhaps to relieve tension, as he gave the news some thought.

Victor heard the hesitancy in his boss's voice. Any attempt to buy would signal a heightened competition. Who else might have their eye on that property—attractive, fertile land just outside the village of La Perrine, almost immediately next to his own land? Not unlikely, at least some of the nearby farms just into Normandy would respond. They could have more money to negotiate. Maybe drive the cost up.

"I would need a substantial loan," Jacques said, finding confidence.

Meanwhile, his first yield—and there would not be much—would be saleable and marketable that winter. He had to have money to market it. Could he manage both? Victor decided to push what he saw as his advantage. "If we miss this one, we may not get another opportunity, especially with this tract being so close."

Jacques looked over at Eddie, occupied with his cloth rabbit in the playpen. He pushed his chair back from the table, nodded. "I agree we should check it out, Victor. Scout the property. Look for springs and natural wells. Outcroppings of rock that would limit use."

"Yes. Of course."

Early the next week, Victor reported that the parcel looked good. A suitable mix of limestone and clay. The old man selling the property had shown him around, driving his truck through sections of Binet Rouge, a varietal Victor knew that Jacques particularly valued. A few days later, they walked through those areas where Victor had asked to take a closer look.

Jacques asked why the owner was selling. "Did he say?"

"He did." He had no children to leave the land to; two sons who would have been in their mid-thirties had been killed in the war. He had one married daughter in distant Marseille. She had no interest, he had said. Too much work.

Jacques understood what the man selling off must have been focused on. Family, for Jacques, had come to be the source of his greatest joy and his deepest anguish. His parents were long dead. His sister, Nina, and her husband were not in his life. His wife had been taken in childbirth. His son, Eduard, was all the family he had, and all he ever would have. And the land. Jacques was torn between hanging on to what he had and pushing through and taking the risk. He'd never been an incautious man. Still, would merely protecting his holdings be smart in the long run? Eddie's wellbeing was the determining factor.

He watched Gisèle playing with Eddie. He knew how much he owed them both. All that Gisèle had done those first several months for Eddie. "I will look into that loan," he said, adding, "Thank you, Victor."

Jacques affirmed the plan in March. Both were taking a gamble. High risk, high reward. The financial plan they worked up looked good to both.

On the first of April, after making an initial offer that turned out to be much the same as two from larger farms, each a good eighty kilometers away in Normandy, Jacques and Victor learned they had been selected. They would need a few thousand additional francs to make it work, and Berlangier came up with the additional funds to secure the contract. The loan had been calculated on the original sale price. The old fellow liked Victor, and he liked the idea of his farm going to a near neighbor. The newest addition to the farm and brandy enterprise had the names of both men on the deed. There was a legal complication regarding the two large parcels, with only the second naming Victor as co-owner. That, they'd agreed, could be managed with certain limitations pertaining to the additional tract.

"Partners," Jacques agreed, clapping his friend on the shoulder.

Victor had the business partnership he had long desired. That night, in the blush of early spring, after it all became legal, they opened a bottle of the good stuff and drank to their good fortune. Once, at the table, Gisèle touched her hand to the ruddy birthmark below her right ear, a small embarrassment to her since early childhood. Maybe the closeness—

"*Santé!*" said Victor.

"*Santé!*" Gisèle agreed, joyful, looking at her husband, at the two men who had become so close.

Those friends, those men, that generous woman—they were partners and confidants. They had been smart. Optimism and good will radiated around the table. Surely, 1948 was their break-out year. What could go wrong?

PART 2

CHAPTER 24

Henri d'Ancel stormed into the apartment, slammed the door, and went to the kitchen cabinet to pour a glass of whisky. Nina looked at the clock over the sink.

"What are you doing here?" she asked, voice tight, rinsing her plate, her lunch break from the hotel just about over. All she needed was to have to deal with her husband's antics.

Henri had been thinking of what he would say, how he could put it. He looked to the mirror above the mantel, checking his appearance as if to confirm the anger he was feeling, then turned to her. "Now, listen to me. I will not be defined by what work I am made to do in this crummy city, Nina. I cannot. I am sick of it." He let out an anguished breath.

She'd heard this before. "It's not one o'clock, Henri. Why are you home, and why are you drinking?"

He set the glass down on a leather coaster atop the small wooden étagère, by the sofa.

"Stop this! You promised. I should have thrown it away. All of it! That shit you always have so handy."

Henri slapped at her hand. Not hard. Not to injure. A rebuke. Taking back what little dominion he had. "This is all wrong," he said.

Nina knew there'd be no good in further confrontation. He had struck out at her before, a week or two ago. More a show of weakness than strength. His constitutional fragility made her all the angrier. Still, she must let him cool down.

"What happened? Just tell me."

"I cannot do this. I am not a welder. I am not an apprentice to some pipe fitter, or whatever it is they want me to do. No. It kills me."

She told him she knew it was only for a while, until he could get back to his music. Once again, she would encourage him and tolerate his behavior. After all, she had once loved him. Hadn't she? Dutiful Nina—still tangled in the backwash of a failed first love. "Do not quit until you have something else. Something better."

Turning from the hallway mirror, collapsing into a stiff, ladder-back chair at the table, Henri drained the glass and set it down. He stared at his fingers. "Do you know what this kind of work does to my hands? How will I ever play again? I have to get out of that place."

Nina shrugged. What were they to do? Henri had been unable to find even temporary work with any club. Not in Nantes. Not in Rennes. He had tried Le Mans too, the city near where he'd grown up. His first wife's home. The list was long: Saint-Malo? No. Too many bad memories there for her. He had sworn he would never try Paris again. Not after the way he had humiliated himself two years earlier at Club Le Caveau. Celebrating the war's ending one evening that summer, he became too drunk to get through even the first set, disappointing three other jazz musicians and the establishment's owner. Fortunately for them, a patron—a young man Henri had seen in the club before—agreed to finish with the group and did well enough to be offered the job. Henri d'Ancel's once promising piano career was done. At least in France's capital city.

Jazz pianists are not beyond getting good and drunk. Nina knew that. She'd witnessed the truth of it on several occasions. But doing so regularly derails even the most promising of futures. Henri's had once looked brilliant. He used an old abandoned upright in the basement of their apartment house to practice. When he did practice, which was rare.

Henri went to the kitchen to refresh his drink. "Just a taste," he said, brushing by her. "Then I need to take a nap," he announced and made his way into their bedroom, where not much had been going on for several months. Watching the pitiable performance, Nina realized it was going to be up to her to survive—alone if need be. Henri did not have the tensile strength to manage even an apprentice welder's training program.

Their first few years together, the second marriage for both, had burned like a grass fire. But, at that point, Nina was exhausted from his moods and his alcohol abuse, from his pathetic moodiness, his inability to hold any job. Her friend Anna Caron's brother, a local pol, had pulled some strings and gotten Henri the work at the factory. Was he willing to learn a trade? He had promised he was. Few men would have had even that opportunity with the economy still in recovery. But he'd complained the labor he was given was mind-numbing. The men he worked with were too far from what he thought of as his social and intellectual peers. It was not that they were stupid, just that none of them were interested in what he cared about.

Nina worked as a maid at one of the nicer hotels. Nantes had enough activity, commercial and recreational, to keep several good hotels busy, but what she took home could hardly keep them both. To supplement what she earned, she kept an eye out for things left behind. Things they might use. She did not think of this practice as theft so much as discreet observation of benign opportunities. Now and again, something useful left in a drawer. Once, a good pair of leather shoes dropped off for the porter to be shined up had gone unclaimed. Once in a while, she'd find a few francs fallen by the bed, or, more rarely, deliberately left for her. Supplemental alms. Justification for a patch of poor luck. She glanced at the kitchen clock. It was a ten-minute walk back to the hotel. Lucien would be looking at the time when she returned.

Somehow, her fate, too, felt unfair. Maybe if she'd not been so insistent on separating herself from family years ago, from her brother Jacques, from her mother, who in those days she'd thought to be especially difficult—always critical of her as a teen— she might have once found some help there. But no. She had willfully shut them all out and could not imagine how to repair the damage. Her parents were long dead, and she was certain of one thing: She was pretty much dead to her only sibling as well. The answers to her predicament lay only with her, not with her wastrel husband. What could Henri do but drink? And even that he did not do well.

The hotel's assistant manager, Lucien, had made overtures. Nina had no doubt he was interested. But what good could come of that? He was young—late-thirties, she supposed. Dressed well. Nicely built. But no. Impossible.

Preparing to return to work, she heard something from the other room, looked in and found Henri had fallen out of bed. And there he lay on the wooden floor, laughing like an orangutan. Could he be that inebriated already? Or had he stopped for a few on the way home? And if he was home midday, did that mean he had quit? Or had he been fired?

"What is the matter with you?" she said, raising her voice, stepping away from the unhappy display, closing the bedroom door. She'd be late for work again. Not that anyone would say anything. She could rattle off any number of excuses if need be. My husband came home sick from work. The toilet flooded. I locked myself out.

Nina returned to the kitchen and switched on the gas burner to heat water for tea. The situation with Lucien was nothing but vexatious. The idea of being with him at the hotel was nonsense. To do so would compromise any self-worth she still possessed and weaken whatever love for and level of commitment to her husband that she still had—a man who might yet turn things around and find a proper job in music again. Stranger things had happened.

As the tea pot whistled, Henri loped back into the kitchen like some large, defeated poodle. He had to come in to speak with her. Penitent. Remorseful.

"Did you quit your job today, Henri?"

"Yes, I did. I cannot do that crap anymore. The monotony, the utter boredom of it is too much." If he expected her to become angry, she did not show it.

"So, you quit. What do you propose we do now? Am I to find a job at the hotel that pays enough to keep us in food, in this apartment? Work extra shifts?"

"I do not know what to think," he said. "I am sorry, sorry I have disappointed you. Sorry I am a failure." He looked to his hands again, as if there might be something they could tell him. Nina contemplated the chipped cups and mismatched saucers on the table.

"Now, listen to me. I want you to go to Paris again, Henri. Find a job. I am serious. A nightclub, whatever. I don't care what it is or where. Give lessons if you must. But pull yourself together." She looked into his face to see if she was getting through. His lack of response irritated her. "You did it once, you can do it again."

"Paris? But how? I lost the only good job. . ."

"Stop! Just listen to yourself," she said, interrupting his self- anguish, not meaning to raise her voice again. "Forget that. There must be other good work in that city. It's big enough."

He looked at the empty table. Empty plates. Plastic salt and pepper shakers. Two people, desperately in search of something. Not this debilitating near-emptiness.

Paris? Had he not been disgraced enough? And even if he were to go there, how could he afford the travel? Train fare, a hotel? Anticipating this complication, Nina went to the tiny pantry and opened a jar that had once held prunes.

"Here," she said, handing him a small roll of money. "Take it. Sixty francs. I was saving for a coat. Mine is worn, but I can get along." He looked at the fistful of notes.

"But, how? What can I do?"

"Find a job. I want you to go. Go tomorrow morning. Go and find something, Henri. Or I will leave you."

CHAPTER 25

Nina had packed a baguette for Henri with a thin spread of gruyere cheese. Something he could carry on the train. What he would do for drink, she knew, would be up to him. She'd warned him against getting drunk.

"You get just this one chance. This last chance. Do you understand that?"

Henri cringed at the admonishment, but she was right. The first morning train for Paris would leave at eight minutes past seven, arriving at Gare Montparnasse just before ten. He told her he had heard of a few new clubs in the Latin Quarter, one on the storied rue de la Huchette in the 5th arrondissement, a narrow and often raucous street. What would the jazz music scene look like there?

"You must be diligent. Do you hear me? You can do this. I know you can."

"A new club? They do tend to come and go," he said, rallying to the possibilities. The nascent Paris night scene was taking form in his mind. St. Germain was a good place to start, he assured her with a rush of nostalgia. They had met Sidney Bechet one evening, maybe in 1938, at the celebrated Caveau des Oubliettes with those crazily costumed waiters. Bechet drew talent to any club he graced. A man just had to try, he said. "And be lucky." A fleck of hope.

The next morning, she told him, "Henri, go be lucky." She kissed him, encouraging him out the door, not for the first time asking herself if this gambit was worth it. Henri had never been particularly reliable, even when sober.

The train was filling fast when Henri arrived at seven sharp, making his way down the platform to the second-class cars, men and women queuing up. Equal numbers of them, he supposed, were on their way up as on their way down. Which group he would identify with was yet to be decided. First class, toward the front, had more room and less noise. It was also next to the dining car. Someday, he would travel with such comfort and self-assurance. One had only to meet the right sponsor or impress the right club owner. What was the expression about risk and reward? Life is a game. *La vie est un jeu.*

He found one half-full cabin—one seat open and next to the window, which he preferred. A car with no children, who tended to be irritable, physically anxious, and pretty much always loud. If he could nap for an hour, he'd be happy. But no. No sooner did he put his overnight bag into the storage space above and begin to settle in than a woman entered with two boys, maybe nine or ten years old. Already arguing, they took the cracked-leather bench opposite him, the woman at the window, the boys scrambling for the seat next to her and kicking their feet. Could he just get up and leave? Try to find another cabin? He admonished himself for not being more discerning. For not finding a car with one seat left and no children. Too late. He had a sense the entire train would be full. And, with almost three hours to go, the boys acting up, and the mother saying nothing, his spirits fell. He could always go to the club car. But what would he buy there? He had no money for much of anything. Maybe a coffee, he thought. Though he would rather have a small glass of whisky.

Both boys soon took to staring at Henri. Whispering. The mother told them to settle down and behave. The red-haired boy insisted on taking over the window seat, which she readily agreed to so as to be able to sit between them. Could Henri stand the noisy boys all the way to Paris? Not likely. He'd escape into the club car. Maybe find a newspaper. He'd forgotten to purchase one. But what about his travel case? He could not leave it there above the seat for the entire trip. And yet it would look odd for him to take it. What a situation. He felt his jacket pocket, thinking that, with any luck at all, he might have a small flask. A blessed sip of something clement. But no. How should he manage?

"Madame, I must meet someone in the club car; I do not know how long I will be gone. With apologies, might I ask you to keep an eye on my bag?"

She looked at him—a hint of suspicion.

"I will return as soon as I can," he told her. The woman considered the request as a weary priest might eye yet another holy-day penitent. But the red-haired boy, clearly the more aggressive, spoke up.

"How long will you be gone, Monsieur?" He stared hard at Henri.

I should have asked someone else, Henri realized, someone like the older lady with a basket of knitting seated next to him. But, somehow, he did not want to disturb her. Maybe he would always make the wrong choice when it came to dealing with people, he thought, castigating himself once again. The woman, however, must have picked up on his distress, a timely benefactor. "I will watch it for you, Monsieur." Looking over her reading glasses. "No need to bother the young woman," she said. "I am off to Paris to see my son and his wife. There will be no bother for me." The red-haired nuisance considered this unexpected interjection, opened his mouth as if to speak, and gave his brother a shove.

Henri did not know what to think. Should he agree? The woman had so unexpectedly volunteered. Who was the woman, anyway? He needed her aid, yet he demurred. He wanted her help, and yet he did not. If he should stop to consider how much his life had been lived on the edge of uncertainty and ambivalence, perhaps he did so then. The red-haired boy was talking again.

"Excuse me?"

The boy wanted to take supervision of the travel bag, doubling d'Ancel's quandary. He would have to call upon a talent for diplomacy, for tact—not at all his forte. Instead, he would feign poor hearing. Henri ignored the boy.

"I do not mind," said the woman, putting down her needlework.

An unspoken *I understand your angst!* passed between them.

"Merci."

The matter settled, Henri smiled at the boy, an awkward attempt to hide his instinctive dislike. He nodded again to the boy's mother and thanked the lady who had, in such timely fashion, intervened.

"Merci," he managed once again, and then, without giving sufficient regard to what came into his head, he asked whether he could bring her anything. Henri immediately wanted to take it back. What could he bring her? He had no extra francs to buy anyone anything. What if she had asked for something? *What a moron I am*, he thought, smiling once again at the rest of his cabinmates, then, as quickly as he could manage, he let himself out the sliding door. There, an old man struggled with an oversized bag, maybe preparing to leave the train at the next stop and needing to avoid the crush of hurrying, uncaring crowds.

The diner was several cars toward the front. The better choice, however, and closer, was the club car, where people went to mingle, to drink, and, maybe, to smoke a cigar. Henri could use something. The soggy baguette weighed awkwardly in his tweed jacket pocket. Walking to the lounge, where he would order a coffee and advance his plan for the day, he gave some thought about how to best proceed to the 6th arrondissement.

Henri knew Paris fairly well, but he wanted to get things set in his mind. The arrival was straightforward: Turn north out of Montparnasse and make a beeline for the Luxembourg Gardens past the street vendors. Always men and boys selling roasted chestnuts and balloons. He walked past the statue of the dour Paul Verlaine and turned left. There were several possibilities nearby. He could do it.

"Pardon," Henri said to a man standing at the club-car door, positioned to enter just ahead of him. Henri had been so distracted in his plans that he had not noticed him. He was a confident-looking fellow. Henri was taken with his smile and his quick-to-get-along kind of demeanor. Henri, optimistic, was taking in the ambiance. The smell of strong coffee brought his gaze to the tall black attendant in the uniform of the rail line. He would buy a coffee and sit somewhere by himself, try to eat that baguette.

"Not at all," the other said to Henri, who noticed the fellow was carrying a handsome briefcase. Maybe an attorney, or a banker. His confidence was unmistakable.

Several people were waiting to give their orders at the narrow zinc bar. Placing only one service attendant there was inconsiderate. People, busy travelers, had needs. Annoyed, Henri fell into line behind the man, who was taking in the room, maybe looking for a place to sit. The car nearly full. The smart looking fellow turned, in that moment evidently sizing Henri up. As the train lurched unexpectedly, Henri stumbled, catching himself on the sleeve of the other man.

"Excuse me."

The fellow righted them both. "*Mais non*. All fine." The man considered Henri. "Let me buy you a coffee and Danish, Monsieur."

"Oh. . ."

"I insist. Perhaps a *tartine*. And they are especially good on this line," he told d'Ancel, who had a sweet tooth and was not of a mind to decline again. The two eased into an open row of seats halfway back in the car. A light fog that had pestered one's view upon first boarding had cleared. Introductions made, the man asked Henri if he lived in Paris. Was he, perhaps, returning home?

Startled by the inquiry, Henri said no, that he lived in Nantes but was considering relocating to Paris.

"Yes, of course. A beautiful city."

Indebted for the coffee and treat, Henri became more voluble. He was a musician, a pianist. No point in revealing he was looking for work. He answered with trepidation. No letters of recommendation, nothing in his pockets or heart but faint hope. "A fine place, Nantes, but I have outgrown it," Henri added, feeling foolish. He asked his new acquaintance whether he lived in Paris.

No, he was traveling to the city on business, something he did all too often, he said, adding that he had recently been to Rennes to inquire about some properties, but that he lived in the village of Épiniac, near the town of Combourg, a small place. He and his aging mother. Someday, he, too, would live in Paris.

"One must only find the right circumstances," he added.

Henri agreed. The man had made his argument for him. So much depended on the right circumstances. "You are interested in properties?" Henri asked, unsure where he expected that inquiry to take them. He knew he owed a kind of social debt to the man for the coffee. To buy and sell properties suggested ready funds. Henri certainly had none.

The other said he was on the lookout for undervalued buildings. "Good money in real estate now." Commercial properties, he added. Undeveloped farms. "The war well over, people are making big changes."

"I suppose so. Combourg, you said?"

"Yes."

Henri considered that significant. "I have a brother-in-law in Combourg," he told him, looking at what remained of his Danish. "What a small world," the man replied, raising his eyebrows.

"Perhaps I know him."

"Perhaps you would," said Henri. "He has an apple business nearby. Orchards. Name of Berlangier."

A skilled and easy liar, Roger Laurent took a moment to consider how he should respond to that news. So, Jacques Berlangier? He looked out the window at the passing farms and rough rural buildings. The vast beauty of the land. None of it was his. "Actually, I am well acquainted with the gentleman," he said. "A hero of France, you know."

"Oh, indeed I do," Henri responded, nodding his head in solidarity. He paused. "Though, for all that, and for all his prosperity, he has not shown any generosity toward his only sister—my wife."

"Oh? Your sister? And why is that, do you suppose?" Both were attentive to the give and take.

"I can only think it is his natural tendency to be a tightwad and an ingrate. Big shot."

"I see. Disappointing, eh?"

Henri looked at the man and nodded. He could not fully discern his attitude. Perhaps he was a friend to Jacques, in which case, Henri should say nothing more. For his part, Laurent found that last the most exciting news he'd heard in weeks, and potentially profitable information. The Berlangier farm? A valuable property. What he did not let on was that he'd harbored a latent envy and general dislike for Jacques Berlangier for some time, not a little of it because of Berlangier's cozy relationship with his late uncle. What could that suggest? He'd thought about that farm before. It was a potential money-maker, a double win.

"Your wife is Berlangier's sister, is that right?"

Henri said yes and took another bite of his nearly depleted Danish and second-guessing that declined *tartine*. "For all the good it does her," he said, licking his fingers.

Roger smiled, a hint of affirmation. "I see."

Henri took one last bite and drew heartily from what remained of his coffee, thanking Laurent once more for the treat and falling silent. He was certain that the other fellow was studying him. But why?

"Lovely day," Henri tried. Maybe he should have gotten a newspaper.

"Yes. Nearly cloudless." There was an unexpected opening there, Laurent thought, acknowledging the favor, a cheap enough investment. That miserably dressed, weary musician may or may not find manna in Paris, as he would evidently attempt to do. But Laurent suspected he may have just found a partner, willing or not. One, perhaps, in need of a clever friend.

CHAPTER 26

Nina was running late by about ten minutes. Or was she? Maybe she wasn't late if no one who mattered noticed or cared. Nina entered as usual through the service doors. Breakfast trays had been left piled on a nearby aluminum cart. Another day of making do.

In the basement service bathroom, she slipped into her gray-and-white work outfit and picked up the schedule, passing Lucien's office as she had to do. She found her cart. His door was open. Was he looking for her? She stole a quick look in and stepped past. Lucien appeared to be going over some papers and had evidently not seen her. Or so she thought.

"*Bon après-midi, Nina*," she heard him say. Had he been watching for her? She would have to step back and return a proper greeting. Should she speak or just wave? The less said the better? He'd know she was just arriving. It was a quarter past the hour. Lucien set aside his adding machine. His looks could be eerily penetrating, with that grin he liked to show.

"*Bonjour, Lucien. Ça va?*" Polite but apprehensive. "How are you?"

"Fine. Busy as ever. And you? A good lunch?"

Was he being smart with her? A good lunch? Was he implying that she had gone home for something else?

With all the smile she could muster, Nina shook her head. She gave him a wave, a let-me-get-back-to-work kind of signal. She looked at the schedule. She'd begin on the sixth floor, where newly arriving patrons would expect to have their rooms ready by three.

"So hasty? Where are you off to, *mon chou?*"

Nina did not like the lovey names, the implied intimacy. What was he thinking? He knew she was married. She'd heard some of the other young women on the hotel staff refer to him by his nickname: *le lécher.* "I begin on the sixth." She had been assigned the fourth, as well, though that would wait. She allowed two afternoon hours for each floor on a typical day. Hours of work she detested. Actually, it was likely he knew exactly where she'd be. Most of those top-floor rooms would be empty, rooms bigger and nicer than the ones on the lower floors. For the most part, they were taken by well-to-do foreigners—Zurich businessmen and the aspirational Americans. A wealthy Belgian family had entertained in the bridal suite—room 602—last month, leaving lavish tips for the staff.

Nina pushed her cart to the open elevator, thinking she had best be prepared for Lucien to show up sometime in the next half hour, checking on things, as he would say, but testing the waters for any heat coming from her. He had, on more than one occasion, exhibited a willingness to take her to one of the rooms with sly innuendos. And, with the hotel manager gone that day, there would be no one to redirect his energy.

Twenty minutes later, as Nina had suspected, Lucien looked in as she was wiping down a mirror in one generous-sized bathroom. The room was a grand double. Irises in the vases. Dark chocolates and a bottle of Chenin blanc on the wet bar. She would place fresh towels on the bed when it had been made up. The room was one of the Marguerite's finest.

"I thought you might like to take a short break," he said. "And perhaps you would care to have these." He offered her what she could see were theater tickets.

"What is this, Lucien?" She saw that they were pricey tickets, and to the gorgeous Théâtre Graslin, a building nearly destroyed in the war but recently rebuilt. "Mozart? Tonight? But how could I possibly use these? Thank you, but I am confused."

Lucien grinned and told her he had acquired them from the concierge. It had been a trade in kind, no doubt. She knew old Bertrand was not opposed to bartering, and he had access to some high-end products. One made the most of his or her position in the city's hotel business. What the nearsighted old man had received in return she did not want to speculate. Nina shook her head. She could not take them, she said, before thinking better of it and holding her tongue, because her husband was out of town.

"So fortunate for you," he said. What was he implying?

"I am sorry, Lucien. I am not able. I thank you. But I simply cannot."

His face showed disappointment; he asked why. Nina said she had no one to go with, did not know Mozart's work. She had never especially liked that kind of music. And, even if she did, she would have nothing to wear. Women donned their best evening attire for such events. Surely, he was teasing. Black dresses. Jewels. Was he mocking her? What did he expect of her?

"As I said, I have nothing suitable, Lucien. No proper dress . . .

He interrupted. "I am less interested in what you wear than what you do not, Nina. You are quite beautiful." Quickly, he moved toward her, and she stepped back. What he wanted should not happen. She saw he had closed the door behind him.

"Stop!" She pulled away again. "Leave me now! And take your tickets. This is wrong, Lucien, and I want this behavior to cease."

The man said nothing more, bowed mockingly, and turned, walking out of the room. What her refusal of him would mean to her work—assignments and schedules—she had no idea. If she'd have to quit her job to escape his insistent advances, she would.

When she finished work that day, just past five, changing once again into her street clothes and passing Lucien's office, she saw his door was closed. She could hear him on the phone, but not distinctly. Had he put the matter aside, of little or no consequence? Or would there be a penalty somewhere ahead?

With a short walk home, Nina entered the apartment where, so recently, she had encouraged her talented if weak-willed husband to take hold of his future. What Henri would come back with, what news, what excuse, could not be foretold. Something like the smell of the hotel came in with her, and immediately she recognized it as Lucien's cologne. What kind of fools were they? Both of them? Henri's lack of drive. Her incessant need to prove herself. All those self-evident truths depressed her as did his fitfulness and her vulnerability. She would have to take another job, and soon. She knew that. The awkwardness of her situation with the assistant manager would not wane on its own.

That night, Nina made a light supper for herself: a slice of ham and a little piece of the gruyere left from Sunday, toast with grape jam, and scrambled eggs. She reheated the water remaining in the tea pot. There would be no Mozart, no fancy dress and eager suitor. Just a quiet evening with a novel she'd begun reading a few days earlier, with the radio for company. Some Edith Piaf, perhaps. Her plaintive "La Vie en Rose," written in the last year of the war, made her feel both melancholy and determined. Like Piaf, the Little Sparrow, as she was called, Nina had given birth at the age of seventeen. Named for her father, whom she loved deeply, her baby Mathis lived only four months. The infant's death, for which she took full responsibility, destroyed her relationship with the child's feckless father and was a contributing factor in her withdrawal from the rest of her family. How the baby had died was not something she ever wanted to think about, much less to explain to her brother.

What was the expression, she thought? You've made your bed; lie down in it? Yes. Well, she was lying in it and had been for some twenty years. The real challenge was to fashion the best life yet open to her. With or without Henri.

In the bedroom, at her dresser, she picked up the creased photo of the baby. How many times had she looked at it? What might he be, her Mathis, had she not been so careless? Also kept there, under a narrow, discolored linen doily, was a photo of her parents taken just before the war. Family was another source of disappointment and remorse. Fathers and sons. Mothers and daughters. Must someone always be at fault? And why was Jacques the blessed one? Still, she would like to have had him in her life. How had he come out so undamaged, and with a fine apple farm—well, except for the tragic death of his American wife, two years ago or more. No, three. There was that. And that was sad. He had a little boy. Her friend Emma Brun, still in Combourg, still helping her ever-reliable husband to run that feed store— Emma had filled her in on the long story. And Nina? What did she have? Where would she wind up?

CHAPTER 27

Meanwhile, Henri had two hours to go yet in his travel. Otherwise a direct shot from Nantes to Paris, the train stopped to drop off and pick up a few passengers in the ancient, stunningly beautiful city of Angers, medieval seat of the ever-unsettled Plantagenet dynasty. Another Henry with mid-career difficulties.

"Angers!" bellowed the conductor.

Henri looked out to the platform and saw several people stepping onto the train, some with large bags, some with nothing at all, a testament to what all of them had so recently lived through and come away with. Most, Henri assumed, were destined for Paris. Each, no doubt, was in search of his or her own distinctive grail. With that stop, with the crush of more bodies, Henri became aware of the temperature. The summer heat in the club car was all but unbearable. Was it too late, would it be stupid to disembark? Did Henri even want to go to Paris and run the risk of once more failing at what he'd set out to do? Were he to get out just there, in Angers, he would only have to cross to the opposite track and await the next train back to Nantes. He could tell Nina he had become unwell. But no. His travel case was in the other car, and the train was moving again. Why must so many important decisions be made with so little time to consider one's options?

Roger and Henri both looked to the door—Roger perhaps to see who else might come into the club car, Henri to see whether one of the young boys from his first car might look in, carrying that mildewed case. Or maybe to say, "The old lady just got off and took your bag, Monsieur." But, of course, nothing like that happened. His fanciful imagination was getting the better of him again. He should be getting back to his original seat. It was the mannerly thing to do. He could not help but notice, however, that Roger was studying him again. Henri was, perhaps less subtly, considering him too.

Ever easygoing, Laurent smiled. What was the man thinking, the way he looked at him? Roger loosened his necktie, something sporting a stout white-and-green–necked pheasant, and asked whether Henri wanted anything else, he appearing not to have heard.

"Another coffee, perhaps?" Roger offered generously. It would be necessary, he knew, to find out more from the musician. What, precisely, was his attitude toward Berlangier? Had they had any recent contact? Disagreements? Evidently, the man's wife was unhappy. Well, people, especially relatives, were seldom comfortable with what someone else had if they did not have it too. Henri d'Ancel was a dreamer; that much was clear to Laurent. To what extent would that make him pliable? Vulnerable?

The train picked up speed, scenery giving way once again to farmland. Horses and sheep. Barns under repair. No one from Henri's compartment was coming to check on him to see what he was doing or whom he was with. There was no turning back. Still, wouldn't he love to have an anise-flavored Pernod to take the edge off and clear the ambient fog in his mind?

Roger was speaking to him.

"*Pardon*?"

Roger asked whether Henri had been to the Berlangier farms. Had he seen the operation? It was a big effort and a great success, Roger told him.

"No," Henri said. They had never been invited. Henri observed how Roger appeared anxious about something. How—why—did he know all of that about Jacques?

"I cannot get over the fact that you know my brother-in-law. During the war, you said?"

Laurent had waited for just that question, expecting such an opening. He explained that he and Jacques, and Jacques's late wife, had done some work together during the war. "Resistance," he said, using the English pronunciation. "All very secretive. Hush hush."

Henri agreed that he knew something about Berlangier's wartime work through his wife. Nina's friend Emma, a woman also in the know, had spoken about it to her. Jacques and her husband had done things. Espionage, maybe. Nina had kept only in loose touch with Emma.

"Highly dangerous business," Roger added.

Henri nodded his head. He'd heard it all before.

"In the war, I met them both—Berlangier and the woman who became his wife. I even attended their wedding." He leaned in. Laurent needed to see whether that connection moved anything in Henri's consciousness. He had little time left to make his pitch.

"You were friends, then?"

"I would not say friends. We shared some common ground."

Roger was assessing how Henri, who was getting fidgety, processed that mini history. He knew not to attempt to force the bait. Go slowly. Show concern. Did he respect and admire the apple farmer? Did he think the man a friend or a fraud?

"Tell me, Monsieur, a man of refined tastes such as yourself. Do you like apple brandy?"

"Not especially," Henri replied, then thought better of it. "Some of it is pretty decent," he allowed, recovering some ground. Laurent offered another withering smile. A woman had come to their seating area, across from them. The crowded train pressed down on Henri. The woman's scent was cloying. She opened a magazine. Roger, pulling his gaze away from her ankles, was speaking to Henri again.

"Henri, I do not wish to disrupt your plans for the day."

But d'Ancel had been daydreaming, looking at nothing in particular. Not the woman. At the fields, maybe. "You are not disrupting anything," he replied, lowering his voice. "I appreciate your company," Henri added, not sure what to make of the inquiry about brandy.

"I mean to say that later in the day we might meet up. If you would like. After you call on these music club owners. *C'est votre plan, n'est-ce pas?* That is your plan, is it not?"

Henri thought a moment, said he had several people to see and did not know when he would be finished with his appointments.

Roger moved the conversation to the idea of their return trip. "Do you expect to return to Nantes this evening, or late afternoon? Or will you be staying in the city tonight?" If so, they might meet up again for the return tomorrow.

Henri said he didn't know. There was no way to know. He did not want to, but he was prepared to stay if need be. He had told Nina he might. If feasible, he'd take the four-fourteen return that day. The afternoon was preferred.

"Of course." Were Henri to stay the night in Paris, Roger would have more time to put together a more careful plan. Such delicate matters cannot be rushed. If not, he would have to improvise. Though in Paris to meet a woman, he could not let the opportunity slip away. "I see. If you decide to travel back today, we might agree to meet for a drink this afternoon, no doubt to celebrate your success."

A drink? The idea appealed. "Yes. Good. Where did you have in mind?"

Roger had a ready answer. "Do you know Chez Félix? It is quiet. Good place to talk."

Henri said he did know the place. In the 7th. He and Nina had gone there once or twice a few years ago.

Roger nodded. "Yes, the Félix. Brazilian flair. Their dark, quiet basement. Just by the Cardinal-Lemoine *Métro*, as I recall," added Laurent, keen to show he knew a smart place. "Easy to find."

"I know it," said Henri.

"Fine. Fine. What time suits you best, my friend?" Roger checked his watch, which Henri noticed looked expensive. "I can take care of my business in a few hours," Laurent continued. "But I do have commitments tonight. Matters that will keep me in the city. I will not be able to accompany you back this evening."

Henri nodded.

"So, we must look to maybe three this afternoon, yes?" What he did not divulge to Henri was that his business that day and that night was highly personal. That afternoon, he'd planned a tryst with the widow of a young police colleague who had been stabbed to death at one of Paris's larger train stations. He'd promised to take care of her. He would begin to do so by taking her to bed, as he had been doing for some months, and would further counsel her on what investments to make with the insurance money she would receive. His company, he told her, made only sure-thing investments. He assured her she must trust him. A policeman. He knew how things worked. He knew investments.

That evening—that night—was quite another matter. No revenge or glib swindle. No property hustle. Just his Sabrina. One night of pure pleasure. The next day, he'd return to Combourg, begin to put a plan into motion, depending on how readily he might manipulate the vulnerable M. Henri d'Ancel.

Henri's first call was to the Joséphine, a delightful little club which, just weeks earlier, the manager told him, had settled on two regular jazz trios. One was comprised of extremely talented American Negroes. Generously, he asked Henri to play something for him, in case he should find himself in need of a substitute, but he was not able to promise anything. He also poured his guest a generous glass of champagne. It was not Henri's alcohol of choice, but it was a free drink. Feeling loose and limber shortly thereafter, Henri adjusted his rumpled shirt, went to the piano, and sailed splendidly through a rendition of "Tenderly" in snappy four-four time.

"Wonderful," the man acknowledged. "My compliments!" And did he know "Come Rain or Come Shine?"

Henri said he did and proceeded to make the best of that one too, even singing a few words in English, perhaps to convince the man he was the real deal.

"Of course, I am not a professional singer," Henri added, equal parts modesty and optimism.

"No, no. Well, no matter." He had two vocalists, the man said, that affable Edgar, again complementing Henri on his talent, adding that he did not just then need another piano player. Would he like to leave his name and phone, just in case?

Henri said he would, and would be happy as well with a refill, if the gentleman was pouring.

Did Henri have references?

"I do if you need them."

Well, they agreed, they would leave it at that for the moment.

The next two stops proved nothing if not disappointing. One club was closed for renovation—no owner or manager on site. The proprietor of the other bar knew the name Henri d'Ancel and asked if he had not once played at le Caveau. Henri's history was still fresh in the minds of some. Henri told the man that no; that was his uncle. Sadly, now dead. He figured, who was to know? The interview went no further.

The proprietor thanked Henri for his interest. *"Bon chance, Monsieur."* Good luck and goodbye. Still, Henri had something encouraging to bring to Nina: The Joséphine. He was getting hungry.

He might just sit in one of the small parks near Saint Sulpice—the baroque church with the big organ—or he could look to something on the Right Bank. He had word of a new club opening in the 18th, in Montmartre. Maybe he'd try there. But first, he needed to eat. Finding a bench and taking the homely baguette out of its napkin, his thoughts returned to Roger Laurent. Obviously, he was a man who knew a thing or two. Henri checked his watch. Ten past one. Henri was to meet the man in two hours.

What could he do for two hours? Should he choose to slug his way over to Montmartre, hill of martyrs, in a pointless search for work? Or should he take the few francs he had left—his return train ticket assured—and buy a whisky, maybe make another new friend? The fates were unpredictable. Two fashionably dressed, attractive young women walked toward him. Both had small dogs trooping energetically before them. The girls were in long, shapely dresses, as was the style. One a dark blonde. The other in a smart, mauve beret. There was nothing desperate in their gaits, nothing uncertain. To Henri's eye, they could have been sisters, twins. He figured they had money. Opportunity, something he so craved. Why could he not be fortunate, someday, as well? He'd pay them no further heed; they ignored him as they passed by on the broad sidewalk. Henri turned west, making his way up the busy rue de Grenelle, anticipating, momentarily, a generous and thirst-quenching welcome from his new friend Roger.

Henri's spirits were in fine shape, a bit later, when Roger Laurent walked into the Félix and spotted the disheveled-looking pianist sitting at a corner table, singing softly to himself. His fingers pressed imaginary piano keys on the small, dark wooden table. He was evidently in a welcoming mood. *Tenderly...*

"How did it go?" Roger asked.

"Oh, how did it go?" Henri took a moment. He stood and sat back down. *"Splendide,"* he said, raising his nearly empty glass. Henri said he had something positive in the works. Club Joséphine could always use an extra jazz piano man. Or that was the luminous cast he chose to put on the noncommittal arrangement he thought he'd struck a short while earlier.

"An extra? *Chapeau*, my friend. So, when will you begin, Henri? When do you start?"

Henri finished the final drops of what had been a long-lasting whisky and looked to the bottom of the glass. "No. I am their substitute. I mean, I would only play if the regular man, and they have two, is unavailable."

"Ah, that is the tricky part, then. And so, we must see what we can do to advance your chances," said Roger without hesitation. Henri gave him a confused look.

"I mean to say that while there is a regular, a fellow able to play, I have nothing. It is only a dream for me that I will actually get to play there." The honesty of this clarification worked to sober him. "I should not have told you that I have the job, Roger. Only in certain conditions would I have that job. I have little more now to show for myself than I did yesterday."

Laurent nodded. The result was much as he had thought it would be. "Let me buy you a drink, Henri. All is not lost. Maybe someday, some night, the regular man will be unable to appear."

"Well, yes. If their man were to become ill. . ."

"Or disabled," added Roger, signaling the waiter. Showing his two fingers and pointing at Henri's empty glass.

"I do not understand."

Roger adjusted his jacket. He leaned forward to speak, confidentially, to a man he could see was both somewhat drunk and vulnerable. The waiter came and set down the two whiskies.

"Accidents happen, Henri. They happen every day. You must only be on the side of those lucky few who have no accidents themselves but stand ready to improve their own situations when others fall."

Henri looked at him with a mixture of confusion and awe. "Improve?"

"Yes. Improve their situations. I help people to do that. I have at my disposal—a hasty word; I do not mean disposal—I have people who help me to help others. I think I can help you. I may even be in a position to help you and your wife to improve your larger situation."

Henri took an earnest pull on his new drink. He said nothing, but looked to Laurent to continue.

One patient spider snaring an errant fly.

Roger steepled his fingers in a show of deep thought. "Let me ask you this, my friend: if something were to happen to Jacques, who would inherit the property, the business?"

"His son, of course. Even I know that. A little boy."

Roger took that in and shook his head, a reflex, not a judgment of d'Ancel's faculties.

Laurent countered quickly. "Not if the child were still a minor." Roger said he'd been down that kind of road before, knew property and inheritance law. He was a man with connections, a man to make things happen. Laurent noted Henri's look of benign confusion.

"If Jacques were to die, and we pray, of course, that he should not—his poor wife, already dead—French law favors the siblings. Your wife and you would own a truly prosperous property. No worries about jazz clubs in Paris. Or in Nantes, or any other city in France. Your fortunes would be made, my friend."

"I do not want to even talk about such a thing."

"No, of course not. I agree, Henri. A horrible idea. But, as a policeman and a hard-working businessman myself, it is my duty to make you aware. Still, you might inform your wife. She should know, if she has never considered the idea, that she is just a few breaths away from financial security. From a life free from worry."

Henri looked to Laurent to see if there would be more. The fellow was a cop and a businessman with connections. What was he implying?

"I only offer what I know of the law," said Laurent, looking at his watch again. A man with pressing business. He asked Henri whether he would be heading home or staying in the city. Would he keep looking for work?

Henri would return home as soon as possible. Not defeated, but with nothing in his hat but a rim of sweat and a particle of hope.

Roger leaned in. "You understand what I have told you, Henri— to know how close you could be to financial security?"

"Yes. I mean no. I do not know what to think." Henri looked confused by the swell of enthusiasm from the other man. What was the man saying? That Jacques's death could be arranged?

"I must return to Nantes and to my Nina," he said. "Let her know of the possibility."

"Yes. Of course. And tell her what else I have said to you," Roger insisted, "Be sure to tell her." And, with that, he pushed his half-empty glass toward Henri, leaving ten francs on the table. "I have appointments yet to see to, and so I wish you safe travels, my friend. But we must plan to meet again. Talk about matters of importance. Yes?"

Henri nodded in affirmation.

"If you wish, I will call on you again, Monsieur. Meanwhile, please take my card. Think about what I have said. Call me, and we will see what is to be done."

Nonplussed, Henri replied immediately, "What is to be done?"

"Accidents happen every day. Piano players, farmers, war heroes. Do I have your permission to make certain inquiries on your behalf, to speak with a few friends? You can always change your mind."

Uncertain, but wary of the chance: "Yes, I, well. . . I suppose so," said Henri who wanted the conversation to be over. He looked to his travel case at his foot and checked the time. He should be on his way to the train station. He was not sure where things stood, but, just then, he was not given to worry about it. Henri pushed the whisky away and stood—one hand on the table.

"I will be in touch," he said. "And I thank you for your friendship."

Laurent tipped his hat, gave Henri a pat on the shoulder, smiled affably and left. Henri looked at the man's card.

R. LAURENT. CAPITAINE: SÛRETÉ NATIONALE.
COMBOURG PRÉFECTURE

Henri put the impressive card into his jacket pocket. Would he keep it or throw it away? Would he speak with Nina about what the man had told him? Maybe. Surely, he would bring her the news of the job possibility. Not bad news. Not good. Truly, pretty much more of the same. As for what Laurent had in mind about the Berlangier property, Henri was, just then, too agitated to be concerned.

"Accidents," Roger had said to Henri. "Sunny days ahead."

CHAPTER 28

Pushing his way through the balky turnstile, jostling his coffee, Laurent entered the *Métro* station at Odéon. He travelled the ten-minute trip to Les Halles, most of that standing, then exited and walked a block, making his way to the fourth-floor Marais apartment. The beguiling Sabrina on his mind for hours. She would be ready. She was always ready. No doubt, he was, even as he made his way up the three flights of stairs. The man always had an abundance of sexual energy. The tumble he had expected with the young widow had been denied him. Her mother had shown up in town for a few days, arriving unexpectedly that morning.

"Call on me again, Monsieur."

Sabrina was a sure thing. That small, lithe body. Her mystical, blue-green eyes. Her small, perfect breasts. Sabrina, who had at her beck and call an even larger number of thieves and rogues than did he, had been his crime partner twice before. She was his own little thief, his *petite voleuse.* Together, he suspected, they could steal the very fountains of Versailles.

Roger knocked, then knocked again. Sabrina had refused to give him a key, though he had asked. Sabrina Toohey—her deceased father a Northern Irish firebrand minister. Her Romani mother, who baited her father, tamed him, and likely killed him, raised her only daughter, leaving a distinctive mark on the young woman's psyche. If Sabrina took anything from the father's side genetically, it would only have been the eyes. Her willful free-spirit soul was irrepressible.

"Well, what have we here?" she teased, stepping away from the door and nodding for Roger to come in. As ever, she eschewed footwear of any kind in the house. Summer temperatures brought out the best in her. He saw she wore a faded cotton, light-blue men's denim shirt, untucked and mostly open. He had given it to her last year, and she wore it with attitude. From the next room, Nat King Cole was playing on her Victrola. "Mona Lisa," the dreamy pop tune released that year, struck him as prescient.

"Come in. Come and sit, Roger. I'll go fix drinks." She winked.

Laurent watched her disappear into the kitchen as he listened to the vinyl record, words he'd heard not a few times before:

Sabrina could go from warm to cold and distant in an instant. Moody, Mercurial, and ever cautious. Like so many others in uncertain times, Sabrina was a woman living between the lines. Entering her flat, Laurent set his travel bag by the oversized tan-and-white striped armchair he'd come to consider his own, rules of rights and possessions running in him as deep and complex as his very vascular system. They had made love in that chair, her wantonness another fascination for the man.

"Martini?" she asked, not expecting an answer, flashing a quick grin, soon carrying two chilled four-ounce conical glasses from where she had been working. She knew he would take anything she gave him. She knew what he really wanted.

Laurent said he was always in the mood for a martini, though it was a drink he would rarely order for himself. She liked them, and that was fine with him. When she set the glasses down on coasters upon her handsome beechwood side table, he stepped toward her, pulling her into his arms, expecting a fevered kiss. Sabrina complied, though without much passion. Running his hands up the front of her loose shirt, he cupped one breast and pulled her more tightly to him.

Sabrina pulled away ever so slightly. *"Minute papillon!* There is no hurry." She detached herself from his embrace and picked up her glass. "Do you want your drink or not? I have been waiting all day for you to come to me. But a girl has her own needs. So, sit with me now. Business first. You said on the telephone you were making a grand plan. Tell me, what naughtiness are you getting up to now?"

Laurent sat back in the big chair, sipping his drink. He looked at her pretty, slightly downturned mouth, trying to settle, as if to say okay; I will behave. For the moment.

"We are in no hurry, are we?" she continued, a tease. The woman took a satisfying sip of the gin and licked her lips, showing him the tip of her tongue. Roger uttered a small groan and pulled off his necktie. He had gone over and over in his mind the game involving Henri d'Ancel. What to tell her. What not to say.

"What is it you have for me?" Sabrina felt his anticipation; she was deliberate, cautious in coming to the business part of their afternoon. She would set the pace. House rules.

"I have something working now that will assure us some income."

"Tell me."

"There is a farm in Brittany. Something that could pay off nicely for us."

"A farm?" She said that she liked income, though she had not much use for farms. "What kind of money are we talking about?"

"Perhaps a million francs, potentially twice that." He needed her on board.

"Oh my. That is a good start." She set her glass down, pulled him to her, and kissed him hard, then said that he might hold off on any further details. Sabrina stood, kneeling in front of his chair, and, having adjusted her long black hair, she began to unbutton his fly, deftly, toying with him, expertly using her fingers, making him groan. Then she cupped his balls, as if to discern their relative worth. Roger closed his eyes and held his breath until he could hold it no longer.

An hour or so later, when they had finished, he got up to take a cigarette from her vanity, recovering with that small act some tacit sense of initiative.

"So, now we may go back to your secret plan, yes? Your little fund raiser? Or do you no longer have the necessary energy to tell me what is to be my part?" Sabrina teased.

He asked how much detail she wanted.

"I want to know what has you so enthused. You mentioned a farm, something you no doubt intend to make your own. I understand you need my people. What is in it for me?"

He could name a figure, or he thought maybe he could try to have another go with her. "Maybe, if we get into your shower together, I will tell you. But I cannot guarantee I will behave."

Her reply was immediate: "Business pays the bills. Showers generate no money."

Laurent offered only as much detail as he felt was needed; He briefed her on the Berlangier property, telling her it was near his home in Épiniac. He shared that a near-ideal situation existed with one vulnerable, middle-aged apple farmer who had turned a simple fruit-and-cider operation into a successful Calvados enterprise. He did not need to mention the personal animus. "He dies. It is sad, I agree. But an unfortunate accident."

"How so?"

"Your cousins—or whatever they are—must connect with my people. I would leave the exact details to them."

"Oh, yes. The details. The murder, you mean. You always leave such details to the others, do you not?" She told him to continue with what he had in mind. The accident. It would not be the first time he'd done something like that. His farmhouse, the property he occupied at that time, had come to him through similar, cold manipulation. As a well-placed cop, astute at finding and playing the middle of any argument, he had little to fear in terms of criminal charges. The local bandits would do his bidding when he agreed to look the other way from their misdeeds.

"Tell me more," she prompted.

"It's a matter of inheritance." The man has a son, he told her, who was too young to inherit, a mere child. Therefore, Jacques's sister would inherit, and she was a woman married to a drunken fool in Nantes.

Her husband would be easily deceived and removed from the equation. "First Berlangier. Then, we shall see."

"Oh? And what of the sister?" asked Sabrina. Would that be her job too? Roger said no, he would handle her. Somehow, he would find a way to manipulate her into giving him ownership.

"I see. And after? You will be spending more time in Nantes? Is that to be your alibi?"

"Perhaps." He would need to set some things in motion soon. There was no time to fiddle. Could Sabrina get her people to act quickly? They would work out the details among the clans; Laurent's hands would remain clean. Sabrina agreed, and he gave her the envelope he had carried in his pants pocket. Inside, the location was circled on a tear-out map.

"My people will do what they do." Sabrina looked at the map, more wary since she had gotten a sense of the dangers and likely difficulties. "Combourg? Of course. And, Roger, I will expect a generous contribution when the fox is through rearranging his den," she told him.

He agreed. That would not be a problem.

She lit a cigarette and said she would need a few days. Was the drunk from Nantes on board with the plan?

Roger said only that he'd been sufficiently briefed. As soon as the first blow was struck, he would have no choice but to be fully on board. "We take the decision out of his hands."

Sabrina took a long drag on her cigarette. "This kind of thing must be done with care and discretion. No one should be stepping out of his or her box prematurely. You understand that, of course?"

He did. But it irritated him to have to say so. After all, it was his show. Not hers. And no one would get hurt who did not need to.

"Now then," Sabrina said, trying to have the final word, "you had best put the cards into the deck, and in the right order."

Roger promised to do his best and looked at his watch. There would be plenty of time the next day to take care of their Combourg business.

CHAPTER 29

Leaning against the hood of his truck, the late August sun setting behind him, Jacques looked out over the expanse of the farm, his fruitful land. No doubt he had greatly enhanced what his father had left—what he'd worked so arduously to develop, defeating blights and scavenging animals and thwarting the unexplained, episodic vandalism. He'd kept at bay, during the long and tragic war, what darkness he could. Those orchards of his mother, his father, his late wife. His farm, at that point, with good help from friends, had prospered. The overfull, lightweight wooden baskets and canvas tarps beneath the taller trees spoke of another bountiful harvest.

Competing against older and better-established orchards of Brittany and nearby Normandy meant heavy speculation. More so, it meant risk. Speculation drove innovation, and that was their ticket. It also meant sizable capital expenditures, more so since they had expanded. Jacques had faced risk. What might it all come to mean ten years from then? Twenty? Jacques thought about Berlangier Orchards, the land and the business it generated. Young Eddie on his mind.

Business was doing better than he'd anticipated, Victor being even more involved in the farm's management than was his father's foreman and right-hand man, Chalfant. The brandy production business, which Jacques had licensed as Calvados Héritage, was showing profits. He could use a new truck, something bigger and more capable. One legal suit from an irate neighbor had come to nothing. But it had been a scare.

Turning to his boy, he saw Eddie standing behind the truck's steering wheel, maybe just to get his father's attention. A tall lad, big for three, he would be getting hungry. The part-time cook Gisèle had insisted Jacques bring in for suppers four nights a week was off that night. The thought of preparing dinner brought him to consider his darling Cleo, gone from him nearly two months ago, old age having finally taken her sweetness away. His heart ached for her. Jacques could not imagine bringing home another dog, yet he knew he should. He looked to the truck, where Eddie was still peering out, then turned back to the pickers. One of the field workers was watching him, which struck him as odd—she was a young-looking woman. He did not know any of the pickers. Once, he knew them all. Long ago. But his property had doubled in territory, so the number of workers had doubled. Too, the seasonal help tended to ignore their bosses, those Victor had jokingly spoken of as their social betters. The woman appeared not the least ill at ease that he had caught her staring. Who was she?

"*Salut*," he called to her, even before he'd considered the appropriateness of the greeting. A word that came to him as welcoming without any tone of familiarity. He added a hint of a wave. She'd been eyeing him, off and on, since he pulled up in the truck several minutes before. His duty, his attention to what they accomplished—their daily labors—meant he must be hands-on should any problems arise. To be present, to show himself, signaled a caring owner.

But what that woman in a large canvas hat with green scarf around her neck expected from him could not be known any more than one could peer down a narrow stone well and see to the bottom. Some realities must always be unclear, just out of reach, such as the soul-wrenching, pointless death of his darling Claire and the more recent, heart-breaking loss of his Cleo.

The woman turned back to her work, every now and again taking another look. She'd not acknowledged Jacques, which irritated him.

What was he to make of such insouciance? She returned to one long branch, nearly out of her reach. He saw her stop, climb down, pull off her broad hat to wipe the sweat from her forehead.

He turned away. Was she merely getting her bearings? Needing to determine what trees she had finished? She called out to another woman, nearby, something he could not make out. A foreign- sounding tone. Not French. Could she be Basque? Both stopped talking when it was clear they, too, were being scrutinized. *Well, we are all innately curious,* he thought. Still, her attention was unnerving. The second picker, an older-looking woman with a red bandanna, was filling a basket of her own. Several full containers lay nearby. They'd leave the harvest there, for the day, well-tarped, tight, and secure, awaiting Victor and his team on Monday. Victor had hired most of those people. Maybe he would know who the women were.

Jacques's contemplative mood was broken when Eddie found the truck's horn. Its sharp noise startled him, but the boy was delighted with himself. Jacques turned to the cab, climbed in, settled the boy next to him, started the vehicle, and pulled away. It was a simple joy that would soon be lost to the weighty years—sodden with purpose—that insist themselves, days that supplant all such innocence. Jacques could not help but think how Eddie's mother would have enjoyed that moment. He missed her terribly.

Driving back to the house, he slowed just past Victor's place, at one tricky spot in the road where heavy summer storms had taken out a bridge and repairs were maddeningly slow. Eddie was looking out his window, eyes fixed on something unseen by his father. A small animal, perhaps? Or something caught up in that troublesome roadside ditch?

Only days earlier, Jacques had driven the boy around the property. The first place he took him was to the tree where, not that many years ago, he had discovered Claire caught in a snare at its base, wet and mad as a hornet. The thought made him smile at such serendipity. Their Eddie would turn four that November. Jacques had shown the wide-eyed lad the newly added orchards, pointing out trees, the several apple varietals, the pyramid-shaped pears. The place where a blight had wiped out a large stand of trees—that section had needed to be cut back, treated, and replanted. Jacques did not expect Eddie to retain much of what was said. The tour was a way of sharing—father-and-son time. It was also a matter of pride, a show of love. Later, near the farmhouse, he walked Eddie around their burgeoning Calvados processing building. The boy took in the acrid smells of the place. The fermentation process yielded an added organic flavor to the building's air. Delighted, Eddie walked along, holding tightly to his father's hand, pointing to this and that, taking in what he might of the strange and marvelously complicated essence of the place.

Proud of his boy, Jacques could not help but wish there were grandparents, or even uncles and aunts, nearby to witness his vitality and joy. To know and love him as his father did. With Jacques's parents gone and his only sibling, Nina, estranged, he was given to think not of Claire's parents—an ocean away—but of her older sister and her caring husband, equally distant but emotionally connected. What would Maddie and Ott think of Eddie then? Ott, with that deep and honest laugh.

Returning home, Jacques set Eddie down for a nap and got himself cleaned up. He had agreed to an invitation to dinner from Victor. That night, helping Gisèle prepare a salad in the kitchen, Jacques told her, "I had the strangest encounter today, in one of our older groves,"

"How so? Wait! Jacques, before we get started, can you open that bottle, just there, on the counter?" Gisèle wiped her hands on her apron; she was busy by the stove. Jacques saw she had gestured to a local product, a hearty red. He cut the foil on the bottle with his folding pocketknife and located the corkscrew nearby. "I'll tell you over dinner," he said, pulling the cork and looking for any sign that the seal had not remained tight, spoiling the wine.

Owing to the fact that she was unexpectedly but happily seven months pregnant, Gisèle had declined any wine. Having already eaten, Eddie was playing in the parlor with Victor's gentle, giant Rottweiler, Gunther.

When the timing felt right, their casual banter behind them, Victor made reference to the daily harvesting and to which sections of trees needed attention. Such detail brought Jacques to return to what was on his own mind, what he had previewed to Gisèle. Both she and Victor could see their friend was troubled. In the telling, he gave only a general accounting of the women, two of them, who had, he thought, behaved strangely.

"You say the one was staring at you?" Victor asked.

"She was."

"In what way? Maybe she wanted to see what the boss looked like, up close," offered Gisèle, leaning into the conversation.

"No. This was different. Not idle curiosity. She was staring."

Victor, questioning the detail, asked, "Not just looking?"

"And in a way that struck you as odd?" Gisèle added, articulating the implied threat.

Jacques said that peculiar might be a better word.

"Fixated," he said. "I would have thought she'd turn away when I looked back and greeted her. That's the normal thing to do. A woman looks at you, and you do not know her, but you must acknowledge her. It is only courtesy. Is it not?"

Victor said he would look at the labor manifest and try to figure it out who it might have been, based on where she was working. "Should be easy enough, one dark-skinned woman speaking something not Breton French should narrow it down."

"I would say there were two."

"Yes, two. All right."

Gisèle asked the question Jacques had suppressed. Could her interest in Jacques have anything to do with Cleo's disappearance? "How many years ago was that?"

"Oh my God. I had not thought of that. But now that you mention it," Jacques said, "it could tie together. You are intuitive, Gisèle!" They both had heard the story of how Cleo had been taken, how Jacques had rescued her, up at a river camp north of Combourg.

"And she had been wounded, poor dog," added Victor, pushing back from the table as if, given the upshot of the strange situation, the obvious should have occurred to him before. "Are you thinking what I am thinking, Jacques?"

"*Merde.* These people are back. You can always tell the snake by its bite. And nothing around here will be the same, with these ravening animals to deal with."

"Easily hired, easily fired," said Victor, as if that would resolve the current question.

Jacques reached for his water glass and accidentally knocked over what little remained of his wine, irritated at himself for making a mess, clearly upset. Victor handed Jacques a kitchen rag to clean up the spill.

"Don't worry about it," Gisèle said. She left the table to check on the coffee, finding she had failed to turn on any lights in the parlor. There, next to Gunther, Eddie lay in his blue overalls and slightly too-large, wooly pullover, asleep on the dog's rug, the dog nuzzled next to him. Gunther was in a position of over-watch. Eddie had made a fast friend.

"Come look," she said.

Jacques saw that his boy was sleeping peacefully.

"It's eight-thirty now, Jacques," said Gisèle.

Victor came into the room, standing behind her, placing his hands on his wife's shoulders.

"He's worn out," said Jacques.

"Leave him here for the night. We can put him in the guest room and see to his needs. Come pick him up in the morning. Tomorrow is Sunday. I think you could use a good night's sleep just now."

Jacques said he thought that was a good idea. He'd come to count on Victor and Gisèle for their support and kindness, and especially for their help with Eddie. The child was clearly missing his beloved Cleo, and the spirited Gunther had, in some sense, stepped in. It was odd how such circumstances change, Jacques thought, one creature knowing how and when to show up in the life of another. "I should carry him in," Jacques said, picking up his child, while Gisèle went ahead to prepare the room. Eddie did not wake when Jacques kissed his forehead, though he felt for a fleeting moment that he wished he had. The boy would sleep comfortably at the Gaillard home. He would take him back to the farmhouse tomorrow.

Returning to his place minutes later, the new-moon night sky pitch black, rain picking up and pattering the windshield, Jacques could not help but think of his boy, at peace and asleep, as a kind of walking, talking crystal ball. He was like an open channel to Claire with her inquisitive eyes and sense of wonder. Jacques could not help but think of her even more as he listened to the music selection on his truck's radio, its refrain a much-told tale: *Plaisir d'amour, ne dure qu'un moment.* That truth was inescapable. The pleasure of love lasts only a moment. The pain of love taken lasts a lifetime. He held that thought a minute more, then reached to turn off the radio, making of it what he could. Heavy rain lashed the truck's windows. Approaching that torn and troublesome place in the road where Jacques had to deliberately slow and work his way around the broken macadam, he sensed the flash of a larger vehicle, its lights off, rushing at him hard from the tree line to his left. The enormous force of impact sent Jacques's truck flying into the jagged concrete abutment on the far side of the ditch. The upended, crushed truck's front wheels were spinning. The dying engine pinged, as if trying, against all odds, to recover. The other vehicle backed away and rushed off, something falling out of its back end.

No more than ten minutes later, the rains intensifying—relentless against the windshield—the ditch filling with water, flooding the vehicle, a familiar vehicle pulled up fast next to Jacques's truck. The driver raced to the overturned vehicle. The man could see, though barely, that Jacques had been thrown to the passenger side; the truck lying on its side. Jacques lay unconscious in the pooling water, his head covered with blood.

Fabien had to get him out. Immediately. How to do so would be the trick. There was no way to pull the truck out or even to right it onto its wheels. The ditch was too deep and sharply cut. More and more water threatened. Fabien hurried to his own truck, grabbing a stout rope and old leather jacket. If he could get his injured friend conscious and reposition him, maybe he could pull him out and secure him against further trauma. He carefully bound Jacques's head and shoulders using the materials at hand, getting him almost upright, the injured man's body affixed to the steering wheel. It would have been easier for a rescue team to get him out safely, but Fabien was the only person there. No doubt there had been a good deal of blood loss. Jacques's situation was perilous, and water was pooling fast. Time was not on his side.

CHAPTER 30

Henri arrived home moments before seven in an agitated, unsettled mood. Was dinner ready, he asked? He embraced Nina, albeit half-heartedly. She had been waiting for his news. Henri was hungry; he could use a drink.

"Well?"

"I have some news." He beamed. As was his habit, he put the best face he could on the improbable story. Yes, he had been asked to play a few selections for one important club owner. Yes, the man was impressed with Henri's skill, what he called his gift.

"You did not try to sing, did you?" she joked, finding, and sharing, the surprisingly improved mood.

"Maybe a little," he said, rising slightly on the toes of his worn shoes, enjoying the small laugh at his own expense. "I did what I set out to do," he assured her. As soon as the man could find a place, he would hire him. "Just a few matters to attend to." The club would be an ideal fit. He could feel it. The owner and he had connected. That was the important thing.

"He is interested in you?" she asked.

Nothing for certain. He could be.

"I see. But nothing firm?" she insisted, irritating him.

"Firm? No. There was someone in the job now," he said. As if that were a small concern. "Should someone get sick or become unable to perform…"

"I see." She gave that clarification some further thought, realizing that there was actually nothing for him. Nothing. "You tried other places? How many clubs did you inquire with?"

Those were not the kinds of questions and problems Henri wanted to dwell on. Then there was the business with the clever fellow he'd met en route, M. Laurent. Should he bring up that discussion? Not just then. He'd have to think about that. Those were troublesome ideas.

"Because if you do get something firm, Henri, I will be ready to go. I promise you that. We shall leave Nantes and try it again in Paris. Somehow. Some way. We put all the disappointment behind us." She intimated, as well, that her job was wearing her out. She seemed agitated but still on something of a high from Henri's generally positive experience with the Joséphine.

Henri managed to take all that as affirmation. "Fix me a drink, will you?" Henri took the proffered brandy and soda as his due. Then, having picked up on Nina's vibes about work, he asked, "Is there something or someone bothering you at the Marguerite?"

"Bothering me?" How did he not know how on edge she'd been for months? Best to say it directly. "I just need a change."

"We both do," he said, taking a large pull on the drink she'd handed him. Henri had to decide how much, if anything, to say about the Laurent conversation. His proposition was not something that should ever leave that room, certainly. There could be problems with the implicit plan, but maybe not. After all, the man was a well-placed police officer. A captain. Would he not be able to manage any awkwardness? Henri fingered the fellow's business card in his pocket, felt an urge to say something about it to Nina. Come to that, he was not certain how they'd left things. Having it both ways. It seemed that even if Henri were not involved, he would be complicit nonetheless because of his ambivalence. He decided to try not to worry. Roger Laurent knew what he was doing.

After their meal, Henri heavily into the wine and feeling the need to assure the woman he loved of his worth and personal charm, he could hold back no longer. He wiped his hands on his napkin and began the story. "Nina, I must tell you. I met a man on the train to Paris." An important contact, he told her. A man of influence. A man with ideas about improving situations financially and, at the same time, leveling the score with Nina's hotshot brother. "He can make good things happen for us."

"For us? What do you mean, good things? I do not understand."

"I will explain. Now, listen." He poured another glass. Skittish as a cat on ice. "Because while I may have to wait for any real piano job to come through, there could be even bigger things ahead for us if we want to put into play something that would make our fortunes and set us up for real success." As soon as he said it, he knew he'd have to be careful about how he presented the idea. He would try not to seem like the engineer of the plot. He set the glass down.

She asked what he meant by bigger things.

"Just wait. I have to think. We have choices." He looked to see whether he was getting through. "Still," he continued, eyes cast down, "there could be trouble."

"What are you saying? Henri? What choices? I do not know when I have seen you so nervous. What trouble? What are you thinking? Just tell me."

Something had to be done. He knew that. Yet, the more he circled the idea, the more he wished he had just kept quiet about it. Yes, he agreed, he was troubled. He hated the idea that he had perhaps reached the pinnacle of his career—short and disappointing as it may have been. He had to act. Decide. There was nothing more he could do there, in Nantes, was there? "There is another way."

"What about the club job in Paris?"

"Stop interrupting! I am trying to tell you something. It concerns your brother's place. The apple farm." He knew the alcohol was affecting him, and, with a shaky hand, he pushed the glass away.

Her voice deliberately quiet, Nina asked what he meant. How did any business about Jacques get into the equation? Irritated, her husband shook his head. He was getting to that. He'd come to realize they could do something different. A reinventing of themselves, as he put it. Why could they not make a success at running an apple farm?

"What? Do you mean—the Berlangier farm? Why? How?" She gripped the edge of table.

Henri asked why not? They could do that. Then, he added he was not opposed to having an unlimited supply of apple brandy at hand, thinking it would be taken as a joke.

"You are scaring me." She sat bolt upright.

"*Listen!* We could be owners. Have people working for us," he attempted. "Well, the farm would go to you, but we would be in charge. Together."

"I do not understand you," she said, fiercely, trying to control her voice. "My God, you look awful, Henri. You are making no sense. The farm belongs to Jacques!"

"I am making sense," he said more loudly. "We are on the edge of something new and exciting for us. You and me. . ." Then, "A simple accident."

"An accident?" Nina's anger reddened her cheeks.

"I think we have a kind of agreement, this man on the train and I. The plan has its dangers. But it's an arrangement that changes everything for us." He wiped at his mouth.

She took a sharp breath. "What arrangements? This person on the train? Henri, I demand you tell me everything. Now!"

Henri looked hard at her. Was she deaf? What had Jacques ever done for her, or for them? The Joséphine was a fantasy. He saw that. He needed a jeweled career as a musician less than he wanted stability. He told her all he needed was one fortunate turn of the wheel. Nina sat opposite him, shaking—she who had given him the necessary travel money.

She took a deep breath. "This makes no sense. What are you saying? TELL ME!"

"It does. It's perfect, and this police captain has a way of getting it for us. Do you understand?" He stopped then and became quiet, waiting for Nina to say something, to ask what, exactly, he had done. Just what was in it for the Laurent fellow was never said, but Henri understood intuitively that the plan constituted some kind of personal retribution. Just why was not important. Laurent knew what was what. Maybe he would want a cut of the profits. Well, that would not be a problem. Like revenge, justice is pliable. Laurent had people to take care of the difficult work. That was the word he used. Difficult. Laurent knew what he was doing.

Nina stood from the table in a state of near shock. "Henri, what did you do? For heaven's sake. If it is something dangerous, you must trust me to help you."

He looked at her, gathering the words, and told her what he and the police captain had agreed to do. It was already a plan set in motion. Too late to stop it.

"This man on the train. Roger Laurent. He knows your brother. He knows Jacques. Understands what we need. What has to be done."

Nina turned white in shocked disbelief and put her hand to her mouth, so as to stifle a scream.

"If and when Jacques is gone," Henri said, "we get it all."

CHAPTER 31

Nina rushed to the phone and rang Emma, frantic.

When the two had been in touch, it was nearly always spontaneous. A "Just thought I would look in on you!" kind of thing. Holidays. Birthdays. Still, for Nina, just knowing she could reach out to her friend should the need arise meant her brother was not gone entirely from her life. Maybe he was only sequestered where the hurt, the disappointments, and the sadness of her self-imposed separation could be contained.

"Emma! Listen. My God, someone is going to kill my brother. Please help!" she screamed. "Tell Fabien he has to do something. Please. Now! He must help Jacques."

"Nina, I cannot understand you. What do you mean?" Emma urged, taking in the sheer urgency of the moment. Nina repeated that Jacques's life was in immediate danger. Thus alerted, Emma, who was reading the paper on the couch waved Fabian over. "It's Jacques!"

"Just send him. Now! Please, Emma. Go to the farm. There is no time to explain." Emma wanted to ask what had happened, but knew time was the only important consideration.

"Yes. Yes, of course. He will go now. He is leaving for the farm now."

The next morning, Fabien drove to the hospital in Rennes where Jacques had been brought the night before, moved from the overmatched clinic in town. The local medical team had stabilized him; their work was nothing but heroic, given what they had to work with, but the small facility in Combourg was not equipped to handle such trauma.

Jacques lay elevated on the bed, his chest and head heavily bandaged, both eyes dark and puffy, his left arm in a fat plaster cast. His breathing was nearly regular again. Fabien looked into the single room to see whether his friend was asleep. Jacques was struggling to reach across his body for his elusive water glass.

"Well, look who is awake. You plan to take some time off from work, do you?"

Jacques stifled a laugh. One that would hurt his ribs were he to let it come. "*Merde*."

"You look comfortable enough," Fabien added, seeing his friend break into that familiar grin of his.

"If you are trying to make me laugh, it's not working."

Fabien found the water glass on the bedside tray and handed it to his friend. "You should see yourself," he told him, waiting for Jacques to take a sip of the water. Then, he held it for him in case he wanted more.

"It's a good thing I cannot. I must look like Boris Karloff in one of his *Mummy* appearances."

Fabien said that, actually, he did, but with more realism. Fabien took in the respirator behind the bed, no longer connected, and saw the IV drip taped to his friend's hand. The air smelled vaguely antiseptic. Jacques adjusted his position in the bed, wanting to get himself more upright, but the oversize pillow he was resting on was too large for him to manage.

"Can I help? Do you need anything?"

"Maybe you can help me sit up so I can take another sip of that lukewarm water. What the hell happened?" Jacques asked.

Fabien could tell from Jacques's tone his friend was hurting and probably still drugged from medication. "You got hit by a truck, one bigger and meaner than yours."

"I remember that much."

"You were unconscious when I found you in a ditch; you'd been driving back from Victor's. He was here a while ago, but you were still out. Gisèle has Eddie with her, at home."

"My God. Eddie."

"The boy is fine. You had left him, after supper, with the Gaillards. Thank God. So, no problem there."

"An accident. What if I had had him with me? My boy." Jacques asked, catching a breath, coming to the reality of the wreck from another, more dire direction.

"That would have been bad. No way to know how bad. And I do not think it was any accident."

"No. Well, I do not remember much. I was driving home."

"And someone decided they did not want you to get there." Fabien related what he knew, which was not much. "Emma took a frantic call from Nina." When he came upon the scene, he said, Jacques's truck had been smashed and driven into a cement culvert; it had been flipped on its side, water building up in the cab. Fabien told him how he'd managed to pull him out. Jacques knew his friend lived nowhere nearby.

"Nina? My sister called? How?" He was struggling to make the pieces fit. "Deliberate, you say? Someone was trying to kill me?"

"Evidently so."

"I cannot think straight yet, Fabien. But who?" He then asked, "What did my sister do?"

"She called Emma. She saved you, my friend."

"I do not understand." His head had begun to ache. His meds were losing their strength.

Fabien told him the two women, friends from childhood, as Jacques knew, had stayed loosely in touch for years. "But whatever prompted her to make such a call," he said, "I have no idea." Fabien shook his head. "There's more." He told him he and Victor had gone back to the scene of the incident early that morning. There, Victor discovered an animal crate by the side of the road, thirty meters or so from the scene.

"A crate? Like to pen animals for transport?" asked Jacques, becoming alert to the implications.

"Yes. Probably pigs, maybe goats. Small animals. It must have fallen out of the back of the truck that smashed into you."

"I know who it was," Jacques said, staring at his friend. "But why would these people be after me again, and motivated enough to kill?" And how would their desperate measures have come to the attention of his sister, in Nantes?

Fabien shook his head.

"But my sister is the key here. This is a mystery worthy of any good detective writer," Jacques said, thinking out loud. "When I am able to do so, I'll find out what happened. And why."

A doctor walked into the room, followed by a nurse pushing a small metal cart with some diagnostic instruments, several wires, and couplings; Jacques recognized it as an EKG machine.

Jacques struggled again to sit up as they entered.

"Good afternoon, Monsieur Berlangier. I am Doctor Mosel. Ernst Mosel." The nurse smiled and put a blood pressure cuff on Jacques, going about her business. Jacques smiled at her and looked at the lean, white-haired man.

"You gave us quite a scare last night."

Jacques asked whether he had been the one who attended to him.

"No," the physician said. "That was the emergency team. In Combourg. They brought you to us by ambulance. An orthopedic surgeon set your arm. But I will be taking care of your health and recovery now." Dr. Mosel explained that he was a heart specialist. He asked Fabien, standing near the bed, whether he was related to the patient. Fabien said no. Jacques said his closest family was his young son, who was not yet four.

Mosel had the nurse attach the precordial leads to the machine. The young woman, wearing a Christian cross on her lapel, was all business.

"I ask only because someone will have to follow up with you. Regularly. Make certain you do not do anything to put undue stress on your heart for at least four weeks. I am serious about this."

"Four weeks?" asked Jacques, wanting to shake the remaining wool from his head.

"In the accident, your aorta experienced some trauma. Your rib cage was seriously damaged. It is possible that one broken rib nicked the outer wall. We will know better after X-rays. This is what we suspect to be a myocardial contusion. We will want to surgically repair any damage if the need is indicated," said Mosel.

The nurse whispered something to the doctor, who was watching the machine's needle jump and settle.

Jacques asked when they would know something definitive. He had to make clear that he had a little boy at home who needed him. He would get whatever treatment he absolutely had to have and then, maybe, get back for further diagnosis. He emphasized the *maybe*. Fabien was listening closely to all that.

The nurse asked the boy's name. "Eduard. Eddie."

"Well, we have an arrhythmia I do not like, Monsieur," said the physician.

"We do?"

"You do. An electrical anomaly. These reactions can be stress-related. Not unusual in cases of such blunt-force trauma. And you lost a good deal of blood. We must stabilize you. You need bed rest," Mosel told him in a tone that said he would brook no argument.

"I understand, Doctor. But I have matters to attend to, and my boy comes first." Saying this, Jacques looked to the nurse, who was removing the twelve leads from his chest.

"You can leave Eddie with the Gaillards for a few days, Jacques, no?" asked Fabien. "He is there now, of course. They will take good care of the boy."

The doctor gave no ground. "X-rays tomorrow, Monsieur Berlangier. Several of them. We will get better readings then. And the orthopedic people will be tending to your rib fractures. There may be more procedures needed. I suspect the broken arm will heal nicely. We will keep an eye on you for a few days. Now, you must rest. Leave your care to us."

A casually dressed woman in a worn green coat stepped around the corner just then and peered into Jacques's room, maybe with a question. Wide-eyed. Jacques thought she might be another nurse, or someone lost. Attractive, and with a most determined look. Searching for someone—then she was gone. It was not so much an interruption as an anomaly that must occur in all hospitals, nothing for Jacques to think about.

Jacques attempted, with no success, to sit up somewhat straighter. He asked about the prospects for surgery. "Can I have a couple of aspirin?"

Mosel nodded to the nurse, who made a note. "Of course. And X-rays will tell the tale." Jacques took everything in. It was out of his hands. Maybe he would know more the next day. Meanwhile, Jacques was feeling sleepy. Perhaps it was the residual effects of the drugs he'd had just after midnight. Doctor Mosel said he would be back to examine him later that afternoon. He told Jacques to rest. The nurse wheeled the cart back into the hall.

"How long?" Jacques asked the doctor.

"A few days. Four, maybe. The tests will tell us more."

Fabien put his hand on Jacques's shoulder; he would see to everything, and he would look in on Eddie at Victor's house.

Jacques said yes; the need for caution was evident. He asked to have Eddie come see him tomorrow. Please. Fabien said he'd speak with Gisèle. Reassured, Jacques smiled and drifted off to sleep. Mosel made another note on the man's chart and nodded to Fabien.

"His hand feels somewhat cold to me, doctor. Is it supposed to feel like that?"

"Yes. Maybe for a few more hours," said the doctor. "His heart is doing what it can to recover. This man is lucky to be alive."

CHAPTER 32

"How long until I get this cast off?" Jacques asked the discharge nurse, a spindly, no-nonsense woman who had wheeled him out the double doors and into the warm autumn sun. He spotted several larks chasing one another in the shimmering sky, playing at something elemental. Those four long days in a hospital bed, he told her, had felt like months. "I have work to do."

"I've heard it before," she said. "Nothing strenuous for several weeks."

"The cast is beginning to itch. Maybe sooner?"

She gave him a look—part reproach, part good humor: "You know the answer to that."

Fabien had gone ahead to bring his truck around to the front doors. The doctor had said four or five weeks. Then they would see.

"You must take it easy. Go slow for several days. *Doucement, Monsieur,*" she told him and offered him an impatient smile.

Jacques spotted Fabien's dark-green truck coming around the lot. With not a little awkwardness, he tried to stand, addressing the woman helping him by name; she was solid behind his chair. "Marie, I do not do slow very well."

"You must not try to hurry the healing," she said, indicating the chest. "The heart has work to do as well. Everything else must wait."

Fabien pulled up, leaving the engine running, waiting for an elderly couple to enter the hospital ahead of him, the woman's arm around the small of her disheveled husband's thin back, each in search of his or her own tender mercies.

"Slowly," the nurse said to Fabien.

He nodded and looked at Jacques, who was trying to push himself up from the awkward chair.

Fabien parked as close as he could to the doors, and, once the couple had cleared the entry, he helped Jacques to the passenger door. The nurse wished him a quick recovery, waved, and returned to her duties. Fabien asked, "When do you come back for another look?"

He had an appointment in two weeks. "But I can hardly drive myself from Combourg with one arm, and I can't continue to impose on you." Jacques attempted to get comfortable, moving a few of Fabien's things from the seat to the floorboard, including a holstered Modèle automatic. "Where did you get this?" he asked.

"It belongs to Paul, but he told me to bring it to you."

"Um. Looks like my own gun, Fabien. You keep it. Or give it back to Paul. If those bastards come for me again, I'll want to have more than a handgun at my side," He looked at it again, maybe reconsidering. He pulled it from the smooth leather holster. "Nice feel to it. Smells clean. Have you fired it?"

Fabien said he had. Just to get the feel. "You never know when you might need one of these." Then, "Listen to me. You just let me know when you need a ride. And it is not an imposition. Or Paul could help." Fabien thought a moment, then added, "Emma can watch the store for a few hours. No problem." The Brun family, Jacques knew, had never shirked what responsibility one gave them. Paul Brun, two years younger than Fabien, and perhaps underappreciated, had been a trusted and worthy partisan, another man to count on when help was required.

Still sore and not a little discouraged at his near incapacitation, Jacques said, "You know, I've had to leave everything to Victor. And Gisèle is taking care of Eddie." Fabien knew Jacques was not used to others taking care of him, not since Claire had died four years ago. Moments later, Jacques added, "And I worry about my boy."

"I know you do. Listen, I've been thinking. You should speak with Emma about what she knows from Nina. What she learned, and how."

"I agree." Jacques decided to consider all that an opening, a second chance. He'd lost a lot of sleep over Nina. For years and years, his sister had been absent in his life. Who was he to fail to forgive?

Fabien said he understood the confusion his friend must be experiencing. "What about this evening? Come over and talk." Jacques regretted what had been lost—all the distrust and attendant acrimony. Not least, he would have to piece together in his mind what had happened and why. Nina was a wound he had tried and tried to ignore. Was there a way back? A way ahead?

"You are right," he said, so softly Fabien was unsure he had said anything. Traffic was light as they made their way north, Jacques in another time and place, deep into another conflict of the heart.

"Come to dinner. See what Emma has to say. After all, you cannot do much cooking for Eddie and yourself in your condition."

"First, I have to relieve Gisèle of Eddie's constant care. Can we swing by their place and let me get my boy? Then maybe you could bring us both home?"

"Let me take you home now. We can pick up Eddie and bring you both to our house later. Give you a chance to think. And rest."

Jacques said he thought that made sense.

Fabien then asked how long it had been since Jacques had seen his sister. Jacques looked out at the fields, the vastness of them. A train was speeding the other way, the rails close to the road. Just a blur. He watched a lean young lad on a tractor. Always work to be done in late summer.

"She disappeared not long after our mother died. Nina left all of it, left me. Not that she would have cared much for apple farming." Jacques added that she had gone off with some character she'd met in an art class she was taking up in Saint-Malo. He got her pregnant. "I tried to reconnect, but she was disinterested. They got married, I think. But it evidently didn't last. She's had a rough time."

Fabien lit a cigarette. He figured it best to let Jacques work through the natural resistance to even talking about such matters. Fabien had no sisters. He and his brothers got on well. They were earnest men taking care of everyday chores. One day was much the same as the one before, more so since the Germans were gone.

Jacques broke the silence. "Nina always kept her thoughts pretty much to herself. Even as a teen." He paused to consider what was, perhaps, her understandable need for privacy. "But I was her brother, for God's sake. I wanted to know how she was doing. Something happened to harden her heart, Fabien. Whatever it was, she was not looking for any help from me."

Gauging what could be said and what should not, Fabien tried, "I am sorry for all that, Jacques." He slowed to take the turn onto the D157. Traffic heading north was picking up. "So, I will bring you home and come back at about seven to take you and Eddie to our place. Yes? We'll have a nice dinner. Home by nine, so Eddie can sleep in his own bed. How does that sound?" Jacques said it would be grand, the best offer he'd had for a long time.

The two remained mostly quiet for the remainder of the drive, both sensing something significant was about to happen. By the time they reached the short gravel drive that would bring them to the Berlangier farmhouse, the skies had darkened. Seeing his crushed truck off to the side of the barn, the vehicle in ruins, Jacques considered making himself a drink, but then he thought better of it. He'd have a hot tea instead. One of the first things he must do, and soon, would be to get that truck replaced. He would have to speak with the insurance people. Then there was the larger, more awkward problem of how to breach the chasm between Nina and him. It was she who had made the crucial first move, an act of courage that no doubt saved his life. Jacques walked over to the mantel and looked at the family photo. How many years had it been since he'd seen Nina? How does any man address that kind of familial sprain, aching in him for well over half his life?

Outside, the brutality of the storm lashing the windows reminded him of the night of the crash, of the truck from nowhere striking his and the fury of it all. It reminded him of his brush with death. That night, he resolved to begin the long road to discovering the truth. The who. The why. And beyond that would be another kind of healing.

Emma greeted Jacques with a ready smile as he entered the house. Still, she kept a distance. "Would you like a drink?" She told Fabien dinner was nearly ready. Jacques said he'd take a glass of red.

Jacques knew and liked the formidable Emma Brun, though they'd never had much to say one to each other. Emma respected her husband's friendships and the work the men did in the war. Had Claire been in the picture, the prospects of the two couples becoming fast friends would have been different. While nothing had ever been said to suggest it, Jacques suspected that maybe her closeness to Nina would have colored her thinking about him.

She handed him a glass of Rhône—a Saint-Gervais, one of his favorites—then said, "Please know that you can count on us to help. And for any help we can offer you in reaching Nina to help you to get to the bottom of this horrible attack."

Jacques leaned toward her, keen to hear what she knew. "Fabien is strong," she continued. "He will help when you need him." He thanked her. Emma's short, dark-blonde hair favored her stocky frame, her own strength evident in her voice. She'd been the vital connection in his rescue. Next, he wanted to understand how Nina was involved. Then, he hoped to discover the identity of his assailants and how those people came into the picture yet again, like some biblical curse. Jacques understood, too, that he and Fabien would soon be making battle plans. But not just then.

Following dinner, Eddie was once again content and playing with the Brun's lazy, outsized cat in the parlor. The conversation turned, as it had to, to the real reason for the evening's get-together. Emma had expected Jacques might bring it up, but Fabien had asked his friend to hold off until they had finished the meal. Emma had been solicitous of Jacques's health. There were plenty of things to discuss without going into the history of the Berlangier family estrangement. The first step in any detective work lay immediately ahead. Fabien went into the kitchen and brought a pot of coffee to the table. Jacques thanked Emma for a delicious meal and added his profound gratitude to the woman for taking the panicked call from Nina.

"Do you remember whether she said anything about how she knew there would be an attempt to kill me? Any names?" He turned to Fabien, including him in the question.

"Only that I must tell Fabien to go now—immediately, Nina said—to find you. She was frantic. Someone wanted you dead, but she did not say how or why she knew."

Fabien offered his opinion: Knowledge of the attack had to have come to her from a source she would take as reliable. "The panic in her voice, from what Emma said, meant Nina knew the source of the intelligence." Maybe it had been her husband?

Jacques said he thought so too.

"But how would her husband come into this? How and why would he know of the murderous plan?" added Fabien. "No one having seen the truck can think it was an accident. And the animal pen you found by the road means one thing."

"Damn. My prior encounter with the bastards who took my Cleo." He looked to Emma. "So, Nina's husband would have to be in the know—maybe complicit," Jacques said.

"It only makes sense that she got the information from Henri," Emma added reluctantly, breaching an implicit line of trust. "I had promised Nina I would avoid bringing Henri to your attention, Jacques. She was insistent about that."

"Why? It is so obvious."

"She knew you would not approve."

Jacques asked Emma whether she had ever seen him. Fabien had let it slip once, a few years ago, about the boozing, having heard Emma commiserating by phone with Nina.

Emma said no. She'd not actually seen Nina for two years. They called each other occasionally. "Now and again, a letter. A lifeline. She called to ask about you when Claire died," Emma told him, her voice going exceptionally soft. "I had written to her."

"She did? You did? I didn't know," Jacques said, astonished.

He looked at Fabien as if he might have withheld that information. "This is the first I have heard."

Emma returned to the matter of the panicked phone call. She said Nina had sounded more upset than she'd ever heard her, except, of course, for the accidental death of her baby over twenty years ago. Little Mathis. In Saint-Malo.

"*What?*" Jacques's face went white. "The death of her baby?

How could that be? When?"

Emma said that Nina had lost a baby less than a year after her marriage to the man she'd met in her art study. She told Jacques about the disappearing husband, noted that the child was not two months old when he passed.

"That was over twenty years ago. She'd lost a child? Mathis, you say? My God. My father's name." Jacques had a revelation. He took a deep breath. "How?"

He only knew she had ceased all contact, not why. He knew she had been divorced and, some years later, remarried. He'd gotten that much. Emma said she had never been sure whether Jacques knew about the child. The baby had died when Nina stumbled and fell, tripping on the cord of her robe while holding the infant. It had been a horrible accident. She fractured her wrist. Her injures could have been far worse.

"What? I don't understand."

"I never got the whole picture. She fell—they did—down a flight of stairs. Late at night. After nursing him. Her tiny one. Nina blamed herself, of course."

"Jesus. I had no idea." Jacques shook his head. "I think I better understand now why she shut down all contact." The silence, he surmised, had been to shield her from shame. But it was just a horrible accident. The other night, Nina had done the brave thing, the right thing. She had called Emma to get Fabien to act.

"I have no choice but to meet her. It's been so long. I must admit I've been unhappy with this imposed silence. It only begins to make some degree of sense now. I want to see my sister, whether she wants to see me or not."

"Saint-Malo is where Eddie was born and where Claire died," Jacques said. "And Nina's baby is dead? Good God, I do not know what to make of that. Or what to think of my sister."

"Well, she made the first move when she decided to help. She must feel something for you," said Emma, looking to her husband, then to Jacques.

Fabien said he agreed.

Jacques pushed back his chair. He had suspected that moment would come, had anticipated the need to decide how to think about Nina, realizing that to see the world—his world—as so many rights and wrongs, goods and bads, blacks and whites, was to miss the many essential complex and relentless grays. And then there was the death of her child, which he could not get out of his head.

"Can you set it up, Emma? I mean, I do not even know how to reach her."

Fabien was taking in the delicate and unfamiliar place his friend and his wife unexpectedly shared. Even so, Emma looked again to Fabien, who, taking a moment, could not help but give a nod that said, *Why not*?

"She is in Nantes."

"Yes." Jacques said he thought it best she not phone Nina. "She might not want to see me. There's no time to believe in miracles. Better I just show up."

Having made her part as clear as she could, Emma spoke more softly when she replied to Jacques's observation about the expectation of miracles. "No. It is a common response, or more accurately a common reaction, to want divine intervention when we find ourselves most vulnerable. I would think most of us do. It's called faith. I will get that address for you."

CHAPTER 33

With he and his remarkable, inquisitive young son resituated back home, Jacques was in an agreeable—if anxious—mood. He'd faired reasonably well with his right arm, which was out of that uncomfortable full cast. His ribs were healing too. The X-rays showed no evident serious damage. No further surgery was indicated.

That day, he'd find his sister. With Gisèle coming to the house to watch the boy, Jacques would travel down to Nantes. What he could not be certain of was when and where Nina worked or what her hours were. He had her home address and knew she had a hotel job in town. Jacques consulted an old map. Nantes was a good-sized city. What startled him was that the map he saw had been Claire's. Her initials were in one corner. Her marginal notes in green ink were distinctive.

Moments after Jacques put the map away, the Gaillards arrived. Victor dropped his wife at the Berlangier farm and then drove Jacques to the station to catch the morning train. The required change in Rennes would mean waiting about an hour for the connection, but that was hardly a problem. The schedule worked well, getting him into Nantes near noon.

He'd assumed Nina had a full-time job, given how evidently unreliable the husband was. It was doubtful he'd find her at home. If she worked nights, maybe. So, he'd locate her place of work. Boulevard Robert Schumann looked to be a likely street for hotels. Within half an hour, he had come upon Nina's apartment building. Emma, of course, had had the address. Two doors down the street, in the direction of the river, he spotted a café. There, he would make his first inquiries, doing so as discreetly as possible, getting the necessary fiction straight in his mind.

He asked one young woman working the uncrowded bar whether she could recommend a good hotel. His plan was to locate a decent establishment, one that would be expected to employ a large staff and drop Nina's name. He'd look for something within walking distance of her flat. He'd get a feel for what could be said and what could not, based on the reception he got.

"Not too pricey," he told her. "Not cheap." A place he might inquire about work, in that he had once managed a small place and worked with customers, but the war had called, and so things were different. Perhaps she had an idea.

Jacques had chosen well, finding someone who met and served all kinds of people all day long. The woman accompanied him outside and pointed north. Past several sidewalk tables. The colorful rush of busy people, people making a life.

"There are several nice hotels," she said, "just that way." She pointed again. *"Bon chance, Monsieur."*

The first one he tried was an old, once-aristocratic kind of place, the name in bold, Roman-style lettering above double glass doors and, within, a renovated grand lobby. The front desk kept two young women busy. Both were attractive, and both were engaged with customers, or would-be customers, which Jacques took as a good sign. Nina would find employment with just such a hotel—a place she felt comfortable—in whatever capacity she might have taken a position. With her native intelligence, she could well be in management. He had no way to know. Finding the desk clerks busy, Jacques walked across the tiled lobby to the concierge, who was seated behind a modest, hardwood desk. He, in another world as he adjusted his dark green suspenders, was startled when Jacques approached.

"*Bonjour.*"

Did the gentleman know the name Nina d'Ancel? "I was told I might find her here."

"Yes? Why do you ask?" the concierge replied, raising his eyebrows. Not so much a challenge as an impetuous curiosity. Or did the old fellow suspect the inquiry was one to portend trouble?

Jacques had his story ready. "Pardon the interruption, Monsieur. I am her brother. This is the last address I have for her." He added that is sister had remained in Nantes after the war, proud Nantes, center of resistance to the Nazi menace. Nina had been there to care for an elderly aunt, who was gone. There had been misunderstandings. Sadly, they were out of touch. Finessing the matter of where he lived, Jacques wanted to make the story realistic, his quest a sympathetic one.

"Yes," the old fellow managed. "Families are given to such troubles." Nina d'Ancel, he said, once again agitating his suspenders, had worked there—maybe some nine or ten months ago. Last fall. Maybe October. "Try the Marguerite."

Jacques thanked the man and made to leave, but the old gent was not quite finished. After all, he had a job to do too. "Can I interest you in tickets to our Musée des Beaux Arts?" Jacques understood he had to demonstrate some polite interest, even if the city's premier museum was far down his list of things to do on that brief stay.

"They have an Egyptian collection. Just this month. Nefertiti, you know. Not to be missed. Very reasonable."

Jacques said his time was short but that he appreciated the offer. He reached into his pocket and gave the man ten francs. Probably about what his commission would have been.

The concierge thanked Jacques and said, as he turned away once again, "Please greet our little Nina for me. And maybe bring her some flowers, like a good brother."

So, Nina's cares were known even to her former work associates. *What next?* he thought, walking out the front doors, finding a taxi pulling up to discharge a young couple. They had what sounded like American accents. "Hotel Marguerite?" Jacques asked.

"You want to go?"

"No, I need the exercise. I can walk."

"Rue Gambetta," he said, pointing generally northeast. "Next to the Botanical Garden."

Jacques thanked him and crossed the street. He figured it could not be far. After all, he was in the city center. Most of the nicer hotels would be located within a kilometer or so. But what then? He could not just walk up to her. Big surprise! Maybe he should phone. Emma had given him the home number. No doubt Nina had more to tell him but could have been loath to share it. Jacques had given serious thought to what he would say. They were actors in the same play, but with different stage direction. Maybe he would have been smart to let Emma take the initiative and just tell her friend that Jacques wanted to see her. He had to thank her. He had questions. But no; that could have backfired. He had no choice but to follow his instinct. Still, he could not be found spying on her—lying in wait at her place of work, thereby frightening her away.

His watch showed the time: just past one. If he expected a sign, he would have to look closer. Contacting an estranged sister was never going to be easy. Claire would understand what to do. She had always had that gift. Instantly, Jacques knew how to lay out his case. His son needed to know he had an aunt—a brave woman who had stepped up and saved his father's life. On behalf of his boy, he had to come find her and put things right.

Walking toward the Marguerite, taking in the sights and smells of the old city and its rich and complex history, he came upon another attractive café, its five or six raised umbrellas. There were tables inside and out. Maybe he could ask to take her to dinner there. Nina probably did not have the opportunity to dine out. Too busy? Too harried? And what about her husband? No, he had to meet with Nina alone. That was the best option. He would figure out the best time to reach her and the way to do so.

Walking on, scooting past a woman pushing a stroller, he spotted the hotel, just across the street and up a block. Two flags of France flew from the top of the tall building, the clever, colorful red, green, and yellow flag of the city just below. And a doorman. Maybe that was the way to play it. He would inquire as unobtrusively as he could, leave word. But with whom? Reception? He could ask that Nina find him there, maybe in the lounge after work. No plan would ever be perfect. He'd brought only the bare necessities in his satchel: minimum toiletries, a book, a change of underwear, and one fresh shirt. Entering the hotel, Jacques decided to take a seat in the lobby and do some people-watching. He would recognize a viable opening when one presented itself. Momentarily, he approached the reception desk.

"Excuse me. I am supposed to meet someone here. I fear I am running late. May I have a piece of hotel stationery?" He was not lying. The man was accommodating his need to the uncertain reality.

"Of course, Monsieur," the man said, handing Jacques a sheet of cream-colored letterhead paper. "I am Lucien, the assistant manager. Please let me know if I may be of any further assistance." He offered a short, somewhat officious nod and a perfunctory smile. Jacques accepted the paper, asked for an envelope, and considered whether Lucien was the person to leave the note with. Maybe. He would take some time to look around, discern mannerisms. Lucien might have been the man to help.

Returning to the generously appointed lobby, Jacques took a seat near a potted Ficus tree and looked around for a moment. Would he even recognize Nina? With a magazine on his lap to stabilize the paper, he wrote: "Nina, please meet me. I am in the city today. Sorry for the long-lost years, but we need to talk. I have missed you. Please. Your loving brother, Jacques."

He looked up just then to see the man who had given him the paper having a word with a woman in a maid's uniform. She looked angry. The man's practiced smile belied his own anxiety. He whispered something. Could that be her? His Nina? Maybe. There was something about her. He recognized the way she stood. As she stepped away, the man abruptly reached to take her arm.

"I said no!" Her anger not quite controlled.

Whatever their problem, she stood defiantly. Was it a disagreement about hours? A guest's complaint? Clearly, the woman was keen to separate herself from the manager—whatever might have been the problem.

Jacques would hold off. Others in the hotel had already noticed, including the woman at the reception desk. She took a step toward them and stopped when the man put up both hands, a sign of everything was fine there. Jacques quickly perceived that if he were to bring the envelope back to the man, a benign, unintentional intervention, the confrontation could dissipate. After all, the man had asked whether he could be of any further help. Jacques still could not see the maid's face, turned away as she was.

"Excuse me, I do not mean to interrupt, but would you be so kind as to. . ." And, with that, the man took back the proffered envelope, irritated, staring at the name.

"I must leave now for a necessary meeting. Can you give this envelope to the addressee when she gets off work?" He then looked to the woman, and he knew. He knew. Yes!

She stared hard at Jacques, startled. She put her hand to her mouth. Lucien looked sharply at the woman, then back to Jacques.

"Give it to her yourself. This is Madame d'Ancel."

CHAPTER 34

Jacques! My God, Jacques! What are you doing here? How did you find me?" Nina pulled her brother to her and let out a great sigh. It had been so many years. Delighted with his one-arm embrace of her, she was not sure what to make of him. "I cannot believe it. Look at you." She blinked back her immediate flood of tears.

"Nina, we have to talk," Jacques said, ushering her away.

Lucien was clearly irritated, caught off-balance. "Make it quick," her boss called after her, muttering something, then stepping toward his office. The man's tone of voice alerted Jacques that his sister had had trouble with that man before. Jacques hated seeing how he put his hands on her.

"Are you all right?" Jacques played the big brother. His Nina had the same dark brown hair as their mother. "You look wonderful. I could not be sure it was you. The uniform. I am sorry, Nina." He took a moment, holding her. They'd spent so much time apart. "Is that fellow mistreating you? I saw how he spoke, how he acted."

"He is nothing. A pig. Pay him no regard. I am just so surprised to see you." She stepped back to take in his physical state. His arm in a sling. She suspected what he had come through. She could only guess at the extent of her brother's injuries. How close he had come to death. She put her hands up to cover her eyes. She needed a moment to bridge so many years.

"Come. We should sit." His good arm around her back, Jacques ushered her to a leather sofa near where he'd been waiting just minutes ago, figuring out how to approach her. Suddenly, there they were. More than twenty years of uncertainty gone with their hurried embrace.

Nina sat, hands in her lap, looking into her brother's face. "How long?" she said. "Jesus. How long is it, Jacques?" And, with that, she could hold back the building emotion no longer.

"Too long," he said.

"I cannot stay here. I hate it. I do. . ." She squared her shoulders, let out another big sigh.

"I know." He handed her his handkerchief.

Gaining control, she looked more closely at him. She saw how he favored his injury. How could any of it be true? "The accident. It was. . ."

"Yes, it was no accident, as you knew. You saved my life, Nina."

"Well. Thank God for Emma and her husband." Nina leaned closer. "I am so sorry about everything, Jacques. And the longer we were apart, the harder it was to begin again." Her voice began to break once more. "I wanted to. You must believe me that I did."

He pulled her to him and kissed her forehead. "*Notre canetonne!*"—our little duckling. It was the endearment their father had given her many years ago. Jacques told her once again that she looked wonderful. "Can we go someplace to talk?"

She had to finish her shift. She looked at her watch. She had three hours left. She would give notice. She'd come to the end of her patience. She found her courage in the face of the unwanted advances of that despicable man. "I cannot do it anymore."

Jacques lifted his damaged arm—the sling doing its work— enough to underscore his physical limitation, and grinned. "Looks like I will have to leave the rough stuff to you," he said. That look she recalled from their teen years. That curly, unruly hair too. His unexpected humor worked well enough to get a small laugh from Nina. That she and her mother had not done well together made her separation from Jacques even more challenging. Her closeness as a child to their father, dead so young, only added to her sense of loss regarding her bad marriage and the horrible loss of her infant, named for their father. What did she have at that point? For his part, Jacques, cautious yet eager, was pleased at how well their long-delayed reunion had begun. Something they'd both needed.

"I have so much to tell you," Nina said. "And so much I want you to tell me." As her thoughts turned to the crash, to the recent attack on his life, she remembered the warning from Henri as to what was to happen to Jacques as well as how Claire had died almost four years before. Her voice broke once again. "Oh, Jacques. I am just so terribly, terribly sorry."

He needed to hold her again. He'd long missed that woman, that part of his own heart. He'd blamed her for how she had pulled away. He had, for too long, harbored a bitterness about their living as strangers, and no understanding of why.

"Yes, of course. Three hours. Where should I go to wait for you?"

She pointed in the general direction of the gardens. "Take a look at our botanical garden. It's lovely. And it's just that way, quite close." She pointed. "Maybe wander. Sit and read. Did you bring a book? You were always reading when we were young."

"I think you were the reader," he said. "I was helping Papa with the farm. You were the family intellectual!" That last comment brought a slight frown. Was he finding fault? Was she too remote? She thought he had said something like that, years and years ago. Siblings so often unsure how to take the other, to correctly interpret what was said and what the statement meant.

"That is not how I remember it," she said softly. She listened to her own words. Was she being defensive?

Jacques shook his head. "Well, no matter," he said, and again gave her that half smile. "Yes, I do have a book. Though it may not be a three-hour book."

"So, just sit and take in the splendor—complements of our Louis Quinze. Those amazing tulip trees, in color. All those gorgeous roses. Gratis. Only the greenhouses charge a fee."

Jacques agreed that her plan sounded appealing. Could he take her to dinner that night? He had seen a café that looked perfect.

"No. You come to my apartment. That works better. And you can meet my friend Anna, my neighbor in our building. She used to live in Combourg too."

"Really? Yes. Your place?" What would her husband think? Jacques was not at all convinced that was the right time to meet the man and confront him. Nor did he want to have the necessary conversation with Nina with the man present. Nina said Henri would not be there. They had argued the night before. He'd gone off. Maybe he was just sulking in a bar somewhere. It was not the first time.

They agreed to rendezvous at five thirty. She would fix drinks. The would have dinner at about seven. She had a pork loin she'd been saving. Did he know her apartment? He did. Emma had given him the address.

"Well, she would," said Nina, and she smiled. "Our Emma Brun is always ready to help."

"I have no fresh clothes to be meeting anyone, except one shirt," he said. "I did not know whether I would even find you. Whether you would see me." He looked at his small travel case.

"Of course, I would see you. You were in pretty rough shape when I saw you—three weeks or so ago. No, four."

"Ah. So that *was* you!" Jacques had had a sense that the woman who had looked into his room the day after the crash could have been Nina, as unlikely as that would have been. But his vision was blurry, and he hadn't seen her for more than twenty years. "You amaze me."

"I took the train," she said. "I had to see you. Emma told me what happened. My God. And I want to know all about your boy. Eddie. Emma said he is a handsome little devil."

Jacques had to hold back—let his own emotions settle. That moment in time—how to begin to process it? He picked up his bag. "I will see you soon."

"Yes. Wait. Does Eddie look like you?"

"He looks more like Claire, I think. His coloring. And I would think he will be taller than me."

She said she wanted to see him.

"I want you to meet him too. There's nothing I would want more. And thank you, Nina. Thank you."

She stood and kissed him on the cheek.

"By the way," he said as he made to leave, "who is Anna? Do I need to be on my best behavior? Does she know about all this? What you did? What happened?"

Nina shook her head. "She knows as much as I know. That you were seriously injured. You will adore her. She is funny, cute, and smart. What more could a young man such as yourself want?"

He chuckled. "I am hardly young, over forty!"

"So, she is close to thirty-nine. She will know some of your old friends. She left Combourg when she married. Her parents owned the bakery in town. Anna Boulant? You have no recollection of her?"

He didn't.

"I will tell you more later. Or she will."

"Okay. That does sound pretty young, now that I think about it. You said she was married?" He laughed.

"She was. Her husband was killed in the war. A partisan. Like you. Leon Caron. "Well, you wouldn't know him. He operated in Rennes. Like so many men and women determined to drive out the Boche. Brave, like you."

"But I am alive. So maybe not so brave as Caron."

"You almost were killed. Luck plays a timely part in all such madness."

He told her he'd see her at five thirty. They would have dinner and talk, then he would catch the last train back. "I don't want to wear you out. Or me. I am still not one hundred percent, as you can tell."

"No. No. You stay in my apartment. I insist. On the sofa, or I will go spend the night at Anna's."

"What if Henri returns?"

"Well, then I guess you will get to find out what kind of shape you are in," she said, amused at her own silliness. "He is the one who told me you were to be killed. As you probably guessed. And Henri knew why."

"Yes. I figured that. But why and to what end I still do not know."

"Soon, Jacques. Comb that hair! I will explain it all, and you will do with the information what you think best." She looked back at the reception desk to see Lucien coming out of his office, his eye on her. "I have to get back to work."

He gave them both a look. Nina would quit. That would be the end of the Lucien problem. All she had to do was find another job, something Jacques knew was not easy to do. Everybody was always looking for the way ahead.

CHAPTER 35

Jacques returned to Nina's apartment, bringing a basket with a sampling of some delicious cherries, raspberries, and sweet peaches. He had to force himself to stop from buying more at the garden gift shops, things he'd not necessarily buy for himself.

While there, looking at so many fascinating flowers and artistic notions, he recalled a purchase he'd made once for Claire—that clever little wooden plaque in the shape of a watering can. What had he said to her that day? The promise of a fine garden. Those seventeenth-century grounds, spread over seven acres, amazed him for its complexity and natural splendor. He admired the many fragrant oleander beds of whorled pinks and whites and enjoyed a trace whiff of apricot. He also stopped to pick up a decent pinot noir at a wine shop near the apartment.

Nina met him at the door, some music he could not quite recall playing softly in the background. He stepped in, finding the smell of something delicious coming from the kitchen.

"Oh, Jacques, right on time." She took the basket. "Thank you. I hope you did not get lost in the gardens," she said, accepting the gifts with a mock bow. "Ah, such wine."

He laughed and admitted he may have lost his bearings a few times; the place was so grand. "I will have to go another time to properly see it all." He took a moment to take in the small, well-appointed home. Seascape blues on the walls of the main room and a few framed prints that suggested his sister had an eye for bright, bold, expressionist work. Claire had spoken of that kind of art. Fauvist was the word she'd used.

"Come in and meet my friend Anna."

The woman looked comfortable on a black leather sofa, playing with one ear lobe. Or, maybe, checking to be sure her earring was in place. Jacques saw she wore a long, dark-blue skirt and a bright-white blouse with a matching blue kerchief. Her hair could not have been darker. Coal black. She had tucked her legs back against the sofa and crossed them at the ankles. Anna wore a smile that was meant to tease. "Do you remember me?"

Jacques unconsciously squared his shoulders. He did not, but he wished he did. Extending his hand, Jacques offered only that his sister had told him she used to live in Combourg. Who did she remind him of with her perfect teeth and remarkable eyes? Yvonne de Carlo, he decided. Yes, as she appeared in *Casbah*, with Tony Martin. Was he staring?

"Well, I left many years ago. My parents had a bakery there for years. They lived above the store. I should say we did. On rue des Princes." She paused. "They are gone now. My parents and their lovely shop." Anna looked at him, letting go of the reverie, thinking him a strikingly handsome man, arm in a sling or not.

"I remember that. A fine, old stone building," he replied. "There is a bike store there now." Jacques tried to recall how long that boulangerie had been gone. What should he say to the woman—a friend to a sister he hardly knew—after missing so many years? How odd was their reunion. Nina rescued them both, or them all, with three wine glasses on a tray, along with some Brie and wheat crackers.

"I was just admiring this painting," Jacques said, studying it. "The rich colors. Is that the word I want? Rich? I am not good with art."

"You have a good eye," Anna interrupted, although it was Nina's artwork. Anna had a keen interest in the painting too. "It's one of Maurice de Vlaminck's most celebrated," she said.

Jacques was amused at her reaction. "Oh? What is the name?"

"Do you know de Vlaminck? Not likely. His several contrasting blues. Remarkable." Anna stood, leaning close to Jacques to examine the piece. Two people momentarily transfixed by something unexpectedly brilliant. An instant, unforeseen bond.

Nina looked at the two of them, decided to add her own thoughts. "This is his *Paysage Cézannien*," she told him, not a little pride in her voice. "It goes back to his early work. The influence of Cézanne, as the title of the work suggests."

Jacques stared for another moment and said, as much to himself as to the others, that his wife had been a gifted artist. Claire. That she, too, painted landscapes. "My late wife did an imitation of Monet's *Water Lilies* on our kitchen wall. It's quite beautiful." He looked from Anna to Nina.

"I would love to see that sometime," said Nina, the most definitive statement yet that she had thoughts of going back—of returning. Coming so confidently as they did, her words gave Jacques a rush of satisfaction. After all, that farmhouse he owned had once been her childhood home. The orchards had been his and hers. And all too briefly, once Claire's. Of course, Nina would come back.

"I hope you do," said Jacques, joining Anna on the sofa, pre- dinner drinks and appetizers lending to the ambiance of the moment. Jacques felt somewhat less like the third wheel. "Well, fine art makes dreamers of us all."

Nina looked at him, seeing her brother in a different light. He was a settled, mature man. What did she know of him, his life, his talents and delights, his sacrifices? His horrible loss? We so often look inward with such intensity, she knew, one may well forget to look out. Nina took a long breath. "Anna knows what happened, Jacques. I told her."

This last news struck him as odd. Nina was sharing the news of the attempt on his life? Was this something he wanted to broach with Anna in the conversation? Plus, he needed to ask about Henri and his possible collusion. Maybe he and Nina could talk later. Nina returned to the kitchen. Perhaps she'd read his body language. And just where was that fool Henri? Should Jacques offer to help with dinner? Make more small talk with Anna? He could smell the roast.

Nina looked around the corner at the two of them. "Probably twenty minutes."

Anna rose and moved to the elegantly set table and adjusted the glasses. Maybe she was nervous too. Jacques knew there was no way their situation was normal. The dinner seemed too fussy. Had Nina invited Anna for moral support? What Jacques made of it was that his sister was on edge. Well, he was too. Jacques glanced up at the off-white ceiling, something catching his eye, and detected a good-sized water stain that had been painted away, though incompletely.

Anna came back to the sofa and sat for a moment, straightening her skirt. A woman looking for a safe space? When Jacques said nothing more, she stood, said she would go wash up, and headed down the short hallway. With Anna out of hearing range, Jacques suggested they hold off any discussion of the attack until he and Nina were alone. Too many nerves on edge.

"Certainly."

The conversation among the three that evening stayed on soft, if not necessarily well-tilled, ground. The recent French Annapurna expedition. Films. Nina asked about Eddie. "How old is he now?"

Jacques said he would be four soon, in November, which also meant, and the fact rattled him sitting there, that was how long his wife had been gone. His Claire. Nina saw the sadness in his eyes. With a lull in the conversation, Anna, having remained pensive on matters of family, felt the need to remark on her husband's death. She said he had been dead well over six years. Anna looked down to the neutral carpet. Neutral colors. Common ground.

"I am certain the men and women he worked with and trusted were all good people," Jacques said. "And brave."

She shook her head.

"I only say that because the kind of work your husband was doing for France is often done with no recognition." Secrecy, Jacques understood, so vital to its very success. He also knew that, for Anna, the Nazis' killing of her husband had injured her as well. She was a war widow. An insidious kind of wound.

Jacques would not speak of his own risks taken. He allowed that, so far as he was aware, resistance people knew only members of their own cells. Too dangerous to know others. All such mixed memories were too difficult to categorize.

"I understand. He seldom spoke of it. He kept it all inside. A banker, you see," Anna told him. "Leon was a banker. He made reports. That's all I know." She took a moment. "I asked him to tell me how I could help, but he said no. Too dangerous. I should stay away from it all."

"In Rennes?"

"Yes. For two years, he did that. Then, he was caught."

Jacques knew that men and women dealing with intelligence information were often exposed by collaborators. Someone noticed something, overheard a name. Their work was precarious in a way different from his paramilitary assignments. Sabotage was a hit-and-run proposition. Blow up things. Disrupt the enemy's timetable. The greatest risk people like Leon Caron faced was never being sure when they had fallen under suspicion and stood most at risk.

"Jacques and my friend Emma's husband, Fabien, worked together," Nina said, sotto voce, as if that information, too, should probably be kept guarded, even then.

Clearly, Emma had told her that much.

"Fabien Brun is one of the bravest men I have ever known," said Jacques, looking at Nina. "I would not be alive today if it were not for his strength and courage." Her brother was speaking of not only their partisan work in the war, but what he had done just weeks earlier and how he'd come to do so.

"Well," she said, "many heroes walk among us. And many of us—maybe most—fail to know it or understand how important they are to those of us who have loved them."

Anna took a sip of her wine and said, "Milton."

"Milton?" asked Jacques. "Sorry. . ."

"John Milton. In his poem 'When I Consider How My Light Is Spent,' he writes, in the last line of that sonnet, 'they also serve who only stand and wait.'"

"Oh my," said Nina, whose English was decent, but rusty. Anna offered that the poem would be just about three hundred years old.

Jacques said he did not know the Milton poem, that he knew few English poems, but he did know about "The Owl and the Pussycat." He chuckled and asked whether anyone wanted to hear it. That bit of whimsy brought a smile to Anna's face. She raised her glass.

"No? Well. Maybe another time," he tried.

Anna had an inspiration. "Wait. Edward Lear, as I recall. A connoisseur of wonderful English nonsense. And, if I'm not mistaken: 'And hand in hand, by the edge of the sand/They danced by the light of the moon,'" Anna added. Jacques could not help but notice how quick the woman was, how dexterous her social skills, especially given that they'd never met and did not know each other. Or if they had met, neither recalled.

"Ah, I did not know that part," Jacques said.

Nina beamed. She asked whether anyone wanted any more of the meat or vegetables and, if not, she would bring coffee. She leaned toward her brother as if inviting conspiracy and said, "Anna teaches in a private lycée: English and English literature for students in their final two years."

"Ah. I thought maybe she was engaged in something like that. Your students are fortunate to have you," offered Jacques, searching for the right thing to say. He wanted to compliment her. He was fascinated by what he was seeing and hearing. All of them more at ease now.

Nina gave them both a smile, more than a little satisfied, and stepped into the kitchen.

"You are being too kind," Anna said, looking at Jacques.

He said no, he was speaking from close proximity to the life of an educator. His wife had been a teacher in Paris after the war. Anna asked what she taught.

"Art history. As well as drawing and painting," he said. "Only for a few years. Before we were married. She was an American, you know."

Anna knew from Nina that his wife had passed away some years earlier. "I am so sorry. We are both alone," she told him. He said yes, for the most part they were just that: "Widow and widower."

Jacques sensed an opening. "My son reminds me in small ways of Claire," he told her.

Anna looked into his eyes and asked what amused the boy.

"What are his loves?"

Jacques said that foremost had been Cleo. Eddie had a lot of natural inquisitiveness. He found fun in building things with his toys.

"I see. Yes. Your son." She peered into her wine glass, then eyed the nearly empty wine bottle on the table and said she had no children. And, she knew she never would. "I am sure your little one is precious to you, building with his toys." The words seemed to be pressing down on her. She looked away and shook her head ever so slightly. She looked to the clock on the far wall.

"I am sorry," Jacques said, feeling the abrupt mood change. "Yes, I am sorry too." She pushed at her glass.

Jacques realized that he had inadvertently introduced the sad scenario. The conversation he saw had unexpectedly gone from bright and breezy to something awkward and almost dark. Anna stood, leaned on the table, and smiled at Jacques in a way that told him she was having a difficult time.

"If you will excuse me, Jacques. I am tired just now. Do forgive me."

"I am sorry."

She nodded, "Of course." She leaned into the kitchen, telling her friend that she had become fatigued. Her eyes were bothering her, she said. "Maybe too much reading," she added, and would it be alright if she skipped the coffee and dessert? Nina came out immediately and looked at Anna, gathering her things. Then, she looked to Jacques. "I understand, Anna. We have had some long days."

Jacques stood too, understanding that the evening was over for Anna, as she walked to the door with his sister.

"We must do this again," Anna tried at the door. Jacques told her how pleased he was to meet her. He said that he would look forward to hearing more about her interests—those kinds of paintings, he noted, pointing to the de Vlaminck.

Anna said she'd like that, adding, "Now, if you will please excuse me. It has been a lovely evening." She hurried out into the hall, where the corridor's one light flickered over the double access doors as if it had its own ideas.

Nina walked with her a few steps in the direction of her apartment, evidently to say something more than good night. When she came back, she found Jacques in the kitchen with a cup of coffee.

"What happened?" he asked. "I would ask you the same."

"Something I said, I suppose," Jacques allowed, thinking he could have been more aware of how Nina might think about his Eddie. Her baby was dead. When the time was right, he'd ask whether she wanted to talk about her child. Or would she want to keep it private? Nina deflected the small confession and said she knew Anna was lonely and could be easily upset. Well, yes. Some losses and precious things that never were are just too painful.

"I feel sorry for her, that she's feeling sad tonight," Jacques attempted, foregoing any urge, for the time being, to speak with her about her Mathias. "But I should tell you that I would like to see her again." He added, "We still have the matter I came to talk about. But, first, how relieved I am to see you again, and to know that you are doing well."

She gave him a doubtful look. He added that he meant she seemed in good health.

"Henri is in a terrible situation," she told him, looking into the sink, rinsing a glass. "And I must find another job. Other than that, Jacques, I am not so bad off."

"Do you want to tell me about Henri? What he said to you, Nina? About the attack that night."

"Come, sit at the table. Have another coffee," she said. "Or maybe more wine."

"Coffee. Nina, it is important I know what he said and how he said it. Was he frightened? Drunk? Anyone else involved? Surely it cannot be someone here, in Nantes."

"Poor man. So lost. So aggrieved. He drinks too much." She fidgeted with her ring. "Was he frightened, you ask? I think so. Yes. There was something about an agreement."

"An agreement?" Jacques waited for what she would say next. "In Paris?"

"No, he went there looking for work. He came back with little or nothing to show for it. There was a man. Roger, I think," she said, thinking the name would mean nothing.

"Roger? Is there a family name? Did Henri give you the man's surname?"

"Yes," she paused, wanting to get it right. "Roger Laurent, I think it was." She looked to see if her brother's face showed any recognition.

"Laurent? Damn him. Why does that not surprise me?" Reddening, Jacques added, "This is unbelievable." He couldn't fathom that Henri would somehow be in league with that man. He was Nina's boozy failed pianist, and Laurent was a brazen grifter. What was there to be said about Henri d'Ancel, except to suggest a kind of moral laziness. How could he fall into step so readily with so dicey, so questionable an individual as Roger Laurent?

"Do you know him? Have you had any bad dealings with such a man?"

"I do," he said, looking at her as if she had just explained the nature of evil itself. "You could say I have."

CHAPTER 36

"You have some loud birds here," Jacques told his sister, walking into the kitchen the next morning and finding her at the small table. "And just outside that window," he added. "Maybe they are just hungry. Like me. What can I do to help?"

Nina gave him a hug. "Good morning. Nothing. Everything's under control. Those are our neighborhood larks and swallows. Arguing or mating. It comes to the same," she said. "Or, at least, that's been my experience. Just sit." She told her brother there was coffee, and asked how he slept, other than for the wakeup call from the birds. "Was the sofa comfortable?"

Jacques said it was fine, though his neck felt a bit stiff. He poured a cup of coffee for himself and topped off the cup his sister was working on.

"Looks like we are out of eggs," she said. "Unless you just want toast and coffee, or these pastries." Nina set a plate of small, orange-scented cakes next to him. "Sorry, I did not know we were so low." Jacques said that, in truth, he wanted nothing so much as eggs, preferably with a slice of ham.

"We have a little ham. No eggs." She rubbed at her upper lip, a nervous tic she'd had since childhood.

Jacques read her anxiety. "No worries. I can go buy some. Where is the nearest market?" Nina suggested he try Marché Leclerc, two blocks west. Would he want to take her bike? No. Not with only one good arm. Anyway, he needed the short walk to clear his head. Anything else?

"Yes, pick up some fresh onions and basil, okay?" She reached for her purse, not knowing whether she would have much to offer. He told her, "No, this is on me."

"I have a breakfast recipe you will like," she said. Everything felt so strange. How was it even possible?

"That sounds promising," he added, wanting to affirm their closeness. Jacques gave her a kiss on the forehead and said he'd be back as quickly as he could, taking the small cloth sack she handed him to carry things home. He was not out the door ten minutes when Nina heard a key in the lock and in walked a heavy-footed, much-depleted Henri.

"Well, look who found his way home."

Henri mumbled his excuses—the same nonsense he had given her before when he hadn't come home. A beleaguered stage actor who had forgotten his common entry line. "It was late. Sorry." Or, "I did not want to wake you." No. It was something else.

"You look like hell. Where have you been?"

Henri decided he had no choice but to tell the truth: He'd spent the night in jail. Sore, disheveled, and smelly; he wanted only something nourishing to eat and to shower. He needed to explain what happened and beg her forgiveness. Why was nothing working out for him? He agreed he had acted poorly. Stupidly.

"Do you think so? You were in jail, Henri? I was worried. What did you do?"

Deflecting the question, Henri sought solace in his perceived mistreatment. "I have talent, Nina: Damn it. I should not be treated this way."

"Just stop! What did you do?" Nina repeated, voice rising. He walked to the sink, splashed water on his face, and sat at the table, not noticing the second cup of coffee before him.

"I got belligerent. I'd had too much to drink, and I called the bargirl a whore."

"Idiot."

"Yes. She was slow, always talking to someone. Anyway, she told the bartender what I'd said to her. She was his wife. The proprietor wanted me to leave. It was just about one, when they close. I refused. I wanted another drink."

"You always want another drink. Why did you not just leave? Come home?"

He allowed that he should have. He was saddened about it. After words with the bartender, he threw his whisky glass at the man, who ducked. The glass missed, hitting and breaking the mirror behind the bar. "After a phone call, the cops came." Henri paused, perhaps looking for something exculpatory to say. "And I went into the lockup," he said as if he could not believe how abused he'd been. Henri then noticed the second cup on the small dinette table.

"Nina, whose is this? Is Anna here?"

"That would be your brother-in-law. The one you tried to have killed, if you recall. He went to the store for some things." She watched to see how he would take that.

"*What*?" He was clearly in a panic. How could that be? "Jacques is here?" He stood, a man beside himself with worry and confusion. "Why? What is he doing here? What does he want?"

"He wants to know the whole story of the attack. That's why. And maybe to restore some sense of normalcy to our relationship, which, in truth, I need very much right now. You owe him, Henri. You came close to killing my brother."

"I thought you hated him."

With anger rising in her voice, she stepped toward him. "Why would you ever think such a stupid thing?" She leaned into his face, which was peaked and puffy. "Hate him? He is my only family. Other than the one we have tried here, in Nantes."

Henri blustered something about their being husband and wife, their intimacy.

"And that has not been particularly healthy. Has it?" She sat, exhausted. Henri remained standing; he pushed at the wooden chair, silent in his shame.

"And the best thing that has happened, ironic as it sounds, is this failed attack," she said. "Which you brought on, Henri. You."

"I'm sorry. I said I was sorry. I do not know why I even listened to that man." His voice was reedy.

"I do not know either. But Jacques will want answers. And I suggest you give them to him."

Henri's reddening face took on a look of abject terror, mixed with pain.

"You need not worry about what he will do. He doesn't want to hurt you. He wants the details."

Weakened, Henri asked whether it would not be best to just forget it, since no one died.

"Well, he could have. And what if his little boy had been with him in that truck that night? Jesus, what were you thinking, Henri, to sign on to a plan to murder my brother?"

Having never seen her so angry, Henri sat, much depleted. He took a moment to calm down, considered saying something, thought better of it, rose, and trundled into the kitchen for a glass of water. On the way back, he took a knife off the table and slipped it into the back of his belt.

Nina saw what he had done. "What are you planning to do with that—kill Jacques? Or yourself?"

Humiliated, he stuttered something about self-protection.

"You disgust me when you act like this."

Jacques came through the door twenty minutes later, with brown eggs, onions, basil, and a clutch of chervil, which he set on the table, taking the measure of the nervous, disheveled man standing half in the kitchen and half in the dining area. Henri did not know where to turn. Both men had enough knowledge of the other to be wary. Henri, especially so. He put the knife back on the table, expecting no one would notice, and then stood next to Nina, who had come around the table. Each looking to see what the other would do.

"I got a dozen," Jacques said, demonstrating a studied calm he did not feel. "The basil looks and smells fresh. I got strawberries too." He gave Nina a look that said, *Now what?*

Nina said thank you and took the bag, returning to the kitchen. Jacques took a close look at Nina's husband, who, if he were any more nervous, would have been vibrating like a harp string.

"We can talk now or after we eat. Personally, I am starved," Jacques said, and sat down. His coffee had gone cold; he got back up to refill the cup.

Henri stood at the same time, offered his hand. Hesitant.

Trembling. "You must be Jacques."

"I must be," Jacques replied, accepting the hand—a reflex— something done out of simple decency. "We have a lot of ground to cover, d'Ancel, but now that we are together, I think it makes sense to eat some breakfast and get to whatever it is you have to tell me when we are all less keyed up and not so hungry." Jacques added that Henri might just want to go wash up.

Henri bristled at that. "This is my house, you know. I am not sure I like how you are giving orders. Coming in here and setting the rules. . ."

"Just stop!" Nina said loudly, interrupting, and placing a bowl of mixed fruit on the table with a measure of fortitude. "Jacques is right. Everything will be ready in five minutes. Then we eat. And go change your clothes. You smell."

Humiliated, Henri headed to the bathroom. Much of the tension in the room seemed to go with him. Nina had prepared three small, delicious-looking ham-and-cheese omelets, *crêpes sucrées* with strawberries, and a second pot of coffee. She also set out slices of apple, more strawberries, and some assorted cheese. Nina and Jacques did most of the talking. Brother and sister catching up after so many empty years. Henri said nothing—an awkward silence, an anxious silence full of meaning. When asked, he told Jacques he was working on getting back to his music. Jazz piano. Jacques figured he did not have to like the man to act civilly. He asked whether Henri favored any style, any one or more well-known people?

"Claude Bolling, I suppose." The young genius from Nice who, he allowed, had redefined French jazz music, along with Art Tatum in New York. "He had his own band at the age of eighteen."

Wanting to show support, and to alleviate her husband's nervous state, Nina added that Henri was talented, but that these kinds of jobs were difficult to find. He was *looking*, she offered, giving her husband a vote of confidence. He needed that. They both did. She picked up her fork. The awkward moment brought them all back to the food on their plates.

Nina asked whether Jacques had a photo of Eddie. He did, and he handed her the one he kept in his new wallet. The smiling, brown-haired boy standing in an apple grove, stretching—reaching for a piece of fruit, tantalizingly just out of reach.

"How old was he here?"

"He turns four in November. My big boy." His pride in the lad without measure.

When they had finished, some cheese left on only Henri's plate, Nina got up. Said she would take care of the dishes. "You men can talk more freely without me being here."

Henri had been steeling his courage. "I suggest we sit in the other room. More comfortable. And I want you to know how horrible I feel about this."

The men took two chairs near the front window, a kind of Juliet balcony beyond the tall, lightly curtained double windows that opened onto their narrow street.

Jacques settled as well as he could, his arm aching. "Do tell me how you came to do this, Henri, and with whom, and why. Everything." The anger in his voice was returning.

Henri lit a cigarette, blowing the acrid smoke straight up as if he meant to follow it, if only he could. "I met a man on the train to Paris. We got to talking. He said he lived in Combourg or quite nearby. Épiniac, I think. I told him my wife's brother lives in Combourg. Making small talk. He asked your name, and I told him." Henri looked at Jacques to see how this disclosure was being received. "He knew you. I had been drinking. . ."

"Yes. Go on. Tell me his name."

"Roger Laurent. He gave me his card." With that, he fished for it in his pocket, finding his wallet—desperate to show it, for something, somehow, to shift the blame. "'Police Captain,' it says. Do you remember him?"

Jacques said he did. Quite well. "Even so, how did this coincidence, this report of a casual acquaintance, translate into a plot to kill me? Because, Henri, I cannot fathom what the motivation might be. What would he, or you, stand to gain from my death?"

Henri wanted just then nothing so much as a stiff drink. Even an after-breakfast sherry would help settle his nerves. He turned in his chair, looking over his shoulder to the kitchen, to see whether Nina was still there, listening. Jacques inferred that Henri did not want his wife to hear what he would say.

"It was all about your farm. The orchards and the business."

"Go on," Jacques told him, taking in the trembling around the man's mouth.

"He said—Laurent said—if you were dead the whole estate and all its properties would come to Nina, and therefore to me, as her husband. She would get it all. We would. Next of kin. He was clear that your boy could not inherit because he was too young. A minor."

"I see. What made you think Eddie could not inherit? Laurent told you that?"

Henri went on to lay out the case as he had been given it. Any inheritance was subject to laws of succession and age-related qualifications. "Napoleonic law," he added, suddenly the instructor.

Jacques thought back to the time Roger had inexplicably made an inquiry about the farm's financial situation. "Well, this will come as a surprise to you, but that is not the case. I doubt Roger Laurent knows any more of property inheritance than you. He was bluffing."

Henri looked ashen.

Jacques continued: "When my wife died, I investigated just how the legal arms of this Leviathan of a legal system work. A special tribunal judge comes into play in such cases, but Eddie would inherit. You and Nina, or more likely just Nina, would be contacted about clarification of next of kin, and so forth. Come to that, my late wife's parents would also be contacted, in case they wanted to take Eddie to live with them in the States. But the fact remains, his inheritance rights are fully protected. And all you would have gained is a prison sentence."

Henri shook his head in disbelief. "I do not know what to say, except to offer my most profound apologies. I have been a fool. A terrible fool." He slumped even further into the chair.

"Yes. Well, the question that remains is how Laurent would profit? He did not set all this up for you and Nina. You can be certain that the end game is designed to feather his nest."

Henri looked away. "How would he do that? I assumed he would ask for a finder's fee, or some agreed-upon monetary settlement."

"His appetites are far grander than the change left on the table when you come to claim Berlangier estates." Jacques waited to see whether Henri was following that line of thought. "Do you know the term 'zero-sum game,' Henri? One winner, one loser. No ties. No second place. Ignore, for a moment, the idea that Nina would not inherit anyway. Nor you, obviously, with me out of the way. So, think: Who then is still *in* the way?"

"In the way?" He did the verbal puzzle instantly. "Me?"

"That is correct, Henri. You. You and my sister, which now makes me angry all over again. If he would kill me so readily, what makes you think you are too strong to get rid of? Or Nina? You were played, d'Ancel."

Henri put his hands to his face. Nina stepped into the room and looked to her husband. His shoulders shook. She decided she had to get something clarified for her own peace of mind. She sat. "You fear him, am I right? This Laurent? Tell me what we can do."

Henri stood, a decision made. "We can get away. And do so soon. When Roger becomes certain that Jacques was not killed in the attack, and he must know that now, he will come for us. Only I can put the blame on him. Do you see?"

"No," Jacques interjected. "Now stop and think. And I want you to listen to me. If he does contact you, you can say that I have no way to know what happened or why. I must have been saved by a passing farmer, A good Samaritan, someone who saw my truck crashed in a ditch. You can string out that story. Can you not? He has no way to know that you let the deal leak to Nina, who then called Emma, sending Fabien. All this is our story. Ours alone. And it is safely hidden. You would be an even bigger fool to leak it. Henri, he knows nothing."

"So, what can I do?" He sat again, hands on his lap.

Nina came to stand with her husband, at the edge of his chair. "Jacques is right. Be smart and say nothing. If this man contacts you again, play dumb. Take no chances with him. Avoid him if possible. Do you understand?"

Henri looked at them both. Said he would think more about it, got up, and said, "I am tired, Nina. So terribly tired. I got no sleep last night. Excuse me now. I must rest."

Nina looked at the clock on the wall. "I thought you were going to work today."

"I'll go in later," he answered, softly, from the bedroom. "I'll tell the boss there was something I had to take care of."

"Lies, of course." Nina looked at Jacques, shook her head. "He is incorrigible. And I need to find another job. The Marguerite is no good."

"I noticed." Jacques told her that he saw a hand-lettered sign by the cash register at the botanical garden's gift shop: Staff Required. "You might see whether they still need someone."

She said she thought that could be ideal and would inquire the next day. She had some experience as a clerk, years back, had done some record keeping.

"Meanwhile, please take this to help, for now. I know you will find something."

She looked at what he had given her: a crisp fifty-franc note. A pensive-looking Blaise Pascal stared back, holding the modest globe—Mother Earth—as if the famed old physicist might somehow make the needed repairs.

"Oh my. This is too much, Jacques. Thank you, but I cannot. . ."

"It's not too much. And, anyway, I missed giving you something for your birthday."

"For the last twenty-some birthdays," she said and laughed softly, giving him another hug.

He agreed, said she had a winning argument, and should go be a botanical-garden girl.

"What will you do now?" she asked, wiping at her eyes. "Keep a close watch on the snake Laurent, for one thing."

"You know him, you said?"

"Oh, I do. There's more going on here than I could have imagined, and now I have some detective work to do. I have a few ideas."

Nina told him to be careful.

"I will. Promise to come see us?" he asked. "Eddie and me."

"Go catch your train. You will see me out there soon, Jacques.

You can show me what to make with all those apples."

CHAPTER 37

Returning to his home in Combourg, Jacques understood that he and Nina had, at least tacitly, said what needed to be said. They'd spoken honestly and had promised to reconnect again soon. Their long-delayed reunion had lifted them both with its hugs, small jokes, and smiles. Theirs was a kind of newfound optimism that could not have been possible absent the horrible events that took place one rainy night several weeks earlier.

Predictably, Henri moped around for a few hours, cursing Laurent, but did manage to get back to work the next morning, bolstered by some small sense of renewal and, maybe, his recent show of something close to courage. His soul was cleansed for having opened up to Jacques about the absurd plan he'd so foolishly become party to. Still, he worried that all the bad salt had not been cleared from the evil tumbler he'd taken hold of.

Nina helped with her unexpected warmth and words of encouragement. She suggested he practice every night, or whenever he could, after work. "Be ready. One never knows when opportunity will stop by to see if you are in."

"I will," he said. That night, the two of them experienced a kind of care for each other they had been missing for all the mistrust that had long pushed affection away. Henri could almost put aside the specter of the soulless, duplicitous Roger Laurent. Or maybe he just tried to forget about it, needing nothing so much as to embrace some manicured sense of recent history.

Back in Combourg, others were making plans. Jacques asked Victor to his house a few nights later, Victor and Gisèle, whom Eddie had come to love for all the care and warmth they had shown him.

"Let me prepare something for us. I can do it," Jacques insisted. "I have one passable beef stew recipe. It was Claire's or her mother's. Besides, you are too pregnant to be working in the kitchen."

"Don't tell her that. She will expect me to do the cooking, and no one wants that," countered Victor, offering the low-timbred chuckle he often made when amused.

Jacques asked again when she was due—this unexpected gift from God, as Gisèle expressed it.

"Two weeks," she said. "Do you think Eddie will be interested in the baby?" she asked.

"Curious, no doubt. Children are fascinated by birth. The origin of the species, however, to misuse Darwin's term, is likely to be beyond his ken," said Jacques.

Victor laughed, and Gisèle added, "Well, I would hope so. So, no talk of the fox and the stork or any other such nonsense." She also made clear that she wanted to hear no discussion of the attack. Let the men hash over that business on their own. She wanted to enjoy a quiet meal. Besides, they would need to involve Fabien in any talk of what might come next, since that it was certain who was behind the attack.

"Agreed," said Victor.

"Fair enough," said Jacques, "but I need to tell you about my reunion with Nina." He smiled to signal his relief at having put right such deeply personal matters. "She's making the best of a difficult time with her husband there, in Nantes."

"Nantes is a beautiful city. Did you get to see much?" asked Gisèle.

Jacques said he did—some—adding that he spent a couple of hours in their grand botanical gardens, quite near where she lives, and which he would never have seen had he not gone to find her. He also spoke of meeting Anna, a fascinating woman. "Bright, and very attractive." Nina had given Jacques's address to Anna. She would write. Victor winked at his wife, who asked whether there might be something brewing.

Jacques shrugged his shoulders and laughed, added that Anna Caron was special. "She teaches English and English literature. And has an eye for paintings."

Gisèle asked whether he was always drawn to the smarty-pants teacher-types. Jacques said the evidence would suggest so. He added that Anna's late husband, a partisan in Nantes during the war, had been killed by Vichy collaborators, in '43. "She's been on her own now for over seven years. I told my sister she could bring her out here anytime she wants to visit."

"Just what you need, Jacques."

"Speaking of getting back into the swing of things, when do you get to put away that sling?" asked Victor.

Jacques said he could probably operate with two good arms again in another week. He was due then, as well, for another cardiac test in Rennes. All felt fine so far. He looked at the empty glasses on the table.

"Victor checked the pantry for a good Burgundy. He said they could all use something from the vine just then. Then he added, "Gisèle is preparing a hearty stew, which wants to be braised with Burgundy, by the way. Might as well see if it's good!"

Soon thereafter, all were enjoying a good meal. Little Eddie, full of questions, asked what is *pregnant* and looked to his father, the source of all knowledge and patience. Gisèle leaned toward the boy in his yellow giraffe-and-monkey wooden highchair and told him it was the time in a woman's life before babies were born. That the baby was inside her, growing and getting ready to come out. The look on the boy's face suggested he did not know what to make of that, unable to identify anyone's reality but his own.

"Your *maman* was pregnant before you were born." This unforeseen turn of the conversation brought Jacques sharply back to the fateful day of Claire's passing. Gisèle immediately knew what Jacques must have been thinking.

"My *maman* is in heaven," the boy said, looking at her then down to what remained on his small plate as if something there could tell him why.

"I know, honey," said Gisèle, looking for a way to steer them away from that heartache. Jacques got up from the table and asked whether anyone wanted anything more.

Victor told him to go sit, to comfort his son who had just walked into the front room. Maybe looking for the dog. "Please, Jacques, leave the dishes and the cleaning up to us."

An hour or so later, the Gaillards having gone home and Eddie asleep in his bed, Jacques mused on what those last few days with Claire had held for them, leading up to the baby's birth and her horrible, painful death late that night. There had been a few things she'd said that had stayed fresh in his mind. Little things.

Jacques recalled how Claire had loved a flower garden. An herb garden too. He remembered the one they'd labored to design and create behind their house, orchards stretching as far as anyone could see. He thought about how the two of them would take a coffee out there and sit in their oversized wooden chairs, Cleo wrapping herself around the feet of one of them. Those were the joys of unqualified affection.

At that point, whenever he could steal away for a short time, even ten minutes, leaving the tasks of the day to his team, Jacques would go out there and sit, her empty chair immediately next to his, recalling bits of what they had said.

"We should talk about names for the child," Claire had told him on one of those occasions.

"Eduard if a boy. Julia if a girl."

She had asked him why Eduard?

"For the Monsignor."

"Yes, the brave and dutiful," she'd agreed.

Unexpectedly, he remembered one other thing: their last hours together in the Saint-Malo hospital, she, far more exhausted and depleted than even she could have known, took her husband's hand.

"Rest now, Claire. I love you."

"I will. I love you too."

CHAPTER 38

If it occurred to Roger Laurent that his business associate and sometime sex partner was acting more keyed up when they met that evening, at her behest, for talk of their precarious affairs, he chose to ignore it. The meeting's purpose was serious business. What she had in mind, he soon learned, was a kind of reckoning of accounts.

"My people will expect their money. You understand that, yes?

These people are less patient than you and I."

Roger sipped from his glass, looked around the bar to see whether anyone could have heard. "I never agreed to any set payment," he said. "And your people failed in their mission. They get nothing. None of them."

She considered that, thinking it was typical of the man who could not see beyond his own hand, who never could comprehend the vagaries of criminal complicity. His was a world of win or lose that always yielded an outcome favorable to him.

"The world does not turn on favors," she said. "I have obligations. Do you not understand? These are not people to screw with, as you must be aware, Roger. They do not like being taken advantage of."

"They did not do the job," he insisted, raising his voice, then checking himself. He shook his head and wiped his hands on the paper napkin by his glass, then he pulled a wallet from his sporty tweed jacket and fingered the bills inside it. "I can give you four hundred francs. That is all I can do. They failed. That prick Berlangier is still walking, although I cannot imagine how."

"Not the point."

"No, no. It is the point, Sabrina." His voice was again momentarily too loud, and he knew it. "I asked you for help in setting this up. That's all. We agreed I could not make the approach directly. Your people were to work with mine."

"And they did. It was a stupid plan, a messy plan, from the start," she said, and looked at the bills in his hand. It was a token payment, which he figured she would take as a rebuke.

Roger laughed. "Look, why not go back to your place, and we find something we both want?"

"Just stop. Forget it. You can find someone else to disappoint," she said, her eyes suggesting nothing but contempt.

"What does that mean?" he said. Did she mean she was disappointed regarding the failed strike against Berlangier or with regard to their bed play? She had insisted on meeting at that corner bar because it was dark and quiet, and she did not want him getting sidetracked by the possibility of sex. Sabrina lit a cigarette, blew the smoke away from them, thinking how to close out the fiasco in a way that did not cause her to lose face with her team.

She looked at the money. "This kind of scheme was never going to be foolproof," she said, taking the bills. "He survived. If you had wanted a sure kill you should have done it yourself. Or told your people how to do it. They love their knives, as you know."

Roger said something about how no close contact would have been feasible for them. "Berlangier was on to these people. He is a tough one, and I have no doubt he would shoot given any threat and provocation, and we agreed that it had to look like an accident."

"Well, I would shoot them too," she said with a smile that suggested she was too smart, and surely too adroit, to work with any of them face to face. "Now you must be certain they do not take a disliking to you, these fine people."

Recognizing the merits of her argument, and not happy with the implications, Roger raised his glass. "Murder, my sweet—I mean any obvious killing—would have attracted too many interested parties. We took the only path open to us."

She put the money into her purse and said, with no apparent bias, "Interested parties will reveal themselves soon. Of that you may be certain."

He asked what she meant.

"For one, your police station house, I would think. The attack, the hit and run, took place in your jurisdiction." Sensing his discomfort, Sabrina asked whether he thought the investigation there, in Combourg, had run its course.

Roger replied that his commander had been much agitated by the whole thing, but, to date, no leads had been found. Or, if they had, they were being kept in the pockets of the investigators.

"Would you not be aware, be kept in the loop? After all, you have some rank."

"The matter was not assigned to me, and, if I try to inveigle myself in it now, someone may think to ask why."

She leaned forward. She gave him a look that suggested there was something he was keeping from her, from his people and her people. Hers operated in the northern parts of Brittany and Normandy. His were more central. But these people were as elusive as they were unpredictable. Roger said he heard there'd been evidence found at the crash site. Evidence that pointed to them.

She asked, "Is that going to be a problem?"

He considered the question. "Perhaps." He added that he had to be careful not to touch something that could stick. As it was, his bosses only accepted, and to some extent supported, his relationship with that element so long as they produced, which often meant turning on one another. Without a doubt, they could yield good sources of information about other criminal activity. "We just have to wait and see what or who turns up." His words came as no surprise, but told her that she would need to cease, at least for a while, any business connections with her crime syndicate.

"I got that," she said, settling back in her chair. She'd have to decide what to do about Roger soon.

Two sides of the same coin, trust and distrust were mercurial elements in the game they'd been playing. They were equally invisible.

Laurent finished his drink, running his sleeve over what remained at the corner of his mouth, realizing he had another set of concerns just coming into focus. His people and her people would be wary of each other, suspicious. One might give up the other for this or that payment, consideration, payback. And what about Jacques Berlangier himself? Surely, he would be putting the pieces of the attack together.

"We have bigger problems than what the police commissioner thinks of my confidential informants."

She asked what he had in mind and reminded him to keep his voice down. Roger signaled for another round of drinks; she waved off anything more for her. Café la Perle was doing an unusually brisk business. Sabrina waited until a young couple passed by their table.

"What, exactly? What bigger problems?"

"Berlangier. That is the one who keeps me awake at night." Laurent took a generous pull on his freshened drink. She watched him, detecting a slight slur, then told him he might want to slow down with the whisky. Admonished, he laughed to himself, even more irritated.

Sabrina put her hand over his glass when he reached for it again. She was right. He was drinking too much, too fast. "How could Berlangier possibly connect you to the attack?" she asked, leaning in, insisting he must steel his nerves. That was the time for patience, for caution. "I have never seen you so nervous, and that whisky does not help."

How could Berlangier tie him to anything? He mumbled something about Henri d'Ancel, then looked at her as a bully might consider an unexpected, unforeseen tougher adversary, then he adjusted his position and leaned toward her. "This d'Ancel is weak."

"Is he?" She thought for a moment about what he'd said about bigger problems. "Set him aside for a moment. Deal with one situation at a time. Start with the attack. Work the puzzle piece by piece."

Roger wiped his forehead with his handkerchief.

"Now, listen to me. This Berlangier might suspect it was one of the local gypsy trucks that hit him. That cannot be helped. And you told me once that he had some history with these people involving his dog, right? But there is no way that piece gets to you. Or is there?"

Roger looked at the whisky glass. She was right. He was making an ass of himself. It was exactly the kind of behavior he'd seen and detested in Henri d'Ancel. What was the matter with him?

"I have to think," he said. "I cannot see how any of this points to me unless the other cops, ones I have no real influence over, pinch the assholes who drove the truck that night."

"But those men are pawns, are they not? They would not know any names but those of their superiors."

Recovering some ground, Roger said if you turn over enough small stones you get to the bigger ones below. The ones that matter. "Even so, they would not expose you, would they? I thought you said you took care of them when they needed you, offered protection. One hand washes the other."

"Yes. Except those times when they just cut off the dirtiest hand among them so as not to infect the other. Or others," he said, looking to see whether she sensed further danger.

"Others?"

He took a moment. "It was you that put those big rocks on the road when you made the initial contact, Sabrina."

She looked at him. "Do I detect a threat from you, Roger, in this telling story of road construction? Big and small stones? This was your deal. I only agreed to help with contacts."

"No threat." He immediately denied having any such intention, then added, "But one or more of your people could do something. Right? Are you certain you are in the clear?"

She frowned at t what he had said, at how he seemed to be concerned with his being discovered as a crook. She knew he had good cover at the police department. Pondering her own options, she'd need to think the situation through. What might that imperious fellow yet do or say?

Sabrina stood, said she had to use the ladies' room. "Your bigger problem is that fool brother-in-law you chose to use as a patsy, as a doorway into this ridiculous scheme. And I blame myself for going along with you." She excused herself. "I will be right back."

Roger reached out to take her by the wrist. His face registered renewed concern. "This d'Ancel? A bigger problem, you think? How so?"

"Did you suppose he would fail to realize his own vulnerability; that he would not see he becomes the next most expendable player, especially once the attack on Berlangier failed? After all, the one to inherit, according to your faulty calculus, was the sister—his wife— not him. He immediately becomes a nuisance. A liability."

"Not necessarily."

"Yes, necessarily. Roger, what additional large holes are yet to be found in this absurd fabric of deception? Your Monsieur d'Ancel was merely a doorway, and one easily blown off the frame. Am I not correct?"

He nodded his head and tried to speak, but she held up her hand and continued her argument. "He would be the next bit-part actor to suffer an unfortunate, and this time fatal, accident. And, if he lives, if he talks, that puts you among those large sharp rocks." She pulled away and walked to the toilets.

Laurent gave her a dismissive wave, as if to indicate he remained unconcerned. The waiter came by to ask whether there would be anything else. Others would want the table. "We will be out of here momentarily," he told him.

Returning shortly, Sabrina's face indicated how angry she was with Laurent. She grabbed her purse, ready to leave.

"We can go to your place. Continue this, and maybe. . ."

"No. We will not be going to my place." She leaned in. "Think, Roger, you never did have a viable path in this fiasco," she continued with her admonishment, "or to that property anyway." Laurent tried to counter that he only needed Berlangier dead, then he would work on the wife. Get her to leave d'Ancel, with whom the woman was already losing patience.

"He explained to me on the train, practically weeping, that he and the wife were in trouble. Finances. His lack of a decent job." He paused to make his culminating point. "I had him eating out of my hand, Sabrina. He loved the plan. Like a hungry hound on a fat rabbit. I knew I could work the man, and at no risk to me. And get back at Berlangier."

"No risk? He was a drunk. You said so yourself. The man was not thinking clearly. And your tender ego is insufferable. Did you plan to sweep his little wife off her feet? Light her cigarette for her, buy her expensive champagne and take her to bed?"

"Perhaps. And why not?"

She considered that and laughed. "Maybe that was all you wanted anyway, Roger. Was it? Another conquest?"

He shook his head. What he wanted more, he insisted, was to see his plan work. To get back at that insufferable Jacques Berlangier.

"So, this was personal? Why?"

"Why?" he asked sourly and took another drink. "A man my uncle loved and trusted more than he did me? This apple farmer? The great Monsignor Arnoux was always singing that man's praises." He looked away, resentment burning in his stomach, a recollection of something said or not said. "Maybe I *was* jealous. But I did think the inheritance would be straight to the sister, since the child could not inherit—the boy. So maybe I was wrong there."

"Maybe?"

The waiter was back.

"You disappoint me. More, you disgust me." She turned to the waiter: "In a minute. Okay? Just keep your shirt on!"

Laurent gathered his thoughts. "If Berlangier had been killed, and we thought he would be, I could have worked them both, Henri and his wife. They're vulnerable people. I could have made them see that the farm could come to them."

"So, what are you saying now? You'd have killed the boy too? He would have died if he had been in that truck. Did you not know that?"

He looked at his beckoning glass. "No," he said. He shook his head, mumbled something about how the plan had never been feasible. "Anyway," he began again, trying to recover the upper hand, "nothing connects any of that to me. There was no communication, no contact, after his train back to Nantes."

"As far as you know," she said, looking into his bleary eyes, maybe to detect how far gone he was. The Roger Laurent she knew, and once might have had some affection for, was always too much the dreamer.

Yes, he knew how to read people—how to gauge a mark, much like his own crime team. But, that time, he had badly misjudged the gambit. He had not thought through the permutations that could come back to nail him.

"And now, I think, you had better head home. Give some thought to those loose ends. Decide how you might tie them up. Maybe there is a first-line hitter or two you might bring in for questioning."

"Hmmm. I had not thought of that. Direct approach. Cut the head off the snake. But doing so would close off all future business ventures with them," he said, a man for whom no wealth is ever sufficient, no game of wits ever fully played out, even if his life were on the line—and he understood that it could be. "Yes, I see what you mean."

A young couple who had been eyeing them from the bar stepped toward the recently vacated table, the determined waiter at their side. "Well," Sabrina said as she picked up her purse and stood again to leave, "such decisions do not make themselves, Roger. Some relationships have their days or nights, and then they are no more." She made an explosive sign with her hands. "All gone."

"When will I see you again?" he insisted, even as she was walking to the door.

"You will not. Take care of business, Roger. For I assure you that I will."

He thought about making a smart comeback but, instead, stepped back to the table and drained his glass. Home? No. He would have to find a cheap accommodation for the night. Then he'd go back to Épiniac on the morning train and figure out what to do about d'Ancel.

At just past six the next morning, two phone calls were made, both from Paris. One local. One to a man, a deliberate fellow, a killer known to Sabrina only by the name of Ferka.

CHAPTER 39

Henri had been reading the newspaper when the phone rang. "Can you get that?" he asked Nina, who was busy preparing to broil a chicken in the kitchen where the phone hung on the wall. He could just as well have gotten up, but he'd become accustomed to having her manage household matters. Besides, he had injured his right hand at work when an oxygen tank toppled over; he had reacted to stop its fall.

"For you."

Henri recognized the voice immediately.

"Hello. This is Edgar from the Joséphine. Hello? Is it Henri? You came to see me some weeks ago. Here in Paris. Yes?'

Henri could not believe what he was hearing. "Yes," he managed. Nerves and unfettered joy wrestled for dominance in his mind, his voice. "Yes, hello, Edgar. . ."

"If you are still interested, Monsieur, I have a need for your piano skills. One of my employees is gone." Henri looked to Nina, who was paying no attention.

"At the Joséphine?"

"Yes. Are you interested?" Henri said that of course he was interested, that he was thrilled. Nina was listening with guarded optimism.

"Who is it?"

Henri shushed her with a positive hand gesture. Made a giddy face.

When could he start? When could he come to Paris?

Could he have a few days? Maybe begin that weekend? He had some matters to see to.

"Yes, of course." Edgar said he understood. Henri's heart was jumping in his chest. His boyish smile brought tears to Nina's eyes. "Oh, my. Friday? Yes. The 20th? Yes, of course." Henri looked at the calendar hanging on the pantry door. Edgar was still explaining the unexpected circumstance, what had befallen one of his regulars. Bad accident. Henri listened even as his mind jumped ahead. He had a job once again, in music. No more welding gloves and burning pipes. No sharp wires to worry about. There would, of course, be matters of payment and schedules for working with the others, Edgar was saying. The club managers would need to be assured of his commitment. Henri said nothing would prevent his acceptance.

Edgar had additional requirements. Nothing troublesome, as he put it. Henri would need to meet the other players. They'd need some time to learn each other's musical mannerisms. But the 21st would be their first live performance. Saturdays were always big at the club. Was he certain about the job?

He was.

Would Henri open with his arrangement of "Tenderly?"

He would. They'd work up a set. Short notice was not a problem. The heavens had heard, had taken notice of his abject distress. The trumpets on high were playing, at last, for him.

"I have a job," he said, beaming, when he thanked Edgar once more and hung up. "Good Lord, Nina. We are going to Paris!"

"Wonderful! Oh, Henri. Oh, my God, at last. And, surely, I can find suitable work too. Where will we live, Henri? Paris is expensive." He said he had some ideas. Maybe in the 10th, or maybe the 13th. I knew a saxophone player who lived there. It has been years. His was a small flat—off rue de Patay. I should make inquiries. Rents are not too bad there. I must think."

"Maybe we could take a day and go look. We should do it soon.

This is so surprising," she said, looking at the calendar.

"Well, maybe. I should go first. Check things out," he insisted. "My luck has changed, Nina. My luck has finally changed."

Sabrina Toohey, restless at home in the Marais, sat in her smart apartment just across the Seine. She'd been giving some thought to her own situation, to her nominal well-being, to her future in the complicated and often dangerous world of brokering illegal deals. It was a life she had once relished, but maybe not so much at that point. Choosing one's associates meant keeping back doors open and knowing how and when to exit, when to seal them off.

Roger had called again, insistent. He had something to explain.

Was she at home?

"No." She begged off, said there were difficulties. "It is best we do not see each other for a while. Not good to poke one's head above the trench line just now."

But he could not leave it alone, and the man had already soiled his britches badly with the ridiculous d'Ancel fiasco. For a cop, he could act stupidly.

Sabrina poured a drink and picked up a magazine, then immediately put it back down. How did one get out of a fast-moving train heading the wrong way without breaking one's neck? Roger was the danger at that point. She set her Martini glass on the table and reached for the phone. A man answered on the third ring. "Ferka, me again." She looked to the door, wondering whether it was locked. "Listen, I have something else that needs fixing. And quickly."

CHAPTER 40

Jacques and his friends had agreed to meet at Fabien's store at closing time. Victor Galliard was the last to arrive, some ten minutes late. All of them wanted to get a handle on what had happened and determine who else was involved. Could there be further strikes, and, if so, in what manner? Was Eddie safe?

The men gathered in the back room. "Who's watching the store?" asked Jacques, clearly in a better mood once Victor came in.

"Gunther."

They all laughed. Rottweilers looked big, but they were a gentle breed. Resting against an old empty barrel, Jacques took a bite of an apple and smiled at his friend and business partner. The irrepressible Fabien was at his desk, mumbling something about having forgotten to order yeast. Victor found the available free chair. He said he'd locked up the barn. "I cannot stay long," he said, checking his watch. Two more consignments needed to be shipped. Gisèle was in the house with Eddie. The other two men would wait for Jacques to say something—make the first move. Fabien asked whether anyone wanted a cider. He kept a few handy in his mini refrigerator. No one else wanted anything.

Taking charge, Jacques said he appreciated their help, their support. "What is done is done," he said. As he saw it, they had to determine, together, whether the threat had passed. "Was the attack in the truck the end of the story?"

"Maybe," said Victor.

"Or maybe not. I just don't know," said Jacques. "But until someone finds Laurent, who's evidently gone missing, I don't have closure."

"What can *we* do?" Fabien asked. "The cops will handle it. Right?"

"Will they?" asked Victor. "I am not sure. And Laurent is a cop."

"Right. So, let's be the cops for a moment," said Jacques. "What do we know, so far? Lay out the facts we have. See where and how they fit."

Fabien said, "The animal pen connects the crime to the Romani. But how is their ringleader, Roger Laurent? If he hired them."

"You think he hired them?" asked Victor. "I mean, directly?

"He strikes me as a man likely to use a cutout. If so, there's a piece missing. Who else? Clearly not d'Ancel. He was just the dupe."

Victor, ready to advance the argument, agreed. "So, besides the farm inheritance scam, to which Henri tipped Nina off, it was personal," Victor added.

"Exactly," Jacques said. "They've been harassing me for months. Even taking Cleo."

Fabien added. "No faces, no names."

"Right. So, we focus on the absent Laurent," said Victor. "He could lead us to whatever piece is missing. Where is he?"

Jacques went to the little refrigerator. He'd been putting it all together, a jigsaw puzzle with pieces still not on the board. He needed a motive and a game plan. "I agree. Laurent appears to be gone. And someone else, someone as smart and ruthless as Laurent, has his fingers in this too."

They agreed that the police captain was the principal bad actor there. But who else?

"We know he got someone to help in the actual strike. But did he arrange it? And, if not, who, and how do we prove it?" said Jacques.

Fabien asked whether it was necessary to prove it. "I am not sure we can trust the authorities. They do their own pruning," Jacques added, taking a swig from his beer.

"Well, I never liked the bastard," added Fabien. "He always acted superior to everyone when he would come to the store. He smelled dirty to me. A cop only for the cover it gave him to pull off nasty deals."

"We need to focus. What I want to know is what help did he have at the top?" said Jacques, tossing the core of his apple into a nearby basket. "Maybe another cop?"

Fabien asked what he meant by that. "Another cop?"

"Maybe," said Jacques. Then he added, "What I mean is that this fellow is careful not to get too close to anything that could poke him in the eye. He stays off the battlefield, uses accomplices and cutouts like Henri d'Ancel. He embraces the undercover tactics of partisan warfare."

"Well, if he has someone else, an unknown partner, directing the action, I do not know how we get to him," said Victor.

Fabien, who had been listening and making notes, asked, "Are we making this more complicated than it is?"

Victor let out a sigh, looked to Fabien, and said, "These people are here one day, gone the next. We never find them."

"No. The only route open to us is through Laurent. He's still dangerous. I hate to say it, but his exposure is one man in Nantes. That man is Henri, and we must not ignore or forget that," added Jacques.

"Where is this d'Ancel now?" asked Victor.

Jacques said he assumed he was at home, in Nantes. Victor made a chuffing sound and said he did not know how they could do anything about it if Roger Laurent had done a runner. "He gets his hands sticky; he uses his police cover to wipe it away." The men's attention was diverted then to a noise from the front of the store.

Emma hurried into the back room. The look on her face, the anguish in her voice, signaled something terribly wrong. "My God! You have to help Nina!" she said, rushing to Jacques. Looking to her husband to understand the urgency. "You must do something. Now!"

"What is it?"

"Nina. She just called."

Fabien came around the desk to support her; the woman was in tears.

"What?" said Jacques, springing to her side as well. Anything involving Nina was likely to suggest danger. "What happened, Emma?"

"It's Henri," she said. "He is dead."

"*What?* Dead? Jesus. When?"

"At the train station. In Paris. Only hours ago. Nina was screaming on the phone. She tried to call you at home."

"In Paris, but what. . .?"

"At Montparnasse," she said, looking from one of them to the other. "In a crowd of people. Stabbed. No one saw anything until he fell. Dead." Emma looked at Fabien, as if he could say something to help her understand.

"This is my fault. Mine. I should have warned him. Here we sit talking about just this kind of threat," said Jacques. Fabien looked to his wife, standing apart from them, once again the unwilling Cassandra.

"Why did Nina not tell me he was leaving? I could have advised him to be careful, told him what to watch for, what dangers to be aware of," said Jacques.

"This is Laurent, covering his ass," said Victor. "But who is to prove it? You know he did not do the job himself. Dirty coward."

"I'll go to Nina," said Jacques. "Or, better yet, call and ask that she come to me. To us. At least until we know more."

"Do you think she is at risk too, Jacques," asked a shaken Emma, who could not have interpreted any motive. Fabien had never said anything to her about a conspiracy.

"Who knows? I would not want to think they would go so far as to try to silence her."

"Who, Nina?" insisted Emma. "Who? Why? I do not follow."

Fabien said they had an idea. "I think Nina will be fine. We need to find Laurent. Make him talk."

"We have to know whether anyone knew Henri was traveling to Paris," said Victor, who stood and walked to the refrigerator. Emma took the chair vacated by Victor. She listened, wanting only to make sense of all the talk of murder and conspiracy.

"But how?" said Jacques. "Henri was probably being followed. Cheap thug labor Laurent uses. Someone was keeping an eye on his place, someone we do not know about. There's plenty of cover and confusion in a Paris rail station."

Fabien said he would ask his brother Paul whether he'd heard anything. Paul would hear all kinds of rumors. "People talk in barbershops. Paul hears more crazy shit than the priests of Marseille. And that takes in every sin and human foible imaginable."

"We can ask him," said Jacques. "But, first, I must make sure my sister is all right. Nina will be devastated. Her husband could be a monkey's ass, but I know she loved him."

"You know we will help in any way we can," said Victor. Jacques gave him a grateful nod, and then he took Emma's hand.

She was a good friend to his sister. His need for affirmation at that moment was as great as his need to give it. He was sorry for all the trouble, for everything spinning out of control following the failed attack on him.

"There is no reason for you to be sorry here, my friend," said Fabien. "None of this was your making. We will do all we can to make someone pay for this lunacy, his attack on you, the death of d'Ancel. We must be vigilant. Someone will pay and pay dearly."

CHAPTER 41

Henri's funeral took place four days later at ten in the morning at the beautiful little Gothic-revival church of Saint-Clément in Nantes. Jacques figured there were no more than ten people in attendance, including two of Henri's cousins, young men from Le Mans. Neither spoke. Theirs was a quiet obligation. Nina must have had their phone numbers. There would be no awkward discussion of what had happened, much less why.

Jacques and Eddie sat with Nina, who, in a long black dress borrowed from Anna, looked both stunning and devastated. How odd the circumstances can be that bring people together, much less create conditions for healing.

"I know you loved him, Nina," Jacques told her, and he squeezed her hand gently.

"It was never easy," she said. "But now, only just the other day, it looked like things could go well for him again. For us. He had been offered a good job."

Fabien and Emma accompanied Jacques and Eddie to the church in a show of support for the bereaved woman. The priest, a short, stooped old-timer adorned in a dark-green-and-yellow chasuble with an odd little black biretta on his head, was much in a world of his own. After the second reading, when he was supposed to call upon the widowed Nina to say a few words from the ambo, he paused, looked up, and continued as if he just could not remember upon what they had agreed. Or, maybe, that he simply could not allow it. *In saecula saeculorum.*

Nina stood, saw no signal for her to come forward, and so sat again. Jacques took her hand and whispered that she would have time to say anything she wanted at the interment, which was not for a few more days. Burial arrangements remained incomplete. Henri had no other family. The funeral parlor in Nantes was waiting for a release from the authorities in Paris.

Anna was at the church for her friend. She and Jacques exchanged a few anxious words. Anna was Nina's virtual sister, a listener and consoler. How inconceivable it was to be killed in Paris, she said. "A man with so much to live for." Not knowing in full the degree of turmoil he had caused Nina, Anna simply decided to put the best face on it all. There was nothing to be gained from blaming the dead. Nothing would be said, of course, about nefarious connections or dangerous associates.

Several times, Jacques sensed Anna looking at him.

After the Mass, no one knew what to say, especially to Nina. Compliment her courage? Offer support? Faces were as long and as straight as rulers. One thing the men had agreed on was that there could be no discussion of Laurent nor of any plans to run what Victor had called the trap lines. The men planned to find the bastard. The implications were clear enough.

The official report on the murder by the Paris police department was that the investigation remained open with no suspects or witnesses. In a crowd of men and women moving from one platform to another at a particularly busy time of day, one man fell dead among them with two punctures to the lower back. His spinal cord had been severed. Dead when he hit the cold cement floor.

As he'd promised, Victor made inquiries at the Combourg station. Would the Paris report be made public? A report was marked for distribution to precincts in Nantes, Rennes, Combourg, any place Henri d'Ancel had business—private or public. Any place he had associates or loved ones. Standard operating procedure. Jacques wanted to know when. To whom could he talk to learn more?

The next day, Jacques decided to beard the lion and drove to the *préfecture*. "May I speak with Captain Laurent, please?"

The nervous young policeman at the desk shook his head. Not that day.

Laurent was making himself scarce. But what was the party line at headquarters?

What did Jacques want to see Laurent about?

"The murder of my sister's husband, Henri d'Ancel."

"A murder in Paris? This is not our concern," the man said, giving the stock reply.

"Who is in charge here?" asked Jacques.

The precinct commander came out of his office. "Laurent is not here." They were deeply sorry, he assured him, but, just then, they were all terribly busy. The report on d'Ancel, he said, and that was from Paris, was inconclusive. "Homicide. No suspects."

Could Jacques speak with another officer? Sorry. No. They were shorthanded as it was. If he might fill out the necessary forms, someone would be in touch. Or he could come back.

Two days later, with Jacques's return to the station, there was a breakthrough. The news could only mean one thing to Jacques and to the others when he shared it later that day. Someone was tidying up loose ends. Someone, or several people, had bagged the thieving Roger Laurent. According to the senior man, one Inspector Algard, he'd not shown up for work Monday and had been absent four days. Yes, someone had been to his home. No, there was no sign of his having taken any personal items. They were puzzled too. "No contact as of today. The mother knows nothing."

The news suggested further complications because it meant perhaps a bigger fish was in the proverbial pond. One with long, sharp teeth and impressive range. Inspector Algard had been forthcoming. The next morning, Jacques drove past Laurent's house in Épiniac, a journey and a destination rife with memories. No sign of anyone there. Maybe the mother would know something.

Victor had asked Jacques whether Inspector Algard had any suspects, and Jacques had said no. What might Roger's mother say? Jacques said he would pay her a visit, and, the next day, he did.

"Did he appear worried about anything?"

Madame Laurent shook her head, utter weariness in her demeanor, and walked into the kitchen. Jacques followed. For a moment, he half expected to see the wrong-footed Roland Thomas there, fiddling with his hat.

She asked whether Jacques wanted to see her son's photo, which she had on the table next to the refrigerator, as if perhaps she had been just looking at it herself. He said no.

Then, once again, in a low, stilted voice she told him, "He always comes back to me."

For his part, Fabien Brun took the news in stride. Laurent was hiding out, or he'd been taken, and, if that was the case, the prick was dead. Fabien reported that his brother Paul had heard nothing about the recent mysterious death of Henri d'Ancel at the barbershop. Paul was grateful to be included and to join the conversation; he had asked the same key questions of a few customers. Had anyone heard of Roger Laurent? Mr. Big Shot. Mr. Fancy Car. All he got were shrugs and disinterest. No one had picked up any gossip. He was gone. Where? No one knew. No one cared.

Men at the police station had again checked his place. There was nothing to indicate he would not be back. He had not picked up his dry cleaning. His keys were on the table by the door. He'd not been to the bank. Jacques said he would not be surprised if that was the end of the train ride for a man with a good-guy disguise covering a long career of nefarious deals.

Having given notice at her apartment, for the first time in some two decades Nina would return to the Berlangier farm. Jacques had insisted she do so for her own safety. She was happy to agree, if only to get away from the long, dark shadows—her husband's and that of the despicable Lucien. She'd picked up her final check and packed two bags. She could not be free and clear of the place until the end of November, but that was not so bad. A few days or so at the farm would help settle her nerves. Jacques would help her find an apartment. She'd want to be near family. She needed to. So much had changed so fast after being stuck for so long. Her return to Combourg would feel strange. She'd find the courage to get through it.

Nina had spent a most welcome hour with Anna just before heading out of Nantes, encouraged by what Anna had to say. Anna was a woman she'd dearly miss, but maybe fate was about to change the numbers on the family playing cards. If so, Anna would know how to play them.

CHAPTER 42

The two women had agreed to meet up for a quick hug and cheery goodbye, before Nina left. Nina thought it would be an I-will-miss-you-and-do-remember-to-stay-in-touch kind of thing. But no, Anna Caron evidently had something more on her mind.

She knocked on Nina's door. The apartment, Anna saw, had been tidied up. Nina's bags were packed.

"Can you come down to my place and talk, please, before you go?" the woman had asked. "Just for a moment? Have some tea?"

"Sure." Nina had an idea that whatever Anna wanted to talk about would involve Jacques.

"Sorry," Anna said. "Just something quick."

"This is exciting and confusing," Anna said, pulling her friend into the flat. "I know you must not miss your train."

"No worries about the train," Nina told her. "There are several. What's going on?"

That was not typical behavior for Anna, who was usually so in control. She took her friend's hand. Anna's was an apartment Nina admired for its distinctive feel, its comfort and elegance combined. She loved the way the sun favored Anna's living room, gracing the *Nouveau* artwork and those unusual accent pieces she had collected some years ago, several of them in her visits to her mother's people in Portugal. The old man—her *grand-père*—was well into his 90s. He lived in a fishing village near Nazare. One figurine on display was a cute little ceramic blue-and-yellow house. There were also a dozen or so amazing white ivory carvings of boats, all settled on a drum-shaped cherry-wood table.

"What has you so animated?" Nina asked.

"I will tell you," Anna said, "but, first, do you want that tea?"

"I will, later. Thank you. Come now, what is it?" Nina asked, sitting on the edge of her chair.

Anna said she had received a letter from Jacques, which was unexpected. It had been in that morning's mail, and she did not know what to think. Or to do.

"A letter? He wrote? Well, that is good of him. But why? What did he say?"

She took a quick breath. "He wrote that he was sorry if he had upset me. At dinner. You know. When I left. . ."

"My brother seems to have more on his mind than he'd told me about," Nina said, grinning. Jacques had matured a lot since she'd left so long ago. "But maybe I am just beginning to better recognize what he truly needs."

"Well, he wanted to apologize for what he might have done or said. And he wanted to make it up to me. Although I could not say even now that it was anything he said."

"Do you want him to? Make it up to you, I mean?"

Anna said she was interested, but didn't know how he would do that, or even what he made of her exit that night. She'd had him on her mind, and now he was calling her on it.

"What did he say, specifically? I mean, he is a busy fellow with the farm and, of course, little Eddie."

Anna set a teapot between them with two cerulean cups. "He wants me to tell you that I should come with you to Combourg for a visit. Not now, of course, not today, but sometime soon. What do you think?" Nina looked at Anna and saw she was smiling brightly.

"To show you the apple trees? A processing building?" They both laughed. Nina sipped at her tea. "You like him. I can tell."

"I do, Nina. He listens. That is rare. And he is a rather handsome man, your brother. He has a beautiful smile. I like that." She also said he had a generous spirit "Yes, I do like the guy."

"His smile? Well, I suppose it is a start."

Anna leaned forward. "I just don't know what I think. That has always been my problem."

Nina gazed into her cup, nodded, and said, "Welcome to the club."

CHAPTER 43

Arriving at the house with her brother, Nina set her smaller bag just inside the door. "It feels so good to be back, Jacques, after so long." The force of recognition, of all that had passed there, registered in her face.

Seeing her tremble, watching Nina holding it together, Jacques pulled her to his side and told her, "I think I may have one or two jobs waiting for you around here."

"No housecleaning." She took another step, smiled, and cuffed him on the shoulder.

Jacques pulled her to him.

The farmhouse, the orchards, and the smells of the place brought another set of memories, not all of them easy or pleasant. But Jacques promised he would put her to work. The Calvados business was booming. Victor would be preoccupied for a while, he told her, when Gisèle had her baby, which would be any day

She looked around, taking it all in. Home. If she realized her knees felt awkwardly weak, she chose to ignore it, shifting her weight from foot to foot, her mood impossible for her to interpret.

Eddie slipped around the door. He looked uncertain. Then, he came into the room to look at her. Nina gave his nose a tiny pinch, and he laughed.

"*Bonjour, tante Nina*," the boy said, and looked to his Papa.

Jacques told Eddie they were a family of huggers, and the boy shrugged his small shoulders and showed Nina the toy truck he was holding. "Well," Jacques said, "only the appliances have changed, and not all of them." The old wooden table was the same. Nina admired Claire's wall painting.

"Oh, look at this. What a wonderful mood it sets for the whole house, Jacques."

"Yes. Claire had a way of making anything brighter," he said. "She was full of promise."

Nina looked back at the front room, taking in the old pieces, as if to figure out where she might help. Maybe the place needed a woman's touch? Eddie, meanwhile, was following her everywhere. Jacques took her bags and showed her to the spare room, the room that was once hers and would be again. It contained one small bed and a gun cabinet next to a desk boasting one taxidermied, green-necked pheasant. She glanced up to where she recalled there had once hung a heavy- wood crucifix, which she had found to be equal parts dispiriting and full of hope.

"Let's sit," Jacques said, and they moved to the kitchen table. Nina looked at the clock, thinking about the way that time itself was so ethereal.

"There are things to catch up on, especially since the business has grown." Jacques admitted that his recordkeeping had fallen behind.

"What did you have in mind, boss?" she said, and winked at Eddie.

Would she like to handle his finances for a while? A month or two?

Yes, of course. With some basic guidance. He could walk her through what had to be done, tell her about his suppliers, his creditors, and who owed what to whom. He could show her where he kept the ledgers. She might find better ways to help him manage, he said, as he patted the sofa, encouraging her to sit.

"Be innovative," he told her. "Look for opportunities." He could not have pleased her more with that assignment. She was an intuitive person. And she was no longer stuck in a lonely apartment, her poor Henri gone. There, at that moment, she could take on real responsibility.

That evening, they shared their first dinner alone—she, Jacques, and an energetic, voluble Eddie—and she told Jacques how happy she was to be out of Nantes, away from that job and the creepy assistant manager. She was taken with her nephew, with his questions and his often-surprising observations. It was clear to her that Jacques had treated him as a smart child. Nothing prepares a mind more than having one's curiosity engaged. The boy's vocabulary was advanced, she said. One subject she stayed clear of was the loss of her own child and the man, little Mathis's father, whom she'd left so long ago. There would be enough time for that. She would mourn Henri and ponder her errant choices. She would move on.

Nina's presence was felt in yet another area. With no child of her own, she was even more attentive to the boy. His birthday was in three days; she had an idea and took it to her brother, an argument already prepared should he say no to her suggestion.

"Eddie needs a dog, Jacques. For that matter, so do you."

"I do?" Jacques asked where that had come from. Had Eddie said anything? She said no, but it was plenty clear that he missed Cleo.

"Well, we all do," said Jacques.

"Not to replace her," Nina added. "That could never be." She understood how important Cleo was to him. "Getting another dog is not to replace; it is to remember. And to start a relationship. You are both entitled to that."

Jacques said he would think about it, but she could tell that he liked the idea. The next day, at breakfast, he sensed Nina's building enthusiasm. She had not yet said anything to Eddie. That would be unfair to her brother and to the child. She did offer the boy a hug, however, and then asked, prompted by Jacques, "What do you say about the idea for a dog?" Startled, Eddie put his hand to his mouth.

Jacques grinned. "Maybe another Brittney Spaniel would be the ticket."

The boy's face lit up. What name would they give him or her? "If we find a girl, can we call her Cider?"

The adults laughed at his ingenuity. *"Cidre!"*

"Yes. A fitting present, young man, for your fourth birthday." Eddie asked about a boy dog. What name could they give him? Jacques said that was a good question. "We can go take a look tomorrow. Now, go get dressed, and we'll have some cereal."

Nina watched Eddie head back to his room, then asked Jacques whether he knew of any local breeders, and, if so, where? Jacques said there was a shelter north of Rennes. Not far. Nina told him she'd like to go along and see some of the countryside, leave the financial accounts books she'd been studying.

"Did I tell you that Anna asked about you?"

Jacques said he had thought about her as well. They had written a few times and talked by phone. "But Nantes is a long way," Jacques added. "Still . . ."

"Not that far. And I think she might like to visit. You did ask. Like, maybe a long weekend?"

Jacques wanted to know who was being visited, her or him?

Nina laughed. "Probably both." She added that Anna could use a respite from her teaching. "You offered in a letter to show her the place. Take her around the property. She'd like that. And I think she'd be good for you. Pick up your spirits."

He said nothing in response.

She studied his face. "Now, with the weather so full of autumn, you can treat her to the colors, the smells. Show off your prize- winning orchards."

"Ours," he replied. Then added, "Berlangier family orchards, Nina. And we have won no prizes that I am aware of." He winked at his son.

"Oh, I think you will," she said, looking out the kitchen window to the converted barn, seeing Victor there talking to one of his team members. "Maybe what these orchards need is a woman's touch again." This last comment made Jacques recall Claire's enthusiasm for any future growth.

He asked whether she had anything specific in mind. She did. She asked if he had given any thought to cider and Calvados promotions. Maybe they could have tastings. They could set up a tent in town for the passersby, the foreign visitors. Would he like that?

"Promotions? I had never thought of that," he said. "Nina, that is a brilliant idea. Maybe have a hospitality room? Is that what you mean?"

Yes. She had some ideas about how they might do that. She beamed in recognition of their ever more comfortable relationship. He appreciated the astonishing, strong woman who was his sister.

"Your son is excited. And I think he needs that dog."

Jacques put his arm around her and told her, "I think we all do."

CHAPTER 44

Anna came to visit the next Friday. A nervous Jacques picked her up at the station, accompanied by a much-enthused Nina. Waiting for them at home, with Eddie providing rubs and much-needed hugs, was one underweight border collie they had named Robespierre. That had been Nina's suggestion, because, she said, the dog looked to have potential to change things, offer them a new start. He had what looked like a distinctive grey ruff, or collar, around his neck. Nina mused that this Robespierre should be able to keep his head.

Anna fussed with the dog and took in the place as a landscape painter looks at the details of an unexpected horizon. She praised Claire's wall painting, the likeness of Monet's celebrated water lilies which Jacques had told her about.

"What colors! What imagination."

They had asked the Gaillards over too, a few days earlier, to say hello, but they could not make it. Gisèle was experiencing labor pains. Nina suggested she might bake an apple pie, then drive over to check on them.

Jacques said that sounded like a wonderful idea. He was keen to show Anna around the place but understood not to rush things. He would let her get her bearings. The next day, they'd all go into town, where she would take in the many changes. She stared at the building that once belonged to her family. "Who was it that said, 'You can't go home again?'" she asked. Nostalgia was a biased lens.

Sunday, when Anna asked Nina how many places to set for dinner, meaning would Eddie be at the table with them, Jacques said five, including one for Eddie.

"Five?"

Yes. Anna and Nina, him, Eddie, and one more. Nina asked who the fifth would be. Jacques grinned and said he had asked Paul Brun to join them. He was a committed bachelor and a fellow who needed to meet some people not in want of a trim or a shave. Besides which, Jacques wanted to thank him for the help he had provided in the unsuccessful hunt for Roger Laurent.

"He is not a musician, is he?" Nina asked with a grin. She gave her brother a look that suggested a difficult history with that breed. Then, she laughed at her own remark.

"As far as I know, he cannot even whistle."

Nina asked what he did for a living, a practical question.

"He's a barber. He has a shop in town."

Having finished the table, Anna suggested they visit the garden, where a brilliant skirt of pink-and-yellow camellias was just beginning to bloom. Eddie clearly wanted to join them, and all three went out, Nina finding Anna a sweater, something she'd forgotten to pack. Jacques saw that it had been one of Claire's favorites.

"Anna seems to like it here," said Nina.

"I thought she would," said Jacques. "Or more to the point, I hoped she would."

"So, am I to take it that this Paul is available?" Nina kidded, trying to get a sense of what pairings Jacques might have in mind.

"Hard to say," he said, then paused to find the right words. "But

I think you might find him a pleasant fellow. You cannot have too many friends."

"Me? No. It's a bit soon for me to be talking with bachelors, don't you think?" Nina's tone suggested she was of two minds on the matter.

Her Henri had been gone only a month.

Jacques shrugged, "Maybe. Maybe not. Hard to tell who is going to strike a match in the heart of another."

At about five that afternoon Paul arrived with a clutch of yellow primroses for Nina, and he proved a delightfully good conversationalist. Jacques had tipped him off about the flowers being one of Nina's favorites.

"Oh, I have always loved these flowers," she told him. "Since childhood." Anna took all that in while considering how thoughtful Jacques was to have arranged it. Nina saw that her friend was smitten by her brother.

After dessert, Anna and Paul, as the Berlangier guests, insisted on clearing the table and rinsing the dishes. "You and Nina go sit," Anna told Jacques. "After all, you made the meal; we can at least take care of cleaning up."

Nina agreed, busying herself by looking for a place to set the centerpiece vase of flowers the considerate Paul Brun had brought. Momentarily, she set them on the mantel, studying the framed photo next to it of her first family. Paul looked in from the kitchen to ask whether the dog had been fed. Nina said yes. Jacques came to her side, maybe sensing a degree of uncertainty.

"Look, Jacques. Look here. This is us," Nina said, intrigued. "I never saw this. Or, if I did, I do not remember now."

"We were young, Nina. My god, look at those clothes."

She leaned against her brother, and he put his arm around her. The warm fire behind them crackled, heightening the mood. So many hard, long days had passed.

"I've tried and tried to figure out whether it was a special occasion when that was taken," said Jacques.

Nina stared at the picture, bringing it closer. "We all look so young. Especially Papa. And look at Maman."

Jacques nodded. "We were young." He added that the picture had to have been taken in 1912 or so. Papa was killed in 1916, so, maybe it had been taken four years before that. "They would have been about twenty-five."

Nina told Jacques she had missed him, had left behind so much. "I missed all of this," she said, dabbing at her eyes with her sleeve. Jacques could see she was looking even more intently at the image of their mother, Adèle. Memories—good and bad—flooding her vision.

"Sweet Jesus, Jacques. Look at her. That long green dress. Those shoes. I must have given her a difficult time."

Jacques did not know what to say, knowing the two had had their problems. He thought back to the graveside service in 1916, when they were all unaware of what would become of them or the Berlangier legacy.

Nina took a moment. "Only now, Jacques, can I begin to recognize what she took on. All she meant to Papa, her helping keep this farmhouse, all the work." She wiped her eyes again. "I failed to recognize what she was trying to do."

"We seldom do when we are that age. We do not even know ourselves."

"I suppose," she said. "And I was selfish." She set the photo back on the mantel, with some flush of emotion she did not fully understand. "Why is forgiveness so hard?"

Jacques said he was working on just that battle too, seeking a general amnesty.

"Really? Forgiveness? Oh, I think I know the people you mean. . ."

"Yes. Something to work on for me. A test of will. We move on. We reconstruct. Maybe we reinvent. Hatred never did anyone much good."

Nina nodded. "Our better selves," she said, and looked back to the framed photo. Choices. The toughest were always the most telling.

"You know, Nina; Maman loved you. She asked me just before she died whether I had seen you or knew where you were. She just wanted to understand."

"I know. Oh, Lord. I'm sorry. So much time. I feel horrible I never told her the same."

"Well," he said, holding her, "I think you just did. I think you said what needed to be said. The journey home—for you, for me, for all of us—is ever unpredictable. But I think, somehow, she knows."

Eddie stepped around the corner of the kitchen doorway as Jacques put the photo back. The loopy-looking dog followed at his heels, turned two or three times in a circle, found a comfortable spot, and settled in front of the sofa, a special spot for the birthday dog.

"I gave Robes. . ." Eddie paused to get it right. "I gave Robes-Pear some water."

Surprised, Jacques looked at Nina and grinned. She laughed and pulled the boy to her.

"I think Robes-Pear is happy to be with you. And I think that is a much better name than the other one," she said, and laughed. Her eyes were shining.

Jacques picked up Eddie and raised him toward the ceiling. Yes, he would have to agree. The name fit a good orchard dog. He reached down to rub behind the dog's ears.

"Oh, Jacques, I am just thinking. What if we were to make another varietal?" Nina asked, one eyebrow raised. Finding confidence. "One with a hint more pear, and we could go with the name Robes-Pear on the label. Include an image of the revolutionary under a pear tree?"

"Well, now. I think that is something to think about. But then we add expenses." He looked out at the trees he could see, those nearest the house. "We'd need another dedicated vat," he said, nonetheless warming to the idea.

"Ah, that is why people take gambles. Right? And it was your boy's idea," she said. "I am just trying to help make the pieces fit. And find a few new ones."

"You are." He paused. "You are doing what I asked, stirring the porridge."

"Which no doubt needed it," she said. "Along with something fresh and new."

"And you are our innovator. Thank you, Nina," he said, and put his arm around her.

The dog got up just then, stretched, and followed Nina into the kitchen. Jacques heard him drinking noisily. "I think Robes has heard enough."

Anna and Paul came back into the room, Paul saying he had to leave, adding how much he'd enjoyed the dinner and company. "Thank you so much, Paul. Lovely to meet you," said Anna.

When he was gone, Anna joined Jacques on the sofa, taking his hand. Jacques pulled Eddie to him, lifting the boy to sit on his lap. He asked, "Would you like to hear a story, Eddie?" The child gave that some thought, then shook his head no. Anna laughed. Eddie was happy enough in the moment.

Jacques looked into the boy's calm, happy face. Robes ambled back into the room. He was getting used to the feel of the house. Eddie climbed down and nuzzled the dog's chin. The warm room seemed to settle all disquiet and uncertainty.

Over the fireplace, Claire looked out from a fine, gilded frame. Claire was there and yet not. One heart-shaped, smooth black pebble rested beside the frame. Jacques tipped his tumbler of brandy to his dear late wife in a moment of repose. Anna watched him as he studied Claire's image for a moment and thought about their work in the war, Paris, the farm, their boy, and all they had meant to each other. Claire seemed to be telling him something: What's done is done. *You have a future, Jack, and it starts now.*

"Your wife, yes?" Anna said. Jacques smiled, nodded, and returned to Anna. Eddie and the dog lay just in front of the couple. Moments later, Nina came in from the kitchen, wiping her hands. "Oh, Jacques, I meant to tell you," she began, "an Inspector Algard called earlier from the Combourg police. He said he must speak with you. Something about a few questions. He sounded agitated."

"Algard?"

"Yes. Is it anything important? Could it be about Henri?"

Jacques took a moment. It was probably routine. Jacques added that they'd met, that they'd talked, he and Algard, a few weeks ago. There was nothing to worry about. "Ghosts in the attic."

The teapot whistled from the kitchen.

Jacques waited until Nina had gone upstairs, told Anna he'd be right back, then picked up the phone. What was Algard up to? He must to talk with his most trusted ally.

At last, Fabien answered.

"I thought you told me Laurent was dead," Jacques said. "Or that they'd found someone, in a lake. Thought to be our boy."

"That's my understanding," Fabien said, curious as to why Jacques was asking. From what Paul had heard, no one was likely to identify whatever was left of the poor fellow. The body was pretty much unrecognizable.

"One corpse. Up near l'Oisette. Why?"

"I know the place," Jacques said. "And I am fairly sure who operates there. I just wanted to know whether you'd heard anything more. Something has changed, Inspector Algard wants to talk."

Acknowledgements

I have many people to thank for their help with this, my first novel. I begin with my wife, Sue, who encouraged me to get on with it when I drifted over three years of scene-building and mid-course corrections. Two friends, both accomplished writers, read through developmental efforts and offered careful, timely feedback. Thank you, Terresa Haskew and Cada McCoy. Thanks to Ashley Carlson for her help, as well. And big thanks to my new publisher, IngramElliott, for giving this novel a new start, and especially to my editor, Angela Glennon.

In the Orchards of Shadow and Light is the first of a three-book series, set mostly in Europe, and all of the work focuses on clandestine operations.

About the Author

Poet, playwright, and novelist, Arthur McMaster retired from full-time teaching, most recently as Visiting Associate Professor of English at Converse College in Spartanburg, SC. His books include: *In the Orchards of Shadow and Light* (historical fiction), *The Whole Picture Show* (poetry), *Musical Muse* (academic), *Birdies Never Die* (golf), *Givings & Misgivings* (poetry), *The Spy Who Came Down with a Cold* (poetry), and *Need to Know* (memoir). Arthur's first career was that of a foreign intelligence officer, with assignments with military intelligence and, briefly, with the CIA. Arthur earned an MFA in poetry at University of Florida. He has received Pushcart Prize nominations. He now teaches in the Continuing Education Department for Furman University (fiction and poetry). He is excited about working with his new publisher, IngramElliott, on the *Orchards* espionage series.

THE SHADOW SERIES

IN THE ORCHARDS OF SHADOW AND LIGHT (BOOK 1)
In the French Resistance, trust is the difference between life and death. In love, it means everything.

In the final two years of the war in Europe, French resistance fighter Jacques Berlangier and his determined, American OSS partner Claire Skiffington struggle to survive a series of hazardous assignments in support of Allied operations. In the war's immediate aftermath, in love and together in Paris, they decide to return to his family's apple farm business in the Breton countryside. There, residual and unforeseen trouble rivals the dangers they thought were well past.

COMING SOON

IN THE ALLEYS OF SHADOW AND STONE (BOOK 2)
In Cold War Berlin and Paris, trust is the rarest currency.

In the aftermath of choosing love over espionage, Kevin Burke settles into a desk job at CIA headquarters, hoping for peace with Nina D'Ancel. But old enemies and new secrets refuse to stay buried. When a cryptic message from Europe draws Kevin back into the shadows, he must confront the ghosts of his past and the dangers of a world where trust is the rarest currency. As Nina faces her own reckoning, their bond is tested by a conspiracy that threatens not just their future, but the fragile hope they've fought to reclaim.

IngramElliott Publishing

IngramElliott is an award-winning independent publisher with a mission to bring great stories to light in print and on-screen. We publish stories with a unique voice that will translate well into film and television. Visit us at www.ingramelliott.com for more information.

Our *IngramElliott* imprint features full-length fiction and nonfiction titles designed with the book lover in mind.

Our *IE Snaps!* imprint features novella-length fiction in popular genres that are designed for a quick read on the go.